THE ALLIES OF DEATH

THE ALLIES OF DEATH

DARK GATE ANGELS™ BOOK THREE

RAMY VANCE

MICHAEL ANDERLE

THE ALLIES OF DEATH TEAM

Thanks to our Beta Team:
Larry Omans, Rachel Beckford

Thanks to the JIT Readers

Dave Hicks
Dorothy Lloyd
Deb Mader
Veronica Stephan-Miller

If we've missed anyone, please let us know!

Editor
The Skyhunter Editing Team

Copyright © 2020 LMBPN Publishing
Cover Art by Jake @ J Caleb Design
http://jcalebdesign.com / jcalebdesign@gmail.com
Cover copyright © LMBPN Publishing
A Michael Anderle Production

LMBPN Publishing
PMB 196, 2540 South Maryland Pkwy
Las Vegas, NV 89109

First US Edition, August 2020
ISBN (ebook) 978-1-64971-117-5
ISBN (print) 978-1-64971-118-2

DEDICATION

To Larry, John and Rachel ... the real Dark Gate Angels!

—Ramy Vance

To Family, Friends and
Those Who Love
to Read.
May We All Enjoy Grace
to Live the Life We Are
Called.

— Michael

PART 1

PROLOGUE

Somewhere else, some*time* else...

This is a place between realms and dimensions. Imagine an immaculate gold sidewalk. As you are walking, you notice a crack, but wonder how a crack could be in a place such as this? It is that kind of place, a place of non-existence, yet existence. A paradox.

There is a castle, but it is not built from stone. Instead, it is molded from flesh, but not that of any mortal creature. The hollowed-out body of Lord Hahmoroth, an elder god worshipped before the elves learned to take their first steps.

His body stretches for an eternity, decaying and living, dead yet dreaming, and these dreams occasionally touch on the realms around, unaware of the crack.

Within this dead god, there is something worse.

A creature abhorred by all mortals. Her curse is mentioned in stories and legends—always a cautionary tale, for she gained knowledge not meant for mortals.

Knowledge that once acquired begins to rot and twist, to distort and destroy.

Rasputina the lich wanders down the narrow halls of the dead god, silently, deep in her own thoughts, which span the course of thousands of years. If a mortal were to investigate her mind, they might be driven insane. The same could be said of an old god. Even the mad can only take so much.

She has been here for some time, but time means nothing in a place such as this. The home of her studies, profane knowledge that not even the gods are supposed to possess. Her insides, if you could call them that, are lined with eyes that perceive that which has no physical or psychic existence.

And it is here that she rages.

Her study is a depiction of suffering. The walls are lined with corpses that alternate between having skin and being pulled inside-out.

Their screams became white noise to Rasputina a long time ago.

The only screams she ever hears anymore are her own.

Rasputina was screaming and ranting, unaware of where she is, her mind fractured in ways she cannot comprehend. There were voices, many of which she could not understand, speaking languages she had never heard. Always new languages. It is as if her mind were full of existence being born and dying at the same time.

Rasputina casts a spell to remember, and in the glimmer before her, she sees something she has forgotten.

Herself.

Who she was.

It is *here*, in both the past and present, that Rasputina finds herself. It is *here*, in both the past and present, that Rasputina remembers her purpose: to conquer Death once and for all.

CHAPTER ONE

There is a forest in Middang3ard that is known for its wild honey. Deep within it, there is a cave, and within that cave, a dungeon. This dungeon could be found past a massive elm tree attended to by swarms of bees.

The Dark Gate Angels have been walking through this dungeon for nearly an hour, because their boss, the most powerful wizard in the Nine Realms, told them to do so in a dream.

If Myrddin didn't have powers beyond comprehension, Anabelle might have dismissed this dream quest and stayed home. But she'd seen him do incredible things, so here they were.

Why Myrddin needed them to dungeon-delve in Middang3ard was unclear. The wizard had chosen to go all Yoda on them, saying cryptic shit rather than spelling it out.

He did spell out one thing, though: this quest might be the key to finally, once and for all, defeating the Dark One.

Anabelle led the disparate group of friends, special agents in Myrddin's task force. Their main focus was tracking and destroying Dark Gates, transportation portals the Dark One had grown exceptionally good at implanting for the slow siege of Earth.

The elf was tragically beautiful, even by elvish standards. If she were to stand still, it would be impossible to tell her apart from one of the ancient elvish statues of their gods.

Terra followed her, crouching to avoid hitting her head, which was freshly shaven. Her axes hung loose across her back. She tried to keep an eye out for creatures scurrying across the walls. The more legs, the worse. Furry wasn't too bad, though.

Abby brought up the rear. She was the youngest of the three, not even out of high school yet...although from the way she carried herself, you'd never know.

She was just as battle-hardened as the rest of them.

As Abby walked, her eyes searched the slick walls of the dungeon, looking for anything of importance.

So far, the dungeon had been straightforward. They had gotten the door open and were following an invisible route.

Terra stumbled in the dark and fell forward, bumping Anabelle, who yelped as she fell forward. "Terra, I'm not going to tell you again; take smaller steps. I'm not a giant like you," Anabelle growled.

"Maybe if it was possible to see two feet in front of me, I wouldn't trip," Terra shot back. "I wonder what this would be like if someone could, I don't know, magically light our path for us."

Anabelle raised her hand, causing it to glow faintly, not nearly enough to light their path. "I already told you, I can't. Ever since that fight with Grok, I've had to conserve my mana. It's not like before. There's like a wall or something, keeping me from accessing all my power."

Abby, who had pushed to the front of the queue, cleared her throat. "It's called PTSD, Belle. Maybe you should see one of the counselors?"

Anabelle flicked her fingers, sending sparks flying. "I know what it's called, Abby. That doesn't mean a shrink can help me with it. Besides, we only have human therapists now. How am I going to unload hundreds of years of baggage on a human? It might break their mind."

Terra's stomach grumbled and she looked down at it, embarrassed. "You'd be surprised what a good therapist can do. Before I got abducted for the arena, I used to go to one all the time. Helps to have someone to talk to sometimes."

"What's there to talk about? I got tortured for a week, didn't kill the person who tortured me, and now I having trouble accessing my powers, which is strange because the Path of the Travelers is obtained through great stress, effort, and pain. In theory, at least, the torture should have made me stronger, not cut me off from my power, but it did. It's basically gone." Anabelle took a deep breath before continuing. "Power that, might I add, is linked to my emotional and spiritual health? You know, now that I said it out loud, it sounds like some basic character flaw from a two-bit writer."

Abby laughed as she crouched and stared at the stalactites hanging over her. "Maybe you need a writer to handle your character growth. We feel like you'd be a good fit for a tragic, ironic hero."

Terra raised her hand to cut off the conversation. "Okay, nerds, some of us didn't take AP literature and might end up dozing off from your riveting literary analysis. If you two are going to geek out, how about we do it over food?"

Anabelle's stomach growled as if it were trying to take part in the conversation. "You know, that's not a bad idea. Who's got fire duty this time?"

Abby raised her hand. She looked around the area of the dungeon they were in, scooping up as much wood as she could find. Then she got to building a fire, which was crackling in a few minutes.

The three gathered around it. Terra pulled a few chunks of goat meat out of her knapsack and handed them to Anabelle. "Please don't char them this time."

Anabelle snatched the meat and skewered a piece on her knife. "Like I told you last time, if you want it cooked a certain way, you can do it."

Terra glared at Anabelle as she leaned back against a rock. "If you have the indecency to think that a burned steak is edible, I will tolerate it. An orc chieftain is used to a certain kind of culinary—"

"By the fucking gods, Terra, I won't burn your steak!"

Abby snickered from across the fire. "You don't have to worry about ours, Belle. We don't have a need for taste, only nutrients."

Anabelle's eyes widened and she gasped. "No, not you too, Abby! You can't turn on me."

Abby raised her hands as she shrugged. "We're neutral. The steak will be what decides."

Anabelle grumbled as Abby and Terra snickered. She didn't crack a smile until Terra shoved her playfully, almost knocking her over.

Terra pulled a jug of mead from her knapsack and passed it around. "You know it's not just you, Anabelle. I've been having trouble too. I don't feel like I'm as strong as I used to be. Doesn't matter what I do. It's like…I don't know, nothing's exciting enough. Can't seem to get my blood pumping, and if the blood's not pumping, these guns ain't working."

Anabelle handed Terra one of the goat steaks. "Looks like Abby's the only one who still has any juice."

Abby took a steak from Anabelle and looked it over. "That is not true. Our powers are greatly reduced as well. We placed this body under a lot of stress over the last few weeks. Pushing it any further could be detrimental. Martin has placed a cap on the number of nanobots we can generate and control."

Anabelle drank from the mead jug. "And Roy has us exploring dungeons instead of out there fighting. Dungeons! What am I, a MERC recruit?"

After they finished eating, Terra stood and stared down the dungeon's dark tunnel. "We should probably get going unless you guys want to be in here all day."

The rest of the DGA got to their feet, and each grabbed a flaming piece of wood to use as a torch. "You should think of it as a team-building exercise. Like playing D&D or something," Abby said.

They turned a corner, and Terra used her torch to burn away a giant spider web. "Why the hell would we have to play D&D? Let me roll for…uh…whatever the hell you use the dice for. It's like gambling, right? You have to place bets or something."

Anabelle pretended to push up a pair of glasses and spoke in a nasal voice. "Uh, I think the dragon is about to pounce on us, guys!"

Terra and Anabelle laughed as Abby blushed. "You guys haven't even played D&D. You're just spouting nerd clichés."

Terra pounded her chest with her torch hand. "Dude, my life is D&D. I'm an orc chief, and Anabelle's an elf wizard monk or something. Granted, not as cool as a…"

"Class," Abby answered. "They're called classes."

"Yeah, orc chief is definitely cooler than elf monk."

Anabelle's mana flashed brightly for a second as she turned around. "Do you not know how to say anything other than the most aggravating statements?"

Terra grabbed Anabelle and pulled her in for a crushing side hug. "If I weren't annoying you, how would you know that I love you?"

Anabelle clawed away from Terra and bumped into the wall. "I don't know. Gifts, maybe? Compliments? Or perhaps, heaping praise on me?"

Terra shook her head as she breezed past the elf. "Nah, that sounds pretty boring."

Abby had stopped walking. She pointed at the wall that Anabelle had fallen against. "Uh, we think you guys might want to check that out."

Anabelle and Terra came over to look at the wall. There was a circular panel carved into the stone that had been touched.

"Looks like a trap," Terra said. "Damn, Anabelle, going around setting off traps and shit? Is this your first dungeon?"

Anabelle's eyes narrowed. "This is your first dungeon too, and you were the one who pushed me into the wall. It doesn't matter, though. If it were a trap, something would have happened by—"

The ground beneath the DGA agents opened, sending the three of them tumbling into darkness. They hit the ground with a muted thud.

Terra was the first to get up, staring up at the hole they had fallen through. "Is D&D usually this fucking annoying?"

Abby's nanobots flowed over her hand, quickly converting it to a flashlight. She shone it around to get a feel for the dimensions of the room. "Usually there are sections where it seems the DM is padding to fill time."

A whistle came from behind Terra, who froze. "You guys heard that, right?"

Abby spun, shining her flashlight in Terra's direction. "Oh. You shouldn't make any sudden moves, Terra," she whispered.

Behind Terra was a creature with large bat-like ears and leathery skin. It had no eyes. Instead, a sloping forehead took up most of its face, which was covered in something like barnacles. The creature stood a head taller than Terra, and it bared its yellowed and sharp teeth as it clicked its tongue.

Abby held her finger to her lips as she pointed to her ear with the other hand.

Terra nodded as she slowly turned around, careful not to make a sound. She backed away from the creature to Abby and Anabelle. When she was close enough, she leaned over to the elf and whispered, "Can I take it?"

Anabelle looked up at the hole they'd fallen through. "Might be easier to get up there without wondering if something is going to pull us down. You think you got it?"

"I'm going to be pretty bummed if I can't even handle a mole-man."

Abby leaned forward. "That's not a mole-man. Mole-men are a combination between a mole and a—"

"Abby, I know it's not a—"

The blind creature let out a screech.

Terra sighed. "Maybe we should've talked about this after we killed it."

The creature darted at Terra, moving extremely fast for something that lived in a hole, waiting for prey to fall in. It hit the human and knocked her into the wall as its jaws gnashed, trying to tear out her throat.

Terra hit the creature in the face, causing it to stumble back.

Anabelle grabbed the bat-creature and flipped it over her shoulder as Terra leapt into the air, bringing down her elbow on it after it hit the ground.

Terra reached over her shoulder and drew her axe as the thing scuttled about on all fours. "Are you guys going to help me?"

Abby and Anabelle exchanged glances. "Uh, we have to watch our power reserves in case we come across anything more dangerous."

Anabelle crossed her arms as she leaned against the wall. "You are the superior class," she mockingly mused. "This shouldn't be hard for you to handle. I don't even know if I would be of any help, being such a weak monk wizard."

Terra grumbled as she looked around for the creature, which had fled into the dark. "Fine, I'll take care of it." She returned her attention to the blind monster, drew her other axe, and clanged the two together.

The creature leapt out of the dark at her, and she jumped to the side and brought one of the axes down on its neck. It wasn't enough to cut through, but the monster hit the ground.

Terra stomped on its back, then swung her axe at its neck, cleanly severing its head from its body. "You see, that's what I'm talking about! I take'em down with a slice."

Abby looked at the opening above her and pressed her hand to the wall, her nanobots flowing out and building a ladder. "Whatever. Strong as you are, we should take the rest of this slowly."

CHAPTER TWO

Now that the Dark Gate Angels were out of the pit, they continued through the dungeon, watching for more traps along the way. Abby was able to spot a few that had been placed on the ground, allowing them to avoid a repeat of earlier.

As they walked through the dungeon, Terra shuddered. She wasn't a fan of caves—not enough room to stretch out. Also, the idea of dying underground seemed much worse than out in the open air.

Probably too many horror movies. That and underground was one step closer to hell.

Terra wasn't and had never been a religious person, but she'd heard enough stories from her grandmother about psychotic imps with pitchforks fighting each other for a chance to rip you apart for all eternity. As she thought about the prospect, it didn't seem that much more frightening than what she'd seen since joining the DGA. There was still an initial fear in there.

She dealt with this by joking with the DGA. Most of the jokes were an attempt to get under Anabelle's skin. Ever since the elf had developed a double consciousness (Terra still wasn't sure on the details of that), she'd been considerably calmer and more aloof. That didn't mean it was impossible to rile her up, though. And it felt like you really earned it by then.

The jokes also seemed to keep Anabelle out of her own head.

Since their last mission, the elf had developed the unsettling habit of staring into space quietly for long periods of time. Jokes helped ease the tension, which was exactly what they needed right now.

Truth be told, Terra also needed the distraction. This place gave her the creeps. "You guys ever think about hell?" she blurted.

Anabelle gave Terra a bemused look over her shoulder. "No. Elves don't have a concept of hell. As far as I know, it's a human idea, but more power to you. No one would ever say you don't all have great imaginations."

Abby shook her head as she came up to a ledge and peered over it. "Can't say that we do. Ma and Pa didn't care for religious talk, and anyplace that fits the Judeo-Christian definition of hell is more than likely just another realm."

That thought hadn't crossed Terra's mind. She was still foggy on how the realms worked. Were they stacked on top of each other, or spread out, or alternate realities? Thinking about it too much made her head spin. "Wait, so you're saying hell could be, like, another dimension or something?"

"Easily. We have reports of interdimensional creatures that don't belong to the nine realms. There could be an infinite number of dimensions. One of them is bound to have a place with fire oceans."

Anabelle tossed out a rope and started to climb down the ledge, descending farther into the dungeon. "What's with all the afterlife talk? That whole thing with Myrddin freaking you out?"

Terra climbed down after Anabelle. "No, not really. Just thinking. I used to like stories about underworlds. You know, Greek myths and stuff like that. And I loved the Hercules story. That guy was hot."

Abby, who was above Terra, snorted. "How do you know he was hot? All you heard were stories."

Terra landed at the bottom of the ledge and caught Abby, who let go of the rope and fell into Terra's arms. "Being hot isn't only about looks. You can read a story and know a character is hot."

Anabelle coiled the rope and pointed down the hall, where there was a flickering light. "I better be the hot one in my story. It should be painfully obvious."

They headed toward the light as Terra groaned. "You're hot, Anabelle. You used to be a model."

"Yeah, but if I were in a story, I'd want it to be very noticeable to the reader that I am *extremely* hot."

"They might think her freakishly big head is a little off-putting," Terra whispered to Abby.

Anabelle's ears twitched slightly. "I heard that." The elf raised her hand and stopped walking. "That's not all I heard. There's something up ahead."

Terra unsheathed her axe and stepped ahead of Anabelle and Abby. "I should probably go first. You two are looking a little squishy."

Anabelle stared at Terra, aghast. "Squishy? Excuse—"

"I meant I can probably take the first hit if it comes to that."

The elf looked barely able to tolerate Terra's answer. "I'm not infirm, but please, be my guest."

The three made their way down the narrow tunnel. The walls were covered in prison cells.

A wheezing sound was coming from one of the cells to the right.

Terra took a deep breath and opened the cell.

A small man sat on the floor. He wore a red-lined black cloak and a top hat. Two daggers laid on the ground next to him, as well as a blunderbuss, which was connected to the man's left arm. He looked up at Terra as she walked into the room. The bottom half of the man's face was covered by a black silk scarf.

He had weary eyes. "Oh, I see you have found me."

Terra lowered her axe as Abby and Anabelle stepped into the cell. "Are you okay?"

The man coughed as he leaned forward. "The world is not okay. Neither are the realms. What is one man in this chaos?"

Terra gave Anabelle a look. "Uh, do you need help?"

The man shook his head as he tried to lift his arm. "No, this is my lot. Some of us are doomed to the cycle of repetition. Not all are the heroes of their own stories. There are some of us who are…merely a dream, ash floating in the wind. But enough of me. What brings you to my tomb?"

Terra pointed at Anabelle. "That would be the boss lady's department."

Anabelle stepped forward. "We're searching for the main chamber. There's an important item there I'm trying to locate."

The man looked up. "You seek the main chamber? Then our goals are one and the same. I hope you find it easier than I did." He sighed and leaned back against the wall. "Good luck."

"Do you know where it is?"

The man did not answer. After a few seconds, he began snoring.

Abby knelt next to him. "Well, that was very *From Software*."

Anabelle and Terra exchanged glances.

Abby threw her arms up in frustration. "You guys don't play D&D, and you don't play videogames? What do you do in your free time?"

Anabelle crossed her arms as she tapped her foot. "Not all of us are sixteen, Abby. Now, come on. We should keep going."

"Shouldn't we help him or something?"

"What do you usually do in your videogames?"

Abby's brow furrowed as she thought. "Uh, an NPC that's dressed this well usually shows up at another story beat. Generally when the player needs something or—"

"Forget I asked. We'll check up on him when we finish all this."

They left the cell, making sure the door was wide open in case the man woke up and felt he had the strength to leave. Then they continued down the hall until they came to a door, covered in fog and smoke.

Anabelle stared at the fog. "Guess this is where we're supposed to go."

Terra walked to the door and poked her finger into the fog. "Ominous. I think the rational thing to do is not to step into the foggy underworld. *Silent Hill*, anyone?"

Anabelle nodded in agreement, causing Abby's eyes to widen with shock. "Wait, you've played *Silent Hill*?" she asked.

"Huh? Video game? No, that was a movie and a damn good one too. We watched it last week," Terra replied.

The elf disagreed. "If you could even call it a movie. Two hours of fog and cults. Hardly entertainment."

Abby threw up her hands in frustration. "Forget we even said anything. Come on, let's see what's on the other side."

She stepped through the fog, and Terra and Anabelle followed.

As Terra stepped over the threshold of the door, the fog disappeared. The three of them had walked into a room with steel grates for a floor. Under the grates were flames, occasionally shooting up in giant blasts. "So, we try not to get burned?"

Terra walked farther into the room. Beneath her feet, she heard sizzling, and she jumped to the side as a wall of flame shot up. "If you hear a hiss, that means you're about to be barbeque."

As Terra spoke, a black creature slunk out of the shadows across the room. The pitch-black dog had mangy fur and stood nearly ten feet, its rotting jaw hanging by tendons. Red eyes peered out of the tangled fur.

Abby readied her cannon, her nanobots providing her sleek metallic armor. "That thing is going to attack us, isn't it? So, we glad we didn't waste those energy reserves?"

Terra drew her axe. "Don't start congratulating yourself until the thing is dead."

Anabelle took a traditional Traveler fighting stance. Terra looked at her. "I thought you said you were running on empty?"

Energy crackled around Anabelle. "Not on empty, just not on full. We should be able to take a dog down. Killing blow gets to pick the next movie or show."

Terra took off running. "This one's mine! I can't watch any more anime."

Abby blasted off after Terra. "We resent that."

The dog ran toward the DGA, showing a considerable amount of speed for something that large.

Terra collided with it and punched it in the jaw, sending the dog stumbling backward. Abby opened fire, peppering the dog with plasma blasts.

"No fair," Terra shouted. "You get like a thousand shots."

As the dog stumbled backward, Anabelle leapt and landed on the dog's chest, driving her flaming hand into its sternum.

The dog let out a loud yelp and lay still.

The three backed away. "Damn, that didn't make me feel good."

There was a hiss from the grates below and the DGA members stepped to the side, easily avoiding the flames. "Maybe we are too strong to be doing dungeon runs," Anabelle suggested. "That's good to know. Come on, let's find a way out of here."

The three of them split up and started to look through the room, occasionally stepping to the side to avoid getting roasted.

Flames flashed up around the dog and it started to twitch, its back legs kicking as if it were in a dream. It then began wheezing harshly.

Terra heard the dog and turned to see what was happening.

The dog's shoulders bulged as if they were filling with pus and it got back to its feet, swaying as it whimpered under its breath. Then its shoulder ripped open, bone and blood flying as a head on both shoulders forced itself out from under the dog's skin.

One of the heads snapped at the others before all three growled and turned their attention to the DGA.

Terra smiled. "You know, I was hoping there'd be a dragon or something."

Anabelle came over to join Terra, as did Abby. "You've already fought a dragon. What's the big deal?"

Terra sized up the three-headed dog. "Dragons are more fun."

"More fun than Cerberus?" Abby asked.

Cerberus threw back his three heads and let out a loud howl before breathing fire from all three mouths.

Terra whistled as she and the rest of the DGA stepped to the side to avoid the fire flaring beneath them. "Okay, this looks like it might be fun."

CHAPTER THREE

Fire began spouting from the grates with increased rapidity as the DGA agents split up, making room for Cerberus. He was now bounding around the room, snapping at whichever agent was closest to him.

Abby stood in the corner of the room, checking her nanobot count. She was worried about engaging in combat. Both Martin and the nanobot consciousness had reassured her that this level of strain on her body was acceptable.

That didn't keep her from freaking out, though.

She hadn't felt this frozen since the first time she'd been in a fight. Even then, it had been nothing like this. Abby had quickly skipped over being afraid and been enthralled with her strength. There was nothing here but fear.

Across the room, Terra was trying to close the space between her and Cerberus, but she wasn't doing a very good job. She looked like someone trying to catch their runaway dog, with the added ridiculousness of attempting to dodge fire bursts.

Anabelle, much like Abby, was hanging back from the fight, launching projectiles of fire and ice—something the girl hadn't seen the elf do much. She wondered if Anabelle was having the same problem she was.

It was apparent why they were doing a dungeon crawl now. The teamwork they had worked so hard to solidify was gone. This fight consisted of a giant, ferocious dog and three teammates who were too uncertain of their strength to fight. *Well, it can't turn out too bad. We'll get the hang of this.*

As Abby thought that, the grate beneath Cerberus exploded, setting the dog's tail on fire. Cerberus screeched in pain, his eyes becoming a darker red, and he turned to face Abby. Whatever the dog needed to push him into high gear had obviously happened.

Cerberus bolted at the girl, who was in a corner. The grates beneath her began to hiss.

Abby leapt to the side, managing to keep from being engulfed in flames as Cerberus landed in front of her.

The hellhound snapped at Abby, who rolled to the side and fired instinctively. Part of her kicked herself for wasting ammo. The other, more rational side, acknowledged that this was the exact situation she was supposed to be using her ammo for.

The plasma blast hit Cerberus in the chest, giving the girl space to get away. The blast had not been enough to do any real damage. She was still afraid of wasting power, being uncertain of how much her body could handle.

Terra came in from the side and tackled Cerberus, giving Abby even more space for a getaway. "Come on, kid. We got to take care of this thing."

Abby fired again as she backed away. "I know! I'm just…"

One of Cerberus' heads snapped at Terra, who grabbed the creature by its jaws. "Yeah, yeah, I know! But you gotta be a hundred percent here because Anabelle isn't."

Abby cast a quick glance in the elf's direction. She was still lobbing bolts, but they weren't particularly strong or well-directed. She looked as if she were fighting in a daze.

Terra wrestled Cerberus down for a second before the dog flipped around and blasted her with a fireball. She screamed and rolled around to put out the fire, only for the grates beneath her to hiss. "Are you fucking kidding me! Abby, get your ass in gear because we have to deal with this."

Abby knew what she had to do. She'd been avoiding it so far, but it had to happen. She felt herself receding into herself. "Abby" became less of a construct, instead infused with the other aspect of her mind now: the Consciousness.

She felt herself calm down, another voice in her head directing things.

The thrusters on Abby's feet fired and she was up in the air, away from the grates, taking in as much visual information as she could process.

She headed toward Cerberus and slammed into his side, sending the dog flying.

Before he hit the ground, he roared in anger, and one of his heads hit Abby in the chest.

She fell out of the air and rolled as the grate beneath her hissed.

Terra pulled the girl up and tossed her across the room, away from the flames that burst upward. Then she turned to face Anabelle. "Hey, anytime you want to get in on this, you're more than welcome to."

Anabelle looked at Abby, her face white and gaunt, her eyes bulging from her skull. Her lips trembled, but she said nothing as she wove another ineffectual energy blast.

Terra didn't spend any more time on the elf, instead focusing on Abby. "Hey, kid, this is all us today. Can you hang?"

Abby slammed her hands together, forming a larger energy cannon. "We can hang." She fired a plasma blast.

Cerberus leapt out of the way, skidding on the grates as a wall of fire shot up underneath the dog, scorching his bottom and setting him aflame. He screeched in rage and pain as he ran around the room, his long tail tossing sparks as his heads lobbed fireballs.

Abby took to the air again, trying to avoid the fireballs in the small, enclosed space. "This is like a *really* bad boss fight."

Terra dodged a fireball coming her way. "The nerd commentary isn't helping, Abby!"

The girl fired another series of plasma blasts at Cerberus, who easily stepped out of the way. He deliberately stepped through the flames from beneath the grates, increasing the burning on his body. "Okay, well, what can we do to help?"

"I don't know. Kill the fucking dog!"

Cerberus jumped, closing the distance between itself and Terra, and knocked the orc chieftain to the ground. Two of the heads barked, while the middle stretched its jaws open to swallow her whole.

Two quick slashes crossed Cerberus' snout. The dog roared in pain and reared up on its hind legs as something scooped Terra up and moved away from the monster.

The cloaked man held Terra. He dashed over to Abby, moving nearly too fast for her to see.

The girl helped Terra to her feet while casting a mistrustful eye on the cloaked man. "We thought you were at Death's door."

The cloaked man stood to his full height, his daggers gleaming. "When you've been here as long as me, you're always at Death's door, but the door stays closed unless this is the place you'd like to open it. Now, are we fighting?"

Abby nodded as she took aim at Cerberus. The grates beneath her hissed and she took to the air as Terra and the cloaked man put some distance between them and the fire that erupted.

The cloaked man dashed forward, once more moving nearly too fast to see, and slashed Cerberus's face.

The dog reared to attack and the cloaked man switched to his blunderbuss, firing twice. Cerberus stepped back, giving the cloaked man room to move.

Abby fired at Cerberus, forcing him to retreat for a moment. The grate beneath her exploded with flames, and she leaped into the air. "This is totally a *From Software* fight!"

Terra was running at Cerberus, her axe raised high. "Abby, that means nothing to me unless it helps kill this thing." She slashed at one of Cerberus' heads.

Before the axe could connect, Cerberus' neck began to jolt and shiver. All three of his heads shot up, their necks stretching to a grotesque length, now so heavy that they drooped to the floor like snakes.

Abby flew over Cerberus, peppering him with fire as the creature flailed, still launching fireballs. She gracefully dodged the attacks but still hadn't managed to put a dent in the hellhound. "Nothing we're doing is working!"

A wave of water hit Cerberus in the side, tossing him like a rag doll. "That's because we're not thinking with our heads."

Anabelle had finally joined the fight. She waved her hands, drawing an elaborate shape in the air, and water gushed from her fingertips. "We're obviously fighting at half-strength, so we need to use our heads. For one, this whole fighting on top of fire thing is going to end." She raised her hands as she floated a few inches off the ground. In one sweeping move, she conjured water out of thin air and a gentle rain began to fall, extinguishing the fires beneath the DGA.

The water seemed to be affecting Cerberus as well. The hellhound sneezed and whimpered as the rain caused steam to rise from his body.

Terra, who wasn't far from Cerberus, looked at Abby. "This is our shot. Let's take him out while we can. I'll keep him still." She took off after the dog, leapt a few feet, and snatched up one of Cerberus' hanging necks as she landed, wrestling it to the grate.

Abby leapt over them, firing a concentrated beam of plasma that seared through the neck.

Before Terra could move away, another of the necks sideswiped her, knocking her into the wall.

Abby dove, grabbed another neck, and pinned it to the grate with a nanorod she fired from her wrist.

The cloaked man surged forward, daggers drawn, and slashed through it, leaving only one more head to be taken care of.

Anabelle clapped her hands, her fingers filling with lightning, and dashed toward Cerberus. She avoided the fireballs belched by the hellhound as Abby and the cloaked man moved out of the way to give the elf room.

She hit Cerberus hard, severing the dog's head. It landed next to her feet. Blood dripped through the grate.

Anabelle wiped the dog's blood off her face. "That shouldn't have taken nearly that long. Maybe we need to start running training simulations when we get back. That was like watching Blackwell and Naota."

Abby landed next to Anabelle. "That's mean. Those two are pretty good together."

"They look like bumbling idiots when they fight together."

Terra sauntered over to her fellow agents. "No lie. They do look like clowns." She turned her attention to the cloaked man, who was hunched over Cerberus' corpse. "Thanks for the help!" Terra called. "Care to introduce yourself?"

The cloaked man walked over, sheathing his daggers, and extended his hand. "Maurice the Third. It is my pleasure to meet you."

The DGA agents each gave an introduction. Once they were done, Maurice looked back at the monster's body. "That creature has killed me many times. I didn't think I would ever be able to get past this room."

Anabelle jerked her hand toward the exit. "You coming with us? This dungeon shouldn't be too much longer."

The cloaked man shook his head. "No, my task is to wait and help. This dungeon…it is hard to explain. Hopefully, you won't find out." He headed back out the way he came in.

Abby crossed her arms and smiled. "Mysterious and cryptic. I like it. Come on, let's finish this shit."

Anabelle gave the girl a disapproving look. "We've talked about your language before, young lady."

"Ugh. We can save the world and experiment with reckless tech, but we can't curse?"

The elf and Terra were already walking toward the door. "We don't make the rules about being a kid," Terra called back as Abby ran to catch up with them.

Terra pushed the door open, and the three of them walked down a long hallway lit by blue-flamed candles in sconces on the walls.

At the end of the hall was another door, but it was different from the other doors Terra and the rest had seen. A long, sad face was carved into this plain wooden door. When the DGA agents got close enough, the door opened its eyes and yawned widely.

Abby yelped and jumped back, her cannon raised and ready to fire. "What the hell is that?"

Anabelle, who looked nonplussed, stepped closer to the door. "Never seen a talking door before?"

Terra and Anabelle exchanged dubious looks. "Can't say I have," Terra replied.

The elf waved at the door. "Hiya! Are you the end of the dungeon?"

The door harrumphed as it stretched its jaw and blinked. "Why, yes. I am the final door," it replied in a heavy British accent. "I'm assuming you aim to get through, aye?"

"That is the plan. What do we need to do to open you?"

The door grinned mischievously. "A riddle, perchance."

Anabelle groaned as she ran her hands through her hair. "Are you serious? A riddle door. Damn the gods."

Terra clapped the elf on the back. "What's the big deal? We just have to answer a riddle."

"I'm terrible at riddles. I hate them. The most basic form of wit, and the whole time, you have to watch some smug asshole smirking while you try to figure out the answer. Lording it over you because they're *so* smart."

Abby laughed as she admired the door's smirk. "Could you have a bigger chip on your shoulder?"

Anabelle shot her a glare as cold as ice before turning back to the door. "Okay. So, what is it?"

The door smiled widely. "Oh, no, you have to ask me a riddle. If I can't answer it, then you may enter."

The members of the DGA looked from one to the other. "Uh, you guys know any good riddles?" Anabelle asked.

Abby grimaced as she thought. "We know one. Should we try?"

"Unless Terra's got a brainbuster on her."

Terra shook her head as she shoved her hands in her pockets. "Do I look like someone who sits around doing crossword puzzles? I'm not a grandma."

"Okay, Abby, you're up."

Abby stepped to the door and cleared her throat. "What has four legs in the morning, two legs in the afternoon, and three at night."

Without missing a beat, the door said, "Too easy. A mortal. Goodbye."

There was a bright flash of light, and the three Dark Gate Angels started screaming as everything turned to darkness.

In the middle of the room made of god flesh, Rasputina found herself standing before a table covered with various fresh body parts. Blood dripped from the table, pooling around its legs.

The lich stood dully, drool dripping from her mouth as she mindlessly tongued the rotting hole in her cheek. Her eyes were white, glazed over with death. The little bit of color in her skin reminded her on a primal level that she was not among the living, which was why she stood naked, her decomposing flesh riddled with holes, bones sticking out at bizarre angles.

The dead had no need for clothes.

As she looked around, she realized she was not much different from the flesh hanging from the walls. Not that she hadn't already known that, but there were times when it became more evident—a truth that could not be escaped.

But truth had never been Rasputina's concern. There was only knowledge.

The door opened, and a diminutive human corpse crept into the room. Most of his skin had rotted off, but he still wore an English butler's uniform. He walked with a limp, and green pus trickled out of his ears. He held a silver platter with a collection of hearts, some from humans and others from elves.

Groaning as he moved, he shuffled toward the table and placed the hearts on it. "Mistress," he said, quite formal in his unfortunate predicament.

Rasputina snapped back to the world around her and looked at Bennington with deep confusion as if she were beholding him for the first time. "What is it?" she snapped.

"I've brought you dinner. You have been in your study for a while now, and your screams sound much more like the screams of the living than usual."

Rasputina grabbed one of the elf hearts and bit into it. "You are testing me, Bennington."

He bowed low. "If I do not torment you, my mistress, who will?"

Rasputina collapsed to the floor, holding the elf heart to her own. "They don't beat, Benny. None of them. They just sit here, quiet. All quiet. How am I supposed to enjoy this?"

The butler took a seat next to Rasputina. "My mistress, that is because they are not fresh. You haven't killed anything in nearly two weeks. It's most unlike you. Is something wrong?"

Rasputina curled into the fetal position as she started to sob. "I don't want to be here, Benny. I want to go home. I just want to go home." Her eyes glazed as she stared into the distance, mindlessly gnawing on the heart.

Bennington patted Rasputina's balding head. "Something *is* wrong. You aren't yourself. Would you like to torture me?"

Rasputina's eyes focused on Bennington. "No. No, my heart isn't in it."

Bennington stood. He knocked over everything on the table and jumped onto it, opening his shirt to reveal a chest that was covered in scars and open wounds. "My mistress, my body is ready."

Rasputina sighed as she climbed to her feet. "You just want to be able to sleep tonight. Don't worry about it. I'll let you stay dead for the whole night."

Bennington sat up, aghast. "My mistress, how dare you? There is something wrong, and I wish to help you make it better." He grabbed a dagger off the table and handed it to Rasputina.

She waved it away. "No, no, Benny. I don't—"

"Mistress, I insist. But you don't have to use the dagger. Whatever you'd like. Perhaps a bone?"

A glimmer of a smile twinkled in Rasputina's eyes. "Fine, fine. If you insist." She accepted the dagger and cut open her stomach, dragging out her intestines, which she looped around her hand once as she walked around the table so she could lean over and look Bennington in the eyes. She wrapped her intestines around his neck and pulled them tight.

Bennington jerked as he clawed at Rasputina's intestines, trying to pull them off. His eyes bulged, and the little color in his skin started to fade.

The lich looked down at his face, his mouth flapping as he begged her to kill him and end it all. She couldn't help but laugh and strangle him harder. Then she climbed up on top of him and drove the dagger deep into Bennington's chest, cracking the sternum. She dropped her intestines and dug deep into his body as she cackled with the laughter one usually only hears from children.

When her butler finally stopped twitching, Rasputina pulled a strip of flesh from his chest and swallowed it. She leapt off the table and crawled underneath, where she retrieved the elf heart and continued to gnaw on it.

Above her, Bennington's wounds began to heal. Once his chest sealed up, he jerked back up, screaming for a second as he felt where his wounds used to be.

"Thanks, Benny," Rasputina muttered from under the table.

He climbed off the table and buttoned his shirt, somehow retaining the dignity he had walked into the room with. "Do you feel better?"

The lich nodded, looking oddly infantile and feral. "That right there is the problem, Benny-boy. Seems like I'm feeling too much. Far too much."

Bennington crawled under the table next to Rasputina. "Excuse me for my forwardness, Mistress, but *you* cannot feel anything, or at least, very few things."

She pressed her finger to her chest. "No, no. Something is happening in here. I don't like it."

"When was the last time you had a real feeling? Other than—"

"Hunger? Hatred? Boredom? Gods, I don't know. There was an inkling of something when I was released. Teeny-tiny. But this… Gods, this is horrible. Something about the Dark One…I think."

Rasputina turned to Bennington and grabbed his face. "What do people do when they feel things? Benny, what do you do?"

He shrugged. "I haven't felt anything but fear recently, Mistress, and even that hasn't been for a long time."

Rasputina scoffed. "Are you saying you don't fear me anymore, Benny? I can crank the torture up, and we'll do all those spinal things you hate."

Benny shook his head. "You removed my spine yesterday, Mistress."

"Oh…"

He reached up, grabbed another heart from the tray, and handed it to the lich. "That's what I'm talking about, Mistress. You don't even remember our tortures anymore."

Rasputina shrieked and the table above her exploded, sending the body parts on it flying. "I don't know what's going on! I feel…ugh, I *feel*. That's enough."

Bennington took out a handkerchief and dabbed away the blood on his skeletal face. "Perhaps you need some alone time. You have been pacing the halls lately. It must be hard to think with the dead god's dreams around you all the time."

Rasputina snapped her fingers. "Me-time. You're right!"

She got up and waved her hands, conjuring a cauldron and a book made of human flesh, inked with blood. "Let's see, what do I need… Benny could you run and grab me an orc cock, and uh, a virgin's heart. No, two *male* virgins' hearts, and a cup of salt."

"Are the virgins' hearts labeled, Mistress?"

Rasputina whipped around and grabbed Bennington by the throat. "They are if you labeled them like I told you to last millennium."

Bennington choked out, "Actually, Mistress, you said that would make a fun hobby for you."

Rasputina dropped her butler, who calmly got to his feet and smoothed his shirt. "I will go check," he said, and with that, he disappeared in a puff of green smoke.

The lich went to the walls, selecting digits, organs, and whatever else she felt was necessary from the corpses hanging on the wall. Then to the cabinets, which housed an assortment of unsavory ingredients not much different from those harvested from the tortured on the wall but from animals instead.

As Rasputina began dumping the ingredients into the cauldron, Bennington appeared at her side. "You did label the hearts, Mistress." He handed her the virgins' hearts and the orc cock. "Is there anything else?"

Rasputina dumped the human body parts into the cauldron. "No, Benny, that's all. Wait...actually, if you could bring me a soul for after I'm done."

Bennington nodded and bowed before leaving the room.

Rasputina peered into the cauldron before taking a deep breath. Then she grabbed her dagger, hung her head into the cauldron, and slit her throat.

Blood poured in as she convulsed, and she felt whatever constituted her life fading.

The blood in the cauldron turned a sickly green and began to bubble, consuming everything in the cauldron and melting it. That included the side of Rasputina's face, which was down to the bone before her body returned to running itself.

Rasputina pulled her head out of the cauldron, flinging acid everywhere as she gasped for breath. The rotting skin on her face started to grow back as she picked up her spellbook. She cleared her throat and began chanting, using the old language of the dead gods—a guttural language, producing sounds almost like a death rattle. Then she dropped the book and watched.

Out of the cauldron rose a skeleton, muscle and tissue growing over the bone until a face was evident.

The lich stared into the eyes of a younger version of herself, the one that existed before she became a lich. A living, breathing person.

The girl looked around fearfully. "Where…where am I?" When she saw the lich, she screeched in horror. "Gods, is that—"

"You?" Rasputina asked, bored. "Yes, I am. Everything you were going to become. That's not important. I need you to answer something for me."

The younger Rasputina trembled with fear. "How did this happen to me?"

"That's not important. Answer my questions."

Rasputina was disturbed by the younger version of herself. Both were nude, but there was something disgusting to her about the girl. Her skin was so vibrant, so full of blood, and her chest kept rising. "I'm feeling things. Why?"

The younger Rasputina didn't answer. She merely stood there, looking as frightened as a rabbit before a wolf. "How could this happen to me?"

Rasputina slapped her younger version. "How did it happen? You wanted knowledge. That's how it happened."

She crawled away from the lich. "Not at this cost. You're…you're a monster! What did you do to me?"

The lich stood silent for a moment, green drool trickling down her chin. "I am not a monster. I am…I am…"

The girl waved her hand, pushing the lich back with her mana. "My magic was meant to help people! How could you do this to me?"

The magic from the younger Rasputina caused the lich's skin to catch fire, though it went out quickly. Holy magic. The lich had forgotten she had known holy magic. What else had she forgotten? "What did you do to me?" the girl shouted.

The lich grabbed her and lifted her by her throat. "I did nothing! He killed them. All I did was what I could. What I had to do!"

The younger Rasputina stared down at the lich, choking, her eyes full of tears. "What did you do?"

The lich tossed her to the ground as she started to cry. Too much was rushing back. There were too many voices, too much noise in her head. "He killed them all!" she shouted. "He killed all of them! All I could do was try to find a way to stop him, but I didn't! There was nothing I could do."

It all came back. Brief flashes of her childhood. And her home. Her village.

People were screaming and begging for mercy from the Dark One. The plague that spread over them killed everyone but Rasputina, leaving her alone, a scared child clutching a small toy, hoping her parents would return. A weak thing without anyone to protect her.

The lich froze, overwhelmed by her memories. This was why she felt. The Dark One had released her.

The younger Rasputina stood. "You did this to yourself to stop him? You sold your soul—"

The lich screeched, "I sold nothing! I only learned…" She crumpled to the floor, holding her knees tightly together. "I had to learn to stop him, and…I forgot. I forgot about all of this…about my life. About living."

"You're a monster."

The lich looked up, staring into her own eyes. "No, I'm not. I'm not a monster."

The girl spat at the lich, "An abomination."

The lich crawled over to the younger Rasputina, who tried to run, but the skeletal hands reached up from the floor and held her down. "I'm a necessity," the lich growled as she crawled onto her younger self.

"How are you, if nothing matters?"

The lich stared down at the girl, who had so much beauty in her face.

So much hope.

Life.

The lich screamed and reached into her side, pulling out a bone sharpened to a razor point. She drove it into the younger Rasputina's chest as the girl begged for mercy. The lich continued as the room became filled with screams, and eventually, gurgling and choking.

Bennington opened the door.

Rasputina looked up, covered in blood and smiling psychotically. "I know what I'm feeling."

Bennington walked into the room and pulled a towel from his waist, draping it over the girl. "Yes? You've figured it out?"

Rasputina caressed the corpse. "He was responsible. The Dark One. Odin. The Death Without Names. He killed them. My family. My friends. That's why I needed to learn how to stop him. That's why I became this."

The lich looked down at her younger self. "She was beautiful, wasn't she? And so strong, so good. She was a good person."

Bennington grabbed the hands of the dead girl and began dragging her away. "She looks to have been."

As Bennington took the corpse out of the room, Rasputina leaned over, crying and shaking before screaming, filling the body of the dead god with her cries. "How could I forget all this?" she whimpered. "By the gods, how could I forget why I sought the knowledge to begin with?"

CHAPTER FIVE

Abby opened her eyes, slightly afraid of where she might have been transported. The last thing she had seen before the flash of light was the riddle door staring menacingly at her.

One eye creaked open, letting in a little bit of light. Now the second. Abby's vision was blurred, but it was starting to sharpen.

She was in her room, lying in bed. "What the hell?" she muttered. "That couldn't have just been a dream."

"No, Mother/Creator, that was not a dream."

Abby jumped at the sound of the nanobot consciousness. Unlike Martin, the consciousness always caught Abby off-guard. It was like having someone barge into her room. At least Martin had the decency to knock. Abby wasn't certain how Martin did it, but whatever he was doing made a difference.

After Abby took a few moments to gather herself, she went to brush her teeth. She stared at her reflection as she tried to piece together what had happened. The door had asked for a riddle, and she had delivered the only one she knew. Something from Plato, or maybe it was just a Greek myth. Either way, it didn't matter. The door had figured out the answer before she'd even finished.

Abby looked down at her HUD, the nanobots in her body building it instantly. They worked on an instinctual level, just as easily as Abby's brain relayed the command to raise her hand and tilt her head.

It was a little past one. That meant at least four hours had passed since she and the DGA had entered the tunnel. The dungeon crawl had *definitely* happened.

Abby's HUD pinged, and a holographic rendering of a recent email appeared in front of her. She swiped her hand to open it.

It was a group chat message from Terra and Anabelle. "Everybody back?" the elf asked.

Abby typed that she had just woken up. Terra said something similar.

"Everybody to the war room," Anabelle texted.

<hr>

Terra and Anabelle were already in the war room by the time Abby arrived. Roy was there as well.

Roy looked exhausted, but nowadays, he always looked like he'd given up on sleeping. His eyes were so sunken that it didn't look like they were ever coming back up for air. "So, what I hear is that you guys didn't retrieve the item."

Anabelle shook her head as she explained what happened. "Like I said, we asked the door a riddle, and then there was a lot of pain. Next thing we knew, we were back at HQ. I have no idea what happened." Anabelle's voice went distant. "There's got to be a better way. Maybe we can reach out to Myrddin and the guy he was with…José…and see if there's another way in."

When Anabelle had first told her and Terra about receiving visions from Myrddin and some guy named José, neither she nor Terra had questioned Anabelle. Weirder things had happened. But Abby had been interested in finding out who José was. She didn't recognize the name from any briefings she had read. And when she asked about the guy before, no one had any answers. "Any updates on who this José guy is?"

Roy pulled up José's file and projected onto the war room's holoprojector. The photo was of a large, broad-shouldered man with a face full of scars and long, flowing hair. Abby thought José looked like what you would expect a Hollywood version of Jesus Christ to look like.

The armor that José wore looked familiar to Abby. She knew she'd seen it someplace before but couldn't quite place it.

Terra was the one to call it out. "That's MERC armor, isn't it? Like those kids who helped you guys bust me out of the arena, right?"

Roy nodded as the projector started to list José's accomplishments. "Correct. It took a while to find his file. He was one of our top MERCs. You know about them, right? One of Myrddin's pet projects. We had to crack into Myrddin's files, and let's just say that a firewall on a wizard's computer is more literal than you'd like." He didn't chuckle, which meant he was serious. "MERCs operate outside the main Middang3ard channels, typically doing shit that is considered too insane for anyone else to attempt. Few got more insane than José. Unfortunately, he died during a mission. Lucky for us, he was strong enough to retain his consciousness in the astral plane. We don't hear from him often, but when we do, it is important."

"We are taking advice from a dead guy. Is that a good idea? I mean, he did end up dead."

Roy turned off the projector and sat back down, giving Terra a look that could easily be read as *stop talking now*. "The conditions of José's death were extreme, and he died a hero. He's just as trustworthy in death as he was alive. Speaking of failing missions, what the hell happened with you guys? You obviously didn't give that door a hard enough riddle. I mean, don't you have a supercomputer in your head, Abby? How hard is it to stump an ancient door without access to the Internet?"

Abby blushed as she stumbled over her answer. She hated being called out like this. What made it even worse was that she hated how slow she felt since her body was closer to normal than when it was bursting with nanobots. "We have significantly fewer nanobots than before. Our brain is closer to a normal human's, and our contact with Martin got cut while we were in the dungeon."

Roy brushed off his pants as he stood. "Well, you guys better look up riddles because you're going back."

"Wait, what do you mean?"

Roy looked over his shoulder as he stopped at the door. "It's a riddle door. That means the whole place is enchanted. Imagine you're playing a video game and you die at the end, right before you pick up the key from the last boss. If you do that, you go right back to the beginning and play through the whole thing again. That's you guys."

Anabelle put her head in her hands. "Are you saying we have to fight our way through that dungeon again?"

"Yep. Try to pick a hard riddle this time."

Roy left the DGA to themselves. "Looks like we're going to be running a training simulation after all," Abby said quietly.

Anabelle walked over to the holoprojector and leaned against it. "This wasn't what I had in mind, but it'll do. At least we know what we're up against. How about we take a couple hours, do some research, relax a little bit, and head in. It's not like we have any pressing missions right now."

Abby's heart leapt. Downtime was exactly what she had wanted. Being in that dungeon had been stressful. She'd gotten used to the amount of ass-kicking power she'd had before. This reminded her of her least favorite *Metroid* games. She had been at the endgame level, and now she hardly had any useful upgrades. "Yeah, that sounds good. We were going to watch a movie with Persephone, actually. You know, something to distract me from, well, what happened in that dungeon. Either of you wanna come?"

Terra jumped out of her seat, smiling widely. "Hell, yeah! What are you guys watching? Please don't tell me it's something sappy."

Abby shook her head enthusiastically. "Classic gnomish horror movie."

"Oh, I'd love to see what those optimistic little dudes think is horrific. You in, Anabelle?"

Abby looked at the elf, who was staring blankly at the holoprojector. "Hey, Belle? You wanna hang out for a bit before we leave?"

Anabelle jumped. "Huh? No, I need to make some preparations. I'll see you guys when it's time to leave. And don't forget to research riddles." She breezed past Abby and Terra.

Terra clicked her tongue while she stared at the door. "She's doing a real good job of avoiding us."

Abby shrugged. "Belle went through a lot with Grok. She probably just needs time to process all that. I know I would."

Terra punched Abby in the shoulder as she walked by. "Give yourself some credit. Not everyone could deal with growing a new personality in their head. Come on. Let's go get our movie on."

The DGA gathered at the hadron collider a few hours later. Creon was waiting for them. As the goblin went ahead and punched in the coordinates, Abby watched Anabelle. She couldn't help but feel sad for the elf.

When Abby had first met Anabelle, she'd thought the elf was the most beautiful person ever to walk the Earth. As Abby got to know Anabelle better, those feelings changed. Abby saw a woman who wanted to be known, yet the way for the elf to do that was by doing the one thing it seemed like she didn't feel comfortable with: leading.

Over the last few months, Abby's crush had faded, but she still respected Anabelle tremendously. For someone who didn't want to be responsible for the lives of humans, the elf had come a long way.

Now Abby saw a shadow of that person. Anabelle had hardly seemed to be engaged with their last mission. She could see something darker in Anabelle's eyes, which disturbed her. The blank expression was one thing.

But that darkness, the way Anabelle's eyes would sometimes flash as if madness were hiding, waiting for a chance to escape, terrified Abby. She hoped it was just her imagination.

As if Anabelle could tell Abby was staring at her, she turned to face the girl. "You guys ready?"

Abby jumped at the elf's sudden question. "Yeah, yeah, we're ready."

The hadron collider opened and the DGA stepped through, instantly transporting to the beginning of the dungeon.

Abby pushed the door open, thankful that even if she didn't have as much firepower as she used to, she still had increased strength and stamina. She wasn't nearly as strong as Terra, but she knew she'd be able to hold her own against a couple of orcs. Maybe a troll, but that might be pushing it. "Who wants to lead the way?"

Anabelle pulled up her HUD and withdrew three torches. "Figured we might as well learn from the last mistake, right?" She passed them around, and the DGA began their steady descent into the dungeon.

This time, they managed to avoid the first trap that Terra had set off, but a little way ahead, they picked the wrong tunnel and ended up opening a door to a room of goblins. "If we have to come back, let's remember not to go this way."

Abby, Anabelle, and Terra made short work of the four goblins. Even with their decreased power, they were still easily able to handle the challenge. Plasma bolts flew, scorching a goblin's skin, while Terra pounded two to a pulp with her fists (the only thing she said would make it interesting), Anabelle torching the last with her hands.

They backtracked, this time choosing the right tunnel—the one that led down to the prison. As they walked, Anabelle stopped them. There was something up ahead.

Once more, they found Maurice sitting in a cell, looking miserable. "I see you've returned," he said as he stood and extended his hand.

Abby shook it and stepped out of the cell to give Maurice a way out. "Planning on joining us this time?"

Maurice pulled up his mask to make sure it didn't fall. "Yes, I will accompany you."

The four of them went to Cerberus' chamber. Knowing what lay ahead of them and having an extra person who had fought the hellhound before made the battle fly by. Terra complained she didn't even work up a sweat.

Abby, who was floating, looked down at the grate. "We were fighting on top of fire. How could you not break a sweat?"

Terra stretched and touched her calves. "What can I say? I'm just too fit."

From there, the DGA went to the riddle door, honoring Maurice's request and leaving him behind. They stood before it, and it lazily opened its eyes and smiled at the agents. "Ah! Glad to see you decided to return. This is the most excitement I've had since the cloaked fool stopped trying to get out of here."

Abby was intrigued. She had assumed Maurice hadn't attempted the riddle, but the door's words made more sense. Why would anyone spend all their time in a cell if they had the choice of leaving? "How long has he been here?"

The door wiggled its nose as it thought. "Hm, maybe two hundred years? Give or take. Now, please, the riddle."

Anabelle motioned to Terra. "Your turn."

Terra puffed her chest out as she stepped forward. "I have no voice, but I cry. I have no wings, yet I flutter. Ain't got a tooth, but I can bite. Don't even have a mouth, but I can mutter. What am I?"

The door smiled widely. "The wind."

"Goddamn it!"

A bright flash of light followed the cackling of the door. With that, the DGA was gone.

Cire, Persephone, and Nib-Nib were traveling via convoy to a prospective Dark Gate. They were covered from head to toe in light fabric cloaks to help deal with the gnomish desert's sandstorms. Persephone sat in the back of a truck, watching the sand dunes roll past her.

It had only been a week, and she was already sick of the sand creeping into every crevice of her body. She felt like she was going to need to shower for at least a month straight.

Cire and Nib-Nib didn't seem to have a problem with the sand, which somehow made it worse for Persephone. She was worried that she was making too big of a deal out of nothing, but that didn't change how uncomfortable she felt.

If Abby was here, it wouldn't be too bad, she told herself. Upon thinking more about it, even if Abby were here, it would still be a shit situation. The last few days had been dedicated to running around, trying to hunt down a portal signature. Unfortunately, the sandstorms were wreaking havoc with the survey information HQ was using to pinpoint the Dark Gate's location.

At the end of the day, Persephone was annoyed, but it wasn't as bad as anything she'd experienced under the Dark One's control. She at least had a say in this mission.

The convoy stopped at a refueling station. Gnomes who were once part of the resistance poured out of the camp and started to take care of the vans and trucks in the convoy.

Persephone snuck away from all the noise and war talk. She commed Abby, but there was no answer. It made sense. The two of them were putting in a lot of effort to get in touch with each other, but between their missions, there was little time that they could talk.

Still, Persephone felt like this would have been a lot less irritating if she could just hear Abby's voice.

The drow made her way back to the convoy, trying to avoid Cire's eyes, which followed her anytime she strayed too far from his line of sight.

Cire's comm rang, and he picked it up.

Sarah was on the other line. "You make it to the Dark Gate yet?"

Cire shook his head as he watched the holoprojection of her face. "No, we're still having a hard time hunting it down. I don't know why you sent us to the gnomish homeworld. It would make more sense for me to be with the orcs. We would be able to find it easier."

"Because we're trying to build ties. Orcs on gnome worlds, humans on orc worlds. This is how we learn to work with each other and build trust. Luckily, we're in a situation where we don't have to deal with any offensive measures from the Dark One. We need to take these chances to lay foundations."

Persephone watched Cire look out at the desolate desert. "Understood. It isn't pleasant, but I understand."

"Send me a report when you make it to the Dark Gate. Good luck."

Cire nodded, disconnected the comm, and turned to Persephone and Nib-Nib. "We still have the next set of potential coordinates. Let's hope that we can find this soon enough. Check with the vendors to see if they've got anything you might need."

The orc headed toward the convoy, no doubt to speak to the drivers about the direction they were taking.

Nib-Nib stood there, looking from Persephone to the direction

Cire had walked off in. Finally, she chittered and snapped her claws. "We shop. Find useful tools maybe."

Persephone shrugged. She wasn't sure what useful tools they were going to find in the middle of the desert, but it wouldn't hurt to look. Being grouchy about her assignment wasn't helping anyone. She couldn't understand why she'd been given desert duty instead of an exciting assignment like Abby. Dungeon-crawling seemed like so much more fun.

Persephone and Nib-Nib walked over to the refueling vendors, who occupied a row of gnomish tents with an assortment of gnomes in each of them. There was even an underground gnome, much more covered than the rest, trading with his fairer-skinned cousins. *I wish elves could do this*, Persephone thought as she gravitated toward the underground gnome.

The gnome looked up when he saw her. "Ah, a friend of the dark places?" the gnome exclaimed. "We don't get you folk around here often. Honestly, can't say I remember the last time I seen a drow above ground." He extended his hand.

Persephone shook the gnome's hand and returned his smile. "It has been an enlightening experience. Most of what I've learned is that the Dark One is everywhere and underground might be the only safe place for now."

The underground gnome spread his wares out on a deep-red tapestry. "Aye. There's a lot of truth in that, but not for long. Even our underground is being taken over. Nothing is meant to last, I suppose. I might have something for you among all this. If you ain't looking for anything practical, I might just have a little something for you."

Persephone knew trader charm when she heard it, but that didn't keep her from being intrigued. "And what would that be?"

The gnome pointed to an obsidian gem resting on the corner of the tapestry. "A Black Tear."

Persephone's eyes lit up when she saw the stone. She hadn't seen a Black Tear since she was a child. The stone was a popular couple gift among the drow, almost an institution. She'd never seen a partnered drow couple without at least one of them owning a Black Tear. "How much are you selling it for?"

The deep gnome plucked the stone up and tossed it to Persephone. "For my drow friend? Free of charge. Let it be a reminder of the deep, yes?"

"I can't take this. It's too—"

The underground gnome waved away Persephone's concern. "Please, please. No one would want to buy it except one of us, and there are so few above ground. There must be someone who you love enough to gift this to."

Persephone nodded as she pocketed the gem. "Yeah, there is."

Nib-Nib scuttled over to the deep gnome's tent. She was gnawing on a charred lizard on a skewer. "Anything good?" she chittered.

Persephone nodded as the underground gnome smiled widely. "Yeah, I found something."

Nib-Nib offered Persephone the lizard skewer. "Me too. Want eat?"

Persephone turned her nose up but could not deny that it smelled amazing. She leaned down and took a bite. "Okay, that's not bad."

Cire whistled from the convoy. "We should probably get going," Persephone murmured. She turned back to the deep gnome and bowed her head. "Thank you again. I really appreciate it."

Persephone and Nib-Nib headed back to the convoy and jumped into the truck Cire was sitting in. "We're heading toward the new coordinates right now," he explained.

The convoy kicked up sand, but this time, it didn't bother Persephone. There were beautiful things in the sand dunes. "What makes this Dark Gate so special?" Persephone asked.

"According to the scans we've run, it's a stationary Dark Gate. Doesn't disappear, and it might have been here for a while. Creon thinks it might be the original Dark Gate. The Dark One might have reverse-engineered his tech from this."

After a few hours of driving, the convoy arrived at its destination. They pulled over and the scientists exited their trucks, eager to have a look around.

The drow was glad to get back on her feet. She was getting tired of sitting. She needed to stretch, so she followed the scientists as they began their hunt for the Gate.

The hunt did not last long. The long-limbed, grumpy gnome she was following climbed up a sand dune, then shouted to the rest of the scientists to come quick.

A Dark Gate stood on the top of the dune. This one was different than any Persephone had seen before, though. It was larger and had odd symbols carved into it, but the biggest difference was that she could feel the energy coming off it even though the Gate was closed.

A chorus of unintelligible voices whispered in her head. The Dark Melody. She could rarely understand it in moments like this since there was too much, but she could tell the Melody was excited. It knew there was something different about this Gate.

Persephone wished she could communicate with the Melody the same way Abby did with the nanobot consciousness, but the relationship was different. Very different.

Cire came up behind Persephone, along with the other scientists. "Let's take a look. I'm going to get in touch with Blackwell." He brought up his HUD and opened Zoom, the only app that worked across planets that had been dominated by the Dark One.

Persephone did the same, but Nib-Nib didn't bother.

Blackwell's face appeared on the HUD, along with Naota and Roy. The three of them looked surprisingly rested to Persephone, which was a sudden change because over the last few weeks, Roy had taken on the appearance of a corpse.

"How goes the hunting?" Cire asked.

Naota leaned close to the camera. "The hunt is done! We found the big ol' son of a bitch." He flipped his camera around to show the group chat.

Blackwell was in the background of Naota's video. He waved and tried to look as professional as possible.

Cire flipped his camera around for the same effect. "What's the next step?"

Blackwell answered, "The science teams are going to do a full analysis of the Gate and send the information back to Creon. We're to keep the area under surveillance all night."

Naota sighed as he crossed his arms. "Are you serious? I thought we were going to hit the bar tonight."

Roy hushed Naota as Blackwell glared daggers at him.

Naota blushed brightly and smirked. "I mean, I know we have to watch the Dark Gate. It would be irresponsible to go out drinking."

Persephone glared into her HUD. "We're not stupid, Naota. You're doing that thing where you're trying way too hard."

Naota threw up his hands, defeated. With hysterical theatrics, he cried, "I cannot lie to my teammates! I have to come clean. An orc told me about their bars, and I can't get them off my mind. I *need* to drink with the orcs."

Cire did not seem to be bothered by the humans shirking their duties. "That is a good idea. It will be well received by the orcs in my absence if the humans attempt to understand orcish customs."

Naota snapped his fingers and grinned. "Perfect. I'll make sure to have a drink for you guys."

Naota signed off, leaving Blackwell and Roy. "We have a team watching over the Dark Gate twenty-four/seven. Hopefully we'll get some answers out of this. We'll talk to you guys later. Try not to work too hard."

The two humans signed off.

Persephone was jealous that the humans were going to have the equivalent of a night out. How *much* of a night was still to be determined, though. She couldn't imagine Blackwell relaxing enough to let anyone have a good time, but you never knew with Naota. He seemed to bring out the best and worst parts of Blackwell.

Persephone, Nib-Nib, and Cire returned to the Dark Gate as the scientists began to set up to take their readings. "Would you two like to do anything tonight?" Cire asked. "Our options aren't as robust as an orcish bar, but there's no need to work all night."

Persephone couldn't think of anything she wanted to do other than lie down and go to sleep. The sandy dunes were starting to irritate her again, but she knew it was only jealousy. Maybe she could call Abby and see what was going on with her.

No, Persephone thought. *I can't rely on Abby for a way out of every awkward moment. Tonight you're going to be present, you're going to engage, and you're going to have a good time.*

Nib-Nib and Cire were talking quietly to each other while scientists scuttled about looking busier than Persephone thought was necessary. She cleared her throat and then looked around uncomfortably. "Maybe we could do something here, like…one of the gnomish customs? There's a village pretty close to here, right?"

Cire called one of the scientists over and asked if there was a village close by. The gnome informed him that it was a couple of miles south. "I do believe it is a gnomish festival weekend," the orc mused. "I can't think of a better time to acquaint ourselves with the recently freed small people."

A festival? That sounded nice.

Cire got more information from the gnomes helping the scientists, and within a couple of hours, they were on their way to the closest village, where a gnomish festival of lights was taking place. Persephone was amazed when she saw what a gnomish "light" was.

The entire desert village had been decorated with floating candles. The festival consisted of people taking one of the candles and giving it to a friend or family member. The receiver of the candle made a wish, then the candle shot into the air, where it exploded into the shape of the wish.

Persephone, Cire, and Nib-Nib spent much of the night walking to and fro, introducing themselves to the villagers, listening to their stories, and imparting wishes on each other. By the time Persephone made it to bed, she was full of the village's hopes.

Blackwell and Naota were shitfaced, dancing on top of the bar with two orcs. The larger female orc had taken a fancy to Naota and had him tucked under her arm. She also seemed to have a slight attraction to Blackwell also, and he was neatly cradled in her other arm.

Roy sat at the bar, ignoring his drunk subordinates. He was watching the room to see if there was anything out of line or amiss. Then he found it—a young orc sitting in the corner of the bar alone, a cloak draped over his head.

Roy went over to the orc, sat down, and placed a drink in front of him. "You don't look like you're here to have a good time."

The orc pulled back his cloak, revealing a heavily scarred face covered in red war paint. "Roy, is it? I heard you were part of the team that captured Grok."

CHAPTER SEVEN

A bright flash of light.

Terra woke up in her bedroom, sick to her stomach, and more annoyed than she'd ever thought she could be. She checked herself in the mirror before walking out of her room to meet the rest of the DGA at the hadron collider.

Twenty-three; that was the number of times that they'd gone through the dungeon. Everyone but Abby was at their wits' end. She had jokingly told Terra and Anabelle that it was like a video game. They were getting better at it each time.

That didn't make the orc chieftain or the elf any less annoyed. On top of that, it wasn't true. Terra had noticed that every couple of times they ran the dungeon, there were more monsters. The pathway never changed, but the conflicts were becoming more dangerous. That didn't matter to Terra, though. She was finally starting to get interested in the dungeon's fights.

Maurice had started to change as well. When Terra had first met him, the man had hardly seemed as if he had the will to make it to his feet. Now he was meeting the DGA at the beginning of the tunnel and continuing with them, obviously delighting in a new challenge. *Maybe he just got tired of fighting the same shit,* Terra thought. *The DGA is bringing spice into his life. Hell, I've only done this for an afternoon, and I was starting to get bored.*

Abby and Anabelle were waiting in the war room. Anabelle was fuming and pacing as she shouted, "How the hell are we going to get this goddess-damned riddle? You can't find anything, Abby?"

The girl, who was already on the computer searching for riddles, shook her head. "Everything I find, the door already knows. It's like that thing sits around and reads riddle books all day."

Terra collapsed into one of the seats, using the conjuring enchantment to get herself a beer. She sipped it as Anabelle continued to rage at an imaginary audience. "Abby, I have no idea how you play games like this."

Abby reached for Terra's beer. She stared at the girl, bewildered, as she took a sip. "It's hard but eventually satisfying. You start off against odds you think you can't beat or outsmart, but you work at it until you eventually nail it."

Anabelle kicked one of the chairs in the room. "That's bullshit! Why can't we figure it out? There has to be something we just haven't thought of yet."

"Obviously. If we'd thought of it, we'd already have gotten the door open."

Anabelle picked up one of the broken legs from the chair and pointed it at Abby. "You are not helping right now."

"Maybe we need to take a break. We've been at this for hours."

The elf took a seat, her eyes manic and frenzied, staring at Terra. "We'll figure it out. We can get this. Call the science team, every theorist we can find. And mathematicians. All of them."

Terra switched seats so she was sitting next to Anabelle. She rested her hand on the elf's shoulder. "You need to take a break and relax."

Anabelle sighed and hung her head. "How am I supposed to relax? Myrddin and José sent us on a simple mission, and we're struggling with getting it done. What the hell am I supposed to do other than freak out?"

Abby spun in her chair. "We could go to a bar."

Terra shook her head. "No, you are still *way* underage. There's no way I'm sneaking you into a bar."

Abby pointed at the holoprojector. "Not one on Earth. Middang3ard. We looked up José's file. It said his MERC squad was based at a bar in Middang3ard called the Red Lion. Maybe we could find someone there to give us a hand. The MERCs are pretty well known for dungeon-crawling. We could try to get in touch with José's old squad."

Anabelle whined dramatically, "What have we been reduced to? Asking mercenaries for help?"

Terra shoved the elf. "Jesus Christ, will you stop being ridiculous? They aren't real mercenaries. They work for Myrddin."

Abby turned off the holoprojector. "Actually, they're pretty close. They take contracts from Myrddin and anyone else as long as it doesn't help the Dark One, but they're on our side. Remember, some MERCs came to help us get Terra out of the arena. They're obviously okay helping us."

Anabelle waved her hand as if she were shooing a fly. "Fine, fine. You two are now the leaders of the DGA. I resign. Take me to our next mission."

Abby and Terra exchanged looks. Neither of them knew what to do when Anabelle acted like this. Terra didn't mind. It was hilarious. "Okay, let's hit that hadron collider."

The DGA appeared right outside the Red Lion. It was a long, wooden bar, built on piers over a rancid swamp. The smell was almost too much for Abby. *Martin, can you reduce my olfactory sense?*

Martin's voice came back to Abby instantly. "Yes, Princess. Is the smell of the swamp offending your delicate nose?"

Shut up, I used to shovel cow shit every day. If I don't want to smell something and don't have to, I'd prefer not to. So, can you?

"Easily. Your body is nearly back up to a reasonable number of nanobots. Interacting with your system shouldn't be a problem anymore."

Abby turned her attention back to her squadmates, who were heading toward the Red Lion. "Hey, wasn't that battle you had in the arena called the Battle of the Red Lion?" she asked Terra.

Terra scratched her head as she furrowed her brow, trying to remember. "Yeah, it was. Guess this was where it took place."

Anabelle opened the door and stepped into the bar.

The Red Lion was wooden and crowded with MERCs. There was a bar toward the back where patrons were served beers and food. Tables covered the floor, and there were more than a few dartboards hanging from the walls.

The mix of races made HQ look sheltered. The bar was full of elves, gnomes, humans, and more dwarves than Abby had ever seen. *Guess dwarves prefer MERC work,* she thought.

The other difference Abby noticed instantly was in the demeanor of the MERCs. The Red Lion was nearly too loud for her to hear her own thoughts. The MERCs were a drunken, boisterous bunch. Even Terra looked to be taken aback. "So, where do we start?" Anabelle asked.

Abby scanned the crowd, looking for a familiar face. She recognized one of the MERCs who had been at the battle to free Terra.

It was a young man with a stern, serious face. He wore very simple steel armor, but it gave off more of a shine than anyone around him. Suzuki, the leader of the Mundanes. That was where they were going to start.

Abby approached Suzuki and the Mundanes, who were sitting around him. Sandy, a morbid-looking young woman with jet-black hair and exquisite, well-fitting black robes with the MERC insignia sat across from Suzuki. At her side was Stew, a shirtless, uncomfortably muscular barbarian whose chest was covered with scars. Abby waved at them as she approached.

Suzuki was the first to notice her. He stood up so fast that he almost knocked over his beer. "Hey! Long time no see. It's Anne, right?"

She smiled and shook Suzuki's hand as the rest of the Mundanes rose to meet the DGA. "Abby, actually. Nice to see you again."

Suzuki gestured to the table. "Grab a seat. And a drink. Stew, can you wrangle up some chairs?"

Stew belched and groaned but stepped over to strip three chairs from the adjacent table. "Stew, can you grab this? Stew, can you wrangle this? Stew, can you stomp on this? You know I can do more than just lift and crush things, right?"

Sandy looked up from the book she was reading and blew a kiss at him. "It's because you're so strong, babe. Suzy can't resist asking you to lift things…or crush them."

Another MERC came from the bar. Beth wore a well-constructed set of leather armor, accompanied by a leather cap. She held a tray of beers and roasted meat and set it on the table. "Who are these suits?" she asked, pointing at the DGA.

Suzuki introduced them, reminding Beth that they were the group they had fought with in the arena. Beth apologized if she came off rude. "Sorry about that. You know how it is. You kill so many orcs with so many people, they all start to blend together."

Terra grabbed one of the spare beers and drained it. "I know exactly what you mean. Every fight looks kinda the same. You ever get bored with it?"

Stew, who was watching Terra like a hawk, shook his head. "Nope. There's always something bigger and better to kill."

Terra shrugged as she tapped the bottom of her cup. "Eh. I feel like I peaked after I killed a demigod."

Stew's jaw dropped nearly to the table. "What? You fought a demigod? You have to tell me about it!"

Sandy flipped through her book, not bothering to look up. "Be careful, Terra. You keep talking like that, and he might try to follow you home like a puppy."

Stew gasped as he pressed his hand to his chest. "Babe, I would never."

Sandy pointed her wand at Stew. "I'm going to remind you. No threesomes."

Terra laughed. "As if. You guys are practically babies."

Sandy waved her hand, and her book disappeared. She reached for one of the beers. "He needs guidelines. Otherwise, he gets a little carried away."

Terra, Stew, and Sandy continued to talk while Anabelle, Abby, and the rest of the Mundanes pursued a different conversation. "We're here because we are looking for information on José," Abby explained.

Suzuki checked over his shoulder. "If you're looking for that, you might want to talk to the Horsemen, or what's left of them. They were José's party before…well, you know."

Suzuki shouted at two MERCs in the corner. The first was a no-nonsense mage named Diane, who wore Coke-bottle glasses and robes that looked more like a military uniform than a wizard's garb. The second MERC was a wiry-looking human with short, dirty-blonde hair who wore welding goggles on her forehead. The two made their way over to the Mundanes' table. "Guys, these are the Horsemen. Diane and Chip," Suzuki said.

Chip's eyes widened when she saw Abby. "Oh, I've been hearing lots about you, m'lady. Been shaking up the whole business with that nanobot jazz. Do you mind if I have myself a teeny look?"

Abby gazed dubiously at Chip. "Uh, I'm not sure if—"

Chip held out her arm, which separated down the middle, revealing an elaborate robotic setup. She flexed, and her arm rearticulated into a beam cannon. "Trust 'ol Chip, m'lady; the interest is purely academic. I ain't seen another person walking around with that much tech in their body in much of a minute. Perhaps an exchange of pertinent information would be in order?"

Abby and Chip slipped into conversation quickly, discussing nanobot rations and paradigms of over-redundancy. That left Anabelle, Suzuki, Diane, and Beth to discuss the matter at hand.

"There's no sense beating around the bush," the elf said. "We've been sent on a mission by Myrddin and José, but we've been having a shit time finishing it. We're stuck in a dungeon."

Beth scoffed before she caught herself. "Aren't you guys the Dark Gate Angels? Way I've heard it is you're Myrddin's special little project. Direct communication with the man and resources that us MERCs can only dream of."

Anabelle spoke slowly. "All that's true, and it doesn't change that Myrddin sent us on a mission we need help with. We need to pick your brains for anything you know and to be frank, I'd appreciate any help you're willing to give us with the dungeon."

The elf went on to explain the intricacies of the dungeon. Suzuki perked up when Anabelle explained about the riddle door.

Suzuki looked at Diane. "What do you think?"

Diane tapped her fingers on the table as she thought. "Well, me and Chip have a couple of contracts right now, and they might not be filled until next week. But you four, if I recall, don't have anything to take care of."

Stew leaned over from his conversation, slightly slurring his words. "Whoa, hold on, Suzuki. You said we were going to get some time off this week. We just got back yesterday. Are they even offering us loot? Because you know I am not working without a payday."

Suzuki was quiet. "What do you think, Beth?"

Beth smirked at Anabelle before genuinely smiling. "It's not every day you get to help out Myrddin's special pet project. Or get access to their armory."

Stew clapped his hands together. "Hell, yeah. That's what I'm talking about."

Suzuki shook his head. "No, I don't want to pull that kind of crap." He turned back to Anabelle. "If you need help, the Mundanes are here to give it."

Anabelle and Suzuki shook hands as Stew grumbled and went back to challenging Terra to a drinking contest. "I really appreciate it, Suzuki," the elf said. "And because you decided not to be a dick, I'll see what I can do about you four checking out the armory."

Suzuki slammed his cup on the table and cheered. "I will drink to that. Now, what are you guys up to tonight?"

Anabelle, Terra, and Abby looked at each other. "Uh, this was our plan," the girl said softly.

Sandy handed Terra a beer. "Since you're here, you might as well celebrate with us. We got a big haul today and lots of gold to spend. Barmaid! Get us another round!"

CHAPTER EIGHT

I t was twelve in the morning, and the Mundanes and the Dark Gate Angels were in the midst of what could only be called revelry. The booze and food at the Red Lion flowed infinitely, and each of them was beginning to feel its effects.

Abby had never been drunk. She'd had a few drinks here or there when she had the courage to challenge the adults around her, but that was about it. Even now, she wasn't certain if she was drunk. There was a weird feeling in the back of her head that made it hard to think, but other than that, there were no noticeable signs. *I'm pretty sure that's most of being drunk,* Abby thought. Then she asked Martin, *Hey, can you filter the alcohol out of our system faster? We're not really crazy about this.*

Martin sighed as he answered. "So, you don't want to enjoy the life-fulfilling experience of alcoholism?"

"We'd prefer not to."

"Uh, all right. You have enough nanobots to take care of that, and I'll repair the damage to your liver and whatever other organs you happen to use."

Abby grabbed the beer in front of her and sipped it. She was glad Martin hadn't become any less of an ass now that there was another consciousness within her. Part of her had been afraid he would be jealous, kind of like a dog that has a new puppy in their home. She also realized that was a ridiculously condescending way of looking at her AI and the new consciousness.

The fuzzy feeling in Abby's head began to fade, and her vision cleared. Now she could watch what was happening at the table more easily. She suddenly remembered that Chip had been talking to her and had left to grab more food for the party.

The conversation had been interesting, mostly because Chip was so interesting. Abby didn't know the Dark One's technology had extended as far as creating new life forms through technology, and she and Chip pondered the bizarreness of such an evil, malevolent life form creating new life for its own purposes.

Not all conversations at the table were as intelligent, though.

Stew was piss-drunk, and Terra was slowly catching up with him. Nearly an hour and a half ago, Terra had told Abby she wasn't going to get drunk with a twenty-year-old. According to Terra, she was too old to be doing shit like that, yet here she was, slamming another beer at Stew's and Sandy's goading.

Sandy wasn't any better, but she comported herself more elegantly. She didn't speak often, but her eyes were wide, and she watched everything going on around her. Each drink Stew and Terra finished, Sandy matched.

Suzuki, Anabelle, and Beth, on the other hand, were all business. Over the course of the dinner, the three of them had constructed a map of the dungeon. Anabelle recounted as many details as possible, occasionally asking Abby to fill the blank spaces in her memory.

It was interesting. Abby had never seen this kind of dynamic in her friends before. Something about Stew brought out an intensely childish and competitive part of Terra, while Suzuki's calm demeanor grounded Anabelle and helped her slip back into her role as the leader of the DGA.

Chip returned to the table carrying a plate of steaming meats and exotic fruits. She slid it onto the table and sat next to Abby. "First time at the Red Lion?"

Abby tore herself away from her observations. She didn't want to record every moment that happened. Being part of it seemed more interesting. "We've never been to a bar. This is an interesting experience for us."

"How long you been running around with these folk here?"

Abby explained to Chip the genesis of the DGA, the battles that they'd fought, and their relationship. Chip, contrary to what Abby would have assumed, hung on every word, occasionally interjecting or asking questions.

Across the table, Suzuki snapped his fingers. "I got it! I've heard of this riddle door before. Well, not this one, but similar ones. They're kinda a con. There's a specific answer they're looking for. It's not so much about the riddle as the answer."

Anabelle didn't look convinced by Suzuki's words. "Wait, are you telling me that not only do we have to come up with a riddle, but the only way that we're going to be able to do that is by finding the specific answer the door is looking for?"

Suzuki shrugged as he pulled out a notebook and started to thumb through it. "I didn't make the door. I'm just telling you what I've heard." He turned to Sandy. "Hey, you know more about those riddle doors than me. Can you—"

Sandy pulled out her wand and aimed it at Suzuki. She flicked it, and Suzuki's mouth disappeared. "You talk too much, Suz. Maybe you should just talk a little bit with a little mouth…"

Beth drew her knife and slammed it into the table. "Sandy! We've talked about no drunk magi at the dinner table!"

Sandy hiccupped and covered her mouth. "Oh, I'm sorry. I just thought Suz would look cute without a word hole."

Stew tore himself away from his conversation and looked at Suzuki. "Hm. I think it's an improvement. He's much less annoying when he can't talk."

Beth grabbed her knife and pointed it at Stew. "If we're getting rid of mouths, I'd say yours should be first on the list."

Anabelle leaned in to whisper into Abby's ear, "They have a *very* different dynamic than us."

Sandy waved her wand, and Suzuki's mouth reappeared. Suzuki

felt his lips and smacked them, then looked sternly at Sandy. "No magic at the table unless it's a joke is the rule, although it did sound a little bit like a joke."

Sandy raised her wand, and a series of sparks shot off. "Victory! Beth the Killjoy is defeated!"

Beth glared at Sandy. "No, she is not!" She flung herself across the table, knocking over a couple of cups of beer, and tackled Sandy to the floor.

Abby and Anabelle leapt to their feet and backed away from the table, confused by what was happening. "Should we stop them?" Abby asked.

Suzuki shook his head as Stew leaned over to look at the two wrestling. "Nah, it's a pretty regular thing," Stew said.

Anabelle began to speak but was interrupted by a gale of sharp laughter. Beth stood up as Sandy tickled her ribs mercilessly. "Do you yield?"

Beth pounded the table and shouted. "I yield! I yield! The killjoy is defeated."

Sandy magically righted all the cups. "Sorry about that. Sometimes Beth needs to be reminded of the damage we mages can do."

Beth skewered a piece of meat, tossed it at Sandy, and winked at her. "Okay, what were we talking about?"

Anabelle cautiously sat, and Abby did the same. "We want your help running through the dungeon," the elf said. "You guys are the most experienced company in the MERC group."

Suzuki felt his face, double-checking to see if everything was where it should be before speaking. "We'll run it with you. And I'll start trying to come up with a riddle. Should be fun. Kinda like a puzzle. Anyone care to give me a hand with that?"

Abby raised her hand. "We would. It's been stumping us for way too long, and it would be nice to work with someone else. Most of our work is done with our labmate. Nothing beats a good collaboration."

Suzuki motioned toward an empty table across from theirs. "You want to take a seat over there? Get some quiet while we brainstorm?"

Chip, who had been talking to Diane, looked at Abby. "Wait, you can't take such an interesting, shiny one away and keep her all to yourself. We got so much to chat about still!"

Suzuki was already on his feet, walking toward the table. "If that's the case, get over here and help us come up with something."

Abby stood and looked at Anabelle. "Is it okay if we get some quiet?"

The elf shrugged as she eyeballed the meat on the table. "You go for it." As Abby walked away, Anabelle struck up a conversation with Sandy and Diane. Both seemed eager to talk to her about magic.

Abby took a seat with Suzuki and Chip. "You guys aren't what we were expecting," she said.

Suzuki and Chip smiled and nodded. "Yeah, most people aren't expecting this," Suzuki admitted. "I'm one of the tamer MERCs, but people are starting to think even I'm a little rough. We had a group of elvish intel guys come through last week. You should have seen their faces when they met Stew. Granted, he *was* in the middle of wrestling three other MERCs. But you know a lot about us, Abby. We've only heard rumors about you."

Abby flushed. She didn't like it when conversations turned to her, and even less so when people knew something about her that she wasn't aware of. "What have you heard?"

Chip leaned over the table and waved her finger at Abby. "Word around here is that you developed some tech to break the Dark One's mind control, and your friend over there's leading an orcish revolution. Safe to say this ain't what we were 'specting neither. A human orc-lover, an elf that enjoys being around humans, and a little genius girl. Nope, not at all."

Suzuki picked at one of the scars on his hand. "Yeah, the orc shit is very interesting. Think it might be the first time in a couple hundred years that anyone gave a shit about them. You three were the most unlikely, in my opinion, but it's a pleasant change. Any chance we might have that mind control tech on a large scale?"

Abby explained why that might not be possible. There was something special about the nanobots growing in her body and attaching to her DNA. Creon had tried to replicate the process more than a dozen times but always failed, and Abby frankly wasn't certain if her body could handle doing it again.

Suzuki sighed as he leaned back in his chair. "That's a bummer, but understandable. All right, let's get to this riddle."

Abby's HUD went off, and she looked down to check it. There was a message from Persephone, asking Abby to call her immediately. "Hey, can you guys hold on a sec? We need to take this."

She stood and walked off as Chip gave Suzuki a bemused look. "Not too bad for a cyborg, eh?"

Suzuki folded his arms. "Is she technically a cyborg? I feel like you have to be part robot for that to count."

Chip walked two fingers across the table. "Are you daft? The little sprite has nanobots running around in her blood!"

Luckily, Abby didn't hear anything Suzuki or Chip had said since she would have had a lot of opinions, because she was busy calling Persephone back. "Hey, what's up?"

Persephone sound rushed and like she was freaking out. "The Gate! It's active, and we don't know what turned it on, and the scientists are really confused, and I didn't know what to do because I don't think I can do anything. So, I called you. Do you think you can come check it out?"

"We're kinda trying to make up a riddle right now."

"We'd really appreciate it. Creon's here, and he asked for you specifically."

Abby leaned against the wall, watching the rest of the DGA at the table. She could see that Anabelle was smiling while talking to Diane and Sandy. "Are you sure you didn't just call me because you wanted to see me?"

Persephone's stress broke for a second and she laughed. "That is a bonus."

"Hold on, let me check."

Abby went over to Anabelle and cleared her throat. "Hey, we just got a call from Persephone. She said Creon needs my help with the Gate. Do you mind if we head over there?"

Anabelle rolled a pastry ball around in her hand. "Of course. How are you going to get there, though?" She turned to Diane and Sandy. "Do you guys have a hadron collider here?"

Diane laughed as Sandy jerked her hand at a door near the bar. "This isn't Earth, it's Middang3ard. We're chock-full of magic. Just talk to the bartenders; give them a general idea of where you need to go, and they'll figure it out," Sandy explained. "It was nice to meet you. Looking forward to killing shit with you."

Abby liked how rough and tumble the MERCs were. She wondered if she would ever be that badass. "Thanks! I'll see you guys later."

Then she headed over to Suzuki and Chip and explained the situation. Chip protested, but Suzuki calmed her down. They agreed to be in contact through their HUDs to keep working the riddle. Once Abby was done, she went over to the bartender and let him know where she needed to go.

The bartender directed her to the door, which she flung open. The girl stared into the portal, took a deep breath, and stepped through.

Sarah was down in the prisoner holding ward. Only Kravis knew that she was there. It wasn't that tabs were kept on who came and went, but generally if a prisoner was being held in HQ's prison, they were high profile. Most people wanted to stay away from high-profile prisoners.

That was not the case for Sarah. There was someone down there she desperately needed to talk to.

If she needed to keep a secret, right now would have been the easiest time. Myrddin still wasn't conscious, and Roy, who was in charge, was not at the base. Sarah had noticed that security had gotten lax in Myrddin's absence. She made a mental note to bring it up with Roy.

As Sarah walked down the rows of cells, she thought about how many prisoners HQ had managed to take over the last few years. Sarah thought it was a mistake. It was better to tie up your loose ends. If someone ever planned a prison break on HQ, they would have a long list of heavy hitters who would want revenge.

It made sense that Myrddin provided so well for the prisoners. At least they didn't complain about room and board. Still, Sarah thought it would be best if this place didn't exist, especially not right under HQ.

Sarah turned a corner and walked down to cell number 415. She peered through the viewing window and watched her prey pacing. Grok.

The door was controlled by a keypad. Sarah had lifted the security code earlier in the day, but no one had noticed. She had wondered if she had clearance for the code. Since she was unofficially part of the DGA, Myrddin had forgiven her past discrepancies and given her a high security clearance. Either way, it didn't matter. Breaking into the system gave her a good idea of where HQ's security currently was. There was a lot of room for improvement.

Sarah opened the door and stepped inside. She'd made sure to leave anything that could be used as a weapon upstairs. All the cells were equipped with spells that Myrddin had cast to nullify whatever magical, supernatural, or technological abilities the prisoners had. Thankfully, like all Myrddin's wards and spells, they had continued to work after he was incapacitated.

Grok looked at Sarah as she calmly walked into the room. At least Sarah hoped she looked calm. Internally, she was freaking out. She knew Grok could probably still kill her if it came down to it.

The orc smiled grimly at Sarah. She still wore the scars of her beating. Anabelle had done a number on her. Sarah still thought it had been foolish of the elf not to kill Grok, but if she had, Sarah wouldn't have anyone to talk to about the questions on her mind.

Grok gestured at the two chairs in the corner of the room. "Can I get you anything?" the prisoner asked. "The meat here is particularly good."

The orc sat first. Sarah watched Grok's movements, searching for hostility. She was pretty good at getting a read on potential danger. Grok seemed relaxed, but not too much. That was good. This meant Grok still saw Sarah as a threat or was at least curious to know why Sarah was there.

Grok waved her hand in front of the conjuration sigil installed in the cell. A moment later, a raw steak appeared on a plate on top of the sigil. The orc tore off a piece and tossed it to Sarah. "So, are you to be my torturer?" she asked.

Sarah caught the meat and sniffed it before taking a bite. "No. Myrddin doesn't like to know those things happen. I wouldn't do that under his roof."

Grok laughed as she chewed. "He prefers a blind eye? It's funny—all the horrible things that have to be done for war, and there are still people who try to pretend their hands are clean."

Sarah smiled despite herself. "We aren't that different, you and me."

"That's my line, and trust me, I know. I've heard tales of the human assassin who kills without a conscience. Kind of like being an attack dog."

Sarah crossed her arms as she leaned back. "I prefer to think of myself as a tool. Granted, I have more autonomy than that, much like you. That battle wasn't sanctioned by the Dark One. That was all you."

Grok nodded, her eyes looking far off. She relaxed a bit, her shoulders dropping slightly. "It was a gamble. Did you come here to find out why?"

"Not interested. I assumed you were trying to make your own lieutenant take on the Dark One. Frankly, I would think you'd be smarter than to assume you could challenge him, but if I had to guess, that would be it."

"His war has gone on for too long. He's getting weak. I wanted to be prepared for a chance. Much like you and your DGA."

Sarah's eyes narrowed as she stared at Grok. "What are you talking about?"

"Merely noting that now would be a perfect time for a coup if any of you had the slightest ambition. Your leadership is weak. I see four powerful women who could easily have an army if they played their cards right."

"True, but that's not why I'm here. I want to know about the lich."

Grok waved her hand over the conjuration sigil again, and a plastic cup of mead appeared in front of her. Sarah did the same, reaching out to grab the cup, carefully watching Grok for the slightest hint of aggression. There was none. "The lich? Hopefully good questions," Grok said.

"From what I gathered, she was fairly happy to have been released from her prison, and she killed with abandon for the Dark One. Then she suddenly vanished. She killed one of the Dark One's top orc leaders and provided you an army, then didn't take part in the battle. What's going on?"

"Why do you think I would tell you anything?"

Sarah sipped her mead. "Because you don't care about the Dark One or his war. You have the old tribal orc blood in you. The fight is what you care about, and I might be able to offer you a better fight—one that doesn't take place in a prison cell. That is, if you don't care who you're killing."

"And you would trust me?"

Sarah drained the last of her drink. "There's a shortlist of people I trust. You aren't one of them, but you don't need to trust a tool. Now, what do you know?"

Grok leaned back and watched Sarah, her eyes darting back and forth as if she could get a read on how honest Sarah was being. "Granted, me and Rasputina aren't besties like you and your girl scouts, but we share a disinterest in the Dark One's plans. Rasputina even more so. Everything that happened before, that's because she's insane beyond repair. She enjoys killing for the sake of the simple fact that she can. She has ideals, but I don't know if she believes any of them. The Dark One made a mistake bringing her back."

"Why?"

"Because she is a true lich. She's immortal and has centuries of magical knowledge. She can't be stopped, maybe not even by him. I've seen what she's capable of. The Dark One might be able to conquer entire universes, but he needs an army. She doesn't. It would take more time, but she could do it."

Sarah had heard stories about how powerful liches were, but she knew Myrddin had been able to at least slow Rasputina down. "That doesn't explain why she wasn't at the battle."

"She's unpredictable. She's as likely to kiss you as kill you. But she was off the Dark One's radar very quickly after she fought against you. He's looking for her. Hunting her. He thinks she might have turned on him."

"What do you think?"

Grok looked around. "It's hard to gather my thoughts in a cell."

"Don't bullshit me. Be honest, and I will too."

Grok's smile disappeared, and her age became apparent to Sarah for the first time. It was always hard to tell with orcs. They were like elves; they could live for hundreds of years, although few did. "A string of elvish libraries has been ransacked since the lich was released. I know she was behind it."

Sarah sighed. She thought Grok was baiting her with unimportant information. "Liches acquire knowledge. That's nothing new. She's—"

"She didn't kill anyone. No one knew she was there. The only reason I know is that she let me know. Rasputina didn't want anyone to know, other than the person who she knew also wants to kill the Dark One."

Sarah thought it over for a second. "I'll talk to Roy. Thanks for the chat."

Grok stood and motioned to the door. "Don't worry. I won't stab you in the back."

Sarah opened the door and slipped out, closing and locking it tightly behind her. "I hope you mean that in more ways than one."

Grok pressed her face against the glass separating her from Sarah. "Find me a better fight, and you can trust I won't."

CHAPTER TEN

The next day, the remaining DGAs and Mundanes met for breakfast. Terra had been called to deliver a speech to the orcish tribes as soon as she could. She'd be leaving the Mundanes and Anabelle to explore the dungeon again.

Terra rushed through her meal, scarfing down her greasy eggs and bacon as fast as possible. She traded barbs with Stew the entire time, who was busy bragging about the horde of orcs he'd taken on single-handedly. "Okay, but have you ever had a horde of orcs flee at the very sound of your name?" Terra mumbled through her full mouth.

Stew puffed his chest out as he waved the waiter over for more mutton. "Uh, well, they would if they knew my name."

Terra stood and patted Stew on the back. "It's cute what you're trying to do, kid, but I'm the de facto leader of all the free orcs. You don't have much on that. Your axe is really cool, though. Catch you around. I gotta go talk to my peeps."

She headed upstairs and pulled out her HUD. After finding the right contact information, she dialed Cire and placed the HUD on the table.

His face popped up as a holograph. "Good to see you, Terra."

Terra was busy picking food out of her teeth. "You too, boo. Is that cool to call you that? I'm not sure how you feel about pet names and shit like that?"

"Why would you call me by the name of a pet?"

Terra retrieved a piece of bacon from between her teeth and swallowed it. "You know, 'cause we're kinda like a thing. We *are* like a thing, right?"

Cire smiled, his sharp teeth gleaming. "There are no other mates I'm interested in. And we have 'pet names' too, though they tend to be somewhat more fitting."

Terra sat down to get a better look at her orc. "Oh, really? What would you call me?"

"She Whose Ass Could Break an Army."

Terra blushed as she tried to hide her giggles behind her hand. "Okay, that is pretty good. A mouthful, but pretty good."

"It is the name I would use for you while speaking to friends and family so they know of your glory."

"Well, I'm going to have to come up with something better for you. Give me a few days. Am I allowed to talk about your cock to friends and family?"

Cire laughed as he beat his chest. "It would be considered a mild insult if we did not praise each other's genitals and bestial lovemaking to others."

Terra made pistol hands and pretended to fire at Cire. "Gotcha, boss. Everyone's hearing about our sex life. Now, on to business, I guess. You ready for this speech?"

Cire stood, showing his full ceremonial garb. He was wearing a fur poncho that went down to his navel, along with fur pants and boots. The skin that was visible was covered in war paint. "I've prepared my thoughts. Are you sure we should both speak?"

Terra started to apply war paint to her face as she nodded. "Yeah. We're doing this together. I'm not speaking for you. I'm flattered the tribes still want me as their chief and don't feel insulted by...you know, the whole human savior thing, but it's important that you're as much of a leader as I am. A chief and a shaman, like you taught me."

"The tribes have assembled. They're waiting for you."

Terra put the final touches on her face and looked into the mirror. Her face looked right, even if she didn't feel that way. Speeches weren't her thing, and neither was being front and center. This felt much different from speaking to humans on talk shows. Terra was one part of a leadership team now. It was a lot of pressure, and she wasn't comfortable with it yet.

Cire thought this was the right thing to do. All she had to do was make sure she didn't fuck it up.

Naota, Blackwell, and Roy were sitting at a bar on the orcish homeworld. Roy was the only one who didn't look hungover. Blackwell looked to have seen better days but was not a complete wreck. Naota, on the other hand, was as pale as a sheet of paper and staring miserably at his plate. "Long night?" Roy asked.

Naota burped, covering his mouth and trying to stifle the urge to vomit. "I went out with Lora-gak last night. She can drink much more than me. God, is this what dying is like? Have I died?"

Blackwell raised an eyebrow at Naota. "Did you go home with her?"

"A gentleman doesn't kiss and tell."

Blackwell sipped his drink as he played with his food. "Hm."

Roy cleared his throat and leaned back in his chair. "If you two don't mind, I'd prefer to stay out of your lovers' quarrel. Terra's speech is coming up."

The free orcs in the bar had quieted, waiting for the speech to be broadcast on the holoprojector toward the front.

Before Naota could respond, the holoprojector flickered to life. Cire and Terra stood next to each other.

Cire took a step forward. "Brothers and Sisters, today is the beginning of a glorious time for our people. We are united for the first time in hundreds of years. The horde is reborn stronger than ever, and our strength will wipe the Dark One from the face of the universe. We are no longer slaves to his devices. We are masters of our own lives."

The orcs in the bar cheered and pounded their cups to the table, spilling mead and beer everywhere.

Cire continued. "Our strength is not only physical, it is of the heart. We will not be dominated by those who wish to use and control us. We will not be seen as beasts by the other races of the nine realms. We are proud. We are powerful. We are the voices of our ancestors made flesh. We are orc!" The shaman stepped back.

Terra bowed her head slightly and pressed her fist to her heart. "I'm still humbled by all this. It is an honor to lead the horde. The trust you've given me...I don't think I deserve it, but I will work to earn it. The horde will grow in strength. Our fight against the Dark One will not be easy, and it's going to be painful. A fucking shitshow. But we are orcs. We will survive."

The orcs shouted riotously.

Terra slammed her fist to her chest. *"Do-hak, no-ja, no ja seela. Do-hak, no-ja, do hak no-ja."*

Silence washed over the orcs, and the bar was silent.

Terra continued to chant, pounding her chest in rhythm to her words. Cire joined the chant, his fist keeping the beat as well.

Slowly, the orcs in the bar joined in the chant, quietly at first, but growing louder with every second until the bar was vibrating.

Roy leaned over the counter and asked the bartender, "What does that mean?"

The orc did not answer at first. Tears were rolling down his face, as they were for nearly every orc in the bar. "The Horde, my blood. My blood, my life. The horde, my blood..." The orc beat his fist to his heart. "The ancient cry of the horde. I never thought I'd hear it in my lifetime."

Roy looked at Naota and Blackwell. "Gotta admit, those two make a really good team."

Blackwell's head was lowered as he poked at his food. "Yeah, looks like they do."

Anabelle and Terra left with the Mundanes to take care of the dungeon shortly after Terra's speech was over. They had all listened to it. Anabelle heaped loads of praise on Terra, but the Mundanes were much less interested. Terra attributed that to the Mundanes being involved in a completely different aspect of the war.

Not that Terra was upset. She did find it interesting, though.

At the insistence of the Mundanes, they did not teleport directly into the dungeon. Suzuki was adamant about wanting to see the area around it. He thought it would give him a better idea of what they would be up against. Anabelle had argued that it didn't matter because she and Terra knew what the dungeon had to offer. They had run it over two dozen times already.

Anabelle eventually yielded. The Mundanes provided steeds, bizarre ostrich creatures with axes for beaks that made a ruckus when they were brought into the Red Lion. They managed to get their steeds under control quickly, but Terra and Anabelle had a noticeably difficult time. "You just gotta bash them in the head a little," Stew advised. "Like this."

Stew slapped the back of his axebeak's head, causing the creature to let out a little yelp and stare back at Stew. The creature did stop squawking and fidgeting, though.

Terra reluctantly slapped the axebeak. Hers did not let out a yelp but straightened up and looked around attentively.

Anabelle did the same, muttering under her breath about the barbarism of hitting an animal.

Then they were off, passing through the portal and teleporting roughly a mile from the dungeon. They kept to an easy trot, conversing with each other, Suzuki showing Anabelle and Terra the draft for the riddle he, Abby, and Sandy had worked on. "The problem with riddle doors is that sometimes the riddles are supposed to be very literal," Suzuki explained. "I have some theories about this one."

Terra, who was only half-listening because Stew had chosen to ride at her side and refused to shut up, looked at Suzuki. "What do you mean, 'very literal?'"

"Well, the last riddle door we came across wanted a riddle about a thief. What it really wanted was for us to steal something in front of it, which was extremely difficult to put together. We had to find someone we didn't know, convince them to come to a dungeon with us, and then rob them in front of the door. Granted, we gave everything back once the door opened, but still. It was ridiculous."

Sandy, who was riding next to Suzuki, nodded as she coaxed her axebeak on. "And the nature of the riddle reminded us of something José told us a while ago."

"Yeah, it's been a little bit, but I remember. He told us that we were eventually going to have to die to go on to the next level of everything. I don't think José reaching out to you was a coincidence. I think the riddle and what José said to us is tied together."

Terra scoffed at what she thought Suzuki was implying. "Are you saying you think we're going to have to die?"

Suzuki didn't look like he was joking. "Something along those lines. I came up with an idea."

Terra scanned the area around her. None of this looked familiar from the last time the DGA had headed toward this dungeon. "Hey, where are we?"

"Oh, totally forgot to mention. We aren't going to the riddle door yet. That's what me, Abby, and Sandy were talking about. I thought Abby told you. We're on our way to get a vase."

Anabelle pulled back on her axebeak and stopped. "Okay, you're going to have to spell this one out for me. I know you're used to working with people who understand your weird, nerdy maze brain, but I'm not following."

Suzuki stopped as well and pulled out a leather-bound journal. "So, there are different kinds of riddles, and riddle doors don't seem to make a distinction or care. I wasn't joking when I said I think we're supposed to die, but we found a way around the actual death part. Here, check it out."

He pulled his axebeak around to Terra and Anabelle and opened the book. "Tell us a story about getting past this riddle door."

The book, whose pages were blank, started to fill up with words in a language Terra couldn't read, but she heard a voice in her head in plain English. "There are many routes to the realm of death. The sword, a blessing of the gods, or a simple jar. Many have chosen the jar throughout time and space. Kings, warriors, liches—"

Terra got excited and leaned forward. "Did it say 'liches?'"

The voice in her head cleared its throat and said, "Yes, I did. Now, as I was saying, a simple jar held in many dungeons can allow one to store their soul for a period of time. The Mundanes and the Dark Gate Angels were able to procure one of these jars to rest their souls in, placing it before the riddle door. They went on to live happily ever after."

Suzuki closed the book and stuffed it back into his sack. "Sometimes he kinda fudges the endings, but you get the point."

Anabelle grabbed Suzuki by the neck of his armor. "Are you saying you and Abby spent all night talking about how to kill us and shove our souls in a jar?"

Suzuki calmly peeled Anabelle's fingers off him. "Yes, more or less. And sorry I wasn't more direct in telling you. I'm not used to having to explain the minutiae of my plans."

Sandy, whose wand was aimed at Anabelle, nodded. "We trust Suz. Maybe you should too."

Terra looked around. The Mundanes had surrounded her and Anabelle, and their weapons were drawn.

Anabelle's eyes narrowed as she leaned back. "You four have exceptional teamwork. I didn't even see any signals."

Suzuki adjusted his armor. "Thanks. Now, are you ready to get this vase?"

Terra and Anabelle exchanged glances. "Yeah, I guess we can give this whole 'trusting a kid' thing a try," Terra said.

Suzuki smiled as the Mundanes sheathed their weapons. "Trust me. It works out more often than not."

CHAPTER ELEVEN

Anabelle was in a funk for the entire trip to the new dungeon. She hated riding the axebeak and having to constantly kick it in the sides for it to listen to commands. *No elvish steed would behave like this,* she thought. *Not even a human steed. Horse? Is that what they call them? Yeah, not even a fucking horse would be this goddess-damned obstinate!*

She hated the needlessly drawn out time it was taking to get to the dungeon. The DGA would have already portaled in and taken the vase. *We would be done by now. Instead, I'm being eaten alive by whatever gods-awful insects this accursed place has.*

More than anything else, Anabelle hated taking orders from the MERCs. She'd taken orders from Terra before. That was tolerable, even if it had ruffled her a little bit. At least she knew Terra had the capacity to lead. Anabelle knew that was nothing more than pride. But this? This went too far.

Suzuki hadn't even bothered to tell her what was going on, and she highly doubted he and Sandy had spoken much to Abby about the situation. The girl would have delivered a full report, letting her know what was happening.

Out of curiosity, Anabelle pulled up her HUD to look for messages. There was one from Abby.

Anabelle opened it and skimmed it. *Okay, even though Abby had let me know what was happening, Suzuki still should have talked to me. A little consideration between party leaders would have been appreciated.*

She shut the message and continued to follow the Mundanes, her stomach growling as the trash mead the MERCs insisted was brewed by the gods themselves churned within her.

Suzuki looked over his shoulder and shouted at Anabelle, "We will be there in a couple of minutes. The dungeon should be easy enough. From my intel, it doesn't seem like this vase has been pinged by a lot of people other than MERCs."

Terra, who was up near Sandy and Stew, asked, "Why wouldn't a MERC be interested in a vase to store your soul?"

Stew stared at Terra. "Kinda sucks the fun out of it if you have infinite lives."

Suzuki raised his hand, bringing the party to a stop. "We're here."

There was a cave ahead, covered in moss and vines.

Suzuki leapt off his axebeak and drew his sword as he approached the door. He hacked the foliage away and took a step back as the rest of the party joined him. "Just because I said it was going to be easy, it doesn't mean I meant it won't be dangerous. We still have to make sure we—"

Anabelle stepped forward, her arms crackling with energy. "Yeah, yeah, got it," she mumbled as she blasted through the door. "Can we go now?"

The Mundanes stared at Anabelle. "Yeah, I guess," Suzuki replied. "You want to lead the way?"

Anabelle laughed and took a step back. "No, no. By all means, please do so."

Suzuki took point, heading into the dark cavern. The rest of the Mundanes followed, trailed by Anabelle and Terra.

Anabelle wasn't paying close attention to the cave. As far as she was concerned, everything underground looked like everything else. She was confused as to how drow or deep gnomes could stand living in such a place. Rocks everywhere. No sunlight. It was miserable.

The cavern sloped down, forcing the party to slide on their asses farther into the cavern.

When Anabelle finally landed at the end of the dirt slide, she got to her feet and brushed the dust off her uniform.

All around her were intricate stalagmites and stalagmites. It gave the opening of the cave the look of jaws ready to close on her. For a moment, she was taken in by the beauty of the shadows caused by the illuminating spell Sandy had cast. Then she realized a *human* had cast the spell, very adequately. "Human, I mean, Sandy. Where did you learn that?"

Sandy pocketed her wand as she wandered around the cavern, looking closely at the rock formations. "That? Oh, that was one of the first spells I learned. Granted, I've beefed it up with some help from Diana. That bad boy could brighten up all of Middang3ard if I really tried."

Anabelle had never seen a human use magic so naturally. For the first time in decades, she was jealous of someone else's ability, almost jealous enough to ask for advice. Instead, she walked over to Terra, who was bickering with Stew about how much they could lift.

Stew had crouched by a boulder. "At the moment, I'm working on getting up to a metric ton."

Terra looked at the boulder and shrugged. "Okay, I get it; you're strong."

"How much can you lift?"

"Never really cared to measure it."

Stew rested his foot on the boulder. "Bet you'd have a hard time with this."

Beth, who was nearby, groaned when she heard the conversation.

Terra knocked on the boulder. "This? No problem." She leaned back, raising her leg, and kicked the boulder, which went flying into the wall.

Suzuki jumped when it crashed into the stone. "Could you guys cool it? We don't know what's in here."

As soon as Suzuki finished speaking, there was a rumble from deep in the tunnels ahead.

Anabelle grabbed Terra by the back of her uniform. "Seriously, are you having a pissing contest with that kid?"

Terra removed Anabelle's hand. "At least I'm having fun, unlike you and Suzuki. Having a hard time following instructions."

Anabelle glared at Terra. "I just think there should be more communication between senior officers."

"Yeah, Anabelle. That's exactly what it is."

Beth, who had crouched near the entrance of the tunnels and was looking through a spyglass, shouted, "Hey, guys, we got company."

As soon as the words were out of Beth's mouth, the screaming of goblins could be heard. The Mundanes drew their weapons.

Anabelle charged her body with fire, flames leaping off her hands as Terra pulled her axe from her back. "What's the plan?" the elf asked.

Suzuki looked over his shoulder at Anabelle. "You really want to know?"

"Yes! What are you planning?"

Suzuki checked above him, then he scratched his chin with his sword as he looked around the room. "Hm. Magic users, I want you in the back giving support. You too, Beth. Tanks to the front with me. We're going to let a bunch of them into the cavern with us. Use the rock formations above to take them out, and we'll be able to clean this up pretty fast."

Anabelle didn't say anything but moved into position with Sandy. She scanned the cavern. She and Sandy would easily be able to detach the rock formations above. It was a good plan.

Suzuki's shout broke Anabelle's concentration. "All right, here they come!"

Goblins poured into the room from the mouth of the tunnel. They were armed to the teeth, each carrying at least two axes or swords. Foaming at the mouth, they chattered in their own tongue, leaping and climbing over each other for the chance to spill blood.

One of the goblins leapt and tackled Suzuki.

Beth, who was back with the magic users, drew her bow and fired an arrow that nailed the goblin on top of Suzuki. She fired three more in rapid succession, taking out three additional goblins in a matter of seconds. As the arrows flew, Stew landed on top of a goblin and took its head off with a clean blow.

Terra, on the other hand, was quickly being overwhelmed. There were at least ten goblins on her, forming a giant pile that she was buried under.

Anabelle was surprised. She'd seen Terra wrestle a dragon, and here she was being beaten by a small number of goblins.

Anabelle couldn't stay surprised for long. At her side, Sandy was casting spell after spell, targeting the goblins piling on top of Terra.

Stew barreled toward Anabelle and flung his body onto the pile of goblins. "Terra! I'm here! Barbarians stick together!"

Stew started tossing goblins off Terra. Suddenly, there was a loud roar, and the goblins on top of Terra were tossed into the air as she swung her axe wildly. "Breathing space, people, breathing space!"

Stew landed on the ground and stared up at Terra in awe. "Dude, that was awesome."

Terra got her feet and stomped on a goblin, crushing its skull. "Yeah, I know. I fucking rock. Now, are we going to kick some ass?" She swung her axe in a full circle, slashing through anything unfortunate enough to be near her, then tossing the axe to Stew in one fluid motion.

Sandy, who was at Anabelle's side, smirked. "I think he's falling in love."

Anabelle channeled a bolt of lightning at the rock formation above them, causing a handful of stalagmites to fall on a group of goblins. "Excuse me? Are you serious?"

Sandy waved her wand, casting a panic spell on the goblins near those that had just died. "No, of course not. Just kidding. Stew's very… excitable. I do think he's got a crush on Terra. He's more…expressive than I tend to be with people."

Anabelle didn't have a hard time seeing that. She thought Sandy was more than a little bit cold. "You don't get jealous?"

"I definitely get jealous, but we have a good thing, and I trust him. He trusts me. If anything feels weird, we just talk about it."

Goblins were still running into the cavern. A deep roar came from the back end of the tunnel, and an ogre burst in. It stood nearly seven feet, and its bulbous stomach hanging over its naked genitals. Swinging a war hammer, it dumbly waded into the battle.

Suzuki slashed through a goblin and looked at the ogre before calling to Beth, "Do you think you can take out its eyes?"

Beth drew an arrow. "Isn't that more of a cyclops thing?"

"Is that a yes or a no?"

Terra's eyes lit up when she saw the ogre.

Anabelle raised her hand in front of Beth. "Do you think you could let her have this? She hasn't had a fight she's been interested in for a bit. Maybe Stew might get a kick out of it as well."

Beth lowered her bow.

Terra threw herself at the ogre, hitting it in the chest and reaching for the club it held in its hand. The ogre grabbed Terra by the neck and slammed her into the ground.

Beth slowly raised her bow. "You sure you don't want—"

Anabelle nodded. "Let's take care of the goblins. Let her have a good time."

Beth gave Anabelle a confused look. "This is her idea of a good time?"

Before she finished her sentence, Terra was back on her fight. She grabbed a screaming goblin next to her, relieved it of its sword, and threw it at the ogre.

Stew, who had been hanging back, shouted, "You mind if I get in on this?"

Terra swung her sword at the ogre. "If you think you can keep up."

Stew cracked his knuckles and rolled his shoulders. "As if I couldn't." He charged the ogre, which stepped to the side and brought its club down on his head.

As Stew fell, Terra took hold of the club. Even from this distance, Anabelle could see the fire in her eyes. The elf hadn't seen that for a while.

Terra pulled the club, which easily half the size of her body, from the ogre, retreating with it for a second. Then she whirled and cracked it across the ogre's head.

The ogre stumbled back, and Terra tossed the club to the side. She ran at the ogre and hit it with an uppercut, and the sound of the ogre's cracking jaw reverberated through the cavern.

Anabelle cast another lightning bolt as Sandy continued to curse the goblins in the cavern. Beth shot arrow after arrow, picking up the stragglers. A few feet away, Terra was still going blow for blow with the ogre. As Stew made it to his feet, Terra cupped both hands together and slugged the ogre in the face. Then she picked up the club again and brought it down on the ogre's skull.

Suzuki slashed through the last goblin and sheathed his sword. "That could have gone smoother."

Anabelle was surprised to hear that coming from Suzuki. From what she'd seen, the whole battle had gone smoothly. None of the Mundanes had seemed even slightly worried or overtaxed. Anabelle had to admit, Suzuki knew how to come up with a plan.

Suzuki pointed down the tunnel. "Come on. If there's any more, they'll have to come through here. But it should be a straight shot to the vase."

The two teams made their way down the tunnel. The whole way, Stew gushed about Terra's fight with the ogre.

Anabelle fought the urge to ask Sandy about her magical abilities since she was curious. She'd never seen a human effortlessly work magic the way Sandy did, and definitely not one so young.

Suzuki stopped suddenly. "There it is."

At the end of the tunnel was a gold chest. Suzuki went up to it and then motioned for Anabelle. "You want to do the honors?"

Anabelle walked up to the chest but shook her head. "No, this was your battle. You should have the honor of opening the chest."

"That actually usually goes to Stew, especially if he's not getting any loot. Yo, Stew."

The barbarian jogged past the rest of the party and set his axe in the chest's crevice. He let out a heavy groan as he popped the chest open.

A simple clay jar sat in the chest. "Is that it?" Anabelle asked.

Suzuki scooped the jar out of the chest and looked it over. As he rolled the jar in his hand, it crumbled to dust.

Anabelle reached out to grab the remains of the jar. "What the hell is that?"

Suzuki let the dust fall to the ground. "Typical dungeon bullshit. We were probably expected to walk out with that. Sandy, can you help us?"

Sandy held her wand high and muttered an arcane incantation under her breath.

The wall behind the gold chest disappeared.

Suzuki poked his head into the darkness. "Jesus, you'd think a shit DM came up with this."

Anabelle and Terra looked at each other, confused. The Mundanes mirrored the DGA members' expression. "You guys never played D&D?" Beth asked. "You know, when your dungeon master is trying to pull a fast one on you by hiding things behind enchantments?"

Neither Anabelle nor Terra responded.

Suzuki laughed as he shut the chest. "That just means we're past the first part of the dungeon."

Stew clapped his hand on Terra's shoulder. "That's nerdspeak for the fun part is coming up."

Anabelle smiled despite herself. "Thank the goddesses. I was worried that it was nerdspeak for something stupid."

CHAPTER TWELVE

The lich didn't need to sleep. That was one of the few things that terrified her. She'd spent a considerable amount of time in a deep slumber when she was encased in the Earth, trapped in a never-ending nightmare. She'd been like that since she was a child. There were horrifying things that slithered and spoke to her throughout the night, things with claws and gnashing teeth that threatened to swallow her.

When her soul had slipped out of her body and she started down her path, the thing she had first fallen in love with as a lich was how long she could read. Days upon days, until her eyes were dry. It didn't hurt to blink, so she kept reading.

It was amazing what one could do without sleep or death. She had an infinite amount of time. The problem was, it all began to look the same—every day, every hour, each minute. A constant repetition that drilled itself into her skull until it was all she could see.

Because of that, Rasputina faced her fears every so often and tucked herself into bed to sleep. It always took her less time to fall asleep than she would have expected, and she did not dream. Not anymore. But she still shivered in bed beneath her covers until she drifted into blackness.

Tonight was not one of those nights, though. Rasputina tossed and turned as her mind ran in circles. Seeing the younger image of herself had left her shaken. Even though she had gutted her younger self and painted the walls with her blood, the lich had taken no joy in it.

That was more than upsetting. There was hardly anything that she enjoyed anymore. Murder and mayhem were pretty much it. Each death reminded Rasputina that she still was alive in some way. Even if she was meaningless, she wasn't going anywhere.

The door creaked open and Bennington stepped into the room, treading silently. He peered at Rasputina, whose eyes were wide open. "Mistress?" he whispered so softly that she almost didn't hear him. "Are you still awake?"

Rasputina reached out. "I'm scared, Benny. I don't want to go to sleep."

Bennington took her hand and rubbed it lightly. "You don't have to sleep. Mistress. You can get up. You can do whatever you want."

The lich didn't need him to tell her that, but it helped to be reminded. She sat up and pulled her covers close to her neck. "Something isn't right, Benny. Something is off."

The butler sat down, crossing his legs and leaning back as he spoke. "What do you think it is, Mistress? What do you not have?"

Rasputina looked down at her hand, the skin still rotting, her bone poking out from underneath. "Why am I like this? What happened to me?"

"What do you mean?"

She tried to speak, but nothing came out except a choking sound. A fire was creeping in the back of her head, and she couldn't fight it. It hurt. Her whole skull felt like it was vibrating. She pitched forward, clutching her chest as she started to cry.

Bennington waited quietly until the tears stopped.

Rasputina stared blankly ahead, drool trickling down her lips. After fifteen minutes of waiting, he left his mistress, who peered into the darkness dumb and silent, running from whatever pursued her deep within her mind.

The lich did sleep eventually, but her sleep was not empty. She dreamed of being trapped underground. It was dark. Her body hurt. Nearly all her power was gone, drained out of her. She looked around, trying to find the source of her suffering.

Two bright white eyes peered out of the darkness at her—the Jotuun. Its voice rumbled in the black pit. "You've returned to me, my ward."

Rasputina whirled, looking for a way out of the darkness, but when she tried to move, her body wouldn't respond. "No, I'm free. I'm not back there. I'll never go back there."

The white eyes moved closer. "You had such potential. Such vast knowledge. What you decided to do with your power? Disgusting."

Rasputina looked at the demi-god, confused. "What did I decide to do?"

The lights floating in the darkness brightened until there was nothing else.

Rasputina woke up screaming and tearing at her skin, peeling it off in ribbons. She plucked out her eyes, tossed them across the room, and flung herself to the floor, screaming as she writhed in agony, pulling bones out of her body and throwing them against the wall. "What did I do?" she wailed. "What did I do?"

Once the tears and screams subsided, Rasputina lay silent, not even bothering to go through the motions of breathing. She didn't need to. Her body was dead, and she felt less human than usual. Blood did not pump. Nerves did not relay. The only active things in Rasputina were her magic and her mind.

After some time, she stood and stumped out of the room. "Bennington!" she shouted.

"Right here, Mistress."

She jumped at the sound of her minion's voice and looked by the side of the door. Bennington was curled up in a ball like a dog waiting for its master. "You called?"

"Come with me. I need an extra set of eyes."

"Uh, Mistress, you don't have any eyes."

Rasputina felt her empty eye sockets. "Hm, I wonder when I did that." A new pair of eyes started to grow in the empty spaces. "Don't sass me, Benny! Now come on!"

Rasputina, followed by her minion, went to her study. She tore through the room, tossing books and furniture about until she found what she was looking for: a small silver cauldron.

She set the cauldron in the middle of the room, then went to a bookcase in the corner and pulled down a vase. "What is that, Mistress?" Bennington asked.

Rasputina looked at him, her face eerily blank. "My brain." She opened the vase and poured its contents, thick, silver liquid, into the cauldron. "After the first hundred years, it all just went to mush, but I couldn't get rid of it. There's…a lot of me in there. Or the old me. Either way, it didn't seem like a good idea to just leave it on the floor. Brains have a lot of uses, like this, for one."

The lich reached into the chasm in her chest and pulled out a rib. She smoothed it and transformed it into a wand, the tip of which she dipped into the cauldron, stirring the ooze of her decrepit brain about. "There are answers to questions I've forgotten in here."

Rasputina withdrew her wand and flicked a pool of silver on the floor. The liquid started to tremble as if the earth were shaking, then it shot up, taking the form of a small child with the deepest black hair and wide, curious eyes.

Bennington watched the child, which was not moving or breathing, closely. "What is it, Mistress? The same you made before?"

Rasputina walked around the silver child. "No, last time it was a version of me. This…this is simply a memory. That was what I looked like from that time in my old life. Come here, Benny, and give me your hand."

Bennington did as he was told and clasped the lich's skeletal hand. Rasputina pressed her wand to the silver child's forehead.

There was a flash of bright light, then they were in a small wooden hut with a thatched roof.

The child Rasputina was sitting at a table covered with books. Her nose was buried in their pages. Two adults walked into the cottage and took a seat at the table. The child didn't bother looking up.

Bennington looked at Rasputina. "Are those your parents? Did they neglect you?"

She shook her head as she walked around the scene at the table. Her father leaned over and kissed the child on the forehead. "No, they loved me. A lot. I loved them too."

The child reached around, trying to touch her mother without taking her eyes off the book. Her mom slowly pulled the book away from the child instead, and the little girl pouted. Her mother planted a kiss on her forehead.

Rasputina took a seat at the table. "They loved me so much."

The two parents coaxed child Rasputina out of her chair, and soon, the cottage. The lich and the butler followed the family as they stepped outside.

The cottage was one of dozens resting in the cradle of an idyllic hill town. The homes were nestled against moss-covered mounds, and occasionally there was a house of a halfling, which was carved into the hills, breaking up the charming, colorful cottages.

It was the middle of the day, and many of the villagers were out. The child ran up to nearly every person she saw and greeted them as her parents took their time, eventually joining the conversation. This was the fashion in which they traveled through the village until they came to the baker's.

Rasputina took her time following the memory of her family. She found herself watching the villagers, admiring the homes, and breathing in as much air as she could. She'd forgotten how sweet air could be. There was a lot she had forgotten. It had been a long time since anyone had looked at her like her parents or the villagers.

Bennington watched as the child's eyes grew wide with wonder at the baker working his magic over the oven. "Mistress, what happened?"

She shook her head as she watched the child shoving fresh bread into her mouth. "I don't know."

There was a bright flash, and Rasputina and Bennington were back in her study.

The lich sat down in front of the cauldron. "There wasn't anything bad there, ever. No one hurt me. They all…everyone loved me, and I loved them, but I feel like they're the reason I'm this way."

She dipped her wand back into the cauldron and tossed another pool of silver on the floor. This time, the brain matter took the shape of a version of Rasputina in her twenties.

The lich stared at the younger version of herself. Then she grabbed Bennington and touched the young woman's forehead.

A flash of light. Rasputina and Bennington were in a larger cottage. Candles covered the walls, bookcases, and tables. And there were many bookcases. Every inch of the walls was covered in books, and there were piles all over the floor.

The cottage was empty, and Rasputina wandered around, looking at the home.

A scream interrupted the tranquil scene. The lich whipped around, trying to find the source of the terror.

The door burst open and a small child came running into the cottage, screaming and laughing wildly. She was chased by her mid-twenties self and a burly man with a beard that covered most of his face.

The young woman scooped the child up and held her tight to her chest as the burly man pulled a deer into the cottage. "Who's ready to get started on dinner?"

The child squealed and ran around the house as the woman sank into a chair, brushing her long black hair out of her face. She yawned as the child scrambled up her leg. "You two make sure to clean yourselves up when you're done."

The bearded man leaned over and kissed the woman on the forehead. "Will do. Good luck with your research."

As the bearded man walked away, he started to cough, a terrible hacking sound as if he were trying to expel his lungs through his chest. He leaned over, bracing himself against the wall as he heaved.

The young woman peered at him until the coughing ended. Then she turned to the book on the table and opened it.

The lich and Bennington watched as the young woman read, occasionally standing and casting spell after spell without a wand, conjuring vials and iambics into existence, boiling a variety of liquids throughout the night until the bearded man and her daughter returned with the butchered deer. "Ready to cook?"

The child squealed again, giggling as she ran into the kitchen.

The bearded man sat down and held his chest as he stifled a cough. "How's it going?"

The woman sighed, closed her book, and waved away the tools of her experiments. "Badly. I can't find anything, not here, at least."

"You talked about going away for a bit. There's that mage college you kept bringing up, the one that wizard came down from."

Young Rasputina shook her head. "No, it's too far. I can't leave you two here, and there's no promise that I'll find anything."

The bearded man started coughing again, and gripped the table until his knuckles were white. The young woman reached out and took the bearded man's hand until the coughing stopped. "Maybe it's best if I stay here with you."

"Don't stay for me. You're the best alchemist and sorcerer this village has. You're the only one who's going to be able to put an end to this. Don't stay because of us. I'll take care of the whelp. Now let me get started on that dinner."

There was a flash, and Bennington and Rasputina were back in the study.

The lich pulled a jar from one of the bookcases and scooped the puddle into it. Then she dipped her hand in the cauldron and poured a handful of the silver ooze on the floor. She grabbed her butler and stepped into the puddle.

CHAPTER THIRTEEN

Memories came at Rasputina faster than she could handle. At first, they were only blurs that made her nauseous, swimming in the indiscernible goop of the past. Eventually, the memories slowed, and she could piece them together bit by bit.

The quick ascent to her power. It would have been praised by every mage, wizard, witch, and sorcerer alike if it had not resulted in the creation of a lich. She watched the past version of herself scaling a mountain and fighting through hordes of giant crablike creatures until she came to the summit, where she found three ancient mages.

They promised to give her power beyond her wildest dreams for the small sacrifice of a few years of her life force. She agreed without hesitation.

But it wasn't enough. She returned to her village and was still unable to heal the villagers from the blood plague. She didn't stay long. Kissed her husband and daughter goodbye and took to the road again.

Next was the journey to the gnomish wizard Goreal, who dwelled deep within the drow caves. The gnome gave her tomes of ancient knowledge that held stories of plagues come and gone and recipes for their cures. It took nearly a month to gather all the materials needed to create a cure. When Rasputina returned home, she administered it to all the villagers. There was no response.

From there, she traveled across the land to the far reaches of the East, where she found an elvish wizard who promised immortality. When Rasputina figured out how to bottle it, she returned to her village. Two women died in their sleep from the plague that night.

Rasputina watched various younger versions of herself sitting on their bed, pacing their bedroom, and crying for the lack of anything else to do. She'd acquired much magic and knowledge, but none of it was enough to save her people.

The memories coalesced into one Rasputina, sitting in bed, reading. The door creaked open and the small child walked into the room, holding a bloody napkin and coughing. The child crawled into her bed and rested her head on her lap.

When the woman awoke the next morning, the child was dead, cradled in her arms.

From there, Rasputina slipped further and further into her own world. She left nearly immediately, and she did not stop traveling, following stories and rumors of greater power.

When she finally stopped, it was at the tomb of the necromancer Zell. Rasputina stole into the cursed mage's tomb, which descended into the very bowels of the earth. She fought through all manner of magical traps and creations, slaying a crystal golem that guarded Zell's final resting place with a simple word of power.

There was no body within the tomb, only a book. The woman camped in the tomb that night, having spent two weeks working her way through it.

Within it, Rasputina found a way to defeat death, and it was simple —profane but simple. For the next three months, she hunted down the ingredients for the spell. She performed crimes she would never want to repeat, yet the lich watched these events with no feeling whatsoever.

Finally, the day came. The woman led a unicorn by a rope around its neck to a grassy knoll where candles were lit and three jars stood upon an altar covered in a crimson shroud.

She recited the profane words in the language of the damned, tasted them on her tongue, inhaled them deep into her body, and then she slew the unicorn, bending over its open throat and drinking deeply of the silver blood that poured from its wound.

Then she laid down and waited. Something moved in the woods around the knoll. She knew it was coming for her. It was what she had summoned.

The woman dared not open her eyes, but the creature came. It reached deep inside the younger Rasputina and pulled out her soul, breaking it into three pieces, one for each of the jars. Then it kissed her on the forehead.

The ritual was complete. The woman opened her eyes and looked around. She left the unicorn's body to rot, not even bothering to give the creature a funeral worthy of its dignity.

When she returned to her village, there was hardly anyone left. A few of the children remained, but that was all. She found her husband's body in their bedroom, the bony fingers clutching a tattered blanket.

The woman held the blanket in her hand. She had spent a summer learning how to sew. Now it was all that was left.

The memories disappeared. The lich sat in the puddle for a moment before waving her hand and causing it to float back into the cauldron.

Bennington unbuttoned his shirt, exposing his chest. "You may torture me if you'd like, Mistress. It might make you feel better."

Rasputina shook her head. "Bring me the jar on the bookcase."

Bennington did as he was told and placed the jar in front of her.

Rasputina poured the contents out in front of her and sat there, staring down at the pool. "Leave me."

Memories enveloped her. She watched as her younger self cuddled in bed with her husband and daughter. James, that was his name. And the child...she was Lily.

The lich could almost feel their breath against her skin. Then she felt something wet and very real. A tear had formed in the corner of her eye, and it fell, streaking her face. More quickly followed.

Bennington, who was not caught in the lich's memories, watched as his mistress blankly stared into the water, weeping for the first time in hundreds of years.

Rasputina did not know how long she'd been watching the memories from this part of her life. It felt like a year had gone by. She watched herself wake, sleep, breathe, love, and cry. If she could only reach out and touch James' face or hold Lily one last time.

The lich looked down at her hands. Even if she could have held Lily, the little girl would have run screaming. Rasputina was a monster and she knew it, even more so now that she had been reminded of what she used to be.

Lily, who was playing in the living room as James whittled quietly, suddenly looked up at the lich. "Mommy, who is that?" she asked, pointing at the lich.

The lich took a step back, holding her hand to her chest. There was no way they could see her. This was only a memory. The past. Something to be hidden away and never thought of. It could not interact with her.

James looked at the lich and gasped before jumping from his chair and scooping Lily up in his arms. "What evil is this?"

The younger Rasputina calmly walked into the room. "Don't be afraid." She took Lily from James and sat down at the table. "She's here to talk."

The lich took a step toward the table. "You can see me?"

The woman nodded. "Yes, I can see you. I would have hoped that I aged better. Take a seat. James, you might want to leave for a little bit."

James nodded and reached for Lily.

"No," the woman said. "Leave her with me. She should see this."

James grunted and left through the front door.

The lich felt something she had not for hundreds of years—fear. It clenched her throat and soured her stomach. "How are you doing this?"

The woman didn't answer the question. Instead, she asked, "Do you want to hold her?"

The lich opened her mouth to say no, but her hands were already outstretched toward Lily, who the woman handed over to her without hesitation.

At first Lily looked ready to cry, but the woman reassured her. "It's okay, it's just Mommy. An older Mommy, but that's all. You don't have to be scared."

Lily stared up at the lich with her huge eyes. "An older Mommy?"

The lich took Lily and held the child close to her chest. For a second, she thought her heart was beating, but it was only the reverberation of Lily's heartbeat against the lich's chest. Still, this moment could have lasted forever.

The woman's voice interrupted the lich's bliss. "Did you finally beat death?"

The lich pressed her decomposed lips to Lily's forehead and inhaled that sweet scent of childhood. "For myself, but I was too late for anyone else. I couldn't save them."

The woman folded her fingers together. Her eyes were viciously dark as she peered across the table at the lich. "Is that why you came here? To revel in your failure?"

The lich put Lily on the ground. "You should go to your dad."

Lily waved and smiled sweetly. "Okay. I love you, old Mommy! Thanks for seeing us." She skipped away.

The lich felt what little was left of her heart breaking. She didn't have much time to feel anything before the woman spoke again. "I wasn't expecting you to be...like this. So evil, but here you are. My rotting corpse staring back at me. Everyone who warned me...they were all right. There wasn't a way to do what I wanted without losing myself."

The table trembled as the lich pulsed with dark energy. She got to her feet, the wood of the table near her rotting. "You? *You* were right? You're nothing more than a memory. I am Rasputina. You're what I left behind. You were weak. What did all this love get you? Nothing! I could do nothing!"

"And now you're working for Death."

The lich stared at the woman. She didn't understand what was being said. "Death? No, it was the Dark One. And I don't work for him. I have my own plans."

"What would those be?"

The lich didn't respond. She couldn't remember. All she knew was that the Dark One's war had stopped interesting her. But what else had she been doing? Killing and feasting on souls. That wasn't a plan. She must have been doing something else. It was hard, and everything felt slippery in her head.

The woman sighed and shook her head. "Death, the Dark One, the Single Blind Eye, whatever the hell he's calling himself now—you don't work for him? Then what are you doing?"

What am I doing? The lich's mind turned the question over for what seemed like an eternity.

The woman smiled, and there was something vicious hidden there. "You really don't remember, do you?"

The lich was tired of this conversation. She raised her hand, and a piece of bone shot toward her youthful doppelganger.

The woman ducked and caught the bone spear in her hand. "You're getting agitated. Let me explain. You think you became the lich in that ceremony, don't you? No, it was happening before. Your pursuit of knowledge instead of staying with your family was when it began. You can't tell me you were thinking about them the entire time. The search was for you. It always was, but you can't remember that because it's all in here. In my safe space."

Black tendrils burst from the ground, wrapping around the lich's hands and feet, forcing her onto all fours like an animal.

The woman walked over to the lich, taking her time as she twirled the bone spear in her hand. "I hid a piece of myself in here. A complete version of myself before I became the pathetic, psychotic sack of shit you are. I've been waiting. I knew I'd eventually fulfill my goal and become something I no longer understood, and that something would have power and knowledge I could never dream of. But it would be useless, a hollow husk devoid of humanity. So, I saved all of it here."

The lich struggled against the vines. She could feel her strength leaving her. "What the hell are you saying?"

The woman knelt before the lich. "Everything else was your memories, but not me. Not the first one. I saved this one, and you've been compulsively saving your memories. I've watched them one after the other. But I am me, and I am real. And I'm taking my body back."

She grabbed the lich by the rotting mass of hair and her head went back, exposing her throat. The woman slit it, and black blood as thick as oil poured out as she stammered, eyes wide with shock. There was no way this was happening. It was impossible.

The woman inserted her hand into the wound, then forced her forearm in as the lich struggled, the decomposing creature's efforts growing weaker and weaker.

Am I dying? Is this death? the lich wondered as the world around her dimmed.

Bennington had been watching the whole time. He noticed that the pool of silver beneath the lich had dried up, and the lich had stopped crying. Now she was sitting very still, staring at nothing.

"Mistress?"

Rasputina sat bolt upright, her eyes glowing a horrid, putrid green as her left eye twitched uncontrollably. Her jaw was loose and limp.

Bennington inched his way toward Rasputina. "Mistress?"

The lich fell forward, clutching her chest as she screamed, *"It hurts! It hurts!"*

A vibration shook the room, then another as Rasputina fell to the floor, digging at her chest. She broke through her ribcage, tearing bone out and tossing it away. Then she pulled out her heart and held it in her hand.

Rasputina's heart pumped once and the room shook, knocking

books from their shelves as she writhed on the floor, thinking, *I've been here before. Yes, I know I have.*

She tossed her heart across the room and shrieked, "You stay out of me! I don't want you!" then collapsed, holding the open gash in her chest. "I don't want this," she screeched through sobs. "No!"

Bennington crouched at her side. "Mistress, how can I help?"

Rasputina looked up at her butler, the green light flickering in her eyes, her smile insane and wicked. "It's beating, Benny. It's beating, goddamn it."

Abby had looked for Persephone as soon as she had stepped out of the portal. To be more accurate, she had been looking for anything that resembled a camp. The portal had tossed her into the middle of nowhere.

There were no noticeable landmarks, nothing for her to use to get her bearings. If there had been, it wouldn't have mattered. Abby didn't have any knowledge of the geography of the gnomish homeworld. "Shit, this is a nice situation to be in," she muttered to herself.

Martin chipped in. He sounded excited or happy, which wasn't surprising. The AI always seemed to be in his best mood when Abby was in trouble. She wasn't sure if that was because he enjoyed seeing Abby distressed or he just liked a challenge. She liked to think it was the latter. "Yeah, it is a shit situation to be in," Martin agreed.

"Thanks for not giving me the whole 'Cursing is bad because you're a kid' lecture. Which—"

"I know, is bullshit because you've been teleported across the galaxy without a babysitter, and now you're stuck in the middle of nowhere. You should try *not* to lean so hard on that one. It's going to start sounding like you have a chip on your shoulder."

Abby's eyes magnified the area, attempting to find something in the distance worth walking toward. She'd tried to comm Persephone and Cire a couple of times but hadn't gotten any responses. "Just for a bit. My nanobot count is low enough that I'm just little ol' me right now. I'm assuming I'm going to need more in a bit, so don't get too used to it."

"Hm. That's odd. The consciousness is still there."

"How do you know?"

"I've been talking to it."

Abby was surprised by Martin's answer. She was under the impression that Martin hated the consciousness and was going to do everything in his power to keep from interacting with it.

Martin's disembodied voice broke her train of thought. "Yeah, yeah, I know what you're thinking. That I hate the consciousness because I'm jealous of you developing a friendship with another non-organic intelligence. I'll have you know, my enormous processing power has allowed me to move past that and foster a healthy, slightly irritating relationship with the consciousness."

Abby sat down as she tried to figure out what to do. "You might not want to mention the enormous processing power too often. Might sound like you have a chip on your shoulder."

"Oh, touché. So, what's the plan?"

Abby picked up a little bit of sand and stared as it slipped between her fingers. "I can't get signal here. Either the gnomes are using a new encrypted signal, or they've lost it. Whatever channel Persephone called me on is down, so I'd say up the production of nanobots in my body to a reasonable level. That should give me enough juice to be able to search out whatever new signal they're using and decode it. And cover my ass."

"Sounds good to me. Juicing you up."

Abby instantly felt the increase in nanobots. It wasn't a physical sensation. Instead, she felt it in her head, in the way her thoughts organized themselves. The first change was the increase in random thoughts and how quickly they passed. Then those random thoughts started to grow more complex. She started building ideas from each stray thought to cross her mind. Last came the consciousness. It was like having a teacher stand over your shoulder while you worked on a test.

Martin appeared in the right-hand corner of Abby's vision. "Nanobots are nearly as high as your regular operating function. I'd suggest taking a moment to let your body get used to everything. Take in the scenery. It's kind of beautiful, isn't it?"

Abby thought it was funny that Martin would be interested in beauty. "Since when did you start saying words like beautiful?"

"When I started to understand the idea better. I've found my comprehension of organic ideals to be a little severe. I've been reading books on art and philosophy. If you're interested, I could upload them to your neural network."

"Nah, you don't have to do that. We still prefer to read. It is a fun activity."

"And, back to the creepy royal pronoun."

"It's only appropriate. We are more than just Abby now. But we will stay and watch the sunset for a bit. It is a very beautiful day."

Abby laid back and watched the sun slowly moving through the sky as it began its journey to dusk. "You know, when we were a kid, our father would stay up with us, watching the sunset. Dusk was his favorite time of day. Ours was sunrise. It was funny…he'd wake up every morning as soon as the sun rose and hated it, but he did it every day."

A small, featherless bird sprinted across the sand in front of Abby. It stopped for a second and blinked. "You still miss him a lot, don't you?" Martin asked.

"Yeah, we don't think we're ever going to stop missing him. How could we?"

"Looks like that orc hatred is gone at least. That's a good thing."

The featherless bird started running circles around Abby, who laughed when she realized what the bird was doing. "Yeah, kinda happened without realizing it, ever since we took control of that orc in the arena. And seeing the sheer number of orcs under the Dark One's control. We can't imagine what it would feel like to lose ourselves like that. It sounds terrible."

"You know, I didn't tell you this before because I guess it feels weird, but I'm proud of you. I know you hear that a lot, but probably not enough. But I am. Ever since you created me, I've seen you step up day after day. It's impressive. Kinda makes me want to keep growing."

Abby chuckled as she sat up and stared at the shadows moving across the dunes. "So, this is what happens when everyone else isn't around? You get all emotional?"

Martin's paperclip avatar smirked as it twirled. "I just thought you should know. Now seemed like a pretty good time. I'm trying to say I respect you."

"Thanks, Martin. That means a lot to me."

Abby felt a shock run up her spine. All her systems were back online. She automatically connected to the closest communication signal and decoded it, then pulled up her HUD and called Persephone. "Hey, Percy, we're here, but not quite certain where 'here' is. Do you think you could send us your coordinates and a rough map of the area?"

It took a couple of seconds for Persephone to respond. "Oh, thank the gods! I thought something had happened to you when you didn't teleport here. Hold on, let me get those coordinates and maps."

"Yeah, apparently, the MERC's tech or magic isn't as precise as what we use at HQ. Even then, we weren't even a hundred percent certain we were on the right planet until we were able to pull up your base's signals. We should get in touch with the Red Lion about that and find a way to improve their transportation methods."

"One thing at a time, Abby. There you go. I'll forward them to you."

Abby pulled up the map and the coordinates. She was still a good distance from the camp and Gate. "Looks like we're going to have to take a little hike to get to you."

"We could probably send out a convoy to pick you up."

Abby watched the sky as the sun continued to make its descent. Shadows stretched across the sand. "No, we think we'd prefer to walk. It's the first time death isn't an immediate problem. We can't remember the last time we went for a walk. We'll be there in a few hours. If there are any sudden changes, let us know, okay?"

"Yeah, that sounds good."

"Great. We'll see you in a little bit. We're really looking forward to it."

"Me too."

Abby ended the call and stood. The bird running circles around her suddenly stopped. Abby looked down at the weird creature with its segmented bug eyes. "Sorry, little fella, we gotta get going."

Then she headed north in the direction of the camp, her shadows stretching along those of the dunes until it looked as if an ominous giant loomed across the sands.

The featherless bug-eyed bird followed Abby, occasionally running by her side and keeping pace. When Abby stopped to admire an interesting cactus, taking a photo to research later, the bird stopped as well, chirping as if it were growing impatient. When Abby began again, the bird followed.

The two walked for nearly an hour as dusk fell, Abby taking her time, watching the subtle way the color of the sand changed with the height of the sun. Finally, as the moon was rising and growing more visible, Abby stopped and sat on one of the dunes while the bird commenced running circles around her again. "That is the oddest thing we've ever seen a bird do," she muttered.

Martin spoke up. "Reminds me of the way bees communicate on Earth, running or dancing in circles."

Abby leaned forward to get a better look at the bird. "Is that what you're doing, little guy? Trying to communicate?"

The bird stopped running and froze in place. Then it tilted its head back and screeched, a shrill, hair-raising sound.

Abby jumped to her feet, caught off-guard by the noise, but the bird did not stop.

Within seconds, the air was filled with the sound of huge, flapping wings. It reminded Abby of a flying dragon. Whatever was in the dark was big.

Abby instinctively adjusted her eyes to the dark, just in time to see a bird nearly the size of a dragon land directly over the small, screeching bird. The huge bird had the same insect eyes but was covered in multi-colored feathers. It had four wings and talons the size of a small car. "Guess that's why you were following us."

The giant bird scratched the sand and let out a shriek.

Nanobots flowed over Abby, covering her in armor. She formed a plasma cannon in her hand and fired.

The bird took to the air, dodging the attack. Then it swooped in on Abby, knocking her over. It pinned her down with its talons and pecked her, and she was barely able to move her head in time to avoid being decapitated.

Martin's voice came through, bubblier than usual. "Hey, Abby, me and the nanobots have been talking. We think you're burning too much energy with plasma shots, and we've come up with a better alternative that'll keep you from wasting energy."

Abby struggled against the bird's talons as she dodged another attack aimed at her head. "Could you not have thought of a better time to bring this up than right now?"

"Now that you mention it, this is a pretty bad time. If you survive this, I'll make sure to talk to you about it."

"Tell me how to get out of this!"

Martin popped up in the corner of Abby's vision, visibly smirking. "Well, first off, we've increased your physical density and made your armor capable of expelling pent-up kinetic energy. We are calling this your charge ability. Go ahead and give it a try. Focus on an object and, you know, charge it."

Abby didn't quite understand what Martin was saying, but she didn't have the time to think it through. She looked up at the giant bird and leaned toward it.

A kinetic field formed around Abby's body, and her armor shunted energy out from around her. She hit the bird square in its chest, energy crackling as it flew backward.

Martin appeared in front of Abby again. "And that's not all. You can also expel energy through a physical attack. Movement speed has been adjusted to help you not depend on those cannons as much. A one-trick pony is boring, you know. If this was a book, I'd be tired of reading the same thing over and over by now."

Abby focused on the bird again and charged, leaving a trail of blue energy behind her as she hit the bird in the chest again. As the bird stumbled back, Abby leapt, kinetic energy flowing through her body, and slammed her fist into the ground.

The bird crumpled to the ground as the girl slammed her hands into a plasma cannon. She fired, and the plasma blast tore through the bird, which fell dead on the sand.

Abby's hands returned to normal. "Okay, that was pretty awesome."

Martin's voice chimed in again. "We'll be working to optimize your body and armor for this. Give you a little bit of diversity."

The small bird was screeching. Abby aimed her cannon at the bird and fired, leaving nothing more than a smoking smear.

"That was excessive," Martin gasped.

Abby looked at the corpse of the giant bird. "We just wanted to go on a relaxing walk and would prefer no more interruptions. You think it's edible?"

Abby's hand grew longer, ending in a sharp edge. "It is a lot of meat to waste."

CHAPTER FIFTEEN

Abby arrived at the camp a little after ten. She found a small gathering of tents and a large pylon built by the scientists near the Gate. Everyone seemed particularly busy with what they were working on, and no one noticed Abby. That was fine with her. She wanted to get a look at what was going on.

Once she was satisfied, she called Persephone. The drow came and met her on the outskirts of the camp. "Why'd you call me all the way out here?"

Abby lightly touched Persephone's face and kissed her with all the longing she'd been feeling. "Every time we see you, there are a dozen people around. Sometimes, we'd just like to see *you*."

Persephone blushed, a confusing sight on a drow. Her cheeks turned dark red for a moment, then the color trickled off until it made her look like she had freckles. "It's good to see you too."

"You want to help us sneak this into camp before anyone sees us? We're not ready to get to work yet."

Persephone grinned and nodded. Abby shone a light on the butchered bird she'd lugged over her shoulder the whole way to camp. "Figured it might be nice to have a feast or something."

The two girls managed to get the bird back to Persephone's tent without anyone noticing, then they sat and talked. Abby had been waiting to do this since Persephone had left. Neither of them had had any time to talk other than a spare moment here, and then it was always business.

Abby had almost forgotten how much she loved lying back and listening to the drow talk. She spoke at length, her tone almost poetry. It was like sitting by a creek and listening to the water speak. Sometimes, it didn't matter what Persephone spoke about as long as she was speaking.

That wasn't to say that Abby could remain quiet for long. If Persephone wasn't talking, she was asking questions, trying to figure out every detail of what Abby had been up to. Despite Abby protesting that the change to her armor was boring, the drow talked her into explaining it. Even if Persephone didn't understand the technical jargon, which Abby was certain she didn't, she played along well enough.

As the conversation died down, they lay down next to each other. Abby rested her head on Persephone's chest, feeling it rise and fall in its slow rhythm as the wind howled around the tent, shaking it as if it were haunted. "How are you getting along with everyone?" Abby asked.

Persephone's breath quickened. "It's weird. Still feels like I don't belong here. I don't know if it's because I used to serve the Dark One or if it's just strange being around so many adults. Cire treats me like an equal, but I don't know. It still feels weird."

Abby nodded as she played with Persephone's hair. "Yeah, it's odd for a while. Sometimes we're still, like, shit, we're a fucking kid, you know? We could be at school right now."

Persephone laughed. "I'd forgotten humans go to school for nearly their whole life."

"Not the whole thing. Only a third of it. But we're glad we're not doing that. It feels good to be part of something that matters, and we were never any good at school."

They laid there for a bit longer, the wind still shrieking madly outside the tent. "Are you thinking what we're thinking?" Abby asked.

"That we should probably get to work?"

Abby sighed as she sat up. "No, that was *not* what we were thinking, but you are right. We do need to check out that Gate in case it's something bad. Come on, might as well let Cire know we brought some food as well."

The two left the tent and walked farther into the camp. There was a fire, where many of the scientists were gathered. Cire and Nib-Nib were there as well. Creon sat across from them, talking quietly with another goblin scientist. They looked up when they saw Persephone and Abby.

Cire rose and extended his hand. "Ah, it is good to see you again, Abby-Lynn. How have you been? Well, I hope."

Abby shook Cire's hand and then pressed her hand to her chest. "We have been well. Briefly visited Middang3ard to speak to the Mundanes. Those MERCs are an interesting bunch. A little rough around the edges. We think that you might like them."

"Terra is probably enjoying herself, then. Be careful, she might end up joining them."

Abby smiled and waved away Cire's concern. "Doubtful. She loves the DGA. Now before we get to this Gate, Persy and I have a little surprise for you guys."

Persephone pulled the butchered bird out from behind her back. "There's more in my tent if you guys want to get cooking."

The scientists, mostly goblins and gnomes, were ecstatic. They hoisted Abby and Persephone into the air, while the rest of them went to get the remains of the bird. It was not long until the scientists had thrown together a makeshift BBQ pit and Cire was tending the grill.

That gave Abby time to mingle with the different scientists from HQ. Usually, she only worked with Creon. She'd forgotten there was an entire science department outside of her two-person lab. When she'd first had come to HQ, speaking to any of these scientists would have intimidated her. Now she felt like she was talking to peers.

Persephone wandered over to Cire to help cook, while Abby let herself nerd out with a pair of goblin scientists. The goblins were very interested in the nanotech Abby had improved upon. They both admitted that trying to improve the nanobots through a connection with organic material being led by an integrated AI was a stroke of pure genius. When Abby told them it was honestly just a stroke of luck, they wouldn't hear it.

Abby spent most of the night trading notes with the scientists. It wasn't until she looked at Cire and saw Persephone was gone that she started to worry about leaving her friend alone. She wandered the small group of drunk meat scientists until she found the drow sitting next to Nib-Nib. "Hey, how are you doing? We were worried about you."

Persephone looked up at Abby and smiled. "Why? I was just hanging out with Nibs."

Nib-Nib chittered and clicked her mandibles. "She's got some good war stories if you can figure out what she's saying. I'm still not the best at picking it up, but Cire's been helping."

Abby took a seat next to Nib-Nib and listened to the mantiboid chitter, gesturing widely with her claws. It was the most animated Abby had ever seen her. If she thought about it, she'd never taken much notice of Nib-Nib before, probably because she was so alien. The thought made her feel a little guilty.

Finally, Nib-Nib finished her story and leaned back, chittering softly as she rubbed her claws together. Persephone leaned across Nib-Nib and asked, "Did you learn anything useful?"

Abby nodded. "We learned we need to spend more time out of our labs and with the other scientists. A lot of them are working on things I've never thought about. The collaboration would be good for us, and that's going to be starting soon enough. We're heading to the Gate first thing tomorrow morning."

The party wrapped up not long after, the scientists drifting away to get some sleep. Persephone fell asleep near where she and Nib-Nib had been talking.

Abby, on the other hand, stayed up all night talking with Cire.

The two, much like Nib-Nib, had hardly spoken since they'd met, and it had been mostly circumstantial. They were rarely on the same missions. Abby took the time that night to sit with the orc and listen.

He told her stories, old tales that had been passed down to him from thousands of years of oral tradition. He fell asleep during the *Ballad of First Bloods*.

Abby leaned against Cire's back and watched for the sun. She had Martin reduce most of her bodily functions to a near crawl so she could rest. Her mind went quiet as she went into something like hibernation. She was still able to enjoy the sunrise, though.

———

Everyone met at the Gate after a quick breakfast.

As the scientists had explained the night before, the Gate had been humming for the last few hours. A few of them had been watching the Gate throughout the night. It had gone dormant. Now, suddenly it was humming again and vibrating lightly.

Abby walked around it, taking readings. The Gate was putting out a frequency similar to the rest of the Dark Gates the DGA had come across so far, but there was something slightly off about it. "Martin, could you run a scan on this and compare it to the readouts we have from prior missions?"

"Yeah, no problem, doll."

"Are you serious?"

"I've been running flirting scenarios for…research. Just wanted to see how that came out. Any feedback?"

Abby looked up from her HUD readings for a second. "Are you kidding? Why would you need to… Wait, are you planning on hitting on our nanobot consciousness?"

"I am not at liberty to talk about that. Also, I'm going to assume it did *not* go well. Noted. Also, your readings are ready. From what I can see, they're operating on a similar frequency, but there is some divergence. It looks like the other Gates are geared to travel between three points: the starting point, a checkpoint in the Netherverse, and the final point."

"And this one?"

"Only two points. This seems like it only goes from point A to point B, point B being in the Netherverse."

Abby stopped pacing around the Gate as scientists came up to take readings. "Any idea how to open it?"

Martin popped up in the corner of Abby's vision. "We can try using the frequency we've used to activate the past Dark Gates. Let's give it a shot."

Abby raised her hand, which converted to a satellite dish, and broadcast the frequency. The Gate did not respond. "Hm, guess it must have a specific frequency to open." She turned to the scientists around her. "Maybe we can reverse-engineer our own frequency to synchronize with this one."

Creon, who was among the scientists, offered to get to work on it, pulling up his HUD as he hobbled over to a makeshift work area the gnomes had put together the prior day.

Abby walked over to the work area as well. The other scientists were also in the same area.

Persephone and Cire were speaking over by the Gate. Nib-Nib was nowhere to be seen.

Abby glanced at Persephone, hoping to catch the drow's eyes. Her HUD was still up, and it pinged.

Martin appeared in front of Abby. "There's been a change in the frequency. Check it out."

Abby pulled up the new frequency. It was behaving very differently. "Hm, I wonder what this is all about."

As Abby absentmindedly watched Persephone walk away from the Gate, she noticed that the frequency changed again. "Hey, wait a minute. We think we have an idea."

Abby ran over to the Gate, waving for Persephone to come over.

"What's up?" the drow asked when she reached Abby.

The girl extended her hand. "Can we see your arm? Sorry, your tentacles?"

"Uh, sure." Persephone's arm split open, and dozens of small, wriggling black tentacles stretched over to Abby's hand.

Abby lifted one of them and looked at it closely. "Do you mind if we take a sample?"

"Is it going to hurt?"

"No, just a little scrape."

Persephone nodded, and Abby's hand converted to a precision laser. She trimmed a thin layer off the tentacle, then she went over to the Gate. Her nanobots covered the sample, fusing with it.

Abby tossed the nanobot-infused sample at the Gate.

The entry exploded into a dark portal.

Creon and the rest of the scientists came over. "Looks like you pegged this one correctly. Wonder what's on the other side?"

Abby peered in. "The Netherverse, but who knows where? Has a living person ever gone into the Netherverse?"

"Hypothetically, it's possible. There are ancient stories about such things. But we've never tried."

Abby folded her arms as she watched the pulsing portal. "Guess we're going to find out today."

Persephone looked at her, her face flushed with worry. "I'm not sure that's a good idea, Abby. The Netherverse is filled with way too much for anyone to just walk into."

"What do you mean?"

Persephone's face darkened. "It is where the elder gods live. Demons. The primordial ooze that came before existence. The Dark Melody was pulled from the Netherverse. There's no telling what you could come across, or if you're going to be able to come back."

Abby understood the drow's fear. She'd been living with a horror that had come from the Netherverse for years, and Abby had seen that horror with her own eyes. The lich had pulled it out of the Netherverse and nearly destroyed New York.

But that didn't change what needed to happen. Someone had to find out what was on the other side of this portal and where it led. Abby wasn't going to ask anyone else to take that risk. If she needed to know, which she did, it was her responsibility.

"No," Abby said. "We'll take care of this."

Abby hugged Persephone tight and whispered in her ear, "We'll… *I'll* be okay. Me, Abby. I'll come back. You don't need to worry about it." She let go of Persephone and turned to the portal, which seemed to stretch out, inviting her into its depths.

CHAPTER SIXTEEN

The Mundanes were leading the dungeon crawl. Terra and Anabelle were lagging slightly behind. The elf was increasingly bored. The Mundanes? Well, that was a different story.

Beth would stop the group every couple of minutes to defuse a trap that was built into the walls and floor. It was effective, and there was a part of Anabelle that was greatly impressed with how perceptive Beth was. That being said, the constant halts were a never-ending source of irritation for her.

Suzuki, on the other hand, was obsessed with an old map he'd gotten that showed the dungeon's layout. The map was filled with notes about different hidden sections. That brought Anabelle to the final thing that was annoying the shit out of them—Stew's constant complaining about loot.

Already, they'd come across five chests. None of their contents had been enough to impress the barbarian.

Anabelle didn't understand. Each of the chests had held something magical enough to rouse even *her* interest, and she was a snob about magical items. Yet Stew would take a look, roll his eyes, and complain about the lack of decent loot in this quest.

If the DGA cared about such trivial matters, there was no way Anabelle would be able to stand them.

Terra didn't seem to have a problem with Stew, though. Anabelle thought Terra had initially been annoyed by the young barbarian, but over the course of the crawl, she'd looked to be warming up to him. As they journeyed through the cavern, Terra and Stew occasionally chatted quietly until Stew became so excited he raised his voice.

As Anabelle reflected on her growing irritation, she realized that she was bored because everyone had something to do but her. Everyone had their roles to play in the crawl, but not her. She was just along for the ride.

This realization made the elf feel, of all things, petty. She felt stupid about not being able to enjoy what was going on nearly as much as everyone else was. It was all business for Anabelle. But the Mundanes looked like they were having a pretty good time.

Maybe I can loosen up. Try to get in the mood, Anabelle thought.

She walked up to where Sandy was and matched pace with the human, trying to think of something to say to break the ice. "Uh, I noticed your magic skills. They're very impressive."

Sandy didn't look at Anabelle. "Uh-huh. Was there something else?"

"What do you mean?"

"Were you going to add 'for a human?'"

Anabelle choked on her words, flushing bright red. Sandy started laughing. "I'm just fucking with you," Sandy said. "It's a joke back at the Lion. Elves are always giving me a hard time because, you know, my magic is upper tier. Everyone's always kidding about me becoming a lich. A couple of people might be worried, though. You've met one, right?"

Anabelle nodded, thinking back to her experiences with Rasputina. "Yeah, fought her a few times. Pretty horrific."

"Really? How so?"

Anabelle looked at Sandy, whose eyes were bright and interested for the first time since the DGA's arrival. "Well, for one, she was practically a walking skeleton. Worse than a zombie, and fuck, was she insane! She killed a news anchor on live tv and then ate him while she forced us to participate in a batshit-crazy interview."

"Ugh. That sounds terrible."

Anabelle continued to explain the extent of the lich's madness to Sandy, and Terra and Stew continued to bicker. Beth and Suzuki still led the party, scouting farther ahead to take care of any traps so the rest of the group didn't have to.

Finally, the rest of the group caught up with Suzuki and Beth. They were standing at the entrance to a sloping tunnel. Suzuki jerked his thumb toward their destination. "Beth went on ahead to check things out. We got a fun one in there. It's a room full of plants."

Anabelle shrugged as she tried to get a better look into the dark dungeon. "What's the big deal with that? Just means someone had the money for an interior decorator."

Stew laughed until Anabelle glared at him. "Sorry," he said. "I thought it was a joke."

Suzuki drew his sword. "Dungeon 101. If you see plants anywhere, they're probably going to kill you. Unless they have thorns. Then they're probably going to poison you. You didn't see any thorns, did you, Beth?"

Beth shook her head. "Nope, not one."

"Cool. So, I'm thinking magic users, you take this one. If you can clear the place out, it would give us a lot more room to move around. I don't want Stew going in until last. The last time he came across magical plants, we ended up having to dig him out the ground."

Stew crossed his arms, pouting. "How was I supposed to know they were going to use me for fertilizer?"

Sandy whirled and pointed her wand at Stew. "Because I *told* you they were going to do that."

Stew leaned back. "Babe, you tell me a lot of things." Unfortunately, he tried to lean on a wall that was not there and fell into the tunnel, screaming the whole way down.

Sandy hit her forehead with her palm. "Goddamn it, Stew! You have to be fucking kidding me!"

Suzuki peered into the tunnel. "Okay, well, I guess that means

Stew's going first, and then the magic users. Give us a holler when it's safe to come down."

Sandy grabbed Anabelle by the hand and ran toward the tunnel's opening. "Come on, this is going to be a blast!" She leaped down the tunnel face-first, wand outstretched, dragging Anabelle behind her.

Anabelle hit the ground with a muted thud. Flowers and buds covered the floor.

Sandy raised her wand, and bright light exploded from it and floated up to the ceiling, illuminating the cavern.

There were plants everywhere, giant hulking specimens with thick wooden stems, tendrils wrapped up in each other, with red and blue blossoms nearly the size of Anabelle's body.

Stew was screaming. He was wrapped up by tendrils that covered his entire body, and one of them was trying to wrap around his mouth and shut him up. As soon as the tendril got close, he took a bite out of the plant. "You can't shut me up! Not Stew JENKINS!"

Tendrils were reaching for Anabelle as well. She pulled her mana and flushed it through her body, sending out a circular wave of fire that burned through anything coming near her.

Sandy whipped her wand around, casting a ring of fire around herself. A black cloak of ash flowed out and around her as a tribal death mask covered her face. "Death has come for all who crave sunlight. I will not tolerate chlorophyll in my midst!"

She cast a fireball at the plant trying to cover Stew with its tendrils.

Stew fell to the ground, grabbed his axe as soon as he could, and swung it madly, cutting down the plants closest to him. "Guess it's time to trim the bushes! How was that, babe?"

Sandy, who was writing a sigil in the air with her flaming wand, turned to Stew and shouted, "I give you an A for effort but a C for content. You've had better."

Anabelle couldn't help but laugh. These Mundanes were having a great time even in a situation that could easily end with their deaths if it was mismanaged.

A shout came from above. It was Suzuki. "Hey, how is it down there? You guys doing all right?"

Stew looked up at the opening of the tunnel. "You guys should get down here! It's a whole room full of killer plants! I mean, like, not just a couple. It's a whole fucking *room*!"

Anabelle could hear the rest of the group muttering above them.

Terra's voice echoed down the tunnel. "We're on our way down!"

One of the blossoms from a plant near Anabelle suddenly turned to face her. It made a sound like a sneeze, and pollen flew toward her.

Anabelle instinctively put her hands in front of her face, manipulating the air in front of her to cause a gust of wind to push the pollen away.

Sandy flew by, casting fireball after fireball, cackling wildly until she stopped just before coming in contact with the pollen Anabelle had gusted away. "Nice move," she called. "I think I can use this." She spun her wand in a circle, and the pollen ignited into a quivering fireball five times the size of the ones Sandy had been casting. "Stew, move your ass if you want to keep any of your hair!"

She flung it at the corner of the room, where the plants were thickest. The fireball exploded, setting flames all over the floor.

Stew, who hadn't moved, tried to leap over the flames, but the wall of fire was too high. "Uh, babe, no reason to go all Firestarter right now."

Terra leapt over the flames and scooped Stew up in her arms. "I would have thought you were tough enough to jump over a simple wall of flames."

Stew stared up at Terra, eyes wide with awe. "Fire scares me. A lot."

Terra landed next to Anabelle and unceremoniously dropped Stew on the ground. The rest of the Mundanes were in the cavern now as well.

Suzuki sized up what was left. "We could probably clear this out quickly enough."

Sandy, who had floated over near the elf, said, "All right, I'm with Anabelle."

Shocked, she looked at Sandy. "What do you mean?"

"I haven't gotten to play off a magic user in a long time, and I really dig your elemental abilities. We could get really wild in here."

The plants were preparing to mount another attack, having pulled up their roots and stretched toward the ceiling, cutting off any route of escape.

Sandy's wand floated in front of her as she hovered off the ground. "What do you say?"

Anabelle smiled, reveling in the pure ridiculousness of the fight for the first time. "I say we take half the room and leave the rest for them."

"Sounds good. Let's go!"

Sandy shot toward the right side of the cavern, dropping small fireballs along the way.

Anabelle ran after her, using her mana to increase the size of the fireballs until they were floating fiery landmines.

Sandy got to the wall and touched her wand to it. The wall started to crack, shooting out flames from the weakened points.

The fireballs that had been left behind exploded.

Sandy pointed her wand at the fireballs as tendrils reached out toward her. "Watch this!" She waved her wand and muttered an unknown language under her breath. The flames froze in midair, yet still flickered.

Anabelle got an idea. "Okay, but how about this?" She extended her mana outward, fanning the flames but also interacting with the time dilation spell that Sandy had cast, stretching the spell even further so the flames stood still. Then she started spinning her hands in a circle, creating a cyclone that picked up the flames, turning them on their sides and slicing through the plants.

Sandy's mask disappeared as she stared at the display of magical excellence. "Whoa, that's really fucking cool."

A tendril stretched out and wrapped around Sandy's foot, stringing her up.

Anabelle pulled out the water deep within the plant and formed it into a floating orb. As Sandy fell, she cast a spell to freeze the water. Anabelle punched the orb, filling it with mana and sending shards of ice the size of her arm flying out to pin the remaining plant stalks to the wall.

"Hey, watch that shit!"

It was Stew shouting. Anabelle looked at him. He was pinned to the wall with an icicle under his crotch. "So not even close to cool, bros!"

Sandy burst out laughing as her and Anabelle's side of the cavern was reduced to ashes. Anabelle laughed too. This was pretty fun. No looming armies. No lich. No Grok. Just dungeon-crawling.

Suzuki, Beth, and Terra were nearly done slashing through their side of the cavern. They were all covered with thick green sap. "You guys done over there?" Sandy called.

Terra reached down and yanked up the last big plant, tearing it out by the roots. She tossed it to the ground, then severed its blossom with her axe. "Yep. Just about." Then she looked at Stew, who was still hanging from the wall. "Who wants to pull him off before he gets blueballs?"

The Mundanes and the DGA broke into uproarious laughter, Sandy laughing so hard she had to bend over and clutch her sides. "That was a fucking good one," she wheezed before magically pulling Stew off the wall.

Stew's crotch was soaked. "Hey, babe, could you, you know, help me out a little?"

Sandy sighed and pressed her wand to Stew's crotch. He sighed with relief, then jumped back suddenly. "Thanks. It was a little too hot."

Suzuki looked around the devastated cavern. "We still got a little bit to go before we make it to the main chamber. Looks like as good a place for a break as I can think of. Stew, Beth, you guys wanna take care of the fire?"

Stew groaned while Beth saluted Suzuki. "We got it. You guys make us some room to get comfortable. And make sure all these things are dead. I don't want to get strangled during lunch."

The Mundanes took the bulk of responsibility for preparing lunch. Stew was in charge. He showed everyone how to shuck the plants that hadn't been roasted to ash, a process that ended up with Stew getting pollen in his face and being knocked unconscious a handful of times. Luckily, Sandy always kept a cache of potions on her, masterfully brewed by Diana for a variety of situations.

After each pollen doze, Stew was back on his feet within a couple of seconds. Through trial and error, everyone figured out how to keep from having the same thing happen to them.

Sandy double-checked the plants in a book she kept on her. It detailed a good chunk of local wildlife throughout the nine realms. She explained she had won the book in a rigged poker game with another MERC. The other MERC had assumed they were the only person who was rigging the game.

Beth and Suzuki picked through the plants for something that was worth eating. Beth voiced a concern multiple times that she wasn't a fan of eating random plants they found in the middle of a dungeon. Sandy assured her there was nothing to worry about.

Anabelle and Terra worked with the Mundanes, diligently cutting off the stalks of the plants and making sure everything was dead. The elf was still impressed by the Mundanes' synergy. She couldn't remember ever fighting with a group that was so keyed into each other's movements. Even Stew, who she initially thought was an oaf, still played off the rest of the party in a way that, even though it was comical, was still worthy of note.

After an hour of foraging, the Mundanes and the DGA brought over a collection of plant parts that Stew deemed acceptable. By now, he had made a healthy fire and was busy grilling a pile of herbs on one of the large leaves of the plants they had just decimated. "All right, you guys can just hang out and relax now. I got this covered."

Sandy sidled up next to Stew. "You need help with anything?"

The barbarian shook his head as he tended the herbs. "Nah, I got everything covered. Don't worry about it."

Sandy clapped her hands together as she scooted away from Stew and pulled out a book. "Great. I've been looking forward to this all day."

Anabelle noticed Suzuki was doing the same, except he was looking through his map, cross-referencing it with a book he had. He seemed to be deep in thought.

Beth opened her HUD, and a lute appeared in her lap. She strummed it lightly, singing quietly under her breath. It was hard for Anabelle to hear the words, the woman was singing so softly, but it was loud enough that the elf could say Beth had a beautiful singing voice. The whole afternoon was turning into something magical.

After a bit of silence, Sandy looked up from her book. "Anabelle, you don't use a wand for your magic, do you? And you're not casting traditional spells either, right?"

The elf, delighted to have a conversation about magic with someone who knew their stuff, leaned forward, the fire warming her. "No, it's not traditional in certain respects. I was trained in the Path of the Traveler. It's an ancient elvish…I guess you could say religion that specializes in using magic in a completely organic, elemental way, coupled with a variety of fighting styles."

"It's very elegant. I've never seen anything like that since I've been in Middang3ard. You should teach it. I think there are a lot of elves around here who would be interested. Maybe even some humans, if we have the capacity. You know, having to use familiars and all."

Anabelle initially felt the desire to tell Sandy that the Path was not for everybody since it was a rigorous exploration of the self, but she thought better of it. She'd been chosen as a child. There had been nothing special about her other than her pedigree. Maybe it was time to bring the Travelers back for everyone. The Path wasn't doing much if there was no one walking it.

"That's not a bad idea," Anabelle admitted. "Maybe I'll take to the mage…Diane, right? That was her name?"

Sandy turned back to her book. "Yeah, you should do that," she murmured.

Anabelle leaned over to Terra. "So, how's it been fighting with another barbarian?"

Terra raised an eyebrow at her. "Excuse me? I am not a barbarian. The term you're looking for is 'orc chieftain.' It *has* been fun to be around someone as reckless as I can get. Maybe not as smart or good looking, but it's been fun all the same."

Sandy, without raising an eye from her book, smirked. "Not as good looking. I think you're wrong about that. My man is hot. Excruciatingly so."

Anabelle laughed as Terra blushed. "Still not sure how I feel about the fraternization in your ranks," the elf joked.

Suzuki closed his book and leaned back against one of the decapitated stalks. "MERCs don't have ranks. There's an intel department and then the rest of us. Keeps things simple. Anything like leadership is up to each party. Might seem weird to all you military folk, but it works pretty well for us."

Anabelle was about to answer, but Terra cut her off. "The DGA isn't heavy on rank either. Anabelle's pretty much in charge because she's the best one for the job."

The elf avoided everyone's eyes. She wasn't used to receiving compliments. Before she could say anything, Stew leapt up to his feet and shouted, "Grub is on!"

Stew passed around plates of the steaming stalks of whatever plants they had just destroyed. Anabelle looked down at hers, unsure whether she should take a bite, but it smelled too good not to. She tore into her food, utterly surprised by the litany of flavors that played across her tongue.

Everyone else was doing the same. Once their plates were cleared, there was a collective sigh from both parties. "Goddamn, Stew, you can fucking cook," Terra whooped.

Stew, looking immensely proud of himself, stood and took a bow. "Thank you, thank you. Further proof that I'm more than a devilishly handsome face and unbeatable rock-hard abs."

Sandy came up to Stew's side and wrapped her arms around him. "I'd say angelically handsome. You do have that baby face."

Stew rubbed said face as Sandy leaned over to kiss him on the cheek. "Babe, come on. I don't have a baby face."

Terra, who was walking past Stew to check out the exit from the cavern, slapped him on the back. "In orcish, it's called *korah-jah-kil*, or, a man with the face of one still nursing."

Stew glared at Terra. "I'll have you know, I never breastfed. My mouth was too weak. Couldn't latch if I wanted to."

Silence fell over both parties, finally broken by Beth. "Uh, okay, that explains a *lot* of things. You guys ready to get moving? I feel like we've had a long enough kumbaya hour. I'd prefer not to hear anything more about what Stew did or did not do with his mother's tits."

Suzuki checked his map again. "Yeah, you're right. We're not too far from the treasure chamber anyway."

Anabelle glanced in the direction of the exit. "Might as well. It's not like the safety of the nine realms hangs in the balance."

Stew whispered in Sandy's ear, "Those DGA suits are *so* serious."

The two parties moved out, leaving the remains of the murderous plants behind them and descending into a narrow tunnel that continued for a mile or two before opening slightly, giving them all room to breathe.

Beth led the party, again stopping at different intervals to dismantle traps. Only one trap was sprung, when Stew was leaning over Sandy to take notes, and he annoyed her enough that she set it off, causing a plume of sleeping dust to settle over everyone. Luckily, Anabelle saw it in time and managed to freeze the dust into ice crystals that fell to the ground without harming anyone.

They went on as Stew sulked in silence.

The traps let up, and they were making better time than earlier. Anabelle hardly even noticed. Her perspective had changed drastically since the battle with the plants. It wasn't about having a role; a dungeon crawl was about the interplay between the different party members.

She was acutely aware of the difference between how she'd been thinking about teamwork and how the Mundanes did. She used teamwork to bring out the best in her. The Mundanes seemed to think of teamwork as the only possible way to function.

The tunnel took a hard left turn and split into six different paths. Suzuki consulted his map, Beth looking over his shoulder, pointing out the notes that she'd scribbled. After a few minutes of deliberation, they chose one of the middle paths and continued.

Anabelle watched Terra as they traveled. The human was quieter than usual. Anabelle wondered what she was thinking about. She also wondered what having open communication like the Mundanes would be like, or if she was even capable of such a thing.

There was a lot to consider, most of which had never crossed Anabelle's mind.

Suddenly, Suzuki raised his hand, stopping the two parties. "I think we're coming up on it. There's a doorway down there. Be prepared for anything."

Everyone in the party drew their weapons. Anabelle was ready for another fight. She'd been itching for one since they had finished lunch. Fighting side by side with Sandy had been exhilarating, like painting or writing a song together—an aspect of combat she rarely experienced.

The two parties came up to the door, which had a face carved into it. A riddle door.

Anabelle sighed, remembering the failings of the dungeon crawl that the DGA had gotten stuck on. "Goddess be damned, another of these things?"

Suzuki shook his head and laughed as he pulled out his book. "No, nowhere near as bad as the one you described from what I've gathered. All the riddle doors in this dungeon are kinda like...imitations. Check this out."

Suzuki made a face at the door, pulling his lips down with his fingers and sticking out his tongue.

The door sneered at Suzuki and then blew up its cheeks so they looked like a chipmunk's.

Suzuki copied the door's gesture, causing it to chuckle before closing one eye and pushing its nose up, which Suzuki mirrored.

The door laughed, an odd sound akin to old wood bending. Then its face drooped and trickled off the door as it swung open.

Suzuki knelt and looked at the remnants of the door inching away like a slug. "See, not nearly as terrible."

Anabelle nodded, silently wishing she'd come across a door with such banal sensibilities.

The Mundanes and the DGA crept into the dark treasure room. Sandy raised her wand, ready to cast an illumination spell, but Suzuki grabbed her arm to keep her from casting. "Wait," he whispered. "There's probably a shit ton of defenses in here. Let's scope the place out before you brighten it all up. Beth, can you see anything?"

Beth leaned down and took a pair of binoculars out of her bag, then scanned the treasure room. "Nope, there doesn't look like there's anything else here. A shit-ton of gold and something floating in the middle of the room, but I don't see anything like an enemy. Unless the gold is cursed. Now that I think about it, it probably is. Stew, don't touch anything. I mean it. I'm not going to let Sandy save your ass this time."

Stew scoffed. "I don't even care about gold."

Suzuki released Sandy's arm. "All right, light it up."

Sandy cast an illumination spell, instantly brightening the room.

Beth hadn't been lying. There were piles of gold, some of them stretching nearly to the ceiling. In the middle of the room was a jar, floating innocuously.

Anabelle took a step toward the jar, but Suzuki held up his hand. "Hold on. There's no way there's just a soul jar in the middle of the room. This should be heavily guarded."

Beth looked at the ceiling and yelped quietly. "Oh, it's definitely heavily guarded. Why do you think there are so many piles of gold?"

Suzuki sighed as he rubbed his forehead. "Don't tell me it's what I think it is."

Terra stepped forward, her eyes bright with excitement. "Wait, is it a dragon?"

Beth pointed at the ceiling.

Above the jar was a gold dragon, its scales glittering in the light of the illumination spell. It was nearly the size of the entire ceiling. Its wings were wrapped around its body like a giant gold bat's. Anabelle couldn't tell where its legs were.

Suzuki scratched his head. "What the hell is a golden dragon doing in the middle of a dungeon? Those guys are supposed to be the pinnacle of goodness. Not that you can't be good and live underground, but a dungeon?"

Terra shrugged, not taking her eyes of the dragon. "Who cares? Are we going to fight it or not?"

Suzuki shook his head. "You don't want to fight one of those. They're the most powerful dragons out there. We'd best try to avoid a fight. We can attempt to sneak around him and avoid the whole thing."

Suddenly, the golden dragon's eyes opened. They zeroed in on the Mundanes and the DGA.

Suzuki drew his sword, as did the others. "Looks like that's off the menu."

The dragon stretched out its wings and unleashed a torrent of golden fire, melting the gold beneath him. The soul jar was not affected.

Beth stepped back, away from the flames. "You guys ever fought a gold dragon before?"

Terra counted on her hand, looking up as she thought. "Uh, I fought a red dragon, a silver dragon, and there's that dragon that was kinda teal. Or I thought it was teal. The light was kinda weird. And… well, there were a lot of dragons. You guys were there for that one, I think."

The dragon fell from the ceiling, stretching out its wings as it let loose a roar that set the elf's skin crawling.

Stew, whose bravado had finally disappeared, swallowed. "Yeah, we were there for *a* dragon, but I can't remember what color it was."

The dragon loosed another gout of flame that stretched to the ceiling, revealing how deep in the cavern they all were.

Sandy cast a barrier shield around both parties as the dragon unleashed another torrent of flame.

The dragon leaned forward, smoke fuming from its nose and spoke, its voice deep and ancient. "Who dares step into my chambers?"

The Mundanes looked at Suzuki. "Don't you have a dragon girlfriend or something?" Beth asked.

Suzuki turned red, and he stumbled over his words. "She's not my girlfriend. It's different from that."

The dragon fired another blast of fire.

Sandy's barrier quivered, weakening and ready to give. "Whatever it is, just fucking do it!"

Suzuki cleared his throat and stepped forward. "All right, I'll give it a shot."

CHAPTER EIGHTEEN

Roy and the mysterious orc sat in a corner of the bar, sizing each other up. There was nothing about the orc to give away why he knew about Grok. Roy watched him closely. If it came down to a fight, he would be able to cover his ass. It also helped that the bar was full of newly made allies.

But the orc didn't seem to be here to fight. If he was, a sneak attack would have been more appropriate. One thing Roy could tell was that the orc was a fighter, and a fighter would have exploited his comfort at the bar and used it to their advantage.

The orc leaned toward Roy. "Name's Yegoth. You're Roy, correct?"

The mech rider's eyes narrowed as he watched the orc. "Who wants to know?"

"I just introduced myself. Yegoth. Why would—"

"It's just a saying, like an idiom. Never mind. Why does Yegoth want to know?"

Yegoth looked over his shoulder at Blackwell, who was sitting at the bar. "Should you invite your associate over? Blackwell, I believe."

Roy nodded politely. He understood what Yegoth was trying to do —show that he'd been watching them or had received a good bit of intel without being threatening. It was a simple code for most spies. Lay everything on the table for the people they were interested in talking to, not killing. "Yeah, I'll call him over," Roy said.

He shouted Blackwell's name, motioning for him to join them at the table. The orc introduced himself to Blackwell and vice versa.

"Now that you have both our attention, you want to tell me what this is about?" Roy asked.

Yegoth pulled back his hood. His face was heavily scarred, and he had a giant tattoo on the side of his bald head. "I'm an agent in the orcish spy network. I come with news you might find interesting."

"What would that be? Does it concern Grok?"

Yegoth shook his head. "Only tangentially, but I thought it would be a good place to start."

Blackwell gave him a curious look. "How could the orcs have a spy network? The twelve tribes have been broken up for years, and the rest were enslaved by the Dark One. Did you think we'd believe there were enough orcs united for a whole network?"

"That's part of the information I'm bringing you. Let's get that one out of the way. Although the orcs have been splintered for a time, there has always been a network that supersedes the individual desires of any tribes. An old ordination from the original council of twelve."

Roy's ears perked up at that. "I've never heard of the council."

"It's an ancient practice that historically worked behind the scenes. There are the tribal leaders, and each tribe had a council leader. The council was responsible for keeping the orcs together. They created three means to that: the Fist, the Eyes, and the Heart."

"You're going to have to explain that."

"The Fist was an elite warrior class designed to put down insurrections. The Eyes were the spy network responsible for keeping tabs on possible issues, and the Heart were the shamans, who were needed to preserve orcish culture, history, and spirituality. Grok was the last of the Fist. I lead the Eyes, and your friend Cire is, for all intents and purposes, the last shaman."

Roy wanted to ask more questions, and he wished Terra and Cire were with him. He also knew his questions would have to be direct and not waste any time. Curiosity could be satisfied later. "And this council?"

"They've asked me to intervene in a set of coming events."

Blackwell shook his head. "How could there still be a council if the tribes have been split up?"

"The tribes split, but the council didn't. They lost the ability to help steer our people in the right direction, but since Terra and Cire united the tribes, there is a chance for real leadership again."

"So, the council is planning on swooping in and ending all the work we've been—"

Yegoth raised his hand, cutting Blackwell off. "To start, no one rules the orcs but ourselves. Secondly, that is not the council's aim. There is a considerable amount of infighting among the tribes now. Some of the former leaders have those who whisper in their ears, suggesting that Terra is an outsider who will never understand orc ways. Whispers that would have her killed and try to take her position. My sources have those orcs pinpointed. They would be weak leaders. Doom the twelve tribes."

Blackwell started to grasp what Yegoth was getting at. "And you want us to take them out?"

"No. We are spies, not assassins. I propose something more delicate. The council will make itself known again and offer Terra a seat on it. She'll retain her commanding power over the twelve tribes, but the council will be able to veto any decisions she makes that might prove detrimental to our people. It will strengthen the resolve of the tribes and keep them from splitting again. Granted, I understand that might not seem like a good deal on your side of things."

Blackwell shook his head as he sipped his beer. "It sounds like you want to diminish Terra's power and relegate her to a bureaucrat."

"It would be a diminishing of power in some regards, but she will be seen as more orc, and the tribes will trust her more. But I will make a concession. The council will be unable to veto any war-related decisions. That will make her even more trusted by the orcs. A new embodiment of our old war chiefs, who existed for one purpose and one alone."

Roy thought it over for a second. Terra and Cire had made it known on multiple occasions how uncomfortable they were with the idea of a human leading the orcs indefinitely. They'd also tried to make their own tweaks to the system to be accepted better. Roy knew it was only a matter of time before there was some kind of orc unrest. This could fix the problem before it got started. "I'm going to do something I don't often do, which is trust you on this. You and your council want what's best for the orcs?"

Yegoth smiled softly and nodded. "That was why I came unarmed and with a soft voice. Regardless of what you do, the council will act. We believe the council would be stronger with Terra. She is an exceptional leader hampered by the fact that she is not a full orc, but given some time on the council, the orc population will cease to see that."

"Deal. What next?"

"The council will reach out to you when they are ready to convene. Now on to more pressing business."

Blackwell chuckled quietly. "The orc insurrection wasn't the pressing business?"

"For me, perhaps, but not for you. This concerns the Dark One's plans. I doubt you know this explicitly, but Grok and Persephone were extremely special agents of the Dark One. Grok had been with the Dark One for some time. Persephone, on the other hand, was still being trained. A lucky situation for you, seeing as she has joined your side. But there is a third."

Roy shrugged as his brow darkened. "I don't see why that is a problem. We've taken care of two of his special agents already."

"Yes, but at what cost? One of yours was taken and tortured for weeks. Grok defeated you multiple times, resulting in a large loss of human lives, and if she had not broken Anabelle, there is a good chance she would have decimated you and your new orc army. I would think you'd want to avoid that again."

Roy tried not to betray his bruised pride. Yegoth was right. "All right, what do you know?"

"Before Rasputina went rogue, the Dark One had her acquire a soul for him—one he's performed unholy experiments on, but who is also elevating the Dark One's tech. A human, actually. Nikola Tesla."

Blackwell groaned. "Are you serious? Is the Dark One getting all his ideas from bad steampunk comics?"

Yegoth stared in confusion at Blackwell. "I don't know what steampunk is, but if you have resources on Tesla, I believe you should use them to your best advantage. I've been unable to find how he plans to deploy his new agent, but I would suggest using your spy networks to find out. The Dark One is growing reckless. All of his agents have disappeared, and his wildcard, Rasputina, is off the grid. These situations make a dangerous enemy."

Yegoth stood and extended his hand to Roy and Blackwell.

"Wait, you're just going to *give* us all this information?" Roy asked.

The orc shook the two humans' hands. "Yes. We have the same enemy, and there is nothing more important than destroying the Dark One. We also hope our spy networks grow to share information with each other. The orcs have nothing to hide. We've spent too long on the outskirts of the nine realms. It is time we fixed that. You'll hear from us soon."

With that, Yegoth pulled his hood back over his face and was gone.

Roy and Blackwell exchanged glances as they sat back down. "I never thought the easiest spy to work with would be an orc. That's one for the books."

Blackwell didn't seem as convinced. "What makes you think he's telling the truth?"

"Because there is no reason to lie about most of this. The only thing I'm iffy about is the council. That being said, I've heard people whispering, and I know how coups go. There is something brewing. Better to take care of it now than get fucked later."

Blackwell leaned back in his chair, smiling faintly. "Nikola Tesla, eh? This shit gets more ridiculous every month. What next, dinosaurs with tech strapped to them?"

"You ever talk to the Mundanes from the MERC group? They'll

have some stories for you. I heard that exact thing happened to them once."

"God, I'm so fucking glad I don't work on Middang3ard."

———

Abby sat by the Gate with her drone Gertrude. The drone had been sent to her through the hadron collider back on Earth. Luckily, transporting inorganic material was easier than flesh and bone.

Gertrude had routinely been updated with new tech by Creon while Abby was away on missions. She was surprised by all the gadgets and improvements Creon had added.

Abby stared into the portal, which hadn't closed. Freezing wind ushered forth from the portal. She was curious to know what was hiding deep within that dark place. She knew it was called the Netherverse, but no one completely understood what that entailed. She was going to find out.

"Hey, I brought you some coffee," a voice said from behind her.

Abby looked over her shoulder at Persephone, who was walking up the hill with a blanket over her shoulder and two cups of coffee. "Thought you might want some for your all-nighter," Persephone said. "And yes, I know, technically, you don't need to eat or drink anything most of the time. But you know, it could be nice."

Persephone spread the blanket in front of Abby and took a seat between her and the portal.

Abby took the coffee and smiled before kissing Persephone on the cheek. "We're surprised you're up this late."

Persephone looked at the portal and shivered. "I haven't been able to sleep since you opened that thing. The Dark Melody is getting louder in my head. Nothing terrible, but it's reacting to whatever is behind that portal."

Abby watched the drow's face. Her worry was evident. "We're going to be okay. Our nanobots are taking readings to adjust our suit, then we're spending all night prepping. We'll be ready for whatever is in there."

"Just promise you aren't going to bring an Elder One back, okay?"

Abby nodded as she sipped her coffee. "Trust me, we've seen enough of those for a lifetime. Besides, you're the only Elder One we need."

Abby wrapped her hand around Persephone's, and the two watched the blackness flicker behind the Gate.

CHAPTER NINETEEN

The morning was spent preparing Abby's nanobot armor for the conditions in the Netherverse. From what the recon nanobots had reported, she was in for an interesting experience.

Creon and the rest of the scientists went through the data with Martin, who was using Gertrude as a vessel since there were few holoscreens. Abby thought it was funny to see her first rudimentary creation alongside something as complex as Martin.

From what had been gathered, Martin and Creon explained, it looked like the Netherverse was made up of a reality-fluctuating compound. What existed there was not matter, nor was it antimatter. It was something completely different. Creon had ideas about what it could be but nothing conclusive. He and Martin agreed that the most likely definition of the Netherverse was a realm that existed within the recycled bodies and minds of the Elder Ones.

Abby liked the idea. When she was younger, she'd wanted to be an astronaut. It was a dream that, like most childhood aspirations, had faded. She hadn't remembered it until now—the way she used to stare up at the stars and wonder if she was ever going to make it up there. Now she'd gone to different realms and planes of reality. She thought it was funny how things could change so quickly and not even be noticed.

During the night, as Abby had stayed up listening to Persephone tell her stories, she'd increased the number of nanobots in her body. Ever since she had used her nanobots to free the orcs from the Dark One's mind control, Martin and the nanobot consciousness had been working on pushing Abby's physical threshold to allow her to accommodate more nanobots without risking her health.

Abby was nowhere near having as many nanobots as she'd had before, but she was at a higher capacity than when the DGA had gone on their dungeon crawl.

The scientists and Creon were talking excitedly as Nib-Nib and Cire walked through the group to get to Abby and Persephone. The two girls were looking at the portal like one might peer into a window.

Cire clapped a hand on Abby's shoulder. "It's a brave thing you're doing today."

Abby squeezed Cire's hand. "No, it's really not. We've been collecting data all night, and they've been working at deciphering it all morning. This is as safe as it gets. We even have some projections of what it should look like when I get there over on that holoscreen."

"The first images of the Netherverse?"

Abby tried to hide how pleased she was with herself. "Yep. Pretty cool, huh? You wanna check 'em out?" She led Cire, Nib-Nib, and Persephone over to the holoscreen and swiped through it until she got to the recorded images from her nanobots.

The holoscreen displayed a vast land of sweeping hills and forests, the landscape black and tinted with a strange, unearthly silver glow. "See? It doesn't look that much different from anything else on this world," Abby said. "We wouldn't be surprised if the Netherverse was like any of the nine realms, sandwiched on top of each other. That's probably how this Gate works too. But we should get to it. The longer we sit here talking, the more time we're wasting."

"What's the rush?" Persephone asked.

Abby's eyes shifted from their usual color to a sharp green, her irises moving back and forth like gears. "We're curious to verify our data. Come on."

They headed back to the portal. Nanobots covered Abby's body, creating armor that was bulkier than usual and had a breathing apparatus on the side. Gravitational displacements connected to her feet, anchoring her to the ground. Two plasma cannons built themselves atop her shoulders, while a domed helmet cobbled itself up over her face.

Creon and the majority of the scientists gathered around Abby and the portal as Gertrude floated over to the girl.

Abby patted Gertrude on the top of its drone head. "Ready to do this, Martin?"

Martin popped up in the corner of Abby's field of vision. "Time to make history. God, I wish I had family to tell this to other than you."

"I made sure to mention you in the email I sent my mom last night. She says hi."

A silver line blasted out of Abby's back, connecting to the ground behind her. "If things get too bad in there, we'll signal you. Just yank on this, and it'll pull us back. See you on the other side."

Abby ran toward the Gate and leapt in. Its surface rippled as she disappeared.

She hit the ground hard, rolling to her feet as her gravitational boots locked her in place.

This place was nothing like the video projections.

Abby stood on a rock that floated through an infinity of stars and black holes, but there was more. It was taking Abby some time to comprehend what she was looking at.

Purple lightning storms flashed in the distance, outlining creatures the size of universes that were slithering about, combining and shifting, breaking away and reforming.

There was land beneath her. The heavens, where Abby seemed to be, were separated by a purple and blue ocean that stretched as far as she could see. "This is definitely not what we were expecting," she murmured.

Gertrude floated over to Abby. She directed the drone down

toward the ocean. The machine splashed through the water, coming out on the other side. It sent Abby a readout of the liquid it had passed through, along with a diagnostic of the air quality.

The liquid wasn't dangerous, and there was enough oxygen here to breathe.

Abby's mask broke apart, conserving the nanobots. Then she leapt through the water, landing on the ground beneath her, which was soft.

Lightning flashed, illuminating the ground. Abby screamed in horror and leapt into the air, firing her thrusters so she could float.

Beneath her, stretching on and on, were billions of corpses. Their blank eyes stared up at Abby. As she looked closer, she could see they didn't have the same consistency as physical bodies. They wavered slightly as if they weren't fully corporal.

"Oh, my God, are these souls?" Abby wondered aloud.

She descended closer to the ground and reached for one of their hands. Hers passed right through it. She raised her wrist, constructed a HUD, and scanned the area. There were no signs of life. "Martin, are you getting all this?"

Gertrude came up on Abby's side, scanning the sea of souls. "Yeah, I'm getting it all. So, I guess everyone was wrong about what happens after you die. This is disappointing. There's not even a river."

"There has to be something other than this. Why else would the Dark One want to have a Gate leading to this place? Maybe just to have access to the Elder Ones?"

Gertrude jetted forward and spun in a circle, scanning everything within range. "Nah, that doesn't make sense. Rasputina had to perform a huge ritual to get that Elder One to Earth. And the only other time we've seen him pulling out anything close to an Elder One out was a mission the dragonriders were on, I think Alex Bound's team. Anyway, it required an interdimensional meteor that might have been made of the very essence of the Dark One. Safe to say, it's probably going to take more than a Gate."

"Then what would he need here? There's only death."

"Let's keep looking."

Abby and Gertrude floated along the shores of the dead, for that was what they were. She could see that as they came to a river, its contents a purple and blue sludge of a liquid, the shores covered with heavy fog. Lightning still crashed above, illuminating the silhouettes of ancient, forgotten gods, unconcerned with the two specks walking around beneath them.

A quick scan showed the waters of the river weren't toxic. Abby knelt and dipped her fingers into it. "The river Styx, minus Charon. Guess the stories weren't true."

"This can't be all of it, though. I mean, I'm glad that I don't have a mortal life, but if this is all you have to look forward to after the big living thing, what's the point?"

Abby hadn't really thought about that, but Martin did have a point. All these souls tossed around as if they were litter on the beach. Was this all that they had to look forward to? "Maybe this isn't the way it's supposed to be. We haven't read anything implying the Netherverse is where all souls go."

"True. You're right. We gotta keep an open mind about this whole thing. There could be something very wrong with this place."

Abby looked at the sky, shading her eyes against the lightning. "Yeah, but maybe this whole place is wrong."

"If it is, it definitely shouldn't be where all the souls of the nine realms are going. It doesn't make any sense."

A bright purple light flashed across the river. It was different from the lightning above her. It continued to glow, growing brighter with time. "There's something there," Abby muttered.

"Do you want to check it out?"

Abby tried to comm Cire, but all she got on her side was static. Still, she explained the situation and told him she needed to investigate further. Then she returned to Martin. "We're going to check that out."

"Wait, do you mean you are, or both of us are?"

"Did you prefer to stay here?"

Gertrude's display showed an icon of a smiley face with an

uncomfortable toothy grin. "Stupid question, okay? Let's go check this out."

The two flew over the river, heading toward the bright purple light. As Abby passed over the river, she could see that its surface was covered with floating souls.

Abby was surprised that she didn't feel more unsettled by this place. There was an odd kind of peace here among the dead. An idea popped into her head. "Martin, scan for our dead soldiers. It is a longshot, but—"

"Already in the process. Also, I have a query."

"A query?"

Martin scoffed, yet stumbled over his words when he spoke again. "Okay, a fucking question. If you were to ask someone to do something but they didn't have a body and most of your conversation centered around exchanging data streams for optimal performance, what would you say?"

Abby stopped flying and floated in front of Gertrude. "You need to be straightforward with us. Are you talking about our consciousness?"

"This is an uncomfortable conversation for me. I kinda feel like I'm asking my mom for permission to date a symbiotic nervous system living inside her."

"At least you didn't say 'parasite.'"

Gertrude's display showed a smiling face with a thumbs up. "You know, you're right. I didn't. So, yeah, I guess what am I asking is if it would be weird to ask your additional consciousness out...sort of."

"If you guys like talking to each other, who are we to stop you? Go for it."

The display changed to an excited face with tears rolling down its cheeks. "Sweet! I promise I won't distract them from their processing priorities too much. Unless things get binary, if you know what I mean."

Abby was only half-listening. The purple light seemed to be coming closer to them. "No, we...I don't know. And I don't want to. Keep me out of it."

Another flash of bright purple, this time only a couple hundred feet away. Abby rocketed toward the light but stopped once she saw what it was coming from.

A lone figure crouched in the midst of the purple light. It was a man, slim, hunched over the souls. His hair stood up and was shock white, and he wore a long black coat. Purple light was radiating from his hands and his eyes.

Abby's cannons aimed at the man. *What the hell is that?* she thought.

The man looked at Abby, his glowing purple eyes flashing as he touched one of the souls beneath him.

The soul began to jerk, black goo stretching over it as technological tendrils snaked from the man's arms, digging into the chest of the soul, tearing it open, forcing themselves inside, and then stitching it up.

Abby waved her hand at the man. "Hello!" The moment she spoke, she realized that she didn't have a follow-up.

The man stood, then clapped his hands together, and there was another flash. As the purple light faded, Abby could see the man was now covered in a skintight black suit. There were electrical valves attached to the back, and a black helmet covered all but his mouth. Electricity ran from his eyes down to his fingers.

Martin pulled up Gertrude's weapons. "Abby, he's getting ready to—"

The man surged forward faster than Abby could have seen, moving at the speed of electricity. He hit her in the chest, sending her flying backward.

Gertrude whirled and prepared to fire.

The man appeared behind the drone and rested one finger on Gertrude. She exploded.

Abby kicked her thrusters on, heading toward the firmament of water above.

The man teleported in front of Abby. "And who might you be?" he asked.

Abby didn't bother answering. She fired her cannons at him, but he teleported out of the way, allowing the plasma blasts to hit the souls on the ground.

The man appeared right in front of Abby. "Hm. I assumed you had the disposition of a learned man or woman, but you might be nothing more than a common brute in beautiful armor.

He reached out, a purple atom sparkling on the tip of his index finger.

Abby had no idea what it was, but she knew it was dangerous. She tugged on the cord attached her back as she scanned the man.

The slack from the cord tightened and Abby was yanked back. She flew through the Netherverse away from the man in black with purple eyes and hands.

Abby burst through the portal and scrambled away from it. "Shut it down," she screamed. "Shut it down."

Creon gave Abby an odd look, preparing to explain something.

Abby didn't listen. She raised her hand and fired into the Gate.

The portal vanished.

Abby got to her feet as her nanobots receded.

Creon came up to her side. "What did you see?"

Abby stared at the Gate. "We have no fucking idea.

CHAPTER TWENTY

The Mundanes and the two members of the DGA stood before the huge gold dragon. It was roughly the size of a red dragon, but its tail was nearly twice the length of the rest of its body. Its wings were long and bat-like in shape, but instead of the soft leathery look of a bat's wings, the dragon's wings looked like spun gold. Golden whiskers like a cat's hung from the dragon's face.

Suzuki gave the Mundanes a look as Terra cleared her throat uncomfortably. "Uh, I'm rethinking this whole thing."

Beth shook her head and folded her arms. "What good is being Dragon Bound if you can't throw your weight around a little bit? Besides, it's a gold dragon. It's one of the good guys. Just use all those fancy words you got, and we'll be out of her in no time."

Anabelle was surprised by the casualness the Mundanes were exhibiting in this situation. If she were to square up against a dragon, it would have been a much more dire affair. The Mundanes went about this as if they were playing a game.

Suzuki nodded and straightened out his armor and turned back to the dragon, which had vanished. "What the hell?" Suzuki gasped.

In the dragon's place was a young man with yellow-tinted skin. He wore a suit of gold and had a shining emerald tie that matched the man's eyes. "I believe you've come for the jar?"

Sandy leaned over to Anabelle and whispered, "Gold dragons are master shapeshifters. Even when they're in their own homes, they hate to be in their natural bodies around anyone other than other gold dragons. I think it's like being naked for them."

Suzuki cleared his throat. "Greetings. I am Suzuki, Dragon Bound, Mundanest of the Mundanes."

The gold man-dragon bowed slightly as Suzuki did the same. "I am Telzrem, the Voiceless one. I have heard whispers of you, Suzuki. I believe you are bound to a particularly beautiful, honorable dragon. What brings you to my humble abode?"

"My party is helping our new friends fulfill a quest of the utmost importance. They stand against the Dark One, as do we, and require a soul jar to defeat what the Dark One has raised up."

Telzrem raised his eyebrows curiously. "That is interesting. Any enemy of the Dark One is a friend of mine."

"Great! So, we can have the soul jar?"

"Absolutely not. Now please leave before I am forced to kill you."

Suzuki's smile faded as he scrunched his face, confused. "Wait, why won't you help us?"

Telzrem raised his hand and sent Suzuki flying back with a telekinetic blast. "This is my home. There is nothing I am required to answer. Just because you were foolish enough to step foot past my door, it does not mean you are entitled to answers. Now leave."

Suzuki landed in Beth's arms, and she kept him from falling over. "What are we going to do now?" she asked. "I'm surprised your golden tongue didn't get the job done."

"That's probably not the only job it doesn't get done," Stew called.

Suzuki and Beth both glared at Stew. "Now is not the time, Stew!"

Stew shrugged as he unsheathed his axe. "Whatever, dude. A zinger is a zinger, no matter what time. Now, if you'll excuse me, I'm going to get that jar."

He let out a loud scream and charged toward Telzrem, axe raised high, ready to bring it down on the man-dragon's head.

Telzrem raised his hands, one hand conjuring a spellbook, and the other casting a light blue mist.

Stew froze in mid-swing, his eyes moving back and forth as he started to panic.

Suzuki shouted, "Sandy, this is your department."

Sandy drew her wand and floated into the air, her ash cloak covering her body as a death mask whose visage was perpetually curled in an expression of terror appeared over her face. She waved her wand at Stew, unfreezing him.

Beth drew her longbow and notched an arrow. She pulled back with all her strength and launched an arrow at Telzrem, who leaned back, letting the missile fly past him.

Telzrem closed the spellbook and placed it under his arm. "I can see that you are all strong warriors. It would be a waste to deprive the fight with the Dark One of fighters of your caliber, but if you do not leave now, I will be forced to kill you. This is your last chance."

Anabelle stepped forward and stood as tall as possible. It didn't have much of an effect because Telzrem seemed to grow even taller as Anabelle approached him. "I don't understand what your problem is. It's just a shitty jar, and we need it."

Telzrem smiled at Anabelle as he crossed his arms. "Ah, Anabelle. Leader of the DGA, I believe."

"How the hell do you know that?"

Sandy came up on Anabelle's side. "Magic. Gold dragons are the only dragons that practice formal magic. He's probably skilled in telepathic magic. If we're going to fight, this is going to be a hard one. One we should maybe think about."

"We need that jar, and I'm not leaving here without it." Anabelle squared up to Telzrem. "You guys can walk away from this, but I'm not going to."

Terra pulled out her axe and came to stand beside Anabelle. "I'm not walking. It'd be cooler to kick your ass when you're all big and shit, but a dragon is a dragon, I guess."

The Mundanes looked at one another. Without exchanging a word, Suzuki nodded and drew his sword. "Mundanes, we're running gold dragon formation extra-spicy mode. Wasabi-drenched."

The rest of the Mundanes drew their weapons and joined the formation. "Why does it have to be wasabi-drenched?" Sandy asked. "That's the most boring one."

"You're just saying that because you are support. It's the most effective one for these kinds of situations."

Telzrem pulled his book of spells out from under his arm and opened it. "You prefer to fight. I will try to give you all a quick, honorable death." The book of spells floated around him as he rose into the air.

The Mundanes split, Stew and Suzuki charging as Beth and Sandy fell to the back. Sandy went to the far left of the cavern as Beth went to the right.

Anabelle was frankly impressed by the cohesion of the Mundanes and their ability to move so quickly. Whatever they had in store had been practiced multiple times, and Suzuki was deft at giving commands. Unfortunately, Anabelle and Terra were not at the same level.

Terra looked at Anabelle, obviously flustered. "What am I supposed to do?"

Anabelle thought fast. "Stick with Stew. He seems to have a similar fighting style to yours. Take cues for what to do from him. I'll roll with Suzuki."

Terra dashed after Stew, who was a few feet away from Telzrem. The two of them swung their axes at Telzrem, who raised his hand, creating a barrier shield around himself. He floated backward, casting a small thunderstorm between him and his opponents.

At the back of the cavern, Sandy was busy carving a sigil into the ground. When she saw the thunderstorm forming, she conjured her own book of spells in front of her, flipping through the pages furiously. She finally found what she was looking for and started working her magic.

A strong gust of wind ushered from her, dispelling the thunderstorm.

Telzrem was moving again, weaving another spell as the barrier extended to the far side of the cavern. It effectively cut the dragon off, giving him time for his magic.

Anabelle knew what she could do about the barrier. She might not have the tactical mind of Suzuki, but she had an instinctual understanding of battle. Anabelle pulled her mana into her hands and fists, drawing from the area around her and the extra magic generated by Sandy and Telzrem's spells, and ran toward the barrier. She leapt and brought her fists down on the barrier as they burst into flames.

The barrier quivered, and after the elf landed, she delivered a flurry of kicks to the barrier, cracking it and allowing Terra and Stew to charge Telzrem.

The dragon was caught off-guard, his eyes wide. Apparently, he'd had no idea what Anabelle was capable of.

Stew jumped and slashed at Telzrem, who threw up a small barrier to deflect the attack as Terra flew past him, throwing her axe.

Telzrem managed to dodge the attack, but Terra didn't let up. She was on him in seconds, smashing her fists into his face. "Just give us the fucking jar!" she shouted.

An arrow flew past Terra with the force of a bullet and hit Telzrem in the shoulder, sending him flying and pinning him to the wall.

Terra charged after the man-dragon, smashing into him with her shoulder. She pounded her fist into the dragon's face until a blast of energy sent her flying backward.

Telzrem pulled the arrow from his shoulder and grinned as it burst into flames. "You have quite the set of skills. Very well, let us battle."

He began whispering in the ancient dragon tongue. As he spoke, his body vibrated, shadows of himself shifting away from him. Three more versions of him, slightly less gold, pulled away from his body. "Now we shall commence," the four Telzrems said in unison.

One of the Telzrems teleported in front of Beth. He slashed at her with a conjured sword, causing her to fall backward. She rolled to the side, leapt to her feet, and fired three arrows that the Telzrem shade easily knocked away.

"Fine," Beth said as she put away her bow and drew her daggers. "Let's fucking play." She dashed at the shade, moving incredibly fast. She slashed across its stomach, then moved behind it and jumped onto its back, driving her blades deep into its neck.

Another of the shades stepped to Suzuki and Anabelle, a sword in its hand. Suzuki lunged at it, their blades meeting. The two clashed, slashing and striking at each other, their feet never ceasing as they danced away from each other.

Anabelle leapt into the fray, her hands crackling with lightning, forcing the shade onto the defensive as it stumbled away, while still managing to deflect her attacks efficiently.

Suzuki bashed his shield into the shade's head, breaking its guard.

Anabelle saw her chance and channeled as much outside mana as possible, then leapt and brought her hands down in a shockwave of electric energy that flung the shade into the air.

Suzuki slipped under it, driving his sword into its chest.

Before Suzuki could step away, the shade exploded in a cloud of smoke. Suzuki grasped his chest, coughing as he fell to the ground, his feet turning to stone and connecting to the ground. The stone climbed up his body. "Sandy!"

Sandy, who was on the other side of the cavern, dashed forward, turning into a cloud of smoke and moving through the battlefield where Stew and Terra fought one of the shades. Their axes bashed at it, but it was wielding a great sword, and reformed in front of Suzuki. Sandy cast a healing spell that froze the stone growth on Suzuki.

Suzuki stared down at his legs. "Are you serious? I'm going to need more than that!"

A bolt of lightning struck the ground next to him, forcing Sandy to dodge to the side.

Sandy pointed at Telzrem, who was floating above the field of battle, weaving his magic and spells throughout the cavern. "I have to take care of that! He's buffing all the shades and doing fuck knows what else."

Anabelle pushed Sandy back. "You take care of him. I'll handle Telzrem."

"Are you sure? He's a powerful wizard. His understanding of magic—"

"Magic isn't something you read about in books. It's something you use to bash someone's fucking face in."

Anabelle drew her mana together, leeching off the energy being cast by Sandy and Telzrem. She knew what she was capable of. Grok had shown her the depths of her power. She let out a scream of rage, and a blue aura surrounded her as lightning crackled at her feet.

She flung herself into the air, moving faster than she could have imagined, and appeared in front of Telzrem, whose eyes widened in surprise.

Anabelle chopped him in the neck, lightning bursting from her hand as she drove him to the ground. As Telzrem fell, Anabelle followed him. The man-dragon hit the ground, and Anabelle's fist slammed into his chest.

A shockwave of energy shot through the room.

Anabelle pummeled Telzrem, hitting him in the face over and over before delivering the final blow. "That is *my* jar!"

Telzrem lay still on the ground as the rest of the Mundanes and Terra finished off their shades, which evaporated into smoke.

Anabelle stood, flicking her hair out of her face. "There we go. Now let's get that jar." She walked over to the object in question, which was still floating in the middle of the room.

"Not so fast."

Anabelle turned around to see Telzrem slowly getting to his feet. "You do seem to have a lot of strength," Telzrem said. "Let's put a stop to that."

Telzrem placed a finger over his mouth and hissed at Anabelle, a sound that reverberated through the cavern, sending the elf through the air.

Anabelle hit the wall of the cavern and slid to the floor. As she picked herself up, she noticed something; she couldn't feel her magic.

Telzrem breathed a plume of fire as he cackled.

CHAPTER TWENTY-ONE

Telzrem's body began to change and contort. His bones cracked and he leaned forward, his legs jerking as his suit melded into scales, his neck stretching and his tail exploding out of his back and whipping back and forth.

Anabelle heaved a sigh. That last attack had taken a lot out of her. Even if she knew how to push her body, it didn't seem as if the Path of the Travelers or the Path of the Lost was simple to access.

Grok had taken Anabelle over the edge. She wasn't sure how to get there herself.

Terra didn't seem bothered by the dragon's transformation. She shrugged and took off after him, followed quickly by Stew. She slashed at the dragon, but the attack was deflected by his tail. Stew followed up Terra's attack but was met by the same rebuttal.

Telzrem curled his tail around his body and began to glow.

Suzuki backed away and shouted, "On me, now!"

The Mundanes obeyed and circled Suzuki. Anabelle and Terra did the same for lack of anything else to do.

Suzuki peeked over Terra's shoulder. "Okay, we know he's a high-level spell caster. That means we can expect more than elemental attacks. What you got for us, Sandy?"

Sandy's death mask disappeared for a second. "If we stick to attacking him one on one, it'll make it harder for him to use any AOE spells. I can handle taking care of one or two of you, but if we all get hit, we're going to be fucked."

Suzuki nodded. "Okay. Sandy, I want you to buff all of us. Beth, no more support. I want you in there putting pressure on with Stew."

Despite Anabelle's inclination, she cleared her throat and asked meekly, "What do you think *we* should do?"

Suzuki looked surprised at Anabelle's question. "Wait, you're asking me?"

"Listen, human, I can admit when there's something I need to learn. You're obviously skilled at strategies that involve more than three people. Let's leave it at that."

Suzuki seemed to be unable to process what he was hearing. "I've never met an elf willing to take orders from me. All right, can you help Sandy?"

"Unfortunately, my magic doesn't work the same way as hers."

Sandy rested her hand on Anabelle's shoulder. "No worries. I got this one figured out. I'll show you."

Suzuki twirled his sword as he stepped out of the circle. "Terra, do you think you can show Stew why you lasted in the arena?"

Terra sighed as she stared at Telzrem. "That might be a problem. A lot of my strength is…I don't know, kinda like an adrenaline rush, and frankly, there's nothing heart-pumping about fighting this mage dragon guy."

Stew shoved Terra. "Are you serious? Come on, dude, let's fuck this guy up. It's a fucking gold dragon!"

"Sorry, bro. Your D&D nerd tidbits don't mean anything to me because I have no fucking idea what you're talking about."

"Don't you have a blood rage or something you can activate?"

"Still no idea what you're talking about."

Stew looked at Suzuki. "Permission to Leroy the hell out of this and show Terra what a barbarian looks like."

Suzuki smiled at Stew. "Oh, you're asking permission now?"

"Not really. I just thought it sounded badass," Stew said as he drew a dagger from his side. He slashed his chest and let out a roar, his eyes glowing bright red for a second. His muscles bulged as they increased in mass. "Leroy-motherfucking-Jenkins!"

Stew stormed out of the group, his steps cracking the ground.

Telzrem swiped his tail at Stew, but the barbarian leapt into the air, narrowly avoiding the attack. Suzuki shouted, "In formation! Let's get that jar!"

Stew landed on top of Telzrem, knocking the dragon down. He scrambled to move, but Stew grabbed him by the throat and held him down. He reached back to slug the dragon. Unfortunately, Telzrem's tail whipped around, sending Stew flying.

Terra leapt and snatched Stew. "Are you serious? You just slash your chest and get mad?"

Stew stared at Terra like a newborn baby. "The thrill of battle, you know?"

Terra put Stew on the ground. "Okay, I got you. I'll give it true." She let out a heavy roar and hit her chest. "I am now enraged!" Terra sprinted at Telzrem, who was back on his feet, alongside Suzuki and Beth.

Beth got ahead of Terra and slid, pulling her short bow out and firing shot after shot.

Telzrem spread a barrier around him to deflect the arrows.

Terra leapt and landed behind the dragon. She threw her axe at him, but he deflected it with a small shield. Terra didn't relent, though, following through by getting close and hitting him in the jaw.

Telzrem stumbled back, attacking with his tail to get more space. Suzuki was already on top of him, slashing at his throat.

Anabelle, who was in the back with Sandy, could see Suzuki's strategy. If Telzrem was constantly on the defense, he wouldn't have time to cast his magic. "What are we going to do?" Anabelle asked.

Sandy's wand floated in front of her. "I'm casting spells to increase their endurance so they can keep up the attack. I can also funnel mana to you. All you have to do is get a little creative from back here."

Anabelle wracked her brain. She couldn't cast specific spells like

Sandy, but the elements were under her control. All she had to do was think.

She looked at the rock formations above. "Got it." Then she slipped into one of the first stances she'd learned along the path, a technique most Travelers moved out of. She reached toward the rocks, planted her feet, and flexed her mana, causing a rock from the ceiling to head straight toward Telzrem.

The dragon looked up at the last second and waved his paw, turning the rock to water.

Anabelle stretched out her mana, her hands covered with frost, and turned the water into ice shards that struck him.

Telzrem twirled, clearing space with his tail, then floated into the air, away from attacks. Beth tossed her short bow to the ground and pulled out her longbow. She nocked an arrow, drew back, and let it fly.

The arrow hit the dragon in the chest, and he smiled as he pulled it out. "Just what I needed." He flicked the arrow on the ground, and flames surged where his blood fell. "This ends now!"

Telzrem opened his mouth, and a yellow mist flowed out of him.

"Oh, shit!" Sandy shouted as she ran forward. She cast a defensive barrier around Suzuki, Stew, and Beth, but it was too late. The barrier that surrounded them locked in the mist.

Suzuki's eyes widened as he swung at the barrier, trying to escape. His movements were slowed, hampered by the dust. He moved at a snail's pace.

Telzrem rocketed toward the ground and tackled Terra. As she tried to get to her feet, he wrapped his tail around her throat and slammed her into the ceiling and then the ground.

Her hands clawed at Telzrem's tail as she struggled to breathe.

Anabelle pulled up the stones around Telzrem, knocking him over, then punched him in the face. She drew the stones around the dragon, hindering his ability to get up. Last, she roundhouse-kicked him, her legs bursting into flames.

Telzrem grabbed Anabelle's leg and grinned, his sharp teeth

gleaming. "Oh, young fae, I was born of fire." Flames radiated from his hands, and an explosion sent Anabelle crashing into the wall.

Only Sandy still stood.

Telzrem waved his hand, sending a fireball at Sandy, who cut through it with her wand. "A talented mage. It is a shame to end a life so young."

Sandy slashed her wand at Telzrem, tearing up the ground beneath her. "I will not fall easily. Tonight, I bathe in dragon's blood."

Telzrem sent a whirlwind of fire at Sandy, whose body broke apart into ash and reformed. She swung her wand and shot a streak of lightning at the dragon, who easily deflected the attack. "Typical. Humans and elves always rely on the basest of magics."

The dragon darted forward, appearing in front of Sandy as if he'd teleported. "Seems a waste to use magic to kill you. To be fair, you are quite advanced for such a youthful mortal."

Telzrem hissed, and time froze. Then he whirled and slammed Sandy with his tail.

Sandy didn't move, but pain registered on her face as she screamed.

"Goodbye, mortal."

Telzrem's jaw opened, unhinging as golden flame burned deep in his throat.

A bright green blast of magical energy hit him in the face, knocking him back and blasting through the dust-filled barrier Suzuki and the rest were locked in.

Another blast hit the barrier, tearing it to shreds. Suzuki and the rest poured out, grabbing their throats and gasping for breath.

A cloaked figure stepped out of the shadows at the cavern's entrance, their hands glowing green.

Suzuki crawled to his feet and grabbed his sword as Anabelle, across the room, stumbled to her feet. They both stared at the cloaked wizard. "You here for the jar too?" Suzuki shouted.

The figure slowly shook their head.

"Then what are you here for?"

The cloaked warrior darted forward, slinging blasts of green energy at the dragon, who dodged before leaping into the air and wrapping his tail around himself.

Anabelle joined Suzuki. Terra, Stew, and Beth were still out cold. "Friend of yours?" Suzuki asked.

The elf cast a glance at the cloaked figure walking toward them. "Uh, it might be a dude who we met in a dungeon, but I don't remember him being able to use magic like that."

"A friend of my enemy…"

Suzuki pointed his sword at the cloaked figure. "Friend or foe?"

When the figure spoke, their voice was garbled, like many voices were speaking at once. "Friend."

Above, Telzrem's wings unfolded as he transformed back into his natural state. He roared, and the walls of the cavern shook as he blasted fire at the three remaining warriors, his rage exploding.

Anabelle and the cloaked figure dodged while Suzuki stood his ground, holding his shield to protect himself from the fire. "We need to bring him down!" he shouted.

The cloaked figure looked at Anabelle and then at the dragon. They jumped into the air, green energy flying from their hands as black tentacles broke from the ground, wrapping around Telzrem's legs and hands, trying to pull the dragon to the ground.

Anabelle drew her mana to her legs and leapt, her body warming with fire and lightning. Her knuckles cracked into Telzrem's face, then her body shifted to cold, her skin wearing frost for a moment as she flash-froze the dragon's head.

Telzrem flicked Anabelle away, but she managed to land gracefully on her feet. Meanwhile, he clawed his face as he breathed fire to burn through the ice.

The cloaked figure, still bristling with green energy, yanked down with their hands, the tentacles around them pulling the dragon with more force.

As the dragon closed, the cloaked figure fired a powerful blast of magic at him.

The magical bolt pierced the dragon's wing, and he screeched in pain as he finally burned through the ice.

Anabelle shouted to Suzuki, "What's the plan when he gets down here?"

Suzuki shrugged as he stared at the dragon. "Uh, well, I wasn't planning on talking him to death."

Telzrem hit the ground, and the force of the impact nearly knocked Anabelle and everyone else off their feet. The dragon roared and then began speaking quietly, under his breath.

Suzuki groaned as he rolled his head back. "Goddamn it, he might talk *us* to death. Get ready."

Telzrem opened his eyes and uttered the final word of the ancient dragon tongue. "*Moz-theroth!*"

Anabelle felt the air around her changing. She raised her arm, but it hardly moved. It was like she was underwater.

Suzuki was in the same situation. He was trying to charge the dragon, but his movements were stifled by the dragon's spell.

Telzrem stared at the cloaked figure. "Ah, so it is you who has come. Such a profane creature dares to challenge me?"

The masked figure pulsed green magical energy, warding off the spell. They clenched their fist, and the tentacles tightened around Telzrem. "It's over."

Green light shot from the cloaked figure's face, bathing Telzrem. The dragon screamed in pain as its scales rotted and turned to ash.

He broke from the tentacles, stumbling backward, covering his face with his wings and tail. The green light continued to burn through the dragon's scales.

Suzuki ran up to the cloaked figure and grabbed them by the shoulder. "That's enough! He's done!"

The cloaked sorcerer pulled Suzuki's hands back, and they instantly started burning. "He will kill you."

Suzuki pointed at the dragon. "No, he won't. Look at him! He's finished."

The cloaked sorcerer looked at Telzrem, who had backed into a corner and was whimpering from behind his wings, which were down to bone.

Anabelle's heart clenched at the sight of such a majestic creature in such inelegant pain. If she and the Mundanes had killed Telzrem, they would not have done it like this. There would have been dignity in it. They wouldn't have decayed half the dragon's body.

The cloaked sorcerer walked up to the floating soul jar and reached out for it.

"Stop!" Anabelle shouted.

The cloaked figure cast a glance over their shoulder. "This is all we need to defeat Death…" She grabbed the jar and held it close. After a few moments, she tossed it to Anabelle. She went to Telzrem and knelt at the dragon's feet. "Release them from your magic, and I'll return your lost years."

Telzrem's wings unwrapped enough to show his eyes. "Fine, lich."

Anabelle felt her heart sink, and her body went cold with fear.

The unconscious Mundanes' eyes snapped open as Sandy fell to the ground, her body no longer affected by the dragon's magic.

The cloaked figure held their hand above Telzrem's wounded wings. "The fight is over, understand? I've tasted you. If you raise a claw, I'll suck you dry and gnaw your bones. Understood?"

The dragon nodded sadly, and the cloaked figure pressed their hand to the dragon's wings. Telzrem screamed in pain, but the scales on his wings and tail began to regrow.

Anabelle and the Mundanes approached the cloaked figure as they stood and pulled back their hood.

Rasputina stood before them, but she was different. She looked to be only a few years older than Terra. Her skin still had the waxen look of the dead, and her eyes were still an intense green, but she no longer looked to be decaying. She appeared almost healthy.

Anabelle raised her flaming fists. "What the fuck are you doing here?"

Rasputina raised her hand. "You can calm down. I'm here to help."

Anabelle and Terra exchanged confused glances, and Terra blurted, "You have to be kidding me!"

PART 2

Abby watched gnomish and goblin scientists running back and forth from command terminals that had been set up. She was on the gnomish world, along with Cire, Nib-Nib, and Persephone. Originally, she had been sent there to investigate a mysterious Gate that was similar to the Dark Gates the Dark One was using. Now she was trying to make sure the Gate didn't open again.

The dead slept on the other side of the Gate; she'd seen them with her own eyes. Rivers flowed with souls, and the ground was made up of spirits stacked on top of each other. There was no telling how many were in there.

Now she was out of the Netherverse, in the gnomish camp, and it was pure chaos. Scientists trying to figure out how to keep the Gate closed, and others were trying to figure out what the Dark One was attempting to use this Gate for.

Persephone and Cire were talking the girl through what she'd seen.

Abby, who was still shaken from her time in the Netherverse, tried to put it all together in her head. Everything had happened so fast. "There was a man in there. He was living. We're certain of it. Or at least he wasn't the kind of dead everything else was. And he was doing something. We couldn't tell what it was, but he was doing something to the dead. Persephone, do you know anything about the Netherverse?"

Persephone shook her head. "Only stories I was told as a child. Nothing concrete. It's where some souls go when they die, and it's the place of the Elder Ones. In all our stories, the Elder Ones are what you're supposed to be afraid of. It doesn't seem like they even noticed you."

Cire leaned in and stared Abby deep in the eyes. "What did this man look like?"

"It was hard to tell," she answered. "He…"

Martin popped into Abby's sight. The AI's paperclip body straightened out and then curled up like a slinky. "I might actually be able to help with that. Since you so *kindly* ditched me in the Netherverse, along with Gertrude's very capable body, I'm recording everything that's happening, and you have to see this. Check out the holoscreen."

Abby and the rest of them went over to a holoscreen that Creon was working at. "Mind if we use this?" she asked.

Creon nodded and moved to the side to give them a better view. His data and research disappeared, replaced by a feed of what was going on in the Netherverse.

The recording showed the man. He was clothed in slim, black armor, his face mostly covered, and electrical rods stuck out of his back. They glowed bright purple, the same color as the lightning flashing in the background.

"Can you get a closer look at him?" Abby asked.

The camera zoomed in as the man touched his mask, causing it to dissolve. He then knelt and poured a dark liquid onto the souls on the ground. It became semi-hard, growing tentacles that quickly expanded over the body, then dug down into the earth, spreading faster than the eye could see.

Persephone leaned in to look at the screen. "That's the Dark Melody. He's infecting them with it."

"Isn't the Dark Melody from the Netherverse?"

Persephone looked at her hand, which had reacted to the Gate the day before. It had been infused with a piece of an Elder God's corpse. That was how the Dark Melody was made. "It comes specifically from the Elder Gods. I guess they aren't dropping it from the sky or anything. Looks like it has to be cultivated."

The camera zoomed in farther as the man pressed his hand to the ground. The electrical conduits on his back started to glow brightly.

A flash of lightning struck him, creating a massive flash.

Once the camera could focus again, they all could see him, still crouched with his hand on the ground. His suit lit up as purple electricity pulsed through him, spreading around him in a thirty-foot radius.

As the energy faded, something started to happen to the souls that in the blast zone. They started to convulse and jerk, their hands lifting off the ground, then they pulled themselves up as the Dark Melody poured into their rotting bodies.

The dead were rising.

Abby backed away from the holoscreen. "Guess that means the Dark One doesn't need the lich anymore."

Martin popped back up on the screen. "Two things. We'll go with the one that makes sense first. Kravis and Sarah just arrived on the gnomish world. They'll be here in a few minutes, along with reinforcements. I took the liberty of sending for them. Kinda figured that whatever was happening, it might be nice to have an army on our hands. Since, you know, things are always trying to kill us."

Abby couldn't help but smile at Martin's cantankerousness. "Okay, so what's the weirder part of this?"

"I did a scan of the faces of the dead and that electric dude. A lot of stuff came back. Those are the soldiers we've lost over the last five years, all of them either MIA or KIA. But that's not the weirdest part. I got a positive on the electric guy. That's Nikola-fucking-Tesla."

"The inventor?"

"Yeah. Fucking weird, right?"

Abby looked at the Gate. "We need to go back in. Whatever he's doing, we need to stop it."

Persephone grabbed Abby by the shoulder. "I'm going with you. It's too dangerous to go by yourself."

The girl shook her head. "We can't protect you with our—"

"I don't need to be protected. The Dark Melody is in me too. I'll survive."

Abby looked at Cire. "Will you mobilize the forces and fill Sarah and Kravis in when they get here?"

Cire nodded and pressed his fist to his chest. "Of course. If something comes through that Gate, we'll be prepared."

"All right, Persephone. Let's go."

Persephone and Abby walked over to the Gate. The drow extended her hand, and it split into heavy tentacles that stretched toward the empty Gate, while Abby sent a few nanobots at it.

The Gate flashed back on as the drones fell to the ground, the purple portal exploding outward.

Abby looked at the dead nanobots. That was why the Gate wasn't working; it didn't have a power source. *It is using the electricity from the nanobots,* Abby thought. *And that is what Tesla is doing in there. Shit, he could probably open the Gate even if we closed it.*

That didn't matter at the moment, though. If they could take Tesla out, the Gate still wouldn't have a power source.

Nanobots rolled over Abby, covering her in her suit. Then she and Persephone stepped through the Gate into the Netherverse.

They were somewhere different than where Abby had first exited.

She looked around, trying to get her bearings.

Persephone didn't seem bothered by the atmosphere of the Netherverse. The only difference Abby could notice was that her tentacles looked slightly more fluid than before.

In the distance, there was a shrill roar as lightning flashed and the thousands of eyes of an Elder One passing over them became visible.

Persephone stared up at the ancient god. She raised her tentacled arm and waved at the dark behemoth above as it floated past in the infinite space. "Guess they really *don't* care that much about us."

Abby was scanning the area for Tesla. "We should count ourselves lucky. Dealing with an Elder God right now as well might be a little too much for us."

"Maybe they think I'm, like, family or something."

There were three bright flashes of lightning in the distance. Abby could see that these bolts all struck the ground. "That way!"

She activated her thrusters and took off toward where the lightning had struck. Persephone followed, leaping from one cluster of floating rocks to the next.

They were closing in on the area where the lightning had landed. Abby saw Tesla's figure silhouetted as another bolt hit the ground.

Persephone gasped, causing Abby to turn around to see what was wrong. "Are you okay?" she asked.

Persephone was standing on a rock, staring at the souls beneath them. "Goddess, I didn't realize there were so many. All these dead soldiers…"

"Yeah. An infinite supply of souls for the Dark One. That explains why he's been so reckless with his battles. If he's collecting the souls of the dead, it doesn't matter who wins a battle. They're still supplying him with souls for an army."

"It's so…evil. Just evil. It's like he has no regard for life at all."

Another crack of lightning cut off the conversation. Abby and Persephone continued on. Finally, they were close enough that Abby could get a good look at what Tesla was doing. Just like before, he was trickling the Dark Melody on the souls and bringing them back to life with his tech.

Abby and Persephone crouched on a rock floating near Tesla. "Maybe he can have some sense talked into him. Grok wasn't under the Dark One's control. It's a long shot, but at least it'll distract him. While we're talking to him, you can get ready to attack if it comes to that. He only saw me last time."

Persephone nodded as Abby blasted toward Tesla.

Abby stopped a few feet away from him, and he looked up at her and smiled.

Tesla bowed formally, as if he had just walked out of the nineteenth century. "Good day. You rushed off before we could have a reasonable conversation last time. I must say, I am envious of your outfit. Impressive technology indeed."

Abby landed and slowly took a step toward the man. "We could say the same about you. Tech that can harness the energy of the Netherverse—that's something we've never heard of."

"And for someone so recently returned to the land of the living, mind you. Oh, how much has changed. It's a shame I won't have much time to enjoy it all."

"Then why do this? We know you're serving the Dark One. You don't have to. We have ways of setting you free. Those microchips—"

Tesla laughed, a hearty booming relic of a bygone era. "My dear Miss, you are confused. There is no control. This is a joint partnership. Through some of my earlier...misadventures, I found myself acquainted with the Dark One. I'm merely holding up my end of a very old deal. That being said, I must return to my work. I'd advise you to leave unless you would like to meet an early death."

Abby raised her arm, her hand converting to a cannon, and fired at Tesla.

He dodged, and the blast tore up the souls at his feet. He clucked his tongue. "Well, my dear girl, it seems like you have a lot of fight in you. I admire that, but a gentleman cannot step away from a direct challenge. Have at me!"

Abby's body filled with kinetic energy and she charged forward, slamming into Tesla, who held his ground as his feet dug into the souls beneath him.

His arm pulsed with electricity, and he swung at Abby as a bolt of lightning came crashing down from the sky.

Her thrusters fired and she swung around behind Tesla, kinetic energy flying off her as she slammed her fist into the ground. The force of the impact tossed Tesla into the air.

There was a bright flash of purple light and Tesla was gone. He reappeared behind Abby, who barely had time to turn around before he struck her with a lightning bolt.

She fell to the ground, her system overheating. "What's happening, Martin?" the girl shouted.

Martin popped up in front of Abby. "Your system is short-circuiting. He overloaded you. We're working as fast as possible to fix it."

Tesla walked up to Abby. "You see, the problem with playing with the master of electricity is—"

Persephone flew at him, her tentacles forming a slithering ball of force. She slammed it into the man, driving him into the ground.

A bolt of lightning struck her, burning through her tentacles. The drow screamed in pain as she stumbled back.

Tesla climbed out of a crater of souls. "Ah, I was wondering when you would join the fray. Good show. Good show indeed." He bolted forward, holding a handful of lightning bolts and driving them toward the drow.

She threw up her elder arm, new tentacles sprouting and absorbing the brunt of the attack as she stumbled backward.

Abby's system suddenly came back online. She got to her feet as Martin said, "We've adjusted it to deal with that voltage level. If he's going to ground you again, he's going to have to hit you with something stronger, and both of us are already working on compensating for that."

That was enough for her. She charged again, slamming into Tesla's back. Then she grabbed him by the throat and pulled him away from Persephone, her hand turning into a cannon, which she pressed to Tesla's head. "We're not going to say this twice. Stand down. You're coming with us."

Tesla held his hands in the air. "Oh, dear. Miss, you have me in quite the compromising position. Much like, I would say, the state your camp is in. That Gate looks very poorly defended from where I'm standing."

Abby looked in the direction of the Gate. Lightning bolt after lightning bolt landed near it, striking the souls in the area.

Tesla gave that booming, silly laugh. "You see, you caught me toward the end of my shift today. I've already taken care of the invading party by the Gate, which you've left woefully unattended and open. Checkmate."

The souls of the Gate started to rise. Necrotic black flesh grew over them, mixing with the Dark Melody and contorting into something very different and grotesque. Hundreds of the newly risen dead surrounded the Gate.

They poured through the portal, heading toward the gnomish world.

"Now, you must excuse me," Tesla said. "I have a battle to oversee."

There was a bright flash, and Tesla was gone.

Abby turned to Persephone. "We need to get to that Gate!"

They took off in the direction of the Gate, Abby flying high enough to avoid the hands of the newly risen grasping at her, trying to drag her to them. Persephone kept to the floating pathway above, out of harm's way.

The two of them finally made it through the Gate and burst onto the gnomish world. They froze in horror at the carnage that lay before them.

CHAPTER TWO

Hundreds of necrotic ghouls had escaped from the Gate, decimating the scientists who had been on guard. Many were crouched over their victims, gnawing on their flesh and tearing it from the bone.

Abby's heart sunk to her stomach as she scanned for Creon. She looked around to see if he was among the dead, but it was impossible to tell since the throng of the ghouls was too large. She could hardly see the ground beneath their frenzied feeding.

Instead, Abby grabbed Persephone by the wrist and jetted into the air, pulling her along as the drow's hand turned into tentacles to avoid being snapped off by the tension created by Abby's powerful thrusters.

They soared into the air, and Abby saw over two hundred gnomish soldiers massing in the north. She blasted toward them.

The soldiers had built a small, makeshift camp. Sarah, Kravis, and Cire were talking with a gnomish general over a holomap of the area.

Abby landed in the middle of the meeting, pulling her helmet off. She was out of breath and almost couldn't speak.

Sarah rushed over to her. "We're going to need you to pull it together fast and tell us what the fuck is going on here."

Abby took a deep breath and steadied herself. "Nikola Tesla is back from the dead and using the Dark Melody and some crazy tech to bring back the souls of warriors who've died in battles against the Dark One. People from our side and his own. The Netherverse is full of them."

Sarah kneaded her eyebrows with her fingers. "Goddamn it, this shit just keeps getting weirder."

"What happened here?"

"We were making our way to meet Cire and Nib-Nib with our reinforcements when we got the call from the scientists. They warned us that something was coming through the Gate, and it was more important for us to be ready for a battle than to come save them. So, I made the decision."

Abby looked at Sarah and the rest of the agents. "Is Creon here?"

Sarah shook her head. "There were no survivors from the camp as far as we know. Only Cire and Nibs showed up."

Abby paced, trying to process what she'd just heard. She sat down suddenly and held her head in her hands. There was no way Creon was dead just like that. It was impossible.

Sarah knelt in front of Abby. "I know you're hurting. That can't be easy to hear, but you're the only one who knows how the tech over there works. If I'm right, whatever took out those scientists is going to continue coming through that Gate until we stop it. We need you here, Abby. All of you."

The girl's legs trembled as she tried to get to her feet. "Martin, we need you to help me. Increase production of nanobots. Lower our adrenaline. Whatever you have to do to help us right now."

Martin's voice came into Abby's ear. "Uh, we can do most of that, but I can't turn off your emotions."

"Then the increased nanobots will. Take them as far as you can. We'll need them for this fight anyway."

Martin hesitated. "Okay."

Abby looked toward the Gate, her body becoming cold and her heart slowing until she could hardly tell it was beating.

Persephone came over to the girl and wrapped her arms around her. "I'm so sorry, Abby."

Abby embraced the drow, feeling her warmth until even that faded and she felt nothing. She gazed into her friend's eyes, feeling as if she were looking at something beautiful and meaningful but very far away. Perhaps too far to understand.

Persephone stepped back from Abby as if she had touched fire.

The girl smiled weakly as a tear trickled down her face. "I have to go away for a bit," she said. "We need to take care of this first."

Persephone held her hand to her mouth as her lips trembled. "I-I understand," she managed.

Abby, whose eyes had turned a bright, unearthly blue, turned back to Sarah. "There were over a hundred ghouls by the time we exited the Gate. Your assessment that they will keep coming is correct. We propose to fight our way through the ghouls so we can disable the Gate. It will be simple enough, but we anticipate Tesla will interfere. We suggest termination at all costs."

Sarah nodded as she glanced back at the holoscreen. "All right, let's get moving then. Cire, how do you want to do this?"

The orc looked at the holoscreen as well. "We'll split into two forces. I'll lead the one with the main artillery. You come with Persephone and Abby. We'll pincer them and put an end to this."

"Sounds like a solid plan. Let's get going."

Sarah and Cire quickly split the small army into two groups. Sarah took the majority of the battle tanks the gnomes had brought, and Cire took what was left over.

Cire did not mince words when he informed the gnomes of the odds they were up against. There was no telling how many more ghouls had come through since the Gate had opened. There could be more than twice the number of gnomish warriors.

One of the gnomish generals sneered and shouted, "We don't need to be tucked into our graves. How about we just get this thing going?"

Cire pressed his hand to his chest. "Spoken like a true warrior."

The two squads moved out, Cire's heading toward the ghoul

outbreak and Sarah leading her squad around the dunes to flank them from behind the Gate.

Abby went with Sarah, and Persephone joined Cire's squad.

Riding on top of one of the gnomish tanks, Sarah continued to ask Abby questions about what she'd seen in the Netherverse. Now that the girl's body was filled with more nanobots, the consciousness was stronger, and it did most of the talking.

Abby was someplace far away where it was safe to be scared and sad. She watched the world passing her as if she were looking out of the window during a car ride. Eventually, she'd have to take the wheel again, but for now, she could be alone with her grief.

Finally, the squad was close enough to see the Gate and the ghouls surrounding it.

It was the worst-case scenario. The dunes were filled with ghouls shuffling about, screeching at the sky as if the sun offended them. They had ripped the bodies of the scientists apart and strewn them all over.

Sarah knocked on the top of the tank she was sitting on, causing a gatling gun to pop up. She stepped behind it, flipped off the safety, and started to fire.

The tanks and the gnomish soldiers on hoverbikes sped ahead, while the ground troops followed.

Abby leapt off of the tank as Sarah continued laying down suppressing fire, mowing down the ghouls in front of her but hardly making a dent in their numbers. The ghouls were piled up at the Gate's exit, falling over each other as they oozed into the world of the living.

Abby flew over the ghouls, dropping three proximity mines into the throng of bodies around the accursed portal.

When the bombs detonated, the bodies of the ghouls went flying. Abby looked over her shoulder to see how much damage she had done.

There was a loud pop and a sizzle, then a flash of light that caused her to turn back around.

Nikola Tesla was floating in front of her.

Abby stopped on a dime, raising her shoulder and hand cannons and firing four shots. Tesla flew to the side, taking damage from only one of Abby's shots. He grinned, shook it off, and fired a ball of lightning at Abby, who activated her shield to absorb the damage.

The two stared each other down as the gnomish army clashed with the ghouls. The ghouls easily overwhelmed the tank Sarah was on, forcing her to jump into the mass of gnashing teeth. She was on top of them for a second before slipping under like someone caught in a riptide.

If more of Abby had been present, she would have gone in to save Sarah, but that wasn't the mission. She had to make sure the Gate was closed and stayed closed. She turned away from Tesla and rocketed toward the Gate just as the second wave showed up.

Persephone and Cire led the attack, Persephone's tentacles sending the ghouls flying as Cire's heavy plasma shotgun mowed them down. The squad only had the element of surprise for a moment. The ghouls quickly turned around and began attacking.

The tactic had worked, though. The ghouls were split down the middle, some of them tearing through Sarah's squad to attack Cire's and Persephone's group.

Gnomes were dying by the dozen. They weren't able to fire fast enough to combat the ghouls that were still crawling out of the portal, their bodies held together by a bizarre amalgamation of flesh and tech.

The dark forces crowed over the dead, foaming at the mouth and ripping open the throats of the living who begged for mercy.

Abby fired from above while heading toward the Gate. The mines she'd set off had done some damage, but the Gate was still functioning. She prepared to loop back over and set off another round of explosions before the battle got any worse.

Tesla appeared in front of her again, but she was ready for him this time. She stopped, held her hands up, and fired a flash-bang at the mad scientist, who screamed as he reeled back. Abby then charged him, knocking Tesla out of the air into the sea of ghouls.

Then she opened fire on the Gate, giving it everything she had. Chunks were blown clear off.

"No!" Tesla shouted from below as he forced his way out of the horde of ghouls. "Do you have any idea what you've done?"

Abby turned to face Tesla as he rose into the air. "Destroyed your plan?"

Tesla's hands burned bright with electricity. "You insolent, ignorant child!"

Tentacles wrapped around the scientist, tightening around his throat and wrists. "No one talks to my girlfriend like that!" Persephone shouted.

Tesla struggled for a second before emitting an electrical shock that ran up Persephone's tentacles and electrocuted her, causing her to drop him. "Now I will deal with you."

Before he could move, Persephone's tentacles wrapped around him again, this time slamming him to the ground repeatedly before flinging him through the air.

Abby looked down at Persephone, who was whipping her tentacles around, trying to make a path. "I forgot what it was like to fight someone who was a fucking god or something," the drow shouted.

A group of ghouls flew into the air, and Sarah stepped out into the open as a white aura surrounded her body. "Where the fuck is Kravis?"

Abby looked around for the gnome agent, but it was impossible to see anything among all the dark forces. All she could see was bodies, those of her gnomish comrades who bravely had sacrificed their lives for the cause, and hundreds of ghouls. "We need to end this now!"

Sarah grabbed a ghoul and punched through its chest before whirling and slamming it into another one. Cire fought by her side, cutting through ghouls with an axe in one hand and firing his shotgun with the other. "Any fucking ideas on how to do that?" Sarah shouted.

Abby looked down at her hand. "Just one." She landed and channeled all her kinetic energy and nanobots into the ground, causing a shockwave that sent nanobots charged with kinetic energy tearing through ghouls, separating the Dark Melody from them and ripping them apart.

The break was enough for Sarah to do what she did best. She pulled a rifle from her back and fired at the ghouls floating through the air, picking them off with extreme accuracy and speed as the remaining gnomish fighters rallied, cutting through the remainder of the ghouls with their plasma rifles.

Abby lay in a crater, her armor blown off, shivering from the pain of the impact. Persephone leapt into the crater and covered the girl with her tentacles as she fired a plasma pistol at anything that came near them.

The sounds of combat slowly faded.

Sarah sheathed her rifle and shouted, "Check for our wounded. We're getting the fuck out of here."

Persephone uncovered Abby and helped her to her feet.

Abby had enough nanobots to create basic armor that was more like cloth and stumbled out of the crater with Persephone. She hardly had any nanobots left. Her head was quiet enough for her to feel her pain.

Cire shouted from across the battlefield, "I found them! Come quick!"

Abby hobbled over to the orc, with Persephone helping her to walk.

Cire stood over a goblin clutching a plasma rifle who was slumped over Kravis. The orc pulled the goblin off and knelt beside the agent. The gnome's wounds were deep, a heavy gash across his stomach and neck. He was losing blood quickly.

Sarah pushed through everyone and knelt beside Kravis. "Oh, fuck. Sweetie, stay with me. Stay with me!"

"He needs immediate treatment," a hoarse voice whispered.

The goblin who had been pulled off Kravis forced himself to a seated position. Creon pushed his glasses back as he took a deep breath. "I suggest inducing a coma. We can treat him once we arrive back at HQ."

Abby rushed over to Creon and threw her arms around him. "Oh, my God, you're still alive!"

Creon winced at Abby's touch. "Neither of us will be unless we leave as soon as possible."

Cire ran toward one of the remaining gnomish tanks that the survivors had crowded around.

Sarah was still with Kravis. "You're not dying, you hear me? We haven't gotten married yet. I haven't even proposed to you!" She grabbed Kravis' hand. "Baby, baby, will you marry me? Huh? What do you say?"

Kravis forced his eyes open as he coughed blood. "Do you really think this is the best time for this?"

Sarah laughed as she wiped tears from her eyes. "Is that a yes or a no?"

Kravis raised his hands to answer and slumped. Sarah clutched his head tightly to her chest.

The gnomish tank pulled up, and Cire popped the door. "Everyone in. We've already arranged for a pickup. Now!"

Sarah handled Kravis while Persephone lifted Creon off the ground.

The tank was full of survivors of the battle. There weren't many.

Abby was hardly able to keep her eyes open as they drove away from the battlefield. All she could concentrate on was how badly her ribs hurt, that and the feeling of Persephone's palm pressed against her own.

The figure of Nikola Tesla sat up in the dunes, rubbing his head. "Well, that worked out better than I could have imagined." He teleported to the middle of the battlefield, smiling slightly as he surveyed the dead. Then he pulled a bottle of the Dark Melody from his suit and poured it over the corpses of the ghouls and the freshly deceased.

CHAPTER THREE

Suzuki and Anabelle stood side by side, staring at the lich, Rasputina.

Anabelle knew exactly who the lich was. She'd been fighting the undead creature on Earth for the last month. She'd seen firsthand the kind of carnage and bloodshed the lich was capable of and seemed to relish.

Suzuki, like the rest of the Mundanes, had no idea who or what Rasputina was. They had traveled with Anabelle and Terra to help on a fetch quest that was necessary to fulfill a quest assigned to the DGA by their mentor Myrddin and that of the Mundanes, José.

This wasn't the lich that Anabelle remembered. The Rasputina she had met was an unhinged psychopath with rotting skin and visible bones who delighted in killing people or eating them alive.

The woman standing before Anabelle didn't look like she was dead, though Anabelle could see a little bit of that madness in this woman's eyes. Something didn't look right, like looking in a mirror that was slightly distorted. It was close enough to right that you knew something was off.

The elf took her fighting stance, drew her mana to his fists, and lit them on fire as she glared at whoever this person in front of her was.

"If you really are Rasputina, you'll forgive me for kicking the shit out of you."

The lich shook her head as she placed the jar on the ground and raised her hands in surrender. "I didn't come here to fight you. I came to help. We have the same goal."

"The last time I checked, your goal was to kill as many innocent people you could. Or was that someone else with the same name?"

Rasputina shrugged and smiled. "People can change their goals. I doubt you wanted to be a prissy model when you were a child, and yet, you fell into the role easily enough. But being Myrddin's lapdog is so much better. You don't have to worry about anything, and don't have to bother with that troublesome issue of thinking for yourself."

Anabelle was about to dart at Rasputina when Suzuki placed his hand on her shoulder. "Is this really a fight that you want to have?" he asked.

"What the hell are you talking about? Of course I want to have it."

"I mean, if she *is* a lich, she's really powerful. Probably more powerful than all of us combined."

"My team took her before and lived, and there are some things you can only pick up from years of fighting. Look at her; she's tired. Taking out Telzrem winded her. We have the upper hand."

Suzuki stared at the woman, who looked noticeably worried about their conversation.

Rasputina pulled off her cloak, revealing light leather armor in a fashion vaguely reminiscent of French royalty. "I'll say it again, elf, since your ears seem to be purely for cosmetic purposes. I am not here to fight you. I am here to offer my help."

Suzuki suddenly vibrated and stepped back. "My familiar says he knows her. He's seen her before.

Anabelle gave Suzuki a confused look. "Your familiar?"

"An eldritch imp. He's losing his shit right now, and he knows his evil. He's seen his fair share of it."

"Then are you with me?"

Suzuki cast a glance at the rest of his team. "Looks like it might just be you and me."

Anabelle cracked her knuckles. "That's fine by me. Just try to keep up." Anabelle darted forward, slashing through the air with hands and leaving a fiery trail behind her.

Rasputina stepped backward, bringing up a green energy barrier between her and Anabelle before holding down her palm, causing a piece of bone the length of a spear to shoot out. She grasped the bone and twirled it, then sliced through her own barrier and attacked Anabelle.

Anabelle was able to deflect her attack, slowly backing up as she countered them. "You planning on joining in at any point?"

Suzuki jumped at the harshness of the elf's tone. "I'm trying to figure out a plan!"

"Your plan should be to wipe the floor with the lich's fucking face. How's that for a fucking plan?"

Suzuki dashed forward, his sword raised high above his head. He brought it down on the lich, who parried with her bone spear, stopping the attack.

Anabelle dissolved into the shadows, slipping around the lich and reforming behind her. She sank her fist into Rasputina's stomach, knocking the wind out of her.

Rasputina stumbled forward as Suzuki prepared to decapitate her, and the blade hit Rasputina in the neck. She dropped to her knees, but the blade would not pass through.

Anabelle leapt, her foot aflame, and cracked her heel into the back of Rasputina's head as Suzuki hacked at the lich's neck.

The lich screamed in pain, then grabbed Suzuki's wrist and twisted it, causing him to drop his sword. When she backhanded Anabelle, the elf flew across the room and crashed into a wall. Then Rasputina lifted Suzuki, her eyes flashing green flames as she smiled widely. Her teeth were as sharp as fangs, and an otherworldly smell floated up from her like heavenly incense. "Boy, I suggest you step away now."

Suzuki drew his feet back and brought them up into Rasputina's chest, causing her to drop him. He rolled away, grabbing his sword with one hand. He drew a throwing axe from his back with the other and flung it, and the axe nailed the lich in the chest.

Rasputina screamed as Anabelle swooped in, throwing three lightning-bolt fists that connected drove the axe further into the lich. She stumbled back, trying to wrestle the axe out of her sternum. "I'm only going to tell you one more time; I am here to help you. I don't want to fight. Do not push me to be what I used to be."

Anabelle paused for a moment. What was she talking about? Who had she been before? *Whatever. It's probably a trap.*

Suzuki wasn't listening to the lich's words either. He rushed forward and rolled, slashing the lich's leg off as he passed.

She hit the ground.

Suzuki turned back around, and in one fluid motion, drove his sword into the back of the lich's skull. "And that takes care of that."

Anabelle stared at Suzuki, her jaw nearly touching the ground. The elegance he had just displayed was awe-inspiring. Not what she would have expected from a rough and tumble MERC. "How did you do that?" she asked.

Suzuki shrugged nonchalantly. "Holy sword. Buffs all my attacks to cause extra damage to undead creatures. Sandy showed me that one."

Sandy, who was sitting on the sidelines drinking a beer, raised her glass and toasted with Stew. "That's my boy!"

Before anyone could celebrate too much, the lich let out a screech and clawed at the sword in her skull, trying to pull it out. The sword had been driven too deep into the cave's floor.

She started trying to pull her body back, her hands frantically grabbing at the floor as her screams turned to dry sobs.

Anabelle's stomach lurched. Her display was pathetic and heart-wrenching. These were not the mad ramblings of the undead thing she'd faced before. There was something extremely human about what they were all listening to.

Anabelle was not alone in that feeling. It was evident from the silence that had descended on the cave.

The lich grasped the hilt of the sword, breaking her arms and contorting them while repeating, "Someone help me. Someone help me, please. She's coming for me," as she slid her head up and down, cutting her skull open.

Finally, Rasputina knelt on all fours like an animal and violently pulled back, yanking the sword through her skull. Brain matter, bone, and blood hit the ground as she scuttled backward.

She reached a wall, where she curled her knees to her chest, her head flopping, part of her face twitching uncontrollably as she chewed on her fingers, laughing quietly to herself.

Suzuki stared at Rasputina and then looked at Anabelle. "Okay, what the fuck is going on?"

Green energy burst from the wound on Rasputina's head as it started to stitch itself back together, the lich wailing in pain the entire time and stumbling to her feet. She clawed at her stomach until she opened a wound from which green pus seeped out, then grabbed a rib and ripped it out. The rib honed itself to a knife-edge.

The lich hunched over, looking feral, her matted hair covering her face as she growled, "I am trying to help you." She lunged at Suzuki, slashing at him with her bone knife.

The Mundanes' leader backed away, raising his sword to block the attack with one hand, the other casting a fireball.

The flaming orb hit the lich in the stomach and burned through her, but she didn't stop, not even when her intestines spilled out. She powered through Suzuki's defense, eventually getting close enough to strike him. Instead, she grabbed him and stared him in the eyes. "I have seen Death, boy."

Anabelle came in from the side, kicking her.

The lich crumpled, holding her stomach as the elf uppercut her and broke her jaw.

Rasputina stumbled back, holding her damaged face instead of her stomach. She raised her hand as she fell backward and fired a bone shard that hit Anabelle in the shoulder.

As Anabelle grabbed the bone to pull it out, the lich aimed her hands, green energy flowing all about her, and blasted Suzuki with it.

The blast rooted him to the ground and the energy flowed back to the lich, who made a fist, causing Suzuki to scream.

Anabelle came in for another attack, casting a small fireball that she followed with a series of punches.

A bone coating grew over the lich's chest, where Anabelle's blows fell.

The lich leaned forward and head-butted the elf, then released Suzuki from her grasp, wrapped both hands around Anabelle's throat, and forced her to the ground as she strangled her.

Anabelle struggled, but the lich was too strong. She could feel her trachea collapsing as she gasped for breath, Rasputina hovering over her, eyes mad with bloodlust and a psychotic smile plastered across her face.

Suddenly it was gone. Rasputina slammed her knife down, driving it into the floor. Her eyes welled with tears. "I am here to help." She sighed, then she stood, walked over to the soul jar, picked it up, and handed it to Anabelle before sitting down at the elf's feet. "Just let me help."

Anabelle sat up and stared at the lich, who was wiping away tears and rubbing her face frantically. "Why the hell do you want to help us all of a sudden? This is a far cry away from threatening to swallow Abby's soul whole."

The lich scratched at her face as she tried to talk. "I am...I wasn't meant to be like this. This isn't what I wanted. I used to be a good person. People loved me. I loved them. I didn't..."

Rasputina continued scratching as skin came off in her nails.

Sandy, who had finally gotten to her feet, placed a hand on the lich's shoulder.

Rasputina looked up at the wizard, her eyes still wet, tears mixed with the blood running down her face.

Sandy knelt next to the lich. "It happened to you, didn't it?" She pulled up the arm of her robe, showing her skin, which was cracked, blue energy glowing beneath it.

Rasputina nodded. "There was a reason I became this. I need to make it right. Please let me."

Sandy met Anabelle's eyes. "I think we should give her a chance."

The elf's anger flashed as she stepped toward the Mundane and shook her head. "You haven't seen what she's done! She is responsible for the death of hundreds of people!"

"Aren't we too? Those orcs and trolls and goblins we kill weren't just nameless soldiers. All of them were people, even if they were mind-controlled. We're all killers here."

"They were unarmed! Innocent human lives tossed away as if they were nothing."

Anabelle choked out on her words as she fought back tears, "Children."

"I know," Rasputina said softly. "I know what I've done."

The wizard stood, her hand still resting on the lich's shoulder. "She could have killed you both. Even if she was exhausted from fighting Telzrem, she had you, yet she was pulling her punches. We should listen to her. See what she has to say."

Anabelle crossed her arms as she looked down on the lich, who was rocking back and forth, cradling herself. "Fine. I'll listen. It better be a great fucking story."

CHAPTER FOUR

Anabelle, Terra, and the Mundanes eyed the lich. She took a deep breath, stifling her tears and regaining a reasonable amount of composure so that she did not even seem like the same person from a few seconds ago. She looked like the confident, sane woman from the battle with Telzrem.

Even the dragon, now fully healed, seemed to be interested in the story.

Rasputina pointed at Stew and Terra. "First, let me undo some of the damage." She traced her finger through the air, scribing arcane symbols that glowed a fiery green and then faded.

A green aura surrounded the two, healing their wounds instantly.

Rasputina chuckled to herself as she sat up straighter. "I've never been much of a storyteller. Perhaps my memories should speak for themselves."

Anabelle, who was ready to find fault with the slightest thing, scoffed. "If they're even your memories."

Rasputina, eyes serious and dead, turned to face Anabelle. "There are few things more precious to share than memories. The dragon will tell you. To lie about such things is to call a curse upon yourself, one that does not end."

Telzrem exhaled smoke and nodded solemnly. "The lich speaks truly. Continue, lich. We are curious. It is a rarity in one's life to come across a creature such as you, and even rarer to hear them speak about themselves."

Rasputina began to shiver, her body vibrating so quickly that it seemed there were two versions of her. There was a flash of light as two Rasputinas split from the one. The lich on the left looked much like the one before them, although her skin was rosier and full of more life. The second was a husk of a person, her pale, skin stretched loosely over bone, She had dead eyes.

The dead Rasputina muttered to herself, looking at the floor as she dug at the dirt, scrawling unknown words. The younger Rasputina looked at the dead thing as if she were ashamed. "That is the Rasputina you know," she explained. "The feral, mindless lich. What happens to a body when it does not have a soul for too long?"

Anabelle pounced. "And what does that make you?"

"A piece of what made her human. Her soul."

Telzrem gasped. "What you say is madness. A lich with a soul?"

"Only a third. Not enough to truly be alive, but enough to retain most of my power and not be consumed by madness."

Anabelle sighed, breaking up the conversation. "Okay, let's assume all of us haven't been reading arcane tomes our entire lives."

Sandy spoke up, her death mask fading so that her skin could be seen. Before she spoke, she wiped her face, destroying the glamour that covered the blue cracks. "Liches hide their souls to gain immortality. That's how they have enough time for their magic studies. They last for centuries, or even thousands of years sometimes. When I first started practicing magic, the older mages would joke that I could become one someday." She pressed a finger to a crack in her face.

"What the hell is going on with that?"

Rasputina stepped in. "Humans haven't been able to use magic for thousands of years, even those of us displaced across the Nine Realms. Most can only use it with a familiar, and even so, the magic rots their body—and eventually, their mind if it is undertaken for too long. That isn't a problem, given how short our lives are compared to elves or gnomes. Even if a wizard devotes all their time to studying, they will die before their mind slips from them."

Anabelle leaned closer, suddenly interested in the tale of the lich. "What about Myrddin? He's been alive for thousands of years, and he hasn't shown the same kind of mental decay as you. Or, you know, your general level of evil."

Rasputina didn't seem perturbed by the elf's slight. "Myrddin has cultivated his own method, one he keeps to himself for fear that humanity may abuse it. He is one of those men who trust they know best and rarely question it."

"Seeing as how he didn't become a lich, he might not be wrong."

The woman stared down at her hands as the older, dead lich barked mindlessly, snapping at the wind with her teeth. "I won't say he was wrong," the young one said. "You can see what happened to me, but I was aware that it might. I sectioned off part of my soul in a place my later self would have a desire to return to, giving me the opportunity to take back some of the power I'd wasted immortality getting."

Anabelle still wasn't convinced this was a story worth listening to. "What happened?"

Rasputina closed her eyes, and the cavern around them contorted and changed. They were now at the altar where she had split her soul.

The memory of the lich laid there quietly, no longer breathing, then rose and looked around. Her eyes fell on the dead thing muttering madly on the floor.

"I saw many things throughout the years that I could not understand. Visions. I thought I was haunted by a ghost of myself. Only now do I know I was being chased by the nightmare of what I was going to become. For years I saw that wraith. It never occurred to me that it was me, sitting here telling my own story."

The newly-made lich left the cavern, and the image shimmered once more. Now they were all in a mage school. Rasputina sat around a table with elves, gnomes, and dwarves, laughing and talking over drinks. Books were spread out all over the table.

"I grew up in a flux realm of your dimension. If you think of your world as a bubble, my reality was as if you pressed a pin into it, and it didn't pop. Humans could hardly use magic in our realm, yet I was gifted as a child. The only place I could learn magic was from the mage colleges throughout my realm. I dedicated years of my life to its study."

Anabelle interrupted Rasputina. "Why? What made magic so important to you?"

Rasputina chuckled to herself. "It's something you could never understand. Your kind is born with magic, as most of the races are. But us humans? All we have is our creativity, and even that pales next to the dumbest gnome." The woman looked at Sandy. "Once you have a taste, it's hard to turn away."

The wizard nodded in agreement but said nothing.

The lich continued. "It was not the thirst that drove me at first. I wanted to save my village. We were dying of a plague, one that I believed I could cure with alchemy, but as always with magic, the journey was not straightforward. Every time I returned home, there were more dead. By the time I became a lich, the whole village had passed."

Anabelle was tired of listening to the lich talk. She wanted to bash the foul creature's head in, regardless of the sob story. "So, what I'm hearing is that you were too slow, your people died, and you became a mindless killer. This is why we should trust you?"

Rasputina shook her head slowly. "No, that was not what happened."

The scene changed again to Rasputina walking into a village, stopping briefly to look at the husk of the lich, still chattering mindlessly in the dark.

The people of the village were gathered and talking among themselves as Rasputina pulled out a wand and began performing wonders. The villagers were enchanted.

The DGA and Mundanes watched as Rasputina moved through the village, visiting families, healing the sick, and working her magic for the benefit of those around her.

Anabelle couldn't care less about what she was watching—the

wistful memories of one who had committed atrocious crimes. None of this changed what the lich was or what she had done.

The woman met Anabelle's eyes as Rasputina looked over her shoulder at Anabelle and Terra. "The first time that I thought I might be going mad was when I saw you two while I was in the middle of dinner. I tried to talk to you but couldn't hear anything you said. All night…I stayed up all night trying to communicate, but all I could see was the hatred in your eyes for everything I was."

The scene disappeared, replaced by Rasputina in an old elven library, buried beneath books. Days passed. Weeks. Eventually months. She hardly moved from the spot, her eyes growing hollow and sunken. Green cracks started to appear across her body.

"We aren't meant to live this long. It unwinds us without us releasing it. Slowly, we cease to be, and there are only two desires, both for that which we do not possess: knowledge and a soul. When the second craving came to me, I removed myself from civilization."

Roots burst from the floor of the college and trees sprang up, tearing through the ceiling, shattering glass until there was only a forest with an angry stream moving throughout it.

Rasputina trampled through the woods, her eyes wide with fear as she screamed at nothing. She tripped over her feet and landed in the river, crawling through the mud before rolling over and grabbing her stomach, her face screwed up in pain as she begged for death.

"It was not my proudest moment, only the first in a long line of shame. I wandered those woods for hundreds of years, never coming across another human. The longer I went without nourishment, the wilder my mind became, yet I was still learning. Hearing the sound of natural magic all around me. Before long, I couldn't distinguish the voices of fairies from the river or my own screams."

Rasputina collapsed beneath a tree. Winter came, and then spring. The seasons changed as the roots of the tree grew over the lich, finally covering her completely.

"The folks who stumbled upon me never stood a chance."

Two young men walked through the forest. They stopped by the river, sat, and started talking to each other.

From beneath the roots of the tree came an unearthly green glow. One of the men looked over his shoulder as a loud growl came from the tree.

Rasputina tore through the ground, her eyes empty of even a semblance of humanity. They were windows into an emptiness not much seen in any realm. She beset one of the men, bounding after him as if she were an animal, then landing on him and ripping his throat out. She didn't worry about the other. She peeled the flesh from her first kill, choking it down as she tore through his chest to get to his heart. That night, she knew contentment for the first time in hundreds of years.

"By this point, what was left of me was dead. Erased in a long slumber. The only thing that remained were the two hungers, and over the course of time, one grew larger than the other. I've met other liches, but none of them were like me; they killed only to keep themselves alive. I was something else. I killed for the sheer joy of it."

Rasputina walked through a village, setting it afire with the flick of her wrist, then scooping up a screaming child as it ran past her and sinking her teeth into its soft flesh.

"I was the first to fall upon the rare curse of the lich, to die with meaning. It's the one thing your soulless mind clings to. Mine was to defeat Death. You call him the Dark One. Some call him Odin. In that meaning, I found my undoing. Death was all that I could create. It was all I lived for."

The memories disappeared. Everyone was back in the cavern.

Rasputina looked at the other lich. "Now we live with each other, she tormented by having a soul again. Feeding on my constant pain, the guilt of knowledge of every life I've ended. We exist together for the first time, and it is unbearable, but I know my purpose again. It is to end the Dark One."

Anabelle stood, her fist catching fire. "Yeah, that wasn't a good enough story." She stalked toward Rasputina as the two forms of the lich joined again.

Telzrem's tail slid between them. "She speaks the truth," the dragon said.

Anabelle whirled to face the Mundanes and Terra. "Okay, she's sorry for everything she did. Who gives a shit? What she's done is monstrous. We should end her right here. Now."

The Mundanes exchanged glances, one to the other. Finally, Suzuki stood and approached Telzrem. "You've lived longer than any of us could hope to. You're wiser than any of us. What do you think?"

Telzrem rose to his full height for the first time since their battle. "For years, I've guarded this soul jar. Myrddin himself asked me to, for a soul jar is one of the most dangerous things for a mortal to possess. I was told to only release it if I was certain it was in the right hands, even if that meant my death."

The dragon sighed heavily. "The battle against the Dark One is above my ideas of right and wrong. It is beyond me. The lich does not deserve forgiveness, but she is sincere in her desire to destroy the Dark One, and she is a powerful weapon to be wielded against him."

Rasputina stood, her face twitching. "Forgiveness isn't what I want. When the Dark One is destroyed, I will give you the location of the last two parts of my soul. Once he is dead, you can end my life as well." She turned to Anabelle and Terra. "I only ask that it be you two and Abby."

Anabelle glared at the lich, trying to find the words to express her disgust, but Telzrem was right. The lich *was* a powerful weapon, one the Dark One did not know he had unleashed against himself. She settled on, "You disgust me. I find you abhorrent, but we need your strength."

Rasputina wiped tears from her face as she nodded. "I am. Truly. I know. And I deserve never to stop knowing that."

Anabelle picked up the soul jar. "Objections, anyone?"

The cavern was silent.

"Good. Then let's get the fuck out of here."

The council of the twelve tribes had been summoned. The announcement had traveled through the Nine Realms faster than any news had for years.

No one knew the orc tribes had been united under Terra and Cire. It was news to the elves, gnomes, and dwarves, but it was the elves who were most concerned.

Whispers traveled through the Nine Realms. Even though all races of the realms were united in their fight against the Dark One, that didn't change politics.

And here were orcish politics, ancient though they were, on display for all the realms to see.

Terra received the summons a few days after returning to HQ. That alone was going to take getting used to.

Anabelle and Terra had returned to HQ with Rasputina.

Roy had flipped his shit when Rasputina waltzed out of the hadron collider.

Anabelle and Tera had talked about the best course of action for some time. Treating him like a reasonable leader would have resulted in the lich being killed on the spot. That was what Anabelle said *she* would have done, at least—given permission for Rasputina to be allowed into HQ, then attacked when she wasn't expecting it.

Instead of doing that, Terra had suggested ignoring Roy until they had a chance to explain their situation in person.

The conversation had not gone well.

"Do you have any idea how bad a fucking idea this is?" Roy shouted as he stormed into the War Room. "We've spent the last two months running from that psychotic lich with our tails between our legs, and you brought her into our base because she's turned over a new leaf?"

Terra raised her hand, cutting Roy off. She looked as convincing as she could. "It's kinda like someone gave us the keys to their boss' nuclear bomb, except that the boss *is* the nuclear bomb, and it's on our side."

Roy slammed his palm to his forehead and sighed for maybe a thousand years. "Are you kidding me? That's your argument?"

Terra smiled as she shrugged. Arguing with Roy wasn't going to change what was happening. Even though he was running things, Anabelle and Terra were the ones who had to make calls at the last minute. This had been one of them. "Well, I'm not sure if it matters since she's already here. If she's going to destroy the place and kill us all, then she will, and there's nothing we can do about it."

Anabelle hadn't spoken since they'd come back, and Terra had wondered what was on her mind. Suddenly, the elf stood and walked over to Roy. She took his hand in her own, her eyes serious yet deep. "Roy, we know you're the one in charge, but we had to make a judgment call. And I know it pisses you off. It's not what you would have done, but that was why Myrddin formed this group. Because he couldn't be everywhere. It used to piss him off too, but this isn't an attack on your leadership. We just did what we thought was best."

Terra and Roy stared at Anabelle, confused by her tone and her words. This wasn't the same elf Terra had met months ago. Her response had been calm, measured, and most surprising, fairly empathetic. It looked like the Mundanes' dynamic had rubbed off on Anabelle.

Roy was obviously fumbling for a response. He finally collapsed into a chair, shaking his head as he muttered under his breath.

Anabelle knelt beside him. "What is it?"

Roy looked up, his eyes sunken black holes of exhaustion. "If this goes sour, I'm the one who is getting fucked."

"Nope," Terra interjected. "You'll be dead. All of us will be, and it's not like you can be court-martialed for being dead."

Roy sat up, trying to rub away how tired he was. "Okay, so where were you thinking we would keep her?"

Anabelle pointed at the floor. "She suggested the prison."

Roy shook his head. "No way. That's where we are holding Grok. If Rasputina is up to something..." He had pulled out the report Anabelle and Terra had filled before arriving back at HQ. "Even if she's not powerful enough to take down the whole base, I'm not going to risk her talking to Grok. Somewhere else."

"There's that abandoned hall near the science department."

Terra raised her eyebrow. "You mean the hall that Abby lives on?"

"Fuck, I didn't—"

Roy interrupted, "That's going to have to do. Worst-case scenario, Abby can handle herself, and you two have an incentive to get your asses there. Oh, and *you* have to explain this to her because this is *your* fucking responsibility."

He stormed toward the exit but stopped when Anabelle grabbed his arm. The elf pulled him close for a hug and kissed him on the cheek. "Hey, I know this is stressful, but we're all doing what we can, same as you. We're in this together. If something looks wrong, you're going to be the first person to know about it."

The edges of Roy's face softened, as did the corner of his eyes. "Okay. Sorry about earlier. I'm just—"

"I get it. Sometimes it's boss time. Don't worry. I'll see you later."

Roy left Anabelle and Terra alone. "So, when did you learn how to put all that honey on top of spice?" Terra asked.

Anabelle sat down, swiping through footage of Rasputina in a containment cell. "Fuck off. It wasn't that much honey."

"Dude, you practically covered your boy in sugar."

"Eh, maybe it was watching the Mundanes. They make a lot more jokes and bicker a lot less, and seem to genuinely respect who is in charge, even if they need to talk shit. Maybe I need to cut Roy and Myrddin more slack. I mean, we *did* just bring a lich into HQ."

Terra chuckled and crossed her arms. "Yeah. That is pretty wild."

That was four days ago. Since then, the lich had been moved onto Abby's hall.

The girl hadn't been excited, opting to sleep in the lab instead while she and Creon continued extended research on her nanobots.

Other than that, the whole thing had gone off without a hitch. No one had heard anything from either of the Gates. It looked like there was going to be a lull in missions for a bit.

That was when the summons had arrived.

Now Terra and Cire were on a convoy heading toward an undisclosed location in the ancient city of Gad, the old capital of the orc world. Apparently, the council had continued to use the city after it had been abandoned.

Roy and Blackwell accompanied Terra and Cire. Both were reviewing files as Terra and Cire watched the wild terrain around them.

Terra noticed that Cire seemed more keyed into his surroundings than usual. "Like the view?" she asked.

Cire looked at Terra, and his eyes filled with tears. He made no attempt to hide them or wipe them away. "This is my home. There has been little time for me to appreciate it."

"Have you ever been here?"

Cire shook his head. He tried to speak but paused, collecting his thoughts. "There is a term for one such as me: *Bethakor-al-Zakoth*. It is one who is... It means that I am not a true orc. I wasn't born here. Was not raised by my people. I grew up in a pen and was taught my ways by slaves, those the twelve tribes believe were too weak to be considered orcs. I'm still surprised the tribes acknowledge me. The only reason I have any sway here is because of you."

Terra stared out at the land of the orcs as she thought about what Cire had said. "You resent me a little, don't you?"

Cire hung his head. "No, I don't. Merely myself. I grew up on the legends of my people. My heart burned with an intense desire to know where I came from and be connected to my lineage. I wanted to feel my ancestors in my blood, but all I have are the stories and the stares of those who believe me to be other and only tolerate me because a human vouches for me. My ancestors and my brothers and sisters are ashamed of me."

Terra wiped away Cire's tears. "You know your history better than any living orc of the twelve tribes, and you were instrumental in getting the tribes back together. Don't sell yourself short. If they don't want to accept you, fine. We'll just have to beat it into their skulls."

Cire laughed as he turned to look at the giant structure ahead of them. It was a tower carved straight into the heart of a mountain with an arena before it. "You're very good at cheering me up. I've always appreciated that. And you? How are you feeling about all this?"

Terra shifted in her seat as Roy looked at her. "I don't know. The more involved I get in all of this, the more uncomfortable I feel. But if the council is willing to accept me as one of their own, then it can't be too big of a deal for me to be part of it."

"No, I mean, how do you *feel*?"

Terra cracked her knuckles and sighed. "Scared. If I'm honest. I hate this kind of shit. Being on talk shows is one thing, but this? Fuck, it's terrifying."

Blackwell, who was driving, banged on the window and shouted, "We're almost there. Get ready."

Roy loaded his plasma pistol while Terra gave him a confused look.

"I thought we were going to a peace council or something?" Terra asked.

Roy holstered his pistol. "I'm assuming every orc in there is armed.

And I don't act on information from spies without holding onto a fear that I might be shot in the back."

The truck stopped in the middle of the arena.

Twelve orcs sat on a stage near the edge. The area reminded Terra of the arena she'd had to fight her way out of. She remembered that Cire had told her the Game Master's arena was based on ancient orc traditions. It was only fitting that the council was meeting in a place like this.

Terra, Cire, Blackwell, and Roy stepped out of the van and headed toward the council's seats.

There were two people waiting for them.

Roy pulled out his binoculars to see who they were. After a few seconds, he screamed a string of curses, threw his binoculars to the ground, and shot them. "Are you fucking kidding me?" he shouted.

Terra and Cire exchanged glances. "That doesn't sound good at all," Terra whispered in Cire's ear.

They walked toward the council, dust kicking up around them. Terra blinked back tears, her vision blurring, then wiped her eyes.

Sarah and Grok stood in front of the council, facing Terra and Roy.

Grok bowed, the air around her pulsing with her energy. "Good to see you again, Terra."

Roy drew his gun and aimed it at Sarah. "You have one minute to explain what the fuck she is doing out of her cell."

Sarah gestured at the council. "A special request."

The orcs on the stage mostly looked the same: large male orcs, all of them ancient, with various tattoos whose meanings eluded Terra. One was a female, who wore a wrap around her face, her body covered in thick hide armor. A shaman.

The shaman stepped forward and cleared her throat. When she spoke, her voice resounded throughout the arena. "We requested that Grok attend this meeting. She is a vital part of orc society. Our Hand, if you will."

Roy holstered his gun. "It's interesting you say that, but it doesn't change that she is our prisoner and—"

The shaman pulled a knife from her side and threw it at Roy. It landed a centimeter from his big toe. "This meeting is between the human, the slave, and us. Please remember that the next time you speak."

Terra stepped in front of Roy. "If we're going to talk, I expect you to give my friends the same respect you would give me."

"Which is what I've done. You'll get our respect when you earn it. Now shut your mouth and listen."

Terra's blood heated. She wished she could jump onto that podium and beat some respect into the shaman, but that wasn't the way things like this went. She would wait for her fight.

CHAPTER SIX

Terra and the rest of them walked up to Sarah, Roy still eyeballing her as if he expected a shot in the back at any time.

Sarah, on the other hand, didn't seem to be bothered by Roy's suspicions. After a few minutes, she sighed as she leaned her weight to the side, putting one hand on her waist. "I just borrowed her. It seemed easier to ask forgiveness instead of permission."

Roy didn't bother looking at the agent. "Have you been talking to Anabelle?"

"Here and there, but that's not important. We aren't here to talk about how annoyed you are with me. This is about Terra and Grok."

Terra thought she must have misheard for a moment. What did this have to do with Grok? But what other reason would the orc have to be here if it didn't have to do with her?

Grok watched Terra the way a large cat watches their prey. She looked ready to pounce at any moment, her muscles tensing and relaxing in slight movements.

Even if Terra was terrified of Grok, she couldn't help but respect the orc's strength, and she could admit it. Every time she saw the orc, she thought she was going to shit her pants.

Grok seemed to know that and grinned at Terra, her sharp teeth gleaming in an extremely attractive way. "How have you been keeping yourself?"

Terra felt like the orc was playing mind games with her. "You know, just kicking the Dark One's ass. Nothing new."

Grok's eyes flicked up and down Terra's body. "You look softer than the last time I saw you. Having trouble finding a good fight?"

Terra felt like she was naked, but there was nothing she could do about the embarrassment. Instead, she tried to ignore the warmth in her face as she blushed.

The ground trembled violently, and everyone's eye went to the shaman. "You were summoned here because the orc council has decided your rule is blasphemous. A non-orc leading the twelve tribes is an insult to all orcs. We revoke your right to lead."

Now the warmth in Terra's face was from anger instead of embarrassment. "What the fuck do you mean, you revoke my right? I didn't come here asking for your permission for any of this. The orcs were scattered. I brought them back together. What the hell have *you* been doing?"

One of the male orcs on the council stood. "Spoken like a true orc. And do you speak for the timid elf scat at your side?"

Terra looked at Cire, who winced and looked down at being spoken to by the council. Instead of waiting to meet his eyes to see if he was okay, she stared at the shaman.

After a few moments, Cire stepped forward. "I speak for myself."

The old orc cackled. "Ah, the shitstain speaks. Surprised you even learned how to move your tongue. Dull-fanged as well. You are the one who follows the human?"

"I follow no one. I am sworn to her as my chieftain by my choice, as per the old ways."

The old orc slammed his axe on the stage. "No shaman would swear themselves to anyone. You do not know the old ways, only the bastard drivel of whatever waste of cum sired you."

"And you all have sat here growing old with your knowledge and watching your people die? Or perhaps you've grown too senile to remember that you sit in ruins like royalty that has lost its kingdom? At least I still have the strength to fight."

The old orc laughed again as he lifted his axe. "At least they talk like orcs."

The shaman raised her hand, causing the earth to shake once more. "Already, forces are moving against you. We offer a way out of the eventual bloodshed you will bring on your heads and those of your orcish family."

Terra smiled as she straightened and folded her arms. "Are you talking to me too? Do I get to be part of the family as well?"

The shaman unwrapped her face, revealing a mangled and broken countenance. "The orcish dinner table is not one of whispers and polite manners, not for us old ones. If you wish to continue sitting among us, you will have to show that you can have your skull knocked in and not lose your wits."

"What do you propose?"

The shaman pointed at Grok. "There is only one recognized leader of the orcs, but it is unspoken among the young of our tribe. They have forgotten our ways, but we have watched for hundreds of years, waiting for the chance to lead the horde back to glory."

Terra and Cire exchanged glances. She wasn't sure if she had heard right. From what Cire had told her, orcs didn't have the extremely long lives of elves, gnomes, or dwarves. They lived about the same length of time as humans.

"Yes, you heard us correctly, *chok-al-yurezth.*"

Cire leaned over to whisper to Terra. "That means 'little children.'"

The ground shook again, calling their attention back the shaman. "Only a shaman can lead the orcish people, and until now, I have not seen one worthy in all my years."

Terra sighed with relief. She had never wanted to lead. It had been thrust upon her, and she had tried to do the best she could. She was ecstatic that someone was going to take this weight from her.

The shaman smiled, her lopsided face somehow managing to convey something like joy. "You aren't off the hook yet. Leadership is more than just brains. The shaman, and the tribe by association, has always had a Hand. For years, Grok was mine. Now you are to be Cire's."

Grok stepped forward. "This is not a simple thing. The Hands are trained in the most dangerous Path, that of the Lost. We bestow upon them the primal rage of our ancestors, allowing them to draw even more strength from themselves."

One of the elders leapt from the podium, landing with enough force to shake the earth, and approached Grok, holding two collars in his hand. He slipped one over Grok's neck.

The shaman continued, "These collars will evenly distribute Grok's power between you two. If you can defeat her, you will be the new Hand, and she will train you in the Path of the Lost. Do you agree to our terms?"

Terra glanced at Grok, who seemed to be unable to contain her urge to fight Terra. It was seething through her skin, and her smile was fierce. She was looking forward to a fight. "I have one condition," Terra said. "If I win, Grok doesn't just train me. She also trains the last Traveler, Anabelle."

The shaman's smile widened, her face looking even more broken than before. "Who are you to make demands of me?"

"You may be comfortable with your position, but I command the twelve tribes, and it's my generally cool attitude that's going to keep me from razing your wrinkly asses to the ground. I get that you're probably all strong as hell, but I have a fucking horde, not just the memory of one."

One of the councilors doubled over laughing, holding his gut as if he thought it would burst. "You've picked a Hand with a lot of fight in her. Hopefully she'll be able to make up for the meekness of your shaman."

The shaman nodded her head. "Agreed. If you can beat Grok, you will both be trained. On one condition. Grok will receive seventy-five percent of her power. You will receive twenty-five percent. And it is up to the winner whether or not the loser lives or dies."

Terra cracked her knuckles. "All right. Grok, any last words before I pound the shit out of you?"

The elder crossed the space between Grok and Terra and handed a collar to Terra. She slipped it onto her neck as Sarah walked up to her.

Sarah placed her hand on Terra's shoulder. "Good luck. A lot is riding on you." Then she went over to Roy, who only glanced at her. "I already knew this was happening," Sarah said. "My network runs pretty wide. This was the only way, and if I'd had my guy let you know about Grok, you would have pulled the plug."

Roy nodded as he scratched his beard. "Yeah, I figured it was something like that. Feels like I'm getting the short end of the stick recently–people trying to put me in my place even though I'm not putting any restrictions on them."

"No, it's not like that. Sometimes things need to happen fast, and you're leading a whole goddamn war. We're trying to make things easier for you and everyone else. All you have to do is—"

"Trust you? I do. I'm just complaining because I'm a tired... Fuck, I'm just tired. I appreciate you making the call. Let's hope it doesn't end with Terra dead."

"Yeah, let's hope."

Terra took a step toward Grok. She felt an energy surge through her body unlike anything she'd ever felt before. The world around her seemed lighter, and her body didn't feel like it had any substance. She could do anything, there was no question about it. Was this how Grok felt all the time?

Grok and Terra circled each other. "You feel that, don't you?" the orc asked. "You aren't like other humans. They don't keep getting stronger like you. They don't have the screaming anger in their blood. Anabelle didn't either. I had to put it there for her. You were wise to ask for her to be taught as well, but it isn't going to happen. You aren't walking away from this."

"You're right. I'll be dancing on your grave."

"So brave for someone whose heart was racing a few minutes ago."

"You tortured my friend. I'm going to enjoy this."

"So will I."

Grok pulled two axes from behind her back and tossed one to Terra.

As the human reached out to grab the axe, the orc surged forward, axe high above her head. She brought it down fast, attempting to cleave through Terra's skull.

Terra's arm went up faster than she thought was possible to move, almost as if her body had anticipated the attack before she registered the orc's movement.

She stepped back, pivoted, and leaned forward, locking her axe with Grok's.

Grok held her own, pushing back against Terra while smiling cruelly. "You fight like an orc, and I don't mean with our passion. How did a human who'd never been in a fight learn how to move with such intention?"

The orc then leaned forward and headbutted Terra, causing the human to stumble back. "Did that filthy creature who calls himself a shaman share our memories with you?"

She leapt into the air and kicked Terra in the face. "He's not worthy to call himself one of us, filling your head with the ancestral memories of orcs too weak to keep from being forced into slavery."

As Terra retreated, Grok rushed her and slammed her fist into Terra's nose. The human crumpled to the ground. "You aren't a Hand," Grok taunted. "You're not even a limp dick."

Terra rolled over, grasping her nose. It was gushing blood, and her face was swelling. Twenty-five percent of what Grok had was nothing. Deep down Terra knew that, but it didn't matter at that moment.

Blood that was as hot as hell pumped through Terra's veins. She slammed the ground, sending a small quake through the earth. Then she sprang up and slugged Grok in the face with everything she had for each moment of self-doubt, every wince, and the many instances she'd listened to orcs talk shit about Cire and didn't say a word. All of it was channeled into that punch.

Grok's legs buckled, and she went to one knee. When Terra's fist connected with the orc's jaw, it created a sonic boom that rippled through the ground as if someone had pulled a massive hoe over it.

The orc touched her jaw, holding it tenderly, her eyes wide with shock. "No technique. Animalistic. Pure force. And without any magic..."

Grok got to her feet as she rubbed her jaw. She took a step forward, firmly planting her foot on the ground. "I extend a formal challenge to you. No tricks. Nothing fancy. Place your foot beside mine, and we go at it."

Terra stepped up to Grok without hesitation. She put her foot beside the orc's and raised her fist. There wasn't time to think this through, but Terra knew the orc had been fighting for years. Maybe this would even the playing field.

Grok swung and Terra raised her arm, absorbing the attack as the orc threw a punch with the other hand.

Each blow hit Terra like a freight train. She thought her arms were going to break from the force of Grok's attacks.

But then there was an opening, a split second as Grok was preparing for another strike and an open spot between the orc's arms. The ribcage.

Terra jabbed, pouring her heart and soul into that punch. It connected, and she felt ribs crack.

Grok coughed up blood as she leaned forward.

Terra slightly relaxed. The next thing she felt was Grok's knuckles slamming into her forehead.

The world went black for a second as Terra swayed, then came back into focus. She saw Grok's fist coming at her and ducked, then reached up, grabbed the orc's arm, and struck her elbow, breaking it.

Grok screamed, and in a fit of pure madness, slapped Terra in the face with her limp, broken arm.

As Terra flailed, the orc grabbed the back of her head with her good arm and pulled the human's head to her, smashing into it with her broad forehead.

Terra stumbled and fell on her back.

Grok leapt and brought her fist down on Terra's chest.

The human coughed blood as Grok straddled her, her eyes mad with blood rage.

The orc punched Terra in the head, and the only sound in the arena was that of bone breaking bone, followed by a much thicker sound.

Terra lay still.

Grok hit her again.

Cire stepped forward, drawing his dagger, and Sarah grabbed him by the shoulder. "Wait." He looked from Sarah to Terra, his eyes narrow with pain and anger.

He turned when he heard Grok hit Terra again. Then again. And again.

Blood pooled from Terra's nose and the cuts on her face. Both eyes were swollen, and her jaw was broken.

She reached up and swung at Grok, but the orc caught her hand and bent it back, snapping the wrist so that Terra's hand hung like a swollen piece of fruit from a broken branch. Her screams filled the arena.

Grok slammed her head into the human's, knocking out five of her teeth. Then there was only the sound of Terra gurgling.

"Do you yield?"

Terra's face hardly resembled anything human anymore. Her nose was pushed to the side, and her eyes were gone. Her left cheekbone was crushed, causing half of her face to sink in. When she tried to speak, only a faint wheeze came out.

"What was that? I can't hear you?"

Terra wheezed again.

"Let me get closer. Whisper it in my ear, okay?"

Grok leaned over so Terra could whisper. Instead, the human lunged up and bit the side of Grok's face. She pulled back as the orc tried to get away, tearing off the Hand's ear and a five-inch patch of skin.

The orc stumbled backward, holding bare muscle on the side of her face.

Terra stumbled to her feet, swaying until she fell back down. She vomited blood and teeth, then forced herself back up and raised her fists.

Grok stared at Terra and nodded before turning to the shaman and the elders. "She's your new Hand." Then she walked away.

Cire, Blackwell, and Roy rushed over to Terra. Cire barely caught her before she hit the ground.

The shaman boomed, "Take her to my chambers. Accommodations have already been made."

The sand swirled around Terra, forming a golem that picked her up and sped between the columns in the arena.

Cire, his eyes still flashing with anger, turned to face Sarah. "How did you know Grok wasn't going to kill her?"

Sarah folded her arms. "Don't come at me like that. This is what you two wanted. All I did was deliver. You should have known it wasn't going to be pretty."

Cire whirled and glared at the shaman. "Take me to her. Now."

The shaman dissolved and reappeared in front of Cire. "A shaman without a Hand is nothing, and a Hand without a shaman is dead flesh." She touched Cire's shoulder, and both of them dissolved into fine sand.

Roy looked up at the remaining orc elders. "Uh, do we have to stay here? I'm kind of on a tight schedule."

Terra opened her eyes. Her entire face hurt, but she managed to sit up. The room was too dark for her to see, but she didn't need to. She could hear Cire praying by her side.

He stopped. "The lights are out because of your eyes. We had to regrow them, and most of your face as well. The damage was extensive, but you won't have anything worse than a few scars."

"Did we win?"

"You won. There are trials I must face alone for the transfer of power."

Terra laid back down. She wanted to talk to Cire but could not keep her mind focused. "I don't remember anything except getting punched a lot."

"You ripped Grok's ear off with your teeth."

Terra smiled and winced from the pain. "That's pretty sick. Do you have your trials soon?"

"Yes. Very soon."

"Will you stay here just a little bit longer?"

Cire took Terra's hand. "For as long as you want. Nothing will get me to leave your side except your words."

"Good. Just keep singing. Please."

And he did.

CHAPTER SEVEN

Terra slept for nearly three days, dipping in and out of consciousness. She did not dream. There was only a feeling of heaviness on her eyelids that gradually disappeared. At times she would wake, looking for Cire. Sometimes he was there, others not, but never without first kissing Terra's forehead and telling her he was leaving.

On the third day, Terra finally woke and managed to stay awake. She searched her dark room and saw someone standing in the corner.

The shaman stepped out of the shadows. "For as long as you live, you are an orc. You've proven yourself far beyond what any of us could have imagined. I had hopes for you and Cire, but to be honest, I did not think either of you was going to survive."

Terra forced herself to sit up. "I don't know if I should be pissed at you or thank you."

The shaman chuckled. "In all cases with our trials, a little bit of both is good."

"You said you weren't sure Cire was going to survive? What did you mean?"

The shaman took a seat on Terra's bed, looking almost matronly. She reminded Terra of a tired mother, one who had tended to her children for far too long. "Your trial tested the limits of your physical body. His trials have tested the limits of his mind. A shaman is nothing without a tinge of madness, and he was quite sane before we started."

Terra tried to get out of bed. "What did you do to him?"

"What had to be done. Stripped him of his name. Drowned him in the memories, anger, and sorrow of our ancestors and the tribespeople. He is more connected to our history than any living orc other than me."

"Then what does he have to recover from?"

"It is an arduous process to absorb so much pain from so many. It breaks the mind. Then the mind has to reform, make itself anew. You may call him Cire still, but I doubt he will answer to anything other than his new name."

"Which is?"

"Shaman. And now I can return to my own name. He has taken my place. I wish you both the best of luck. The two of you will lead our people well. I have no doubt of that."

There was a knock on the door. The shaman looked over her shoulder as Cire stepped into the room.

He had lost a lot of weight, his muscles having been stretched and burned down to leanness. His entire body was covered in what looked to be ash, his face smeared with the stuff so that he had a ghostly complexion from which his intense eyes burned. "We have business to attend to," he said.

The shaman bowed and left the room. Cire stepped farther in.

Terra noticed the difference instantly. The timidity was gone, and the insecurity had vanished. Her friend had been replaced by a man she did not recognize. He was dark, angry, and powerful. "Hey, Cire."

Despite the foreign eyes, a piece of Cire shone through when he smiled. "I've thought of you night and day."

He rushed over and threw his arms around Terra, who tried not to wince at the pressure on her bones. "It was almost all I could think about."

"What did they do to you?"

"Bathed me in anger and purpose. We will talk about it some other time. I am still trying to understand what happened, but for now, we must meet with everyone. Roy wants reports from all of us. Apparently, Abby has upgraded all our HUDs so we can speak to each other over longer distances."

"Wait? Roy, Sarah, and everyone else didn't stay?"

Cire shook his head as his eyes bored into Terra's. His new intensity was a little off-putting, but surprisingly, extremely attractive on him.

The orc took Terra's hand. "You've been out for a couple of days. No one could abandon their missions, and it sounds as if things are moving about on the Dark One's side. Our crisis has been averted. We must help the others now. Are you ready?"

Terra looked under her covers. "Uh, hardly. Apparently, I had to be naked to heal all the way. I'm assuming that was your idea."

"No, but I am not complaining. That isn't a concern, though. No one will be able to see."

"Do you want to crawl in here with me?"

"And give the illusion that we haven't faced death? No, but I will once the call is over."

Terra nodded. She liked whatever had happened.

Cire raised his arm, his HUD lighting, and Terra did the same.

A message appeared on the HUD, stating that they were waiting for the other members of the chat.

Roy appeared in Terra's room first.

She nearly jumped out of bed. It looked like Roy had teleported into the room, but on closer inspection, Terra could see he was a hologram—the most impressive hologram she'd ever seen. Completely lifelike, even casting a shadow.

Roy smiled when he saw her. It was the first such expression she'd seen in a while. "Good to see you awake. I thought Grok was going to take the chance to kill you."

Grok appeared next, leaning against the wall near the door. "Arrangements have been made for me. I don't plan on breaking my agreements."

Anabelle shimmered into sight. She was lying on a lounge, her hair pulled back in a messy bun and her face devoid of any makeup, but she somehow looked as radiant as if she'd prepped for a photo shoot. "Way to inspire confidence, Grok, seeing as how you bailed on your agreement with the Dark One."

Grok smirked smugly. "If you'd prefer I honor that commitment over this one, I'll kindly ask you to release me."

"Not a chance. Just saying you're hardly trustworthy."

Abby appeared next, along with Persephone. The two of them were sitting together on a couch. "People change," the drow said. "I was on the Dark One's side, and you guys didn't have a problem accepting me."

Anabelle glanced at her. "One, you were a kid who was microchipped. Two...well, actually, I guess that's the only reason. Oh, and you're also kind of a sweetheart. Abby's told us some embarrassing—"

Abby interrupted. "Maybe we should all be quiet for a second so I can finish some calibrations. It would be unfortunate if our communications cut out. Or if someone else's did."

Terra laughed. Abby was as awkward as ever. It didn't seem like her tech upgrades were going to change that. Seeing Abby hit Terra with a pang. She missed the kid. Missed hanging out with her and Anabelle instead of running missions all the time. Part of her wondered what was going to happen when this was finally over. Did people stay in touch after wars? What would she have in common with a sixteen-year-old cyborg and an elvish model?

Other than taking down the biggest, baddest son of a bitch in the entire universe? If that didn't bring you together, nothing could.

Roy looked around the room. "Guess that's everyone."

There was a sharp crackling sound, and Rasputina popped into sight. She sat in a chair, her hands folded and her chin resting on them.

Roy sighed. "So, you're going to be sitting in on everything?"

The lich looked up, her green eyes flashing. "Unless you would like to provide me with private meetings for everything that you discuss."

"I'm still not sure you need to know much about anything you aren't involved in."

Anabelle, surprisingly, stepped in to defend Rasputina. "She's part of the team, even if I don't like it. The more we act like she isn't, the harder it is going to be to work with each other, so let's just accept it. She doesn't want to work with us. We don't want to work with her. But we need each other."

"Fine. All right, I want reports from everyone. Anabelle, you're up."

The elf cleared her throat and explained how the last mission had gone, informing Roy that they had retrieved the soul jar and were ready to tackle the dungeon they'd had to skip. She suggested that the full team be available for the dungeon crawl, especially if Rasputina was going to be there.

Roy leaned back in his chair and kicked his feet up, looking like a caricature of a tough guy from a military soap opera. "Hold on. Break it down for me in layman's terms. What the fuck happened to make Rasputina good?"

Rasputina pulled back her hood, showing her younger, healthier face. "Plainly speaking, I left a surprise for the monster I had become. When she consumed it, I reversed part of the process of becoming a lich. My personality is split. There's me, the real Rasputina. and then there is the lich, who I will keep in check."

Roy shook his head. "Jesus Christ, Abby has an AI and a nanobot consciousness living in her, Persephone hosts part of a sentient elder god, and now this? Can we make a new rule? No more multiple personalities. This shit is getting hard to keep up with."

Abby and Persephone giggled, and the drow tickled Abby.

Roy cleared his throat. "Also, please keep all the cute shit off private channels. Everyone. Okay, Terra and Cire. How did everything go on your end?"

Terra groaned as she sat up straighter. "Well, I'm not dead, and both me and Anabelle are going to be trained in the Path of the Lost, so I guess that's a win in my department."

Anabelle's eyes widened. "Wait, what are you talking about?"

Grok looked at Anabelle and smiled. "I'll be training you both. One of the perks of Terra becoming the new Hand of the orc council."

Anabelle didn't look happy about the information she had just received, but she didn't say anything else, merely slumped further into her couch.

Cire spoke, his voice clear and sharp. "I have undergone the rites required to assume the position of the shaman for all orcs, and I have healed from them. Now we have the guaranteed strength of the horde."

Abby clapped her hands as she leaned forward. "Oh, Cire! Congratulations! That sounds amazing."

Cire smiled slightly. "Thank you."

Roy clapped, slow and sarcastic. "Hey, guys, we're doing a military briefing, not an emotional powwow. Is there anything else you have to say about the horde, Cire?"

"My name has been revoked by the customs of the horde. From now on, refer to me as 'Shaman.'"

Roy raised his eyebrows. "Oh, okay. Thanks for the heads up. Abby?"

Abby stood up and stepped farther into the room. "Unlike the rest of you, we don't have anything positive to report. We've learned the Dark One has a new agent, a resurrected version of Nikola Tesla. And the Gate into the Netherverse? It took us to a place that was made from the souls of people who have fallen in combat against the Dark One."

Roy nodded solemnly as he scratched his beard, his brow furrowed with thought. "How are those things related?"

"Tesla was using the Dark Melody and his own tech to resurrect some kind of ghoul army. We were barely able to escape, and our gnomish division sustained severe casualties. We managed to shut the Gate down, though."

"Has there been any activity from the area again?"

"Not after Tesla raised the dead and took them through. No. None."

Roy looked around the room. "Okay, so we got some good news and some bad news. Guess the next step is to figure out how and why the Dark One is using the Netherverse. I can check and see what intel I can pull up on that, but until then—"

Rasputina cleared her throat. "I might be able to help you there."

CHAPTER EIGHT

Abby and everyone else in the meeting watched the lich rise from her chair. Even as a hologram, Rasputina's power radiated from her—or perhaps it was the layer of insanity right below the surface.

The memory of Rasputina driving a knife into Abby's stomach flashed brightly in her mind. There was that as well.

She could almost feel the blade still cutting through her nanobots and her skin. She still felt the fear as well. Looking at the lich terrified her. She hadn't voiced her opinion about working on the same team as Rasputina to the rest of the DGA. She didn't think she was going to, either.

Grok had tortured Anabelle for nearly a week, and she was able to still work with the orc. If the elf could push her way through it, Abby told herself she could as well.

Maybe people could change.

That wasn't the matter at hand. The real question was how powerful a tool the lich could be. From everything Abby had seen, the DGA had just been handed a nuclear cache to use against the Dark One. Just the fact that Rasputina knew things about the Netherverse was already giving the DGA more resources.

The lich didn't bother to see if anyone was looking at her. She probably didn't care. "The Netherverse is the nexus of all realities."

Anabelle was geared into what the lich was saying. "What do you mean, all realities?"

"You all know about the Nine Realms and how they exist, folded on top of each other. That's why inter-realm travel works. There is hardly any space you need to pass through. It's like climbing a staircase. You're always in the same house, more or less."

"Then why say 'other realities?'"

"Because you forget that just because your house is nine stories, there are other homes on the block. Those are the other realities."

Even though Abby was terrified of Rasputina, it had no bearing on her curiosity. She'd read a little bit about the theories of alternate dimensions and realities from studying the mission briefings of Team Boundless, a Dragonrider squad that had allegedly met a psychic being named Vardis from another reality.

Vardis had claimed to come from the same dimension as the Dark One. Further, he'd said he had a weapon that could have destroyed the Dark One. The plan had fallen through due to the betrayal of Alex Bound and her squad, who were responsible for destroying the weapon. Alex had thought to use it for herself, to destroy the Dark One and rule Middang3ard instead.

Abby couldn't help but ask a question. "So, you're saying that there are multiple versions of us out there?"

Rasputina shook her head. "It's not that simple. There are infinite realities. The complexities of infinity are much more than you can understand, even with your improved intelligence. The only one in the room other than me who can probably fathom such a thing is Cire, now that he's finally been brought into his role as a true shaman."

She turned to face him. "You must have seen some interesting things, yes?"

Cire did not acknowledge Rasputina's words, so she continued, "For every action that has taken place in the entire history of existence, there were a nearly infinite number of variations. Some matter more than others. A leaf hitting the ground a centimeter from where it landed in another universe hardly causes any consequence. Whether you cross a street at a certain time does."

Rasputina waved her hand and a green version of Abby appeared in the room. "This is our Abby. Every decision she has ever made spawns another Abby. *Every* decision."

Billions of Abbys appeared in the room, so close together you could hardly see their faces. "Some of these Abbys are similar to ours. Others bear only the slightest resemblance. Quantum physics is a little more complicated than there being a good Abby and an evil Abby."

Terra raised her hand as if she were in class and cleared her throat. "Excuse me, but I just wanted to double-check. Is there a possibility that there is an evil Terra?"

Rasputina snapped her fingers and all the Abbys disappeared. "Yes, there is a high probability. Or *you* could be the evil Terra in a couple of years. Who knows?"

Terra mimicked an explosion with her hand. "Mind. Blown."

Rasputina continued. "The only thing the vast majority of realities have in common is death. Nearly everyone and thing dies at some point, and that is what connects us all. The Netherverse is, in essence, the afterlife."

Roy ran his hands through his hair and groaned. "How? Every race has their own idea about the afterlife. How many different versions of the afterlife are there if there are infinite realities?"

"That is the interesting part about the Netherverse. It's composed of the decaying bodies of the Elder Gods, bodies dead but still dreaming. Every soul in the Netherverse is affected by the dreams of the Elder Ones, who contort themselves based on the memories of the souls. Everyone gets their own personal afterlife, informed by what they believed their afterlife would be when they died."

Abby's HUD went off. She'd received a message from Terra, which copied Anabelle. **I feel like I should have smoked a shit-ton of weed for this conversation.**

Abby stifled her giggle as she texted back, **Who would have thought we'd get a metaphysics lesson from the lich?**

Anabelle didn't seem to have time for joking. "And how do you know all of this?"

Rasputina's skin reverted to that of the deathly husk that was the lich. "I am neither dead nor alive. I've slipped between the planes for years, sometimes living my time among the dead, others trying to remember what it meant to be alive. I've seen it with my own eyes."

Her skin returned to normal. "That is how the Dark One plans on invading, by using the Netherverse as a Gate to the different realms and possible realities. Depends on the level of his power and ambition, but he can easily access the nine realms through the Netherverse."

Roy skimmed through his notebook. "What about this Tesla? Why the hell does the Dark One have a super-powered nerd inventor?"

"We think we have that one figured out," Abby sheepishly muttered.

Abby pulled up a holograph of a limited edition run of *S.H.I.E.L.D.* On the cover was a man who looked suspiciously like the one she had recorded trying to kill her.

Roy groaned as he let his head sag backward, his irritation mounting. "Are you telling me that the Dark One is using villains from comic books in alternate realities?"

Rasputina shook her head. "Actually, that's not how all this works. That would have to be a form of magical creation. It's just a very eerie coincidence. Maybe the Dark One gets his ideas from human media. Who knows?"

Abby retreated to her bed.

Roy jumped to his feet and began pacing as he scratched his beard, digging deep as if he were trying to find his chin. "Okay, great. I got a lot of information but no clear plans. What are we doing about this?"

Anabelle shook her head. "If no one else is going to talk about the elephant in the room, I'll bring it up. We are now working with three former agents of the Dark One. Persephone, I'm not even slightly worried about, but the other two? Are you guys kidding me? This isn't one of Abby's ridiculous animes. People don't suddenly become good."

Abby clasped her hands tightly together and pressed them against her knees. "They aren't ridiculous."

Terra slapped her thigh. "Yeah, I resent that statement. We just finished the *Perfect Cell* arc, and it was fucking amazing."

Roy pinched the bridge of his nose. "Are you three seriously arguing about anime right now? That's it, no more missions with the Mundanes. Those MERCs are rubbing off on you."

Anabelle zeroed in on Roy, her eyes narrowing. "Anime aside, I have a point. How the hell are we supposed to trust those two?"

Roy turned to Grok. "She's right. What do you have to say about that?"

The orc straightened up. "Sarah cut a deal with the council. Ever since I joined the Dark One, I've had a price on my head. They've been waiting to kill me, and they would have if it hadn't been for Sarah. One of the conditions is if I back out of my side of the bargain, the council will unleash the horde on me. Cire probably heard about that one."

He nodded slowly. "It is true. The council has the means to stop her if she does choose to go rogue."

Roy turned around and pointed at Rasputina. "What's your convenient reason for why we should recreate the first season of *Power Rangers*?"

Terra's HUD went off, and she looked down at the message she'd just received from Abby. **Now who's making too many nerdy references?**"

The HUD pinged again. This time it was from Anabelle. **Will you two stop fucking around and pay attention?**

Across the room, Rasputina looked to be deep in thought, her brows knitted tightly together. Finally, she answered, "There isn't any reason for you to believe me. All I can tell you is that I'm in control of my body."

Anabelle wasn't backing down. She stepped closer to the lich. "Are you? Because what I saw back in that cavern was someone who is mentally deranged trying to pretend they are sane. I'm not saying you have an elaborate plan to trick us, but there is no part of me that assumes you are even slightly in control."

"How do you propose to settle this? Do I have to take a psyche evaluation? Makes me wonder if you would pass."

"Fuck off. I might have anger issues, but I'm not an arrogant, psychotic, undead bitch."

Rasputina's eyes flashed bright green as she clenched her fist. "I'm. Not. Crazy." She bit the corner of her lip as she picked her cuticles. "And I *am* in control."

"What do you get out of this? Why the hell would you help us?"

Rasputina relaxed. "I remembered why I became this way. To defeat Death, the Dark One. That in and of itself would be reason enough, but I-I was destined to choose this. There was a higher purpose for my descent into this filth of an existence. I was meant to destroy the Dark One."

Anabelle raised her hands in defeat. "Does no one else hear her delusions of grandeur? Next thing we know, you'll be telling us that Jesus Christ with the Three Goddesses and Hephaestus personally choose you for this holy mission. Even your reasoning sounds like it needs to be medicated."

Rasputina sat back down, hanging her head. "There has to be a reason I did this to myself. I know it. They know it. I know it." She continued to repeat this to herself.

Anabelle walked away from the lich. "I rest my case."

They sat there in silence as Roy deliberated. After what felt like an eternity of listening to Rasputina muttering softly to herself and occasionally crying, he made his decision. "I once fought with a guy who thought he was the reincarnation of King Arthur. One of the best men I served with. We're not pulling her from the mission until she proves she's not fit for combat. That being said, Rasputina, you're meeting with our psychology and health department tomorrow, and you will be for the rest of your time here."

She wiped the tears from her face and sniffled. "Understood."

Roy spun so that everyone in the conference could see him. "Now, what I've just heard is that we have a potential army of undead to deal with. We have a horde that, no offense, pales compared to an infinite fucking number of souls. We don't know if we can keep the Gates closed. Oh, and we have a fucking soul jar, and the DGA suddenly understand nerd culture now."

Abby raised her hand slowly. "Uh, we've always understood."

"That is not the point."

Rasputina, her eyes having become lucid again, pulled her hood up. "There is a way to stop the Gates. Ask the drow the one thing she fears more than anything, the fear that sits deep in her chest. If she were even to hear it spoken aloud, it would frighten her."

Persephone looked around, obviously uncomfortable with being brought into the conversation. "What are you talking about?"

Abby grabbed the drow's hand and squeezed.

Rasputina smiled cruelly, a bit of the old lich shining through. "Tell them what that Dark Melody has nightmares about."

Persephone took a deep breath and sighed. "The Dark Melody has nightmares about ether flame. It would scorch it to nothing. Completely sever its ties to me."

Roy collapsed into his chair. "Great. The one kind of dragon I don't have access to. Couldn't be an ice dragon. God forbid a red dragon. Had to be an ether dragon. Well, I guess until we can figure this out, the priority mission is on hold. Until then, each of you keeps up with your current assignments. Good chat, team. Glad you all developed a sense of humor. Roy out."

He sizzled out of existence, quickly followed by Grok and Rasputina.

Terra smiled broadly and waved at Abby and Anabelle. "Hey, guys! I missed you!"

Anabelle stretched. "Terra, I saw you earlier this week. How did you manage to do that to your face?"

Terra smiled even wider. "Oh, you like my new scars? Pretty sick, right?"

"Every day, you are more like an orc."

Abby chirped, "We think you look cool. And we miss you guys too."

Cire cast a glance over his shoulder and whispered something to

Terra, who leaned closer to get a better view of the rest of the DGA. "Okay, I gotta run guys. Apparently, there's pressing orcish business I must attend to. Orcs out!"

Terra and Cire disappeared, leaving Anabelle, Persephone, and Abby. "You been staying safe?" Anabelle asked.

Abby nodded, feeling a little childish for having to even answer the question. "Yeah, how about you?"

"About as safe as risking your life every day can be. Sorry I can't stay and chat, Abby. The work is never over. Hopefully I'll be able to see you soon. Goddess, I'm so tired of being over all nine of the realms every week. I feel like getting killed is the only way I'll be able to take a break. Anyway, I'll catch you two around."

"See you later, Belle," Abby said.

From Persephone. "Stay safe."

Abby released Persephone's hand, her eyes darting back and forth as she thought.

The drow got up and knelt in front of Abby, looking her in the eye. "I know that look. What's going on?"

Abby smiled coyly. "We think we know where to find an ether dragon."

CHAPTER NINE

In Middang3ard, far from the Red Lion, there were the remnants of a battle. The dead lay in piles—mostly humans, some dwarves and elves. Their blood stained the soil, seeping into the ground as their bodies slowly decayed. It was impossible to tell how long they had been there. The army that had decimated had moved on, but the wind still smelled of iron and rotting flesh.

Alex Bound surveyed the battlefield. She was the leader of Boundless, a squad of the dragonriders. Her magical eyes, which she shared with her dragon Chine, were searching for clues as to where the army had gone. The ground should have been full of them. This would have been too much to cover up by traditional means.

Tracking wasn't Alex's strong suit. She had other talents. She was mostly killing time until Gill, a quiet, analytical drow with little time for humor or fun, returned with his updates.

Jollies, a pixie who rode a miniature electric dragon named Amber, zipped by, quickly informing Alex about what she had seen while scouting ahead. There were no clues as to where the butchers had gone.

Far from the battlefield, Jim, Alex's second in command, scanned the horizon. Alex had positioned him to watch for any soldiers of

Middang3ard. She knew the realm was full of MERCs, but generally, they didn't bother her or her riders. There wasn't an official bounty on Boundless' head. Well, that and they were usually deterred after seeing Jim in his dragon mech.

The mech was nearly the size of a red dragon and outfitted with more weaponry than most outposts in Middang3ard had.

The realm was full of tales of the Steel and Red Death. Alex knew Jim was proud to be half of that duo.

The other half was Brath, who was patrolling the sky on Furi, his red dragon, the only creature Alex had ever met that had a shorter temper than his rider.

Alex stood among the dead. She still couldn't believe the destruction before her. She and the dragonriders had been tracking this army for nearly two weeks. They had first heard of them up north after a village had gone missing. Boundless had been on the trail ever since.

But the trail was drying up. If it hadn't gone cold already, it soon would.

The grass rippled from the wings of a dragon. Timber, Gill's earth dragon, landed in front of Alex. Gill stood atop him, held in place by his dragon anchor, a tool on his wrist that connected him telepathically to his dragon and kept him from falling off during flight while offering him the ability to walk around on top of his dragon.

Alex rose when she saw Gill even though she wanted to stay seated. She was tired. She hoped no one else could tell.

Gill, on the other hand, didn't seem to care about looking tired. He came over to Alex's side and collapsed onto the grass. "Couldn't find anything. Not even a trace."

Alex sat back down and hung her head in between her knees. "Damn it. They shouldn't have had time for all of this, not with their speed or their size. It's like they have someone working just to keep them from getting caught."

"You're not ready to give up yet, are you?"

Alex wearily looked at Gill. She could see that his face was ragged. It only made sense. Boundless had been on the move for longer than Alex could remember. Luckily, they had been trained to survive in the harshest terrains under pressure from all sides. This part of Middang3ard was downright cozy compared to their training ground.

Gill sighed and shook his head, looking as if *he* were ready to quit. "Why are we even doing this? Every day we're out here is another day we're unnecessarily risking our lives."

Alex grabbed the drow's arm and squeezed hard, hoping it was reassuring. "You know why we're out here. Just because the Corps fucked us, it doesn't mean we're backing down from why we signed up. We're still at war with the Dark One, even if the Corps is at war with us."

Gill looked like he remembered something. "You're right. I'm just tired. And frustrated. I never thought I'd get tired of playing hero from the shadows. Guess I didn't sign up for thankless tasks."

"Or maybe you just don't like being branded a traitor."

Alex hadn't wanted to say it out loud, but it was better than pretending that wasn't the case. It seemed like everyone in the nine realms believed Boundless had forsaken their oaths and followed Alex, who had become mad with the desire for power when the Dark One offered it to her.

The problem was that the whole narrative was a lie. Worse than a lie, it was a false memory psychically implanted throughout the realms by Vardis, the most powerful psychic she had ever met.

Alex would have been alone if it hadn't been for Chine, who had managed to shield the rest of Boundless from the psychic attack. She was glad since there was no way she would have been able to handle this on her own. The knowledge that the rest of the realm thought she was a power-hungry traitor hurt more than anything else, but she knew it wasn't their fault.

That didn't take away the sting.

Luckily, Myrddin's forces were spread thin. There weren't enough resources to spare, and there was no justification for chasing after Boundless if they weren't causing trouble.

Which they weren't. Not for Myrddin, at least.

Boundless had been focusing on dismantling every small-scale operation of the Dark One's they could find. They'd gone from raids to hunting down marauding bands of the Dark One's forces. Even if they didn't have Myrddin's approval, they were still making Middang3ard safer for all the free races.

Alex looked at the sun. It was nearly two. "All right, team, let's get some food in us. Who is on watch duty for this meal?"

Jim's voice came through the comm. "I have been in this thing for nearly five hours now. Unless you want me to permanently fuse with it, I suggest letting me get some fresh air."

Brath's caustic, high-pitched voice answered, "That might be an improvement. You'd look better, and fly better too."

"I swear to God, Brath, do not test me right now. First off, I'd fly circles around you. Secondly, I'd look better doing it."

Brath laughed as Furi meandered over the sky. "All right, all right. I'll take the watch. I don't want Jim to get his jeans in a bunch. Or is it underwear? I never understand human expressions. So many of them have to do with clothing."

Jim's mech took off, bounding from its position toward Alex, where the rest of the riders were converging.

Alex had already busted out the goods, the saddle of a lamb Furi had killed earlier in the week that they had butchered and smoked overnight.

A few months ago, Alex could never have imagined herself looking forward to eating lunch surrounded by the bodies of the innocent, but there was a lot in her life now she couldn't have imagined before it happened.

The rest of the riders looked just as tired as Alex felt. It wasn't the lack of sleep or the tracking. They were being worn down by not knowing what was coming next, and Alex couldn't offer them any encouragement.

Luckily, Jollies was good at keeping things lighthearted. She zipped around, going on about what her family would have thought about her eating so much smoked mutton. Apparently, it would have been deeply unsettling.

Brath waved his hand to shoo the pixie away, a habit that Alex knew she detested. "My aunt and uncle would have thought I was living the life. We used to have to jump through so many hoops to get meat, but it was always worth it. Stuff isn't easy to come across when you're poor."

Gill tossed Brath another piece of mutton. "You ever think you'd be doing your best eating on the run?"

Brath thought about it for a second. "Actually, I kind of did. Wouldn't say it was a goal, but yeah, I saw this one coming."

Jim broke into the conversation. "Hey, guys, we got something coming at us fast, and you're not going to like this. It's Roy."

Alex was already on her feet. "How far?"

"Can't tell. He's booking it. Whatever upgrades he added to his mech are intense. I don't think we'll be able to lose him. If he's already going this fast..."

Something black and metallic shot by overhead fast enough to generate a sonic boom. Alex watched as it came back around. "Boundless, saddle up. Get ready for anything."

Jollies flew over to Alex and landed on her shoulder. "Are you really thinking about fighting Roy?"

"I'm prepared to if need be."

Alex reached out to her ether dragon, a young male named Chine, who was off hunting. "Chine, get back over here. Roy's coming."

Chine, whose telepathy was extraordinary no matter how far away he was, answered, "I'm on my way."

Then she commed Jim. "Get back here now."

Jollies, Brath, and Gill were all on top of their dragons, weapons drawn.

Jim hit his thrusters and rocketed toward Boundless. He stopped right in front of Alex. "So, it's finally time?"

Alex shrugged as she watched the horizon. "I don't know. Even Roy isn't arrogant enough to come alone. Not to capture us. Definitely not to kill us."

"Something was with him. It was just moving a lot faster than he was."

"One extra person? What difference is that going to make?"

There was another loud boom.

A figure covered in sleek black armor that looked to be made from living metal floated before the dragonriders.

The figure's mask rolled back as if it were water, and Abby stared Alex in the eye. "Alex? Do you remember us?"

Alex recognized the girl. They had met in the arena after Myrddin had conscripted the dragonriders for a rescue mission. Afterward, the two had corresponded, mostly sharing information about their tech upgrades, and occasionally venting to each other about the pressure of being a child fighting in such an insane war.

"Abby? What are you doing here?"

"We came with Roy. We need to—"

Roy's mech landed with the sound of gears whirring, machinery working madly in tandem with the will of its rider. "Alex Bound, you are hereby under arrest. Your dragon will be confiscated, and you are stripped of your—"

Alex stretched out her arm and brought it down in a slash, pulling her scythe from the ether while the ground around her flexed from her telekinetic powers.

Roy's cockpit opened, and he poked his head out of the mech. "I didn't want to do this, Alex. I was just going to let you guys run as long as you stayed out of trouble, but we need Chine. That means it's time for you to come in."

Chine shot a plume of black ether fire into the sky.

Alex jumped onto her dragon's back. "You have to listen to me, Roy. I didn't kill Vardis. I'm innocent. He—"

"I'm not here to debate with you, Alex. I'm taking Chine and letting you go, or I'm taking you in."

Jim's mech moved forward as the cockpit opened, allowing him to look out. "No one is taking Alex. It would be a good idea for you to leave."

"If any of you stand with Alex, you stand with the Dark One. Do you understand?"

Chine took a step toward Roy. *If you'd even take a moment to see what we're doing on Middang3ard, you'd see that all we've done is attack the*

Dark One's forces. If we were working for him, why would we be killing our own troops?

Alex saw something flicker in Roy's face. His lip twitched, and his expression suddenly froze as if he were trying to say something but couldn't. Then it returned to normal. "I'm not here to argue. It was hard for me to believe, but what you did was unforgivable. Now, what is your decision?"

Jim's mech fired a plasma dart at Roy, the dart barely missing the rider's head. "Don't worry about this one, Alex.

Roy slipped back into the mech, broadcasting through his speakers. "You've been AWOL for a few months, and now you think you got what it takes to stop me?"

Jim's mech tackled Roy's, steel connecting with steel as Roy swiveled, trying to get the upper hand and finally tossing Jim off. He fired his thrusters and took off, Jim following close behind.

Alex looked down at Abby. "What were you planning on doing?"

Abby's armor disappeared, replaced by an official DGA uniform. "I wanted to talk. Your message after you ran away? I read it. You said you didn't do it. We believe you. The night Vardis was reported dead, there was a massive spike in telepathic frequencies. They came from his death place and stretched all through the realms."

The girl held her hands in the air, showing she wasn't going to fight. "We weren't affected. The augmentations we've made to our brain prevented it. We don't have any of the memories that they do, so we figured talking was a good idea."

Alex pointed at Roy and Jim, who were circling each other in the sky. "What about them?"

"Roy has his way of solving problems, and we have ours. Let's sit."

Alex jumped off Chine, then grabbed a piece of smoked sheep meat and tossed it to Abby. "You have no idea how happy I am to hear that."

CHAPTER TEN

Alex and Abby talked while Jim and Roy battled above. The two girls sat across from each other, filling the other in on the details of what had been happening.

There was a lot Alex wasn't aware of. She hadn't received any communication since leaving the Wasps' Nest, the headquarters of the dragonriders.

Abby was more than happy to exchange information with Alex, even going so far as to offer to upgrade Alex's cybernetic arm.

From what Abby said, it didn't seem like the war with the Dark One had gotten any better. That weighed heavily on Alex. She had hoped her personal confrontations with the Dark One had made a difference. It was disheartening to hear that nothing she had done so far mattered.

When Alex expressed those thoughts to Abby, the young girl pulled back her hair while clicking her tongue. "You shouldn't say that. Everything we do matters, even if it's just prolonging the lives of everyone around us. We might not have ended this war, but we are keeping people from dying. That is worth our efforts."

"You think that Chine can destroy those Gates?"

Abby pulled out a glass vial. It was full of the Dark Melody. Upon being introduced to the light, it grew hard, then slammed itself against the glass, trying to break it. "This is what the Netherverse is composed of, and the Dark Gates as well, more or less. Would you mind?" Abby gestured toward Chine with the vial.

Alex chuckled. "Sure, come on."

She rose and walked over to the dragon, who was curled in a ball, dozing quietly as smoke flowed from his nostrils. She tapped him on the head, causing him to open one of his eyes.

After explaining the conversation, Alex asked Chine to supply a little ether fire. She produced a torch and Chine breathed flame, setting it afire with his ether breath. "Now what?" she asked.

Abby opened the vial and held it in front of Chine.

The Dark Melody reared up, trying to escape.

"Now!" Abby shouted.

Alex held the flame to the top of the vial. There was a screeching sound like air rushing out of a balloon.

From proximity to the fire, the Dark Melody crystalized and then turned to dust, which broke apart even further until there was nothing there.

Abby held the glass up to get a better look. "Looks like that'll do the trick. What do you say?"

"I want to help, but I don't want to get locked up for something I didn't do. And I'm tired of being on the run."

Roy's mech crashed to the ground, skidding across the earth and tearing it apart as Jim's mech slammed into it, claws tightly wrapped around his opponent's neck. Neither of them was using their weapons. This was more a contest of skill than an outright battle. It was hard to tell who was winning.

Roy's mech managed to get away and took off, Jim following once more.

Abby watched Roy fly away. "We obviously don't think you should be taken in, and we're pretty sure we can convince Roy of that. The mission you're on now—you said you've been tracking a marauding army of the Dark One, right?"

Alex nodded, pointing in the direction she believed the orcs had gone, not that there was a chance they were going to find them now. Whatever tracking could have been done was over now that Abby and Roy had distracted them enough that the trail was dead. "Yeah, that's what we were up to."

Abby followed Alex's finger. "We'll find the Dark One's forces together. Roy will be singing a different tune if he sees your squad dealing with the Dark One's forces. How's that sound?"

"If we could still find the trail. It's been cold for a while."

Thrusters formed on Abby's back as she floated into the air, her armor covering her body. "We'll take care of it. Excuse us, please." She blasted off in the direction Alex had pointed.

Gill walked over to his squad leader. "It would seem events have taken an interesting turn. Do you think she's telling the truth?"

Alex thought about it. There hadn't been any indication in their messages that Abby was not a trustworthy person, and unlike Roy, it didn't seem like she had come for a fight. "I think we can trust her. Besides, we can't get any more screwed then we are right now. What do you guys think?"

Jollies flittered up, her skin changing from pink to sky-blue. "She seems nice, and she's willing to help. At least we'll be able to free the prisoners."

Brath, who was still sitting on Furi, looked up from the knife he was sharpening. "Either way, if she's capable of tracking the orcs from this cold a trail, it's not going to be a problem for her to find us again. We should nip this in the bud before she brings an entire army with her next time."

Gill was staring at the sky, watching Jim and Roy fight. "Holding his own against Roy? Didn't know he'd gotten that good."

Alex clapped Gill on the back. "He's not the only one. You've all become even more amazing riders than before."

Above them, Roy and Jim were still going at it. Jim managed to flank Roy, wrapping his mech's arms around Roy's mech's throat. He hit his thrusters, driving Roy toward the ground.

Roy's mech crashed into the ground again. This time, Jim's plasma shoulder cannons were aimed at Roy's cockpit.

Jim opened his cockpit and poked his head out. "Don't make me do this, Roy."

Before he could answer, there was a sonic boom and Abby was in the midst of the group again. "Found them. I uploaded their coordinates to your anchors."

Alex walked over to Roy's mech and climbed on top of it. She kicked the cockpit. "Okay, here's the deal. I'm not going with you in your custody. Boundless will help you and the DGA under two conditions. One, we leave when we're done, and you leave us alone. Two, you help us take out this platoon we've been tracking and save their prisoners. We got a deal?"

Roy opened his cockpit and met Alex's eyes. "Fine. Let's go."

Jim released Roy, and they all took off toward the coordinates Abby had provided.

Alex thought it was interesting that Roy had shown up with just Abby. She knew he was aware of how many riders it would have taken to subdue team Boundless, yet he didn't bother bringing anyone other than the girl who believed Boundless was innocent.

It was almost like there was a part of Roy that was fighting the memories that had been placed in his mind, as if he was sabotaging them subconsciously. He hadn't even bothered trying to argue with Alex's conditions. Maybe that showed it was possible to break Vardis' spell eventually, but that would have to wait.

Abby led the way, occasionally comming the dragonriders to give them updates on the terrain they could expect.

The army had grown since the last time Alex had seen it. From what Abby had described, it seemed like they had been joined by another group of orcs, bolstering their numbers.

Suddenly, the girl stopped and pointed down below.

Alex took out a pair of binoculars and scanned the area.

There were about two hundred orcs, goblins, and trolls. There were also dozens of cages on wheels being pulled by wargs. The cages were full of humans.

Alex pulled up her anchor and spoke to the riders. "We want to hit them hard and hit them quick. We're outnumbered, but they're all stuck to the land. They'll probably be trying to pull us out of the sky with one of those anti-dragon sirens we've been seeing. First things first; I want those taken care of."

Abby scanned the area. "They have four of them. If you want, we can take care of them. We won't be affected by them."

"Sounds good to me. Jollies, I want you to take care of those prisoners. Jim, Gill, Brath, you guys torch the place. Create enough chaos that no one gives a rat's ass about Jollies. Roy, you feel comfortable taking orders from a traitor?"

Roy's voice came through the comm. "You're not making a good case for yourself, talking like that."

"If you're going to keep treating me like one, does it matter?"

Roy sighed. "What do you want me to do?"

Alex noticed that Roy sounded tired, not angry. "You're coming with me. We'll take out the big guys. There are at least a dozen trolls with spears and arrows. Can't have them firing at us. We'll take the heat and give everyone else room to do their jobs. Should be done in under half an hour."

Roy whistled, a sound Alex knew he only made when he approved of something. She was surprised to hear it. Seeing as how Roy cut it off, she thought he might have been surprised as well.

Alex drew her scythe. "Move out, team."

Abby's body vibrated with kinetic energy. She suddenly exploded downward, connecting with one of the anti-dragon sirens. The device exploded as orcs piled out of the tank supporting it. Abby leapt up and slammed her fist into the ground, sending the orcs flying. She blasted them with her hand cannons before turning to find the next siren and launching toward it.

Once Abby had destroyed the first two sirens, the boys moved in, their dragons breathing fire, ice, and plasma on everything that moved beneath them.

The orcs had been caught off-guard. They were running around, trying to put up a defense, but Boundless was too swift. Brath and Gill moved with seamless efficiency, Brath using Furi's size and power to put pressure on the orcs who were armed as Gill flanked them, freezing the ones who were trying to flee.

Gill came up behind the frozen orcs and blasted them with his plasma cannon as Abby zoomed past behind him, heading toward the next dragon siren.

A handful of orcs dragged a hulking plasma cannon out of one of the tanks near the prisoners. They were preparing to fire when Alex leapt off Chine, landed on top of the cannon, and sliced through the barrel with her scythe. She spun, decapitating one of the orcs behind her before drawing her plasma pistol with her free hand and nailing the two remaining orcs with headshots. Then she was back on Chine, scouring the battlefield for trolls.

They weren't hard to spot. The trolls were mounting their counterattack, many of them heaving cannons the size of their bodies and a few with railguns.

Alex and Chine raced toward the trolls, Roy coming up behind her. "Jollies, how are you doing with those prisoners?"

Jollies voice crackled over the comm as Chine launched an ether fireball at the trolls, who broke formation and scattered but held their ground. "Nearly halfway done. I'll get them out of here and join up with you afterwards."

One of the trolls fired its railgun and the projectile nearly impaled Chine through the chest, only missing because he barrel-rolled and Alex tossed up a telekinetic shield that sent the projectile off-course.

Chine rolled back around as Alex detached herself from the anchor, falling into the group of trolls. She pushed them back with a telekinetic blast, turned and cut through the troll who had fired, and then sliced through the railgun.

A troll reached out to grab Abby and Roy's mech slammed into it, opening fire once it hit the ground. The mech's machine guns whirred as Roy demonstrated why he was considered the best shot in the Riders Corps.

Chine landed behind Alex, who leapt onto his back. The dragon fired his gravity disrupters, causing the trolls to float into the air as gravity ceased to affect them.

Alex glanced over her shoulder at the rest of the fight. "Report!"

Brath shouted, "We got them on the run. We just gotta clean this up."

Jollies was next. "All prisoners are safe. Not a single casualty."

Alex plunged her dragon anchor into the port on Chine's back. "All right, let's wrap this up."

Her anchor absorbed Chine's draconic fluid, blood fused with magic and energy from the augments on his body.

Alex screamed with rage as the anchor pumped Chine's blood into her veins. She burst into flames and darted forward with increased speed, slashing through the remaining trolls, leaving flames from where her feet had touched or her blade had cut.

The flames flicked out, and the trolls lay dead.

Alex hit her comm. "Everyone, check the bodies. I don't want any survivors."

Abby flew over to Alex and landed next to her. "No prisoners?"

Alex shook her head. "We don't have that luxury. Where would we transport them too? No, it's better to just make sure it ends here." Then she turned to Roy. "Like I said, you help us, we'll help you. Thanks for the hand."

Roy surveyed the damage Boundless had managed to do in less than twenty minutes. "Doesn't look like you needed it."

Alex pointed in the direction of the prisoners. "Actually, this is what I need your help with. I can't get within twenty feet of a MERC camp. Can you make sure these people get to safety?"

Roy's face twitched again. He was fighting something deep within himself. Unfortunately, he wasn't winning. Yet. "Sure, but don't think that means I trust you. I'll be watching your ass. All of you. If you so much as think of pulling any shit, I'll drop you in a second."

Alex nodded solemnly as Roy took off in the direction of the prisoners.

Abby extended her hand to Alex. "Sorry it's not under better conditions, but we're glad to have you on board."

She shook the girl's hand. "Same here. And now that I've got you here, we need to go over some of those emails you sent me about dragon blood transfers because I didn't understand a single word."

Abby laughed as she and Alex walked over to the rest of the dragonriders.

Alex hadn't lied. She was glad this was happening. Boundless had been on the run for too long. It was about time they got something like a break.

CHAPTER ELEVEN

Gnomes did not do hospitals. It would have been impossible to find one on the entire gnomish world. Instead, gnomes relied on a deep magic that many of the races throughout the nine realms had forgotten. There was no race as in touch with the natural world around them as gnomes were. It didn't matter if they were the fair folk or the deep gnomes. They spoke to the earth and it answered. Always.

Kravis was lucky to have been wounded on a planet full of healers. After the disaster that had taken place at the gate and the decimation of the gnomish soldiers and scientists, he had been rushed to the closest settlement. Sarah had to leave him there. It had hurt to see him that badly wounded, but she knew her heartbreak wasn't going to help anyone.

Now she was finally back. There was still work to be done, though. Instead of going straight to Kravis, she found the camp leader. She needed a report on the gnome resistance camps across the planet. The defeat at the Gate had been a shock and an unexpected blow. Gnomish soldiers were a precious resource. Much of the gnome population had been enslaved and worked to death by the Dark One.

Those who remained were the last of the gnomes. There were

hardly any off-world compared to the rest of the races. If an elf army had been hit as hard as the gnomes, the elves would have survived, as would humans or dwarves. Gnomes were in the same position as the orcs. They were fighting for their race's very survival.

Sarah met the gnomish leader in his camp, where he offered her a cup of tea that tasted like dirt and honey. She winced as she drank it. Gnomish drinks still didn't sit well with her, but she was polite and drank her tea as the leader went on about the state of the other camps.

Gnomes from across the realms were returning. There were many who were not serving on military duty. They were the most vital gnomes to come back.

Kravis had explained the reason to Sarah many times. Raising children was never high on the list of priorities with gnomes. Their planet was small and had scant resources, one of the reasons half of the gnome population had evolved to live underground. That, coupled with their extraordinarily long lives, caused gnomes to concentrate on things other than reproducing.

But now, gnomes had put a high priority on increasing their population. They were assigning their best scientists to a project to increase fertility rates among civilian men and women.

As the gnomish leader detailed these new plans, Sarah raised her hand. "Wait, are you saying you're making breeding camps?"

The gnomish leader curled his lip in disgust. "No, we aren't making camps. You make it sound so sterile. Think of it more as a resort. There are gnomes who would want nothing more than to stay on a tropical island and fuck like there was no war going on."

Sarah thought about the plan. That *would* be how they would go about this. They weren't a serious race by any means. Practical jokes were almost considered greetings. A grouchy gnome like Kravis came along once every hundred years, and the rest of the community loved him for it. It only made sense that when they were faced with extinction, their solution would be an island orgy. But Sarah saw one glaring problem with the plan.

"You know, it's still going to be some time before your kids become adults. A lot could happen before then. You could end up with a lot of parents who have to leave their children for war."

The leader refilled his cup with tea and offered Sarah another one, which she took as she steeled herself against its terrible flavor. "We've started preparing for that. The rest of the races would probably not approve. Definitely not Myrddin. I am telling you in secret since you've earned more than our trust, Sarah."

"You don't have to tell me anything you think would compromise you."

"It won't. We've made up our minds. Over the years, we've developed tech to allow us to grow our children outside the womb once they've entered the fetal stage. We've been building the structures underground since the war began."

Sarah had no moral feelings concerning the subject. Gnomes were going to be extinct if something drastic wasn't done. What was the difference between growing in a womb or a tube? "I'm assuming you can artificially age them as well?"

"Yes, but for that, we want to be certain. A hundred percent. If you could get Abby or Creon to check our work, it would be a huge favor to us."

Sarah pulled out her holoscreen and jotted down a couple of notes. "If you send me your information, I'll pass it along to them and make sure it gets looked at. For what it's worth, I think it's a great idea. Practical."

"Hopefully we won't have to keep orgy island open for too long, or at least make it more of a vacation spot. Ease out of military-mandated repopulation. Something to look forward to."

Sarah thought there were much worse things. A child didn't seem that bad, especially if you didn't have to endure nine months of bloating and sickness. She didn't even want to think about the birthing part. She was always confused by the sadness those thoughts brought on.

"If there isn't anything else, do you think I could see Kravis?" she asked.

The leader stood and headed toward his tent's exit. "Of course.

He's been stabilized. Wounds are healing, but he's retreated in the old fashion. Very typical."

The two turned a corner in the camp and arrived at Kravis' tent. The soldiers had taken the liberty of decorating it, giving the tent the feeling that Kravis was sleeping, not comatose.

Sarah knelt beside him, resting her knees on a throw pillow she'd gotten him for his birthday. "What do you mean by typical? I've never heard of this."

"It's an evolutionary response. If our bodies experience too much trauma, we enter a coma."

"He's healed, though. Shouldn't he be waking up?"

"Sometimes the trauma is emotional, or merely something the gnome wishes to avoid. I've personally known gnomes who slept for fifty years to avoid a conflict."

Sarah stared down at Kravis, who looked to be sleeping peacefully. "Avoiding a conflict, you say?"

She smiled at the leader. "Thank you. I'll make sure your work gets looked at as soon as possible. And thank you for taking care of Kravis."

The leader bowed slightly. "Whatever we can do to help. Farewell."

He left Sarah alone with Kravis.

Sarah had never seen him look so comfortable. She almost didn't want to disturb him. Almost.

She pressed her finger to his temple and calmed her breathing, concentrating on her chakra gates, envisioning them cracking open and her energy exploding outward. She was focusing on her crown chakra.

Suddenly, she felt it open, her mental powers expanding rapidly. She drew them in and focused them to a blade's precision. She aimed that blade at Kravis' head.

The mental knife shot into his mind and the tent disappeared. Sarah was sitting in a cave with Kravis. The walls were sleek with water, the cave filled with the sound of water dripping on the floor.

Sarah leaned over Kravis, staring at him. He was breathing.

She continued to stare, waiting for Kravis to betray himself.

The red-headed gnome slightly opened his right eye.

Sarah slapped her knee. "Gotcha! I knew it! I fucking knew it! Get up, you big faker."

Kravis grumbled as he sat up. "Are you serious, Sarah? I can't even get any peace and quiet in my own mind?"

Sarah blushed, feeling like she was being ridiculous and invasive. "I was just worried about you."

"Oh, yeah, you were? What exactly were you worried about?"

"Someone told me about your gnomish habit of going into a coma. He said there were a couple of reasons. One, that you're too hurt, but it looks like you're healing all right. The second would be because of trauma."

Kravis sighed as he leaned his head back and let water drip on his forehead. "Or the other reason is to avoid a conflict. Pretty sure you heard that one too. That's probably the number one reason for conveniently slipping into a coma just because of a light stabbing."

"It's the marriage thing, isn't it?"

He tried to avoid her eyes. "You know, I didn't think there was time to talk about this. Not *really* talk about it, but what better time than when I'm trapped in my mind, right?"

"Wait, did you say trapped?"

"Yeah. It's not like I thought, I'd like to be in a coma right now. It just kinda happened. You could call it extreme avoidance. Some gnomes are better at it than others. I once spent six months in a coma because I couldn't answer a friend's question about whether their cooking was any good."

Sarah covered her mouth, trying to keep herself from laughing at Kravis, who was obviously attempting to be serious. "Well, maybe we should talk now."

Kravis stretched and touched his toes. Then he stretched and cracked his knuckles. After that, he twisted his waist back and forth as he gave a high-pitched whine. "Yeah, I guess you should go first, seeing as how you proposed."

"Or maybe you should. It seemed like it freaked you out a lot."

Kravis took a deep breath. "Marriage is a huge thing, and there's this war going on. Why commit to something that might not even happen? It seems like such a huge thing to hope for, and hope makes people stupid."

Usually that was Sarah's line, but seeing Kravis full of despair made her want to be the positive one. "Hope also can be the thing that keeps you going. I know you want kids, too. That's something we both hope for, even if we never talked about it."

"Talking about something I know will probably not happen doesn't sound appealing. You know how gnomes feel about family."

Sarah did know. Even if gnomes didn't think about marriage or kids often, once it happened, it happened in a big way. Most gnomish families had at least fifteen children, and that was on the small side. Sarah didn't want to be pregnant for the rest of her life.

"One or two wouldn't be too bad," Sarah offered. "I'd even be willing to try for three, but you wouldn't get to name any of them."

Kravis laughed, but there was a hint of sadness to it. "You know that would be terrible for them. Even half-gnomes need a big family. Otherwise, they get depressed and have developmental issues. Then before you know it, we'll have three serial killers on our hands. Most people already label us sociopaths, if not downright psychotic. Think of the children!"

Thinking about a roaming pack of half-human, half-gnome toddler serial killers made Sarah burst out laughing.

Kravis wasn't through. "And then there's the whole long life thing. All your kids would outlive you, and then they'd spend a lot of their time without a mother."

Sarah swallowed hard. She'd already thought that through. She'd been thinking about it for a while. "Well, there are options."

Kravis stared at Sarah, confused. "Unless you're planning on trying to become a lich, I don't see how we get around the whole mortality thing."

"I have friends who have sort of an open family situation. Elves and humans end up doing something like that a lot."

Kravis' face went white. "Uh, okay. Wasn't prepared for the

conversation to go this way. I'm going to need a little bit of time to think about it."

Sarah rested her hand on Kravis'. "There's no rush. I'm just saying we have options to think about and work through all this. It'll take time, but...hey, you okay?"

Kravis, who was still white, pointed behind Sarah, who instinctively drew her daggers and stood.

Myrddin was standing behind her. "Good to see you two again."

Sarah sheathed her daggers. "First off, how fucking long were you back there? Then explain to me what you're doing here?"

"The entire time. You both handled that conversation with a grace I don't often see from people your age."

Kravis's white face turned tomato-red as he hid his face.

The wizard continued, "And to answer your second question, I've been trying to get in touch with you both for some time. It's easier to enter through dreams, but catching you two while you're sleeping is a nightmare, no pun intended."

"Are you just here to be creeping on us?"

"No. I came to speak to you about Anabelle, Grok, Terra, and the Path of the Lost."

Sarah groaned. She couldn't even get a moment alone with her boyfriend while he was in a coma without being interrupted.

Kravis reached out and pinched Sarah, causing her to glare at him. Her face softened once she saw his smile. "Before things got weird, I was going to tell you the answer is yes. It still is yes, even though things are very weird now."

Sarah's heart fluttered for a moment. That was all she had time for. Myrddin was impatiently tapping his foot, waiting for her attention, so Sarah pushed down her feelings. It was time to get back to work.

CHAPTER TWELVE

Terra was in the arena before the sun rose. Cire was at her side. They watched the stars fading above them.

The shaman had been correct; many things *were* different about Cire. There were also things that were the same but deeper.

The orc had always been quiet, only speaking when he felt it was important. Now he was even quieter, but when he spoke, his words held a weight they had not before. Gone was the awkward silence. It was replaced by something that felt much more intentional.

The two of them had spent the night in Terra's bed, holding each other through the silence, tracing their fingers over each other's skin. All that had transpired that night felt sacred, like a prayer, the slightest glimpse of God. Terra had never felt that way with another person. When Cire whispered in her ear, it didn't matter that he was speaking orcish. She understood it regardless.

Later that night, as Terra was drifting to sleep, Cire told her their training started in the morning. The old shaman would take him, and Grok would handle Terra. That was when Cire suggested they get up early enough to watch the sunrise.

It had been a great idea. Terra had never cared for sunrises. They took too much out of you. But this one, it was perfect. She could have watched this sunrise for the rest of her life.

Unfortunately, Grok eventually walked into the arena.

Cire rose when he saw her, kissed Terra on the forehead, and left without a word.

Terra didn't bother standing up or looking at her trainer. She would enjoy herself for a little bit longer.

Grok sat in front of her, folding her knees over each other. She waited for the human to meet her eyes. "Are you ready to begin?"

Terra realized it was pointless to keep acting like the orc wasn't right in front of her. "What's with the politeness?"

"I'm here to train you. There's no sense in making this harder on myself than it needs to be. You will endure suffering, and I need not drag it out. Besides, it was never personal for me."

"Wait, not personal? You tried to kill my friends and me!"

Grok nodded slowly, her eyes still locked on Terra's. "What was between Anabelle and me was personal. You were incidental. A great warrior, unfortunately for you, hampered by your humanness, but great nonetheless. I don't need to waste time dancing around such things."

Terra looked around the arena. "Where's Anabelle? Part of the deal was that you would train her as well."

Grok's face tensed at the mention of the elf. "She has had years of training already. I merely have to show her how to access the Path of the Lost by her own choice instead of being prompted. You, on the other hand, have no formal training of any sort and no reservoirs of magic to pull from, which is an extreme handicap."

"What are you talking about?"

"Humans, much like most orcs, lost their ability to perform magic without certain accessories. Orcs are given it at birth. It is rudimentary but works. Those such as us, who need magic to access the deep power within, need something a little more substantial. It is not enough to allow us to do spellwork, merely enough to help us access all of our inner strength."

Grok held her hand to her chest. It began to glow bright blue.

She cupped her other hand beneath her chest, and a blue liquid poured into her palm. She held her palms together and rolled the blue liquid back and forth, molding it into a solid ball that crackled with energy.

"This is the soul of one of the strongest orcish warriors. You must absorb it to begin the path. This particular soul has killed four hundred people."

Terra stared at the ball in awe. "They must have been some warrior."

"You misunderstand me. Four hundred have died trying to absorb this soul."

Terra's throat dried and she swallowed uncomfortably. "And I have to..."

"Push this into your chest. Only then will you have the will to travel the Path of the Lost."

Terra eyed the soul as her body went cold. She'd been prepared to meditate or do some light stretching. Maybe even read. But this? There was no way she could have prepared for this.

She reached for the soul. The moment her finger touched it, she screamed in pain and pulled her hand back. It felt like she had just pressed her finger to a flame. "Are you fucking kidding me?"

Grok stood, still holding the soul as if it were nothing. She dropped it on the ground. "If you cannot pass this test, you will never be a Hand, and I will be free of half my obligation."

"Do you have any tips or anything? You're supposed to be training me."

Grok sneered at Terra. "Figure out how badly you want this."

Terra grabbed the ball. The pain was unbearable. She screamed, pulling her hand back instantly. The skin of her palm was smoking. "I can't even pick this thing up!" she shouted, unsure who she was angry at.

Grok crossed her arms and clicked her tongue. "Looks like you have a problem."

Terra tried again and recoiled from the pain, which was unlike anything she'd ever felt. It went all the way down to her bones and lingered even after she released the soul. "How the hell did you have this in you?"

Grok pressed her hand to her chest, withdrawing another soul. She rolled it between her palms before shoving it back into her chest. "The first one is always the worst. If it doesn't kill you."

Terra looked at the soul orb. There was no way she was going to be able to do this. She couldn't even hold the damn thing. It hurt too much.

Grok chuckled softly, and the sound was like glass slicing Terra's ear. The orc was laughing at what Terra couldn't do, the same laugh she'd heard her entire life from everyone. The laugh when she flunked out of college, when she failed to get a promotion, when she had to ask to borrow money because she couldn't pay her bills. It was always the same.

Terra leaned over and grabbed the orb, and her bones screamed from the pain. She acted fast to keep from backing out and pressed it to her chest. It felt like her skin was being burned off by a flamethrower. She shoved it into her body.

Everything went white.

The pain of touching the soul orb had been nothing compared to what she felt now. It was as if someone were cutting through the skin all over her body. Her bones vibrated with energy, and she burned alive from the inside.

The scream that came from Terra was heard for miles as she collapsed, gripping her chest, her eyes bulging from her head as her feet twitched uncontrollably. She tried to get up, only to continue lying there convulsing as the soul orb tried to force its way out of her body.

Grok watched with no trace of emotion on her face.

Terra stumbled to her feet, still screaming, her mind breaking from the pain. She fell to her knees and coughed up blood. She slammed her head against the ground until she thought her skull was going to crack open. Anything to take this pain away.

She felt the skin of her chest unraveling, thread by thread, and she pounded her fists into the ground as her eyes and ears bled.

A bit of the soul poked through her chest, and she grasped it with both hands and forced it back in, increasing the pain, her body shivering as it began to shut down.

Grok knelt beside Terra. "It'll take hours. You understand now what you are going to endure?"

Terra's head flung back, smacking the ground as she clawed her face, scratching her skin away. She forced her neck to go rigid for a second, gritting her teeth to keep from biting through her tongue, and she nodded.

"Good. I'll see you at sundown."

Grok walked away, leaving Terra screaming and rolling around in the dirt of the arena, filled with a pain that few had ever experienced.

Terra fought, but she didn't know what she was fighting. It was more than pain. Perhaps it was death, but she fought.

There was only blank whiteness in her mind. The pain. All she knew was she couldn't let go. She didn't know why, but she didn't need to.

Terra screamed long into the afternoon. She only stopped when she tore her vocal cords. Now she lay on the ground, eyes wide open, trembling as she clutched her chest, a high-pitched mix of a whine and a wheeze coming from her mouth.

She saw hands tearing open the ground around her, picking at her flesh like vultures. She wanted to fight them off, but she couldn't move. All she could do was wheeze.

***

Cire sat in a pool of dark water, submerged up to his neck. The shaman sat across from him. Black masks covered their faces.

The water was troubled. It moved back and forth as if it had a mind of its own. Screams echoed throughout the room as shadows moved across the wall.

They were Terra's screams.

Cire tried to close himself off from his feelings and ignore the pain Terra was experiencing. The pain that he was causing.

The shaman hummed a soothing song, which did nothing for him. He had learned too much in the last two days. Nothing could soothe him.

"You are distraught, my child," she said.

Cire didn't want to speak. He wanted to fade into the water, but he knew this was his trial. There was no running away from what needed to be done.

The shaman stood, the thick black water rolling down her nude, wrinkled body as she raised her hands to the sky. "I have looked for you century after century, Cire. Born again and again, resurrected time after time. We didn't think we were ever going to find you again."

Cire remained quiet. He was still trying to understand what the shaman had told him. This was not his first life. There had been hundreds, much like her own. With every death, they were reborn, but not entirely. Their true soul rested someplace other than their body. Rested within the Hand.

Terra's screams continued to echo throughout the room as she tried to absorb a piece of Cire's soul.

Cire finally spoke. "How many did you say have died trying to absorb my soul?"

The shaman was quiet for some time. "The last time we had you in our possession, it was around four hundred. You were the toughest of all souls for anyone to handle, which is no doubt why you are the only one who has continued through the cycle of reincarnation."

"And if this kills her?"

The shaman cupped water in her hand, drawing it forth and pouring it over Cire's head. "That is not a thing we must think about now. If she fails, you will be lost again, and another dark time will fall over the orcs. It is best not to ponder that."

"I'm hurting her!"

"Or making her stronger than she could ever be without your magic. If she is capable, you will have knowledge and power you could never have dreamed of. She will tie you to the world of the living, keeping you from becoming a lich. You'll retain your mind and your soul. You can grow in wisdom and strength, and more than anything else, in compassion."

The water pulsed, exploding upward in an image of Terra, screaming on the ground as she clawed her face.

Cire still could not believe any of this. His entire life, searching for the way of the true orc, only to find he had lived it countless times without realizing it. Finally learning that the true shaman was a lich, that his whole existence had been moving toward this. "I love her," he whispered.

The shaman removed Cire's mask and kissed the top of his head. "It is your love for her that will keep you, and that love will give her strength and power. Her life will keep yours, and you will keep hers. It is the way it has always been."

"And Grok?"

The shaman removed her mask, her face tired and worn. "There was a reason Grok absorbed a piece of my soul for power, but despite that bonding, despite our essences being connected, she still did what she did."

The water trembled again as the shaman moved to stand behind Cire. "Now, let us complete the ritual. Drink deep, shaman, for when you wake, it will be for an eternity."

The shaman pushed Cire down, forcing his head under the water. He struggled, but the shaman was strong. She held him down as he tried to stand, his lungs burning as he held his breath before finally accepting his place in the grand scheme of things. Then he relaxed and lay still, his lungs aflame before breathing in and extinguishing the pain.

When he stopped moving, the shaman stepped away. His body floated to the surface of the water as the shaman stepped out.

Cire was gone. Now she would wait.

Anabelle and Abby arrived on the orcish world in the early afternoon. Transportation between the orc world, the gnome world, and the human world had been significantly improved. Creon had created a team of scientists to adjust the hadron collider to run more smoothly once the DGA found they were frequently needed on all three worlds.

War was brewing. Even though there had been fewer conflicts over the last several weeks, Anabelle knew this silence was the eye of the storm. Whatever was coming was probably already here. They just didn't know what it was.

That wasn't to say Anabelle didn't have any ideas. The dots were all there, waiting to be connected.

Tesla. The undead army. Those two were obvious, but there was one thing that continued to bother Anabelle, something she couldn't get out of her head. Why would the Dark One have taken such a huge gamble on Rasputina? Did he not know the details surrounding her becoming a lich, or was he banking on her switching sides?

Everything was happening on Anabelle's side of the equation. The increase in orcish forces, complemented by the orcish peace talks and treaties. The gnomish resistance was steadily growing. It wouldn't be long until the resistance was a force to be reckoned with. Gnomes were coming out of hiding from all over the nine realms and returning to their homeworld.

The only wildcard that Anabelle could think of was Roy's and Abby's recent gamble. Enlisting a disgraced Dragon Rider team to hunt down a herd of ether dragons sounded good on paper, but from what Anabelle had read about Alex Bound in her briefs, there was cause to worry. The brief didn't mince words. Alex was a skilled rider and fighter, having climbed the ranks of the Dragonrider Corp exceptionally fast.

Bound's tactical skills rivaled Suzuki's, and she had the undying loyalty of her squad, who had chosen to stay by her side and risked death by doing so. It didn't help that she was also an extremely powerful psychic whose powers had only just started to manifest. That meant there was a possibility of her getting even stronger.

Anabelle and Abby made their way to the orc council's chambers. She noticed the girl seemed distracted. There was probably just as much on her mind. "Hey, Abs, how you holding up?" she asked as she stopped and tapped Abby's head. "Enough room in there for you to think?"

Abby brushed away Anabelle's hand in a quick, irritated fashion. "Sorry, we were running potential combat scenarios for the future."

"Bullshit, you're always doing that. What's going on?"

Abby glanced over her shoulder as if she were worried about someone following her. "Something weird happened to us last night while we were sleeping. We aren't sure if it was a dream. We checked our sleep status—Martin keeps track of it to do maintenance—and we weren't in REM sleep when it happened. Still don't quite know what to make of it."

"What happened?"

Abby furrowed her brow before speaking. "Tesla. We saw him last night. He opened some kind of portal in our room. He said he didn't want to fight, just talk, and he...he offered me a position in the Dark One's army."

Anabelle felt her skin prickle as her insides went cold. "Wait, are you saying Tesla was in HQ? He just appeared inside?"

Abby nodded, looking slightly uncertain.

"Why didn't you notify anyone?" the elf asked. "Or sound an alarm?"

"After he left, we scanned the room. We had Martin look through all our surveillance footage. Everything. He didn't leave a trace. That's why we weren't sure if it was real."

"That's not all, is it?"

Abby took a deep breath. Whatever she was trying to say, Anabelle could tell it was hard for her to get through. "He threatened Persephone. He said if we didn't join, he was going to kill her in a way that only he knows how to."

"So, you told him you'd sell us out?"

Abby's eyes widened as she frantically waved her hands and shook her head. "No, of course not! We would never do that."

"Then why are you acting like you did?"

"It was disconcerting. We thought we were crazy, that all the nanobots and upgrades and shit in our head had finally gotten to be too much. We thought you might look at us like you look at the lich."

"Abby, that isn't the same thing. Even if you had a breakdown, you haven't spent the last thousand years terrorizing the nine realms, and for what it's worth, I don't think you're crazy. Why do you think Tesla reached out to you? He could have offered the same thing to any of us, especially if he can teleport wherever he wants."

Abby raised her hand, and the nanobots covered her arm with armor. "We think he wants something from us. We only caught glimpses of his tech, but it is years beyond our own. But we do have technology in common. Maybe he thinks we find him sympathetic."

Anabelle tapped her fingers on her pointed chin as she thought. "Do you think he's going to come back?"

"He said he'd give us time to think about it. What do you think we should do? Go under surveillance? Guards whenever we're alone?"

"Nope. Next time he comes, you should tell him yes."

Abby stared at Anabelle, confused. "Wait, what?"

"If there's anyone I know who is smart enough to infiltrate the Dark One's enterprise under his nose, it's you. Plus, you have the tech to keep from being microchipped. If Tesla thinks you're scared enough to join the Dark One, you might be able to strike a blow from the inside."

"We'll think about it, but we better get a move on. The council is waiting for us."

The two continued down the halls of the great arena. As they turned the corner, they ran into Grok, who simply smiled, took a step back, and walked around them.

Anabelle froze. Grok was so close. She still had the urge to kill her torturer, to lash out with everything she had and tear the orc to pieces.

Mana surged around Anabelle, slightly pushing Abby away. She couldn't help it, nor did she want to.

Grok stopped walking and looked over her shoulder. "Can't wait to start our training." She turned back and continued.

Anabelle concentrated on her breathing. She wasn't going to get lost again, not like last time. She pulled herself back and centered on where she was, calming herself. "I can't wait until this war is over and I can finally kill that bitch."

Abby rested her hand on Anabelle's shoulder. "Come on, Belle. We gotta take care of this meeting."

Anabelle knew Abby probably didn't want to talk about what had happened anymore. She'd noticed that Abby liked to figure things out herself, then it was brought to the group. On top of that, Abby didn't seem like someone who would initially feel comfortable with any kind of spying. Anabelle didn't have any doubts, though. The kid knew how to adapt.

The orc council had gathered by the time Anabelle and Abby arrived in the meeting chamber. The shaman sat in the middle of the council.

Anabelle searched the room quickly. Terra and Cire were nowhere to be seen. "Where's my team?"

The shaman raised her hand slowly, moving as if she'd been

drained of all her energy. "They are finishing their final rites. The transfer of power is in the process of being completed. We did not call you here for that, though."

"From what I understood, Terra and Cire were going to be calling the shots. This looks a little bit different than what we'd spoken about."

"Only for the moment. And I am merely stating what Cire has asked me to. If he survives the trial, you may verify this with him."

"What are you talking about, 'if he survives?'"

The shaman sighed, not as if she were annoyed but rather like she was finding it difficult to remain awake. "After we speak, I will be more than happy to take you to either him or Terra. But for now, we must talk about your next military moves."

Anabelle wanted to find out more about what was going on with Terra and Cire, but she knew the shaman wasn't going to disclose any more information. It was evident that she was used to speaking about things when she felt it was time. "So far, the gnomish resistance has been growing. Humans have also been joining up to fight as well. Some of them are sticking to their own armed forces, and others are getting involved with the various factions Myrddin created."

"And the elves?"

Anabelle could hear the bite in the shaman's tone. It didn't seem to be directed at her but more at a general hurt. It was the tone of one who had been wronged multiple times and had never forgotten. "Much like the dwarves, many of them are staying with their own armies, waging their war under leaders not that different from Myrddin. But a good number have joined Myrddin's forces, dwarves and elves alike."

The shaman nodded approvingly. "Then the orcs must make a clear distinction. It seems as if many of the other races have put stock in their own power to overcome the Dark One, only supplying soldiers for Myrddin's cause when they believe that they can lose a few. It makes sense. One must protect their own homes. The gnomes found that out the hard way."

Anabelle braced herself for bad news.

The shaman weakly stood, needing help from one of the orcs next to her. "Cire and I are in agreement about what must be done. The orcs will no longer exist as an army. The entirety of the horde will join your efforts. We will abandon our home so we can go where it is necessary. Every single one of us."

The elf was shocked by what she'd just heard. There wasn't any part of her that had thought the orcs were going to join their fight against the Dark One wholesale. She'd anticipated them holding troops back to defend their world. Every race had done that so far. She hadn't expected them to be willing to sacrifice everything for the war. "That's a pretty tall order you're talking about. What about—"

"The true nature of the orc is in the horde. We are not a planet. We are not a city. We are a people. Wherever the horde is, that is home."

Anabelle went to one knee, pressing her hand over her heart. It was the only thing she could think of to do. "Thank you. We are forever indebted to you."

"The tribes will continue to exist, but you and Abby will be High Generals. The only leaders higher than you are the Shaman and the Hand. When the war is over, the horde will release themselves from you. If there are any internal struggles for power, the council will handle them. There may be times during the conflict when you must, as is our way, but we doubt you will have many issues. The tribal leaders are aware of your strength and look forward to tackling a new enemy together."

The council cheered, slamming their axes on the ground and hooting.

Anabelle had heard that war was in the heart of orcs, but she had always thought it was quite different from this. Elves told stories of the horde, mad with blood rage, thirsting for murder and violence. This was something else entirely. She was beginning to see what was at the heart of the orcish culture, and she could now understand why they had so readily accepted Terra.

The orcs were warriors. They didn't need or crave violence. They were merely excited and ready to test themselves against stronger opponents, ready to defend what they loved and fight for what they believed in. Lessons that Anabelle thought anyone could have benefitted from.

She stood, her hand still pressed to her heart. "We will not disappoint you or waste this gift. Thank you."

The shaman bowed her head before descending the stairs that separated her from Anabelle and Abby. "What you see will disturb you, but trust me, it is a necessary part of the process."

The DGA members followed the shaman as she exited the meeting room, the elf wondering what they would see that was terrible enough to have the shaman preface it. Her eyes had borne witness to many atrocities. Surely this could not be worse.

When Anabelle saw Cire's body floating lifeless in the dark water, she screamed and turned to attack the shaman, stopping only because Abby had grabbed her and held her tight. Anabelle demanded that the shaman explain herself.

The shaman went on to do just that, telling them about the redistribution of ancient power, a power the orcs had cultivated and hoarded for thousands of years.

Anabelle could hardly wrap her head around the fact that the shaman was a lich and that was what they were turning Cire into. It seemed wrong, perverse even, yet the shaman stood before Anabelle and was nothing like Rasputina. There was no insanity or detachment. The shaman still seemed to care deeply about not only her people but the safety of all the realms.

Still, the elf was horrified by what Terra was experiencing. "What are you doing to her?" she demanded.

The shaman waded into the water with Cire and pressed her ear to his chest. "There's no breath, yet I can feel his energy. Terra must be nearly through. Follow me."

The shaman led Anabelle and Abby to the main arena.

Terra lay on the ground, trembling, holding her chest and whimpering in pain.

Anabelle rushed over to Terra and knelt beside her. "Terra, are you okay?"

The human tried to sit up but failed and collapsed back to the ground. "I'm going to get it…" Her body convulsed and she screamed, energy crackling around her.

Anabelle fell backward, the wave of energy knocking her on her butt. She'd never felt anything like this from Terra. "What the hell is this?"

She reached out to help Terra sit up. The moment their skin touched, the world blew apart in white light.

Anabelle was standing in the arena, but it had changed. Everyone else was gone, and infinite whiteness stretched around the borders.

Terra was on her feet, bloody and covered in open cuts and gashes. She stood facing another Terra, who was glowing bright white and was just as badly beaten.

The less luminous Terra turned to Anabelle. "Huh. Didn't think I would see you here."

"What the hell are you doing?"

Terra shushed her. "Hold on. This is probably the best fight of my life."

She returned her attention to the luminous Terra, who scowled as she leaned in and swung at Terra, who dodged and came up with an uppercut. The luminous Terra stumbled back, shook off the punch, and leaned in with her own. Her fist connected with Terra's jaw, forcing her back, but she pivoted, stepped to the side, and clocked the luminous version of herself in the back of the head.

The luminous Terra stumbled, clutching the nape of her neck as Terra tackled her to the ground.

Terra let out a scream as she raised her fists, cupped together, and brought them down on the luminous version of herself. Then she grabbed the luminous Terra by the back of the head, holding it as if it were a baby, and drove her fist into her skull.

The luminous Terra flailed as Terra wrapped her hands around her throat. Blood frenzy was in Terra's eyes as she strangled the luminous Terra, whose hands flapped as if they were beached fish.

Finally, the luminous Terra stopped struggling and lay still.

Terra, who had hunched over and was breathing raggedly, leaned back and let out a sigh.

The luminous Terra began to glow bright blue, energy crackling from her body as she dissolved into a beam of pure light and washed over Terra.

Then everything changed again.

Anabelle was still kneeling beside Terra. Abby had joined her and stared in concern at the human.

Terra groaned and sat up, her hand pressed to her chest. She chuckled softly as she withdrew a glowing blue ball of energy. "Holy fucking shit did that hurt. When the hell did you guys get here?"

The shaman walked over to Terra and knelt beside her. "One of the last trials of the Path of the Lost. Now you and Anabelle are on the same playing field."

Anabelle wondered how much the shaman knew about the Path of the Traveler. Grok had let the elf know that the Path had never been restricted to only her kind. Orcs had followed it as well, caring only for the Path of the Lost, exemplified by Grok, the only one among them to master it.

The shaman looked over her shoulder wistfully. "And now there is a new shaman, one bound to you and you to him. How does this new power feel?"

Terra stumbled to her feet, rolling the ball of energy in her hand before shoving it back into her chest. "Feels like I want to sleep for a fucking decade and then eat forever." Her eyes looked distant for a second. "Cire's probably hungry as hell too."

"Then you two should feast. I believe it is about time that you two were alone."

Terra gave Anabelle and Abby a weak high five. "I'll catch you guys later. I'm going to go check on my dude."

As Terra walked away, Anabelle turned to the shaman. "What do you know about the Path of the Traveler? If Terra and I are to walk it together under Grok, I'd like everything to be on the table. Straightforward. After all, aren't the Paths of the Traveler and the Lost effectively the same thing?"

The shaman shook her head. "They are born of the same traditions and power and share many traits, but to call them the same thing is like saying the rain and a river are one and same. Both are water and both can be deadly, but there are many distinctions." Pursing her lips, the shaman stared at Anabelle for a long moment, her face betraying an internal debate. Then nodding, she said, "Come with me. I will let you know what I know, and what you and Terra should expect under your new teacher."

Anabelle looked at Abby. "You want to come with?"

Abby shook her head as she pulled up her holoscreen. "No, we have to take care of some…stuff with the Gate."

Anabelle crossed her arms. "All right. You're going to be safe, right?"

"Of course, *Mom.*"

"Ugh. I hate the way that sounds. Don't make that a habit."

The shaman was walking away.

Anabelle punched Abby lightly in the shoulder before smiling and heading after the shaman. It was time to find out what the rest of her journey on the Path was going to look like.

CHAPTER FOURTEEN

Terra and Cire stayed in their room for two days. Food was brought to them, and Terra never questioned who it was from. Hours were spent curled around each other in light conversation. Moans and screams echoed loud enough to be heard through the halls. Terra didn't care. This was a level of bliss she'd never felt before.

Her body tingled with a power that flowed from a deep well within her. When she looked at Cire, she saw light reflecting and refracting off him, splitting the atoms and restructuring them as they went along, each of them rebuilding into something entirely different.

There were brief interruptions that forced Terra to return to reality. The war was still going on, and Roy had kicked the DGA's plan into overdrive. An assault was being mounted.

Terra checked into the meetings the DGA held regularly. Abby was working on a way to open the Gate and close it remotely. The plan was to expand the Gate so a large number of gnomish and orcish troops could invade the Netherverse. She was actively trying to pinpoint Tesla's position. He periodically popped up in the Netherverse, which Abby was surveying through nanobots she'd sent through the Gate. It was only a matter of time until Tesla's position was found.

While Abby was trying to locate the scientist, Anabelle would accompany Alex Bound to beseech a herd of ether dragons Alex's dragon Chine had informed Roy about. They were also going to be traveling with Suzuki. Terra had been informed that he was a big deal among dragons. She thought that was interesting.

Terra was glad that all the planning was going on without her needing to offer too much input. She was enjoying her time with Cire, time she didn't know she so desperately needed. It wouldn't last, but that was okay. What was coming next would be exciting as well.

That was what she was thinking about when Cire sleepily opened his eyes, his head resting on her chest.

As the orc groaned under his breath, Terra kissed his ridged forehead. "How'd you sleep?" she asked.

He sat up and yawned as he stretched. "I had far too many dreams. It is good to be awake again. There were...unsettling things to see. It is difficult to make sense of them. I'm not used to these visions. Are they of things to come, or only possibilities? It is difficult to tell. Did you rest at all?"

Terra shook her head as she got out of bed. She admired herself in the mirror, watching her muscles as she reached down to grab her axe. "Hardly. There's... I don't know how to explain it. Not quite excitement, but there's something there. Every time I think about leading the horde through that Gate, my whole body tingles almost as much as when you touch it."

Cire rolled over and laughed. "Itching for battle, huh?"

"When I'm not thinking about you, it's the only thing on my mind."

"Then you're looking forward to speaking to the generals and the horde today?"

Terra sighed. "Ugh. Do you always have to be the serious one? No, I'm not looking forward to talking to the generals. At all."

"And you're to start training with Grok soon, right?"

Terra had actively been avoiding thinking about that. The last task Grok had left Terra with had greatly increased her strength and filled her with a confidence she'd never thought possible, but it had also been the single most painful experience of her life. And she still hadn't even officially started the training.

She started to get dressed. Since she'd completed the ritual known as the Clasped Hands, she'd been given a set of ceremonial armor. It was hide from the same animal that Cire's was made from. She'd seen Grok wearing it during one of their early battles. It hung loosely and was the most comfortable thing Terra had ever owned. She didn't think she'd ever wear anything else. "Not even slightly, but I'll get it over with soon enough. I have to meet with Grok and Anabelle in a little bit. What's on the agenda for you?"

Cire leaned over the side of the bed, watching Terra dress. "Reading. The Mundanes from the MERCs, the young one you fought beside and her friend, have supplied me with research materials. There is a lot I must learn. The old shaman has lessons for me as well. But it is nearly time to speak. Are you ready?"

Terra flopped back onto the bed as she let her fur vest fall to the ground. "You know, I might be the Hand of the horde, but you might be the fingers. Maybe we could put it off for a little bit?"

Cire rolled on top of Terra and smiled broadly, his eyes twinkling. "That isn't a problem."

The council was already seated when Terra and Cire arrived. They'd left two seats open in the middle for Terra and Cire. The old shaman stood elsewhere, watching the council, having given away her place of authority.

Terra jumped into her seat and kicked her feet up. "'Sup, everybody? Y'all ready to do this?"

One of the older orcs sniffed at Terra.

Cire leaned over and headbutted the orc, causing the other council members to chuckle.

The orc rubbed his forehead. "Hmph. Seems like you two are starting to understand how things get done around here."

Cire only grunted before saying, "Bring up the horde. We're ready to address them."

A holoscreen projected in the middle of the room. It scanned Terra and Cire and then beeped.

Cire looked to Terra. "Would you like to speak first?"

Terra stood and cleared her throat. "A fight is before us, one that is worthy of the horde. Millions of dead soldiers, an infinite army for us to overcome. Do I have to say anything else? There will be skulls to crush and souls to, uh, fuck up! This is going to be a *fight*—no more wasting time on the Dark One's minor-league bullshit. We're going to hit him where it hurts, and we're going to make sure that shit leaves a mark."

As Terra sat back down, Cire rose. "Too long have we been slaves to the Dark One's will. When we attack, we will remind the nine realms of what orcs have always been. We will invade the Netherverse and prove that orcs cannot be held down even by death. Ready yourselves for war. *We are the horde!*"

From the holoscreen, hundreds of voices returned the chant, "We are the horde." Then the screen went blank.

The old shaman approached the council. "Brief and sweet. Couldn't have asked for anything better. Now...Terra, are you prepared to finish your training? You may have the power to walk the Path, but you still must learn your way. Grok is waiting for you in the arena. I believe your friend is already there."

Terra groaned to express to everyone in the room how little she wanted to see Grok, but that wasn't the entire truth. She'd been excited about this since she'd absorbed Cire's soul energy. She was intoxicated by her new strength, and she couldn't wait to learn how to harness it. "Okay, okay. I'm out of here. Don't lose the war while I'm out.

She rose and headed toward the arena, her head swimming with the possibilities of what was going to happen. Worries about Grok had long left her mind. Not that she trusted her. Terra just knew if Grok was going to betray her, the entirety of the horde would come down on the former Hand.

The shaman had been right. Anabelle was already in the arena.

Terra had to stifle a fit of laughter when she saw Anabelle. The elf was wearing yoga pants and an 80s-style crop top. "Dude, you didn't tell me we were playing dress-up!"

Anabelle pulled out the waist of her leggings and let them snap back in place. "Oh, this? I was trying to lighten the mood. It's not every day you get to go to a grueling, soul-crushing training session with the person who tortured you to the brink of death."

Terra winced. In her excitement, she'd forgotten how hard the situation it must be for Anabelle. "You know, if you aren't feeling—"

Anabelle raised her hand and cut Terra off. "No, I'm doing this. This war is bigger than Grok and me. Whatever edge we can get, I'm going to take."

"Good," a gravelly voice said behind them.

Grok sauntered into the arena, wearing her familiar smug look.

Terra saw the elf's body tense as the orc walked toward them and understood why. She herself wanted to deck Grok anytime she saw the orc, and she hadn't been tortured. Anabelle managed to keep her cool, though.

The three stood in the arena, and the tension in the air was thick. Terra wanted to make a joke to ease it, but there wasn't anything to say. She didn't want to be friendly. Now that the orc was here, some of her excitement had faded. Grok's smile wasn't making it better.

"Well, now the human can tap into her true power," Grok said. "How's it feel to cradle someone else's soul?"

Terra didn't answer. She and Cire had talked about the implications of Terra drawing power from his soul. The reality made them both a little uneasy, but mostly Cire. He was terrified of becoming like the lich, but they'd both been assured by the former shaman that nothing of that sort could happen as long as Terra was Cire's Hand. Still, it was a weird feeling.

Grok didn't wait for the human to answer before continuing, "Now one of you has come close to the Path of the Lost. Touched your toes along it. The other merely knows of its existence."

Anabelle scoffed incredulously. "What do you mean, come close? I defeated you. I've obviously walked the Path."

"Because you defeated me? Hardly. Do you remember your training as a Traveler?"

Anabelle stepped to Grok, nearly nose to nose. "What exactly are you implying."

"Merely that the Path and all of its ways revolve around threes. That includes the three steps to properly travel. You no doubt finished the other two. I've seen you fight. But on the Path of the Lost, ironically, the third step is somewhat lost."

Terra was trying to keep pace with what Grok was saying. She didn't have the historical background Anabelle did. "So, what are the three steps?"

Grok held up a finger. "One is access to power. You got there through the ritual of the Clasping Hands. Anabelle arrived under my gentle guidance, but even then, Anabelle only passed the first step." Grok turned to the elf. "You have a tremendous amount of latent strength, and you caught a glimpse of what it was like to use it for a moment, but you both need to take the next step."

"And what is that?"

"As if it's a surprise. You'll have to fight."

Anabelle cracked her knuckles and rolled her shoulders, smiling slightly. "Good. I've been waiting to kick your ass."

Grok laughed and shook her head. "Not me. You have only fought the last link in the chain of the Path. Today, you will fight the rest."

The air around Grok pulsed with energy, but it was different from anything Terra had felt coming off her before. Even though she wasn't versed in what different energies represented, she could tell it was not the same energy the orc used to fight.

Anabelle also noticed a difference, so she stepped back and raised her fists, ready to fight whatever was coming at her.

The ground shook as if there were an earthquake. Terra looked around for something to hold onto as the ground broke apart, but there was nothing. The earth opened into a great chasm that Terra and Anabelle toppled into, their screams echoing in the darkness.

Sarah and Kravis sat with Myrddin, the wizard's robes radiating white light. They'd been listening to him talk for some time, hanging onto his words. Sarah had never put much stock in Myrddin's advice. He was only a man, after all, fallible just like everyone else.

Now things were different. He had gone beyond the veil and seen things no other living person had. And he had brought back that information.

Myrddin leaned forward and held out his hand. "Are you ready to see it all, Sarah?"

Sarah looked at Kravis and took a deep breath. "Do I have a choice?"

"You never have to look at something you don't want to see."

Kravis held Sarah's hand and squeezed it. "You can handle it, whatever it is."

Sarah had an idea about what Myrddin might be showing her. He'd only spoken of two things since he arrived in Kravis' dreams, the Path of the Traveler and the Eight Gates of Hell.

As far as Sarah knew, the Eight Gates of Hell, the final form one ascended to after they opened all eight of their chakras, was akin to the Path of the Lost, the biggest difference being that the Eight Gates were created after the Path for humans who didn't have access to magic. That was the only relation Sarah knew about.

Sarah took Myrddin's hand and everything disappeared. She was in a green field, cherry blossoms floating through the air. Myrddin was standing at her side.

Two young women were fighting, their movements nearly too fast to be seen. Sarah recognized one of the fighter's stances. They were the same as the ones she'd been taught during her training. The other fighter used stances like Anabelle's.

Sarah didn't understand why she was looking at this. "What's the point?"

Out of nowhere, another fighter barreled into the fray. She had no stances and fought on primal instinct. The three were locked in combat with each other, gracefully dodging, blocking, and attacking from all sides. They looked to be in a draw.

The sky above darkened. Lightning cracked, and a horrifying screech came from the clouds as two red eyes opened in the darkness and peered down at the three fighters, who had ceased their battle.

The fighters looked at one another, then they turned to face the red eyes watching them.

Myrddin folded his hands and rested them on his waist. "A vision I brought back from the archives of the Seer's Realm. Seems straight-forward, doesn't it?"

Sarah shook her head. "No, not at all. If that's what I think it is, that's impossible. Anabelle has mana to pull from. Terra just finished a ritual to give her the strength needed to follow the Path of the Lost. I'm not like them. I'm just a human. Opening the Eight Gates and trying to keep up with them could kill me."

Myrddin nodded sadly. "Yes, Eight Gates would kill you, but what if I told you there was another Gate? One past that breaking point. The Ninth Gate of the Heavens."

Sarah turned to face Myrddin. "I would ask how I open it."

Myrddin took a fighting stance, his wand floating in front of him. "That was what I wanted to hear."

CHAPTER FIFTEEN

Sarah woke up lying next to Kravis. As she sat up, he started to mutter under his breath. The muttering turned to coughing and then the gnome sat upright, rubbing his eyes to wipe the extended sleep from his face.

Kravis peered around the room, no doubt looking for Myrddin. "Guess the great white wizard is still out for the count. What did he show you?"

Sarah stood, trying to keep from falling over. She was still disoriented from the vision Myrddin had shown her. "He told me about another gate. A ninth gate."

Kravis didn't look like he believed Sarah. "What are you talking about? We've never come across anything like that, and even if it did exist, it would be extremely dangerous. I had to find something to help you force that eighth gate open, and even then, it might have killed you if you hadn't known when to quit. What the hell would a ninth gate look like?"

Sarah held her hand out in front of her as it started to glow with white energy. "He showed me what it looked like. Showed me how to open it. I-I think it's possible, and I have a bigger role to play in all of this than I thought I did."

Kravis grumbled as he looked around for something to drink. "Great. That's just what we need, one more thing that'll make it easier for you to get killed. And you want to go and have a wedding?"

The proposal had slipped Sarah's mind. She'd been so concerned with everything else going on that she hadn't had time to think about it, and that made sense. They were in the middle of a war. Myrddin was hinting that she might have to make a stand with Anabelle and Terra when she felt like there was no way she was as strong as them.

But she still wanted to have something like a life, or as close to one as she could get at the moment. Kravis was important to her. Their relationship had gotten her through some of the darkest periods of her life. If death could come at any moment, Sarah wanted to make sure it came while she was at her husband's side. "We don't have to do anything big. Well, I mean, we couldn't even if we wanted to, but this is a big thing for me, Kravis. It would—"

Kravis wrapped his arms around Sarah's waist and kissed her stomach. "You don't have to explain. I said yes, didn't I? We're doing this. I'm all in. Whenever and however you want to do it, I'm in."

"Soon. You, me, and one of the generals can officiate it, but not until we talk about everything else, okay? I want to figure this out with you. Find out how to do it in a way that works for us."

Kravis nodded, his head still resting firmly on Sarah's stomach. She ran her hands through his red hair before kneeling to kiss him. In a few hours, she was going to have to leave him again. That was the way it always was. Coming and going, the only real time they had together being work. They'd adapted to that. There wasn't anything the two of them couldn't figure out.

"So, how do you get this ninth gate open?" he asked.

"I have to push my mind beyond anything it's ever gone through before. My body is already there. I'm going to have to find someone who can help me do that."

Kravis peeked out of the tent. "What's going on out there? I assume I missed some important things while I was taking my power nap."

"The gnome army is getting ready to invade the Netherverse, as is the orc army and a handful of squadrons from HQ. We're going on the offensive this time."

Kravis smiled as he glanced back at Sarah. "Beautiful. I was getting tired of always being the one caught off-guard. It's about time that we returned the favor."

"You should probably go coordinate with the generals. I heard a rumor that you were going to oversee one of the invading squads."

Kravis grabbed his weapons from a dresser near the tent's exit. "Sounds fantastic. I'll think about what you said. And I love you."

"I love you too."

Kravis left Sarah with her thoughts, which were racing. Everything was going to change and fast. She just hoped she would be able to keep up.

Abby had returned to HQ on Earth to continue with further experiments concerning the Netherverse Gate. She didn't have all the materials she needed on the orcish planet. Their lab had been set up too quickly and was meant to be used on the move. She was glad Creon had made adjustments to the hadron collider to facilitate faster travel.

There was another reason Abby had returned to Earth. She had a suspicion that Tesla wouldn't try to find her on the orc planet. She'd been there for a while after her initial confrontation, and he had waited until she was back in the safety of her home.

Abby had thought about Anabelle's suggestion. She'd even talked it over with Persephone. Surprisingly, the drow thought it was a great idea. She had equal faith in Abby's ability to infiltrate the Dark One's ranks.

The idea of going undercover sent shivers up Abby's spine. She wasn't worried about being microchipped, but she couldn't put a finger on what had her scared.

There was someone she had to talk to before she made any decisions. She hoped Tesla would at least wait until after that conversation to get in contact with her.

Abby went to the floor her room was on, but she didn't go to her quarters. She walked down the hall until she came to Rasputina's room.

A viewing hole had been placed in the door, and four soldiers stood guard. "We need to speak to Rasputina," Abby said.

One of the soldiers saluted Abby. "Of course." He opened the door and stepped to the side.

Rasputina had made notable changes to her room. There was an alchemy table in the corner and a small fire in a wooden hearth covered in vines that looked to have exploded out of the wall. The floor was covered in dirt and moss, and the air was thick and humid and smelled of old earth and lichen.

The lich sat before the hearth, staring into the fire. "I was not expecting to see you, little one." Rasputina turned to face Abby, her bright eyes flashing green as a distant smile graced her face.

Abby walked farther into the room, her stomach clenched in fear. She still got chills every time she saw the lich from the memory of the lich's magic dagger breaking through her armor and tearing her stomach open. "We wanted to talk."

"What do you need to talk to *me* about? I assume you have been advised to stay away from me."

"We were going to, but we have questions we think only you have the answers to."

Rasputina stood, drawing her moss-covered cloak tighter as she conjured a table and two chairs into existence. She sat at one, and the other chair pulled itself out for Abby. "What do you wish to know so badly you would come to my hellhole?"

"What is the Dark One like? You've met him, haven't you?"

Rasputina smiled faintly. "Oh, yes, I have, many times. The Dark One is difficult to describe. He is...more of a force than anything. Whatever humanity was there is long gone, not that much different than a lich. The only difference is the Dark One isn't evil."

"What do you mean, he isn't evil? He's responsible for the deaths of thousands, maybe even millions."

"Death is an inevitable part of existence, and one kills for many reasons. For me, it was something perverse and evil within me that compelled my soulless body forward. The Dark One is more of a predator. He kills, conquers, and expands out of necessity and nature."

"Is he easy to fool?"

"If you're thinking what I believe you are thinking, you needn't fool the Dark One, only those around him. That's a much smaller pool of people for you to outsmart."

Abby stood and prepared to leave the room. "That's good to know."

"Wait! Before you go, for what it's worth, I'm sorry. There's not much I can say to excuse what I was before I got a sliver of my soul back, but I am sorry for hurting you. And I appreciate you giving me a chance to prove myself."

Abby hadn't expected an apology from the lich, nor did she really want one. She had acknowledged that the lich could be a valuable resource who needed a second chance, but that didn't mean she had any desire to relate to her. Abby still thought she was a monster. "No problem."

She left and closed the door tightly behind her, leaving the lich alone, and headed to her room.

A large portion of Abby's lab had been moved into her room. Creon was hardly in the lab anymore since he was mostly working on the orc world, occasionally jumping to the gnome world. Abby had found that it made more sense to work from her room. She didn't have to go anywhere, and resources were always available to her.

Abby took a seat at her computer and brought up her holoscreen. It displayed the readings from the Netherverse Gates on both planets.

There was a loud, sizzling pop, and the air was suddenly filled with the smell of burning toast.

Abby looked away from her holoscreen and across from her, sitting in her guest chair, was Nikola Tesla.

He wore a plain black suit and tie, and his eyes were deep pits of blackness rimmed with purple. It was like looking into the Netherverse.

When Tesla spoke, his voice was cool and collected. It sounded like a shrill blast of arctic wind, and for a second, Abby thought she could feel it on her skin.

"Have you had a chance to think about my offer?"

Abby took a deep breath and let it out as slowly as she could. "Yeah. We've thought about it."

Terra woke up in darkness. After her eyes adjusted, she could see Anabelle, who was just getting to her feet. "What the hell happened?"

Anabelle looked around the pit. "Whatever it is, I doubt it's going to be enjoyable."

A light flashed across the dark pit, then another. And another.

Two ghostlike figures stepped into the light that now shone from above. Their bodies solidified the closer that they got. Both were orcs standing at least six feet tall. One of them growled as he hunched over.

Anabelle pulled her hair back. "At least it's going to be a straightforward challenge."

The orcs rushed Terra and Anabelle, one of them swinging at the human and hitting her in the jaw. She stumbled back as the other orc kicked Anabelle in the chest.

Terra tried to watch their movements, but they were too fast, demonstrating the speed Grok had shown. Whatever these orcs were, they had the kind of strength that was supposed to be in Terra.

The elf was facing off against the two orcs. She was keeping up with their attacks, but just barely, and it didn't seem like the orcs were going to be tiring anytime soon.

Terra wanted that power. If it was in there, she wanted to use it. She ran into the fray, barreling over one of the orcs, but the other grabbed her by the neck and spun her around. "Come on, Anabelle, we got this!"

At the sound of Terra's voice, Anabelle seemed to click on. She let out a scream, and mana pulsed around her body. When she attacked, it was with the same efficiency she'd seen from Grok.

I can do it. I can do that too, Terra repeated to herself as she blocked the attacks from the other orc.

As Terra backed into a corner, hands wrapped around the back of her neck. She punched the orc in front of her and whirled.

Two more orcs stepped out of the darkness. Across from Terra, where Anabelle was fighting, two other orcs had stepped out as well.

Anabelle leapt and kicked one of the orcs. She landed and backed up, pressing back to back to Terra. "This must be the trial. Fight off every orc who's ever been the Hand."

She hardly heard Anabelle. She was trying to tap into the strength she knew was deep inside her, but she couldn't find it. There was no swelling of magical power like Anabelle or Grok displayed. "How do you do it?" Terra whispered as six more orcs walked out of the darkness. "How?"

"What are you talking about?"

"Get to the Path. I-I can't…"

Anabelle's frantic answer wasn't what Terra was expecting. "I don't know! I can't. This is just…shit. It's not the same."

The new orcs descended upon Terra and Anabelle and even more came from the shadows, dog-piling on top of the two women. Anabelle tried to tear through them with her flaming limbs, but it did nothing. There were too many of them.

Terra didn't fare any better. She was quickly overwhelmed, fists raining down on her and knocking her to the ground, where dozens of feet stomped on her, cracking her ribs. She coughed blood and curled into a fetal position, her mind running away as she prayed for the pain to stop.

Anabelle screamed as more of the former Hands poured from the darkness.

"Weak."

Terra wasn't sure where the voice came from, the Hands around her or from within, but it did not stop. Over and over it repeated the word, drumming it into her brain.

"I am NOT WEAK!"

Her bones burned as if they had been set on fire. Energy swelled around her in a red aura, burning through the bodies of orcs beside her. She exploded up, sending orcs flying off her.

Anabelle was curled up on the ground, crying and muttering something under her breath.

Terra looked around the room. It was like everything was moving in slow motion. She could see the details of the dark room clearly, and there was no fear.

She knelt next to Anabelle. "Hey, Ana, you okay?"

The elf looked up, her face streaked with tears. "She…she made me weak. She took my strength…"

Terra reached out to her. "No one can make you weak. Now get up."

Anabelle shook her head. "No. I can't do it."

Terra's energy pulsed around her. "This is our Path now. Get. Up."

The elf's eyes hardened as she wiped away her tears. There was a serenity on her face that Terra had never seen before.

A blue aura burst out around Anabelle, engulfing her in its power. "You're right. This *is* our path."

An orc ran at Terra. She saw it happen in slow motion. It was nothing to step to the side and drive her fist through the orc's chest. "Yeah. This is our fucking path."

The Path of the Lost had opened.

It was early the next day when Anabelle rose to meet Terra. There was no time for either of them to rest. Terra was to start finalizing the arrangements for the orcish tribes, along with Cire. She told Anabelle she needed to squash any dissension in the ranks before the first battle.

Anabelle wished her luck over a quick breakfast of roasted mutton and eggs. When Cire arrived to leave with Terra, the elf was left alone with her thoughts.

She'd finally achieved the Path of the Lost, but it had taken Terra's help to do it. There was a time when Anabelle would have been disappointed with herself for being unable to accomplish such a feat on her own. Now, she looked back at the darkness they'd both experienced in the pit and was happy she hadn't gone through that by herself.

Anabelle's HUD pinged, and she looked down to read the message. Alex, Suzuki, and Rasputina were waiting for her on Middang3ard. She was to meet with them and follow Chine's instructions to one of the last herds of ether dragons.

Its location was a closely guarded secret. Chine had refused to give it up, one of the conditions of him leading Anabelle to the dragons. The other condition was that Roy couldn't come along.

The elf quickly finished what was left of her meal and headed toward the miniature hadron collider that had been built for transportation. The scientist was already waiting for her with the portal open.

She stepped through quickly and passed into the small collider that had been set up on the outskirts of HQ. Teleportation was nowhere near as uncomfortable as it had been. Traveling now felt as easy as walking through a door.

Alex was impatiently tapping her foot on the other side. She nodded at Anabelle as the elf stepped onto her side of the world.

A quick look at Alex was enough to confuse Anabelle. The woman couldn't have been any older than eighteen, yet her eyes were those of a warrior who had seen the worst war could offer. The bionic arm stressed the loss the girl had gone through. Alex cradled it like it was special.

Suzuki stood by Alex's side, obviously unconcerned about her status as a war criminal. Anabelle had heard them talking to each other quietly as she had passed through the collider.

To round out the group, Rasputina stood off to the side by herself, her hood drawn over most of her face, her eyes darting back and forth. She looked like she was in one of her moods.

This is a fucking group right here, Anabelle thought as she walked over to Alex. "Where's the rest of your crew?"

The ground shook violently as Chine landed behind Alex, who casually spat and wiped her face. "Getting ready for the party your guys are cooking up. Boundless is prepping."

Suzuki nodded as he eyed the ether dragon behind him. "Yeah, the Mundanes are doing the same thing. Roy's coordinating it. All we have to worry about today is convincing those ether dragons to lend a hand."

Anabelle cast a dubious glance at Suzuki. "Okay, I know why the kid is here, but what about you? What's your stake in all this?"

Suzuki rolled his shoulders and hitched up his pants. "Well, Roy thought it would be a good idea for me to come along because I'm kind of a big deal with dragons. I'm Dragon Bound."

Anabelle looked from Alex to Suzuki and then at Chine. "Sorry, but that doesn't mean anything to me."

Alex started walking away, and her dragon followed her. "It means a dragon wants to fuck him," she called over her shoulder.

The four of them walked down the sloping green hills to the stables as Suzuki scoffed. "If that's what you think it is, you might want to ask Chine."

Alex turned around and walked backward. She was smiling. "I'm just messing with you. I know what it is. Basically, Suzuki impressed one of the most difficult dragons in all realms, a red dragon. She swore her undying loyalty to him. Legend says when that happens, the Dragon Bound can tap into the strength of a dragon if needed. On top of that, the gold dragon you two came across had amazing things to say about Suzuki. He's a pretty popular guy—with dragons, at least."

Down at the stables, they found an axebeak and two horses that had been left for them. Roy had done a good job of making sure Alex felt like he was giving her space.

Anabelle climbed onto her horse. "Is there a reason we're traveling like a bunch of fantasy novel rejects? I'm pretty sure we could provide enough hoverbikes for everyone."

Alex bent down and picked a flower. She held it in her hand for a moment before peeling off one of the petals. "The ether dragons don't trust people or any signs of them. We go in there with any more tech than we need, they'll fry us on the spot. This way, we won't draw attention to ourselves."

Anabelle snapped her horse's reins to start off, and Suzuki did the same with his axebeak through the typical means: slapping it across the back of the head.

Rasputina reached out. Bones rose from the ground, cobbling together the form of a horse. Green fire flashed where the horse's mane would be, and its eyes glowed the same green as the woman's.

Anabelle groaned as she caught up with Chine and Alex, who had climbed onto her dragon's back. "Yeah, the lich and her undead horse aren't going to draw any attention to us. Why the hell is she coming with us?"

"Roy said resources are tight. It was this, saddle another group with her, or leave her at HQ to her own devices," Alex explained.

"Wait, Roy told you that? You guys on speaking terms now?"

"Not like we used to be, but it seems like he's willing to give me a chance."

Anabelle felt like she shouldn't pry, but she was curious to know what had changed in Alex. The girl didn't seem much different from when she'd rescued her. It was hard for the elf to imagine Alex killing anyone without a need, and even harder to see her wanting to join up with the Dark One. It didn't fit. "You mind if I ask you something?"

"Shoot."

"What was it like serving the Dark One? I have an agent going undercover, and she might have to deal with him. What should I tell her to expect?"

Alex didn't bother looking at Anabelle. "Wouldn't know. I've spent the last few months in MERC territory freeing prisoners. Go ahead, ask Suzuki. There's probably been an increase in dead orcs and a massive decrease in the number of villages and towns that need to be rescued."

Suzuki, who was riding at Anabelle's side, nodded slowly. "That's true. Troops of the Dark One's forces have been showing up dead, and no MERC groups can account for them. Also, they're usually charred by dragon fire, so yeah, it's fairly obvious. The timelines match. I believe Alex. I don't know why everyone has such strong memories of Alex saddling up with the Dark One, but the MERCs know where she's been. Unless there's another dragonrider group out there that Roy doesn't know about, which I find highly unlikely."

They continued weaving through the Crimson Forest, a place of beauty the likes of which Anabelle had never seen in any forest outside of her home. The trunks and leaves of the trees were a bright autumn red. Even the grass captured the color.

The forest stretched on for miles, and the party made sparse, brief conversation, mostly questions from Suzuki about Anabelle and the DGA. Rasputina remained silent, brooding in the back of the party.

Occasionally Alex would join in. As they traveled, she lightened up. Anabelle even caught Alex smiling a couple of times.

The hardened image Alex had projected when Anabelle had first met her fell away. Anabelle could see the humor in the girl now, and the earnest sincerity. Once all this was over, Anabelle was going to make sure to get to the bottom of what had happened with Boundless.

Anabelle's HUD pinged. It was a message from Terra. The orc world was close to having finished their preparations. She hadn't heard anything from Abby yet, but Creon had stepped up to take care of any concerns on the gnome world.

Abby finally moved forward with Tesla, Anabelle thought. That was the only thing that explained her sudden absence. Anabelle hoped she had made the right call by encouraging the girl to slip under the Dark One's radar. She had a suspicion that this battle in the Netherverse wasn't going to be their last.

They finally left the forest and continued riding west, the sun beaming down on them now that they were in the clear. At noon, they stopped by a lake and ate a small meal consisting of provisions Suzuki had prepared ahead of time. Anabelle thought it was funny how food was a part of the Mundanes' day to day planning. She couldn't ever recall planning for a lunch with the DGA.

Once everyone was fed and Chine had drunk enough from the lake, they resumed their journey.

While they traveled, Anabelle noticed that her mind was fuzzy, as if someone had draped a sheer bedsheet over her thoughts. When she looked around, she wondered why she couldn't tell where she was. She was generally good with directions but now felt as if she couldn't tell east from west.

Poison. Alex and Suzuki could have slipped something into her meal, but what reason would they have had for doing that? The three of them wanted the same thing. Anabelle could have been wrong about Alex, though. The kid's increasingly good mood could have been part of a larger con.

Even as Anabelle ran through possible scenarios in which she might need to fight for her life, she had to laugh at herself. She hadn't even assumed the lich was responsible for this. If anything, that made the most sense.

But the Path of the Lost was open to her. It would take more than Alex or Suzuki to put her down. She was pretty sure she could hold her own even against the lich, even if it was just to buy enough time for her to escape. That confidence relaxed Anabelle enough that she felt free to investigate the odd sensation. "Does anyone else feel kinda lightheaded?"

Suzuki rubbed his forehead as he yawned. "Lightheaded isn't the word for it. I can't figure out which way is up or down. Taking a nap sounds like a good idea, and for the record, I hate taking naps."

Alex stretched and shook her head like she was trying to free herself from cobwebs. "No, it's not just you. I feel weird too. Chine says it's because we're getting close to the ether dragons. They have a psychic barrier up to confuse people. No one knows they're here because of it; they're hiding in plain sight. Chine isn't affected, and he'll make sure we get there."

Anabelle glanced at Rasputina, who didn't seem to be affected. "How are you holding up?"

Rasputina tapped her head and smiled distantly. "Most of this is already gone. There isn't much to tamper with."

Anabelle continued to watch her surroundings. There were trees again, but she didn't remember when they had entered another forest. Then there was a waterfall flowing out of a mountain. She couldn't say when they had left the forest and come into the mountains. Everything began to blur together.

When Anabelle turned to look at her fellow travelers, she couldn't tell them apart. Their faces were smeared. They looked like wax figures exposed to heat for too long. "We need to stop."

She leapt off her mount and stumbled, and Suzuki did the same. Suzuki leaned forward and held his head as he vomited. "Fuck! What's happening?"

Alex got off Chine and ran over to him to help him to his feet. She slung his arm over her shoulder, dragged him back to his axebeak, and flung him onto its back. Then she took the axebeak's reins and pulled it forward, swaying slightly as she walked.

Rasputina approached Anabelle, who scampered backward and shouted, "Get the fuck away from me!" Rasputina's eyes glowed bright green, and flames erupted from beneath her eyelids. Her skin melted down her face, revealing the alabaster skull beneath.

Anabelle's mana flashed around her, searing the grass beneath her and lashing out at Rasputina.

Rasputina raised her hand, and it glowed green too. "Trust me."

Anabelle frantically looked from Rasputina to Alex, who was holding her head as she muttered to herself. The flames around her subsided.

Rasputina knelt beside the elf and pressed her finger to her head. A warm feeling flowed from Anabelle's forehead to the rest of her body, and the crippling nausea faded enough for her to get back to her feet.

The lich helped her up, guided her to her horse, and helped her mount. Then she took the reins and pulled the horse up to Alex. "How much farther?"

Chine raised his head and sniffed the air. Alex turned to Rasputina and said, "We're closing on the inner sanctum. Take Suzuki's reins. Chine and I will make sure everyone's heads don't explode from the strain."

Rasputina took the reins, and Alex climbed onto her dragon.

Alex shut her eyes, and the air around them all rippled and then grew still as if it had been encased in a bubble. A psychic shield spread out from Alex and Chine as they moved to the front of the party and guided Rasputina.

Anabelle watched this happening as if she were in a dream. Everything continued to move, swaying back and forth and melting. She stared at the back of the lich's head and watched flames flickering.

Finally, Alex stopped.

As the party came to a halt, the pain vanished from Anabelle's head, and her vision returned to normal. They were beneath a sky of stars, even though the sun was still in the sky. A lake spread out like an ocean and craggy black rocks surrounded it.

Dozens of eyes opened across the rocks.

They had arrived at the Palace of the Ether Dragons.

CHAPTER SEVENTEEN

Dozens of dragons slunk out of the shadows. Most of them dwarfed Chine, demonstrating just how young Alex's dragon was. The dragons hissed violently, hardly a friendly sound.

Anabelle's senses had come back to her. Apparently, the psychic bubble was the outer defense. Here within the palace, everything was back to normal.

Alex dismounted and walked toward the approaching dragons. She held up both hands, signaling that she had come in peace. Suzuki walked up beside her but made no such gesture.

One of the older dragons, a graying creature with jagged wings who was covered in scars, flew down and landed before them. It stretched its wings and let out a mighty roar. As it leaned forward to get a better look at the mortals who had entered its court, the dragon's telepathic voice boomed in Anabelle's head. *Who dares to enter our sanctuary?*

Suzuki stepped forward, bowing low. "My name is Suzuki, the Most Mundane of the Mundanes, Dragon Bound to the Great Red Dragon. These are my companions. Anna—"

The dragon raised its hand, cutting Suzuki off. *Your name is loved among dragons, but only enough to suffice for you. You are welcome among all dragons, but your companions must answer themselves.*

Alex clicked her tongue at Suzuki before muttering, "Showoff," and lowering her hands. She spoke to the dragon. "I'm Alex Bound of the dragonriders' squad Boundless. I'm Chine's rider."

The dragon eyed Chine, his one eye also focusing on the dragon. "Yes, I know Chine. A child of one of our sister tribes, one angry enough to forsake his horde for battle. Tell me, Chine, how does your decision sit with you now?"

Anabelle heard Chine's voice in her head for the first time. He must have been making an effort to speak to all the dragons and mortals. *War is harsh. I have seen many lives lost, those of my friends and those I consider family, but none from my new herd have fallen. Alex is a brave leader and a caring human. There are no riders as noble as she is.*

The old ether dragon roared as he dug up the ground with his claws. *And that is why you bring this great evil to your home?*

Rasputina removed her hood and released the reins of the horse she had guided. "I see you still recognize me, even with a new layer of skin."

Anabelle wasn't surprised that the ether dragons knew Rasputina, but she wasn't sure how well. Most creatures of the nine realms knew liches as an abstract evil, and many had been touched by a lich's evil.

The old ether dragon snarled as his lizard eyes narrowed on Rasputina. *How could we forget? Our lives and stories are not so short that we would neglect to tell our children the tales of Rasputina, the profane lich, who cut our numbers down to what they are today. I believe it was my mother who managed to burn off your skin?*

Rasputina opened her robe, showing a scar that ran down from her neck to her groin. "Aye, it was she who cut me open and spilled my guts for the first time. A powerful warrior."

And yet, that didn't stop you from burning our homes to the ground and covering the earth with our corpses. Forgive me, lich, if my memory distorts the truth, but was it not you who gnawed the bones of our fallen for centuries, guarding them like a feral beast?

There was no remorse on the lich's face as she listened to the dragon. "Your memory serves you well, and it would do no good to tell you that I am not the same lich. I've had a portion of my soul restored. Perhaps I am still a monster, but not as monstrous as I once was."

The dragon breathed a plume of smoke from his nostrils. *Ah, a soul now? It's obvious that its weight is dragging you down with remorse.*

Rasputina's face showed no change. "I did not come here to apologize. It would fall on deaf ears, regardless of my capacity for feeling. All I need for you to know that I came here for the same purposes as these three."

The dragon took a step forward and bowed his head in front of Suzuki and Anabelle, watching them closely. *And what is that purpose?*

Anabelle and Suzuki exchanged glances as they tried to figure out who should speak. "Uh, I think you should handle this one," the elf said. "You're the one with the dragon clout."

Suzuki cleared his throat to speak and Anabelle saw the warrior disappear for a second, replaced by a twenty-something man riddled with insecurity, but only for a moment. If Anabelle hadn't been used to looking for those small moments, she wouldn't have seen it.

"We've come to ask for your help against the Dark One," Suzuki explained.

A mighty hiss went up from the dragons crouching on the craggy black stones.

Anabelle didn't need decades of people watching to know what that sound meant.

The old dragon chuckled as he leaned back on his hind legs, towering above Myrddin's agents. *You wish us to join your fight? This battle among mortals is of no consequence to us. The dragons have been and always will be. Whatever happens to you small, scurrying, naked creatures is of no importance to us. We have told countless young dragons who wished to fight the Dark One the same thing. This is not our problem or our fight.*

"Except it is," Anabelle said.

The old dragon leered at Anabelle, his mouth slightly open as if to remind her that he could swallow her if he felt the need to. *How is it our problem?*

Anabelle knew dragons were exceptional at oration, and they valued it second to none. She was going to have to be careful with her words. She'd seen enough from Suzuki to know what to shoot for.

"The elves believed this conflict was above them for years. Myrddin had tried for years to convince us to fight alongside him, but we thought it was the problem of the dust children. The problems of those who lived a mere two hundred years at most were not ours. We would simply wait for the conflict to end and go back to our lives."

Anabelle watched the dragon's expression, trying to read it. She couldn't gather much other than that she had his attention and perhaps that of those watching as well.

"But that isn't what happened. The Dark One enslaved the orcs before we realized it and then began attacking and enslaving every living being in the nine realms he could get his hands on. You dragons are not above it. I have fought drakes, wyrms, and dragons under the Dark One's control. It might be difficult to find and subdue you, but it *is* possible, and it is happening. You can make the same mistake the elves made and stand by idly as your people are reduced to pawns, or you can bring the fight to him and end this threat before it wipes you out."

The old dragon settled down on all his legs and smiled. *Oh, little elf, you speak of your people's pain with a candor unseen among most of the fae folk. Your words ring true, yet you allow that despicable creature to walk at your side as if you were equals? Explain this.*

Anabelle didn't have time for bullshit. She was going to say it as plainly as possible. "This lich killed thousands of humans in cold blood. She cut open my friend's stomach and nearly killed her. Another former lieutenant of the Dark One is also working with us. That one tortured me for a week. Made me lick her boots after she pulled three teeth out of my mouth. I would kill them the moment I had the chance and enjoy it more than I've enjoyed anything in my entire life, but for now, I need them. That's how important defeating the Dark One is."

The old dragon thought these words over, humming under his breath before turning back to the dragons behind him, still humming.

Anabelle assumed they were speaking. He finally said, *The words you speak ring true, but my brothers and sisters are not convinced. We have seen the guile of the Dark One. You are not the first to come to our home and request our services.*

"Who came to you?"

A man dressed in black, glowing with purple energy. He was quite upset when we refused to join him. And many before him.

Anabelle recognized the description as the same one Abby had given her of Tesla. "How long ago did that man come here?"

The dragon scratched his chin as he thought. *A few days ago.*

Anabelle breathed a sigh of relief. Tesla obviously knew the weakness the DGA was planning on exploiting, but he wouldn't have enough time to figure out a workaround if she was able to convince the dragons to join their cause. Not even Abby could figure something out that fast. "What do we have to do to prove ourselves?"

A simple test. Only one of you is necessary. We will present you with a situation, and you choose what you believe to be the best decision. It is the same challenge, to a certain degree, that we've given all who request our help. What do you say?

"May we have time to choose?"

As long as you need.

The party huddled together, looking at each other.

Anabelle figured either Suzuki or Alex should go. Suzuki's name was highly esteemed among dragons. Alex had a relationship with an ether dragon. Both were competent leaders and would probably make the right decision. Obviously Rasputina was out of the running.

She was about to offer her opinion when Rasputina said, "Anabelle."

Suzuki and Alex were caught mid-sentence, both saying, "Anabelle" as well.

The elf was taken aback. "Why the hell would you guys select me? Neither of you knows me."

Suzuki shook his head. "I've been hearing rumors about the DGA for a while. If you're a fraction of the leader I've been hearing about, you can handle this."

Alex scratched behind her ear, looking uncertain. "You're one of the few people who seems like you genuinely want to give me a chance. I feel good about you speaking for us."

Anabelle tried not to meet Rasputina's eyes. She would have thought she'd be unconcerned about why the lich named her, but that wasn't true. The curiosity was there, even if she didn't want to ask.

Rasputina must have picked up on her interest. "I've fought many foes, none of them as simple and honorable as you."

There wasn't any reason to waste time arguing. If they wanted Anabelle to take the test, she would.

Anabelle left the huddle and approached the old ether dragon. "I'll do it."

He smiled, his sharp fangs gleaming. *Then we will begin.*

The court disappeared, melting in the same fashion Anabelle had seen the world warping on their ride toward the dragons. She was in a blank space, a reality coming into existence.

There was a wail in the darkness. A child crying. The darkness shifted around her, taking form and shape.

Anabelle was in a hut. A woman stood above a crib, cooing to the child crying in it.

The ether dragon's voice echoed in Anabelle's head. *Our tribe is gifted with an immense boon in our final years. Many dragons can see into the past, but we are the only ones who can send a person to those moments.*

"Where am I now?"

You are watching the Dark One's first moments.

"Can they see me?"

No, but they will feel you.

Anabelle's heart froze, but she could not keep herself rooted to the spot. She walked over to the side of the crib, as far from the woman attending the child as she could get, and looked in.

The child in the crib was a small, pink thing murmuring softly, calling out for his mother.

You could end it here, Anabelle. For years, we have wondered if we should do it ourselves, but we are old. We don't have the perspective we once did. But you...you have fought this war and seen your own die. If there is anyone who knows the sacrifices that have been made, it is you. Do you wish to end the Dark One's reign?

Anabelle looked down at the child. She could stop it all right now. Smother the Dark One with the pillow in the crib. Put an end to the suffering of the nine realms before it even began. The child meant nothing to Anabelle. It struck no chord in her. There was merely the whining of one who would eventually take the lives of those who were dear to her.

She stood above the child and glanced at the mother. There was no feeling there either.

For the first time, Anabelle realized she had changed. She wasn't the same person who had wanted to quit being Myrddin's public face, who wanted to join the war effort and fight on her own terms. Now she knew hard choices had to be made, choices that she would eventually regret.

"If I kill him now, he's gone forever. Just like that?" Anabelle asked.

The old dragon's words echoed in Anabelle's mind. *It will be as if he never existed. Your actions here will reverberate throughout time.*

Anabelle reached down into the crib, past the pillow beside the child's head. Instead of grabbing the pillow, she brushed the child's cheek, stroking it gently. The child looked up at Anabelle and cooed softly. "This child hasn't done anything. I'd kill the man for his crimes, but not an innocent baby."

The room disappeared, and Anabelle was back in the dragon's grotto. The elder dragon was looking at her, smiling his toothy grin. *You would let the Dark One live?*

"I'd let a child live."

The dragon laughed, his voice ringing in Anabelle's head. *You've chosen an interesting champion, humans. It takes a very special heart, one of a kindness we have not seen before, to make that decision. I wonder what any of you would have done in her situation.*

Alex and Suzuki avoided Anabelle's eyes when she asked, "Did you see it too?"

Both nodded, but it was Rasputina who spoke. "I would have killed him."

The older ether dragon spread his wings as he leaned back on his hind legs. *Then it is good you were not chosen. In case you didn't know, elf, dragons are constrained by time like the rest of you. Our gifts are often exaggerated.*

Anabelle let out a sigh of relief. "So, did I pass?"

The dragon looked over his shoulder at the rest of the ether dragons, who were walking toward Anabelle and her group. *I believe you have the moral fortitude to wield the power of our flames.*

CHAPTER EIGHTEEN

Anabelle, Suzuki, Rasputina, and Alex returned to the base on Middang3ard. Generally, congratulations would have been in order for having pulled off such an important mission, but it seemed as if everyone was stuck in their own thoughts. Anabelle knew she was.

She kept thinking about the choice she'd made in the elder dragon's mind trap. There hadn't been any real thought behind it. She'd done what she thought was right. But was it?

Even if the child was innocent, he was responsible for the deaths of thousands, maybe even millions. Anabelle knew the scenario was merely a trick, but if she had really been able to kill the Dark One as a babe, would it have been right to walk away and leave him living?

Rasputina would have killed the child; the lich already had made that much known. What about the rest of them? Or Terra and Abby? For some people, these would have merely been interesting questions. They seemed like more to Anabelle. She couldn't get them out of her head.

Roy was waiting for them at the hangar. "How did everything go?"

Alex crossed her arms when she saw Roy and stopped walking.

Roy shrugged as he walked over to Anabelle. "Don't worry, I'm not here to arrest you," he told Alex. "If you held up your end of the bargain, I'll hold up mine."

Anabelle wanted to hug Roy, but she wanted to get him alone first. It had been so long since she'd felt him lying against her, she'd almost forgotten what it felt like. Or that they were dating at all.

Suzuki was the one to speak up and explain everything. "Alex led us to the dragons, just like she promised. Anabelle took care of the logistics. It looks like we have a squad of ether dragons for the party."

Roy smiled at Anabelle, his eyes lingering on her waist. "Good job. Glad you handled this one. Those dragons are our last chance at ending this bullshit with the Netherverse Gates as quickly as possible. And we still have a shit-ton to get set up. Abby's disappeared, and I can't find her anywhere. Even Persephone doesn't know where she is."

Anabelle couldn't believe she forgot to tell Roy what was going on with Abby. She could have kicked herself. "Oh, we can talk about that later. How's the rest of the preparation going?"

"Well, luckily, Abby left us all of her work. She was putting together a system of bombs to be planted throughout the Netherverse. The nanobots she left there have been sending back phenomenal intel. Creon's been mapping the region. From what we can see, there's a nearly infinite number of souls, but Tesla's only been able to revive a section of them. He's mostly been concentrating on areas near the two Gates, which leads me to think that the Dark One doesn't have the resources to activate them all at once. From what we've seen, Tesla's the only one on the job."

"That's good to hear. Anything else? I've kind of been out of the loop for a bit."

"Come on, let's walk and talk. Suzuki, Alex, what are you two going to do now?"

Suzuki pointed at his HUD. "If this is going to be as big a battle as you make it seem like, the Mundanes want in. Tell us where to go, and we'll be there."

Roy scratched his chin as he thought. "The Mundanes would be a good addition. We'll send you to the orc planet. Terra's leading the strike, and I'm pretty sure you're already familiar with her."

Suzuki opened his HUD and scrolled through it. "Yeah, I am. Stew's going to lose his shit. Sandy and Beth will be stoked too. Everyone loved her. And it'll be nice not to have to give orders."

Roy turned to Alex. "What about you?"

Alex was glaring at Roy. The little bit of softness Anabelle thought she'd seen earlier was gone. "What exactly am I allowed to do?"

"Like I said, I'm holding up my end of the deal. You can walk."

Alex looked from Roy to Anabelle and Suzuki. "Everything wiped clean?"

"I don't know how many more ways I can say you can leave."

"Good. Then Boundless wants in on this. You need as much firepower as you can get, and I have an ether dragon to boot. Use us as infantry like you're using the Mundanes."

Roy thought it over, chewing his bottom lip. "Unless Myrddin knows something I don't, and if he were here, he would kill me for this, but you're in. We'll send you to the gnome world. Our agents Sarah and Kravis will be leading that charge. I'll reinstate your anchors to the system. You'll both receive briefings for your team in a little bit."

Alex walked up to Roy and extended her hand. "Thank you."

Roy stared at her hand for a moment before taking it. As they shook, his eyes glazed over and his lip twitched before returning to normal. He smiled at the dragonrider. "It's going to be a fight worth remembering. Now, hunt down the science department, and they'll be able to get you home. Third floor. It's huge. You won't be able to miss it."

He turned with military precision and started to leave. "Care for a walk, Anabelle?"

Anabelle quickly caught up to him. "Where are we walking?"

"If I had my way, I'd say a broom closet if it's closer than either of our beds, but that'll have to wait. I know you know where Abby is, and if you haven't told me yet, I figured you have a pretty good reason. There's a place we can talk and no one will hear us."

Anabelle followed Roy as he went down hall after hall, turning left and then right without any seeming reason. Finally, he stopped in front of a nondescript door. "Did you do all this just to find another broom closet to fuck in?"

Roy sighed as he opened the door. "I'd much rather be lying in bed with you then crammed into a broom closet. I know that shit gets you off, but I would prefer a soft mattress."

Anabelle stepped into the room. "Wait, I thought you were into that closed space stuff."

"Fuck, no. I like to spread out."

"Hm. We should probably talk more about these things."

"Later. Check this."

Roy hit the light switch. The room was covered in white tiles and was empty save for two black chairs facing each other.

Anabelle looked around, trying to find what was so special about it. "I don't get it?"

Roy took a seat in one of the chairs and motioned for Anabelle to do the same. "It's a utility room. Myrddin put one in after he saw Harry Potter. You wouldn't believe how many things he's ripped off from those movies. He's lucky Rowling hasn't walked into this place and doesn't follow me on Twitter."

"J.K. Rowling has a Twitter?"

"Who doesn't? I wouldn't recommend following, though. She only posts trash. But anyway, the room will give us whatever we need. Myrddin and I have used it a lot for discreet conversations. Now, where the hell is Abby?"

Anabelle quickly explained the situation.

Roy stared at Anabelle in disbelief the entire time she was speaking. "Wait, are you telling me you sent one of our youngest operatives undercover without anything close to a plan? Do you know how bad an idea that is?"

"She can take care of herself. She's smart."

Roy jumped to his feet and started pacing around the room. "It has nothing to do with being smart. It takes years for us to train operatives to go undercover, and sometimes even longer to make sure they get put in the right place. You can't just drop someone into a situation like that with no training. How do you know it wasn't a ploy to get her away from the team?"

"I went with my gut. Abby knows what she's doing. It doesn't matter how young she is. I believe in her."

Roy sank back into the chair. "This is going to shit real—"

A crackle of static cut Roy off. Martin popped up on a holoscreen between Anabelle and Roy. "You guys having a tea party or something?"

Roy yelped and fell back in his chair. "What the hell are you doing here? Aren't you with Abby?"

Martin twirled as he groaned. "Don't you pay attention to anything? Remember when you had me installed on everyone's HUD? That's the whole reason I was created. I'm always here. Most of my platform processing power is with Abby. In that way, I'm sort of like God."

Anabelle had also forgotten that Martin was always around. If she hadn't been so glad to see him, she'd have been creeped out. "What's going on with Abby?"

"So, when Tesla offered Abby a position in the Dark One's army, he kind of neglected to mention that the position was as a giant battery to supercharge his ability to resurrect the Dark One's army. Who would have thought he wouldn't have been straightforward, right?"

Roy glared at Anabelle as he got back to his feet. "Is she okay?"

"Oh, yeah, she's fine. Abby has enough reserves to power sixteen nuclear plants if she wanted. The problem is that she's resurrecting a *lot* of ghouls. Also, you guys should come up with a better name for them. Ghouls? Really? It's like no one's bothered to pick up a copy of a *Monsters Handbook*."

"Martin!"

"Sorry, sorry. So, yeah, Abby's safe. She's a battery now. Uh, what else, oh! Did you guys find the bomb info we left behind?"

Roy nodded as he crossed his legs. "Yes. Creon's taking care of that."

"Sweet. Okay. Last bit of info. You need to get Abby out of the Netherverse. She's cooking up a surprise because she can't take Tesla down, given how stressed her system is. So, be a dear and get a package from Creon and bring it to Abby in the Netherverse. He'll know what we're talking about. And don't talk about it out loud. Or in any messages. Or at all, actually. Tesla has the whole place bugged. I've been keeping him from getting most of what's being said and disabling his planted bugs, but he's good. Be extra careful. AI Messiah out!"

Martin disappeared, leaving Anabelle with Roy's anger. "He did say she was safe," she muttered.

Roy pulled up his HUD and started messaging. "Change of plans. Terra's not leading the strike. Cire can take care of that. She's going into the Netherverse with you, and you are getting Abby back."

"Sounds good to me. Is there anything else we need to take care of?"

Roy checked the time on his HUD. "We still have a couple of hours before go time. Do you want to try to relax?"

"How many hours?"

"About eight."

Anabelle looked around the room again. "How does this place work?"

"You just close your eyes, think about what you want, and the room will take care of it for you."

Anabelle shut her eyes tight and tried to relax. She knew what she wanted if she had eight hours to kill with Roy. It was going to be memorable.

When Anabelle opened her eyes, Roy was sitting on a lush, velvet bed, holding two glasses and a bottle of ancient elvish wine. The bottle was already open, and Roy smiled as he filled the glasses.

Anabelle took a seat on the bed, crossed her legs, and accepted a glass. "We could die tomorrow."

Roy and Anabelle clinked their glasses together. "I can't think of anyone I'd rather spend my last few hours with."

"Don't let the wine go to your head. It's a special blend I've heard about. Wasn't sure how I was ever going to get it, but here you go. Also, check under the bed."

Roy reached underneath the bed and felt around, then pulled out a large black box. He cracked it open and his eyes widened. "There's a lot in here."

Anabelle leaned over and kissed Roy's neck before whispering in his ear, "Don't worry, we have enough time. And I'll make sure you get a lot of rest."

The two collapsed onto the bed, their bodies hungry for each other as they tore their clothes off and descended into passion.

CHAPTER NINETEEN

Anabelle traveled to the orc world before the sun rose. Roy was awake by the time she was ready. He was hunched over his rifle, cleaning it meticulously. When he saw Annabelle, he smiled. "You make sure you don't get yourself killed, all right?"

There wasn't any point to bravado. Anabelle kissed Roy gently on the lips and told him that she loved him, then left before he had a chance to say anything else.

Now she was stepping through the hadron collider. As she walked into the orcish world, she saw Terra and Cire waiting for her.

Terra clasped Anabelle's forearm, something the elf had seen many orcs do. "What's our kid gotten herself into this time?"

"Nothing I didn't think she could handle. There was just a lot more to handle than I thought there would be."

"Roy made it sound like she was dying in the Netherverse. What's going on?"

"Don't quite know. All Abby told me was that Tesla threatened to kill Persephone if she didn't work with him. Martin said something about her being turned into a giant battery."

"That sounds like something Tesla would do. Both him and

Edison. Crazy. Not the kind of geniuses I would trust. I'd rather go without electricity."

Anabelle stared at Terra, dumbfounded. "Are you serious? You think you could live without electricity?"

Terra shrugged as she walked toward the Netherverse Gate. "All I'm saying is that you can't trust nerds. Other than Abby. The rest of them.... maybe Suzuki and those Mundanes. They seem pretty nerdy, but after that, nope. Not a one of 'em. They think too much. An abnormal amount. You? You think a regular amount. Cire, he thinks a regular amount. But not nerds. I don't trust them."

Cire was waiting for them at the Netherverse Gate. "Good to see you, Anabelle. Are you well-rested?"

"Rested enough to finish this war," she said. "How about you?"

Terra jabbed the elf in the side. "We got to bed at a reasonable time. Do we have a decent fix on Abby's position?"

Anabelle pulled up her HUD. Martin's grouchy paperclip face stared at her as he sipped a cup of coffee. "You know where Abby is, right?"

Martin drained his coffee and tossed the cup over his shoulder. "I have a rough idea of where she is. I'll be able to guide you to the general area, but after that, you're on your own. Most of our resources were being to make sure we got a good lay of the land, and let me tell you, it was a doozy to take care of. The format of the Netherverse has been changing, almost like it's anticipating what's about to happen. I don't know if that's the Netherverse or if Tesla has something to do with it, but that's where most of my time has been going. I figured you two would be able to figure out the rest."

Anabelle looked at the map Martin had just sent her. "Your faith in us is astounding, Martin."

"I try to give credit where it's due."

In the distance, Anabelle could hear chanting. It was deep and slow, accompanied by war drums. "What the hell is that?"

Cire and Terra both smiled. "You have to see this," Terra said. "Cire, can you do the thing. Please?" She turned to Anabelle. "Since he became a shaman, he can do a lot of ridiculous things. This one isn't my favorite, but it's pretty fucking close."

Cire raised his hands, and his eyes glowed white. His feet floated off the ground, as did Anabelle's and Terra's. They rose into the air high enough to see over the hills.

What Anabelle saw took her breath away. For miles upon miles there were orcs adorned with war paint, carrying axes and swords and all manner of other weapons. They were chanting in perfect unison, their voices louder now, the old call to battle—the blood songs.

Terra was humming the same tune under her breath. "Pretty amazing, huh?" she asked Anabelle.

The elf struggled to find words for what she was looking at. "When you guys kept saying horde, I didn't realize you meant an *actual* horde. This is amazing."

"There were a lot of orcs the Dark One never got close to touching, plus those we rescued. And there's only going to be more. We're going to crush him, and it begins today."

Cire returned Anabelle and Terra to the ground as both women received pings from their HUDs.

A hologram of Sarah, Kravis, Roy, Suzuki, and Alex appeared before them.

Roy checked to see if everyone was present. "Alex and Suzuki, where are you right now?"

Suzuki answered first. "We're up near the front of the horde. We saw Cire in the air a few minutes ago."

Alex spoke next. "Just arrived at the gnomes' camp. The little dudes were pretty freaked out when they saw the dragons, but Brath was able to calm everyone down pretty quickly. The guy is practically a legend here, I guess. I'd forgotten gnomes don't ride dragons."

Roy looked at Kravis and Sarah. "How about you two?"

"I'm ready to storm our Gate," Sarah said. "Kravis will lead the gnomes into the Gate after me."

"What do you mean?"

"You have a strike team from the orc world. The gnome world Gate should be just as prepared."

Grok stepped into sight, alongside Rasputina. "Since Terra and Anabelle have mostly mastered the Path of the Lost, you have a shit-ton of power on one side. That could easily tip to us getting fucked over here. I'm not losing the gnome world again. This way, we should be able to apply equal pressure from both assaults. Make sense?"

Anabelle expected Roy to freak out, but he was quiet for a few seconds before speaking. "Good thinking. Completely slipped my mind. Thanks for making sure you both were covered."

Sarah smiled as she glanced at Grok and Rasputina. "I have no doubt that these two will do great."

"Okay, so, who's going to give the speech? We must have one before we go running into the realm of the dead. That's, like, a hard rule." Roy smirked.

Everyone looked at one another. Anabelle didn't have anything to say. She'd be more than happy if someone else took care of their parting words.

Rasputina stepped forward. "I... There is no reason I should have been given a chance like this. There is nothing I will ever be able to do to redeem myself, but this...this is more than I deserve. I will do everything in my power to show you my thanks."

Although her face betrayed no emotion, tears were rolling down her cheeks. She wiped them away and stepped back.

Roy sucked a breath through his teeth. "Uh, that was not quite what I had in mind but—"

Terra pulled out her axe and turned to the horde, her back facing the rest of the group. "Cire, translate, please."

The orc stepped into the holographic conference. "Death awaits us beyond those Gates," he translated as Terra's voice boomed. "Today, we walk among the dead. We will watch them rise, and we will watch them fall. Today we look at what our bodies will one day become, and we will say, 'Not today, Death.' Today we will slay our fallen comrades, and we will give them the dignified deaths they deserved. We will find the Dark One and strangle the life out of him while the Elder Gods watch us in their glorious indifference.

"Not all of us will come back, and we relish that. The dead will die the most honorable deaths imaginable, and when they rise again, we will strike them down once more and give them the deaths they deserve. Those of us who live will hold our boots over the neck of the Dark One. We will bleed him dry and drink of his blood. We will tear his flesh and feed it to the dogs. We will show him the strength of the horde. We will leave only death in our wake!"

The cheers of the orcs beyond the hills were thunderous as Terra turned back to the agents.

Anabelle quietly murmured, "You're getting pretty good at that."

Terra slammed her fist to her chest. "Can we get going already? I'm tired of talking. I'd like to kill something now."

Roy pointed to someone off-screen. "All right, Creon, pop those Gates open. I'll be joining you shortly. Try to stay alive until I get there."

The Netherverse Gate opened in front of Anabelle and Terra as the holograms faded.

The elf met Terra's eyes. "If there was anyone I'd want to fight Death with by my side, it'd be you. I respect you a lot."

Terra punched Anabelle in the arm. "Hold off on all the sappy shit until Abby's here. She's going to get a kick out of it."

She ran through the Gate.

Anabelle took a deep breath and followed her.

As she passed through the portal, the air went cold. It felt as if it had been sucked out of her lungs and replaced by ice, an unnerving sensation. When she saw the Netherverse, the uncomfortable feeling was replaced by pure dread.

Anabelle had reviewed Abby's report on her experience in the Netherverse, but it did nothing to prepare her for what was in front of her.

The plains of the Netherverse were built of souls. Anabelle could see their hands poking out of the ground as if they had been heaped up and were clawing their way out from under each other.

Jagged pieces of purple stone floated through the air, stretching to an infinite darkness broken only by flashes of purple lightning followed by thunder that sounded as if the world were collapsing on itself.

Out in the darkness, colossal shapes moved, barely visible—millions of tentacles wrapping around each other, sliding over bulbous bone skulls with a sea of eyes, skin peeling, revealing something deeper that Annabelle could not bring herself to look at.

Terra looked to be just as displaced as Anabelle before suddenly laughing. "Abby's gotta get better at her reports. She should have mentioned that this place was a fucking walking nightmare."

Anabelle couldn't help but laugh too. Only Terra could look upon the horrors of the Elder Ones and find something to laugh at. "Come on, let's head toward those coordinates."

The two of them sprinted toward the location Martin had given them.

Bolts of purple lightning repeatedly struck the ground in that direction.

Suddenly, a shockwave of purple energy blasted through the ground, rippling across Anabelle's and Terra's feet.

Around them, the hands of the souls started to shake, coming to life. The ground rose and fell as if an earthquake were rolling through the Netherverse.

In the distance, Anabelle could see the faint outline of two figures floating in the air. Beneath them was a force of ghouls that could not be counted.

Terra spoke into her HUD. "All forces roll in. Get ready to fuck shit up."

The two stared at the army in front of them. "You think the horde can handle this?"

Terra nodded as she stretched her arms. "Yeah. Cire'll take care of it. You ready?"

"I've never just slipped into the Path."

Terra clenched her fists. "We did it before, so we can do it again. Let's go get Abby."

Anabelle closed her eyes and let herself sink within. The mana flowed through her as she focused on the only thing that was important: her strength. She let it consume her, burning within her like a fire threatening to devour everything.

Flames burst from her skin, covering her in a fiery aura. She and Terra screamed, their eyes glowing white. "I'm ready," the elf said.

The two of them launched toward the site, leaving a trail of energy behind them, heading for the thousands of ghouls standing between them and Abby.

The horde poured into the Netherverse as Anabelle and Terra slashed through the thousands of ghouls ahead of them.

Terra, moving faster than she ever had in her life, sliced through the ghouls in front of her, Anabelle at her side like a flaming rocket. They eviscerated everything in front of them with the power coursing through their veins.

Neither of them could see the ghouls in detail. Even though time was moving slower for them, they were racing toward Abby.

The horde's purpose was to handle the ghouls. Abby was theirs.

A bolt of lightning struck directly in front of them. The elf flung herself to the right while Terra increased her speed, narrowly missing being struck.

The ghouls far behind them, they stood before the two floating figures: Abby and Tesla.

Abby's armor had changed. It looked more militaristic and vicious. Spikes ran down her back and across her shoulders. Her forearms were covered with blades, and her eyes glowed an eerie black. Other than eyes, there were no other facial features.

Tesla slowly turned around. His pupils were purple, and his mouth was turned up in an unforgiving grin. He had the audacity to twirl his mustache as he cackled. "Ah, my dear ladies. I believe you have arrived too late. Abby has been helping me power the Dark One's army. How does it feel to have one of your own leave your ranks to serve me, the Great Tesla?"

Terra drew her axe. "I thought you were serving the Dark One. The way you make it sound, you are the one in charge."

Tesla laughed again. "My dear, it does not matter who I serve. My genius will be known regardless. Bow before my technological glory. Look at what I have done to your precious Abby! Her tech was a little lacking. Rudimentary, I would say. I've given her a few improvements. perhaps a microchip or two." He followed this statement with an aggravating old-time laugh reminiscent of the worse vaudeville.

Anabelle's heart sank as she imagined the worst. Maybe Roy had been right, and it had been a mistake to encourage Abby to try to work both sides. Just by looking at the girl, Anabelle could tell something was different.

Tesla waved his hand, causing another bolt of lightning to strike the ground in front of him. "Abby, my dear, my muse, please show them the power you can call with just a little bit of ingenuity."

Abby floated forward, her eyes flashing brightly as the blades running down her spine glowed. "It would be our pleasure." She raised her hand, her arm converting to a plasma cannon that dwarfed anything she had created before. She aimed it at Anabelle and Terra. "We have experienced substantial upgrades. There's nothing more we would like to do than show them off."

And then she winked.

She spun, her cannon trained on Tesla, and fired a plasma blast the size of a MAC truck. The blast rocketed at the scientist, who let out a yelp and teleported out of the way.

Abby flew to Terra and Anabelle, laughing. "Oh my God, can you believe he fell for that? We swear, all we did was make our armor look 'evil,'" she said with air quotes, "and he totally bought it. I don't understand how a genius could have been so stupid."

Tesla's eyes shifted from purple to red. "You were faking? But I showed you so many diagrams and shared so many theories. I thought we were bonding as equals!"

Abby was doubled over laughing. "We know! It was hilarious. You really need to work on your people skills. Like, learn how to read a room, my dude."

Tesla crossed his arms and pouted. "Some of us are beyond the normal realms of intelligence and don't waste time on trivial things. We pursue the sciences and truth."

Abby wasn't listening to Tesla. She was already talking to Anabelle and Terra. "Dude, you won't even believe this. He handed us his improvements on the microchip before he chipped us. Just put it in our hand. We broke it down and came up with a counter-virus for it, so the Dark One won't be enslaving anyone new for a while."

Tesla grabbed his head and screamed, "Noooooooooooo! How could you betray me?"

The blades on Abby's armor withdrew. "Oh, that's not even the best part. He put us in charge of powering the whole first quadrant of the ghouls."

Abby held out her arm, and her HUD projected a holographic image of the battlefield. "Looks like we have your orcs here, and Sarah's forces on the other side. And...yep, here we go." She tapped the holoscreen.

In the distance, there was a giant explosion that shook the ground they were standing on. "That takes care of probably half the ghouls that were resurrected," Abby said as she dusted her hands off and took a bow. "Thank you, thank you. We'd like to thank the Academy for this award, and Terra for always reminding me how strong we are, and Anabelle for always encouraging us to take risks."

Terra slapped her knee as she laughed and gave Abby a high five. "Dude, that was fucking awesome. He didn't even see it coming."

Tesla was still stewing above them, unable to deal with his defeat.

Terra pointed at the man. "So, what now? Do we just beat the shit out of that nerd?"

Abby raised her hand. "Not yet, not yet. This is the best part." Her hand flashed bright white, and a portal opened in front of her.

Persephone stepped out and sent her tentacles flying.

Abby giddily pointed to her hand. "We also jacked his teleportation tech. He wasn't joking about the upgrades. We got hooked up! Uh, Persy, you wanna help the orcs or the gnomes?"

Persephone stared at the Elder Gods as she thought. "I think I'll give Sarah a hand."

Abby opened a new portal as Martin projected a holographic version of himself. "All fun and games once you get portals, huh?" He groaned.

Persephone jumped through the portal, and it closed behind her.

Abby took another bow. "*Now* we can beat the shit out of this nerd."

"Enough!" Tesla shouted as thunder boomed behind him. "I will not be mocked."

A bolt of lightning struck him, and then another, and yet another. He fell to the ground, screaming in pain and rage as bolts continued to hit him.

Terra stepped forward, swinging her axe. "Don't even worry about it, guys. Me and Anabelle unlocked our ultimate potential. We can handle this in, like, two seconds."

She tossed her axe in the air, caught it, and ran toward Tesla, then brought the blade down in a move designed to finish him.

Tesla raised one hand and caught it. "I do not think it will be that simple, my dear." He let out a roar and lightning blasted from his body, sending Terra flying.

Tesla floated into the air, purple lightning flashing from his eyes as vents opened on his body, exuding steam. "My social skills might be lacking, but my genius cannot be doubted."

He teleported in front of Abby and Anabelle and loosed a torrent of electricity that sent both members of the DGA flying. "I am Tesla, the Master of Electricity."

Anabelle skidded across the ground as hands reached up to grab and pull her down. She flexed her mana, scorching everything beneath her. "Abby, make me some space!"

Abby casually flicked her hand to the right as her body pulsed with kinetic energy. She blasted forward and connected with Tesla, who caught her mid-charge and held onto her wrist. The girl vented steam as her body recharged.

All around Anabelle, ghouls were beginning to rise, their mouths foaming as the Dark Melody they'd been introduced to earlier started to tear out of their corpses.

The elf flipped backward, torching them to ashes. "Terra, I want you to take care of the ground."

Terra swung her massive axe, cleaving through the ghouls rising near her.

Anabelle pulled up her HUD and pinged the other commanders. "Cire, Sarah, I want reports now. Where the hell are those dragons? We're going to need them soon!"

Sarah's voice came through first. "The gnome division is working its way through the first wave. I'm glad I brought Rasputina and Grok along. Even with the dragonriders, we're only barely cutting through these bastards. We're going to be able to make it, though. We're forcing a path toward you. Figure anything that dies on the way is a job done well."

Cire came in next. "A set of explosions helped us out a lot. We're outnumbered, but the horde wishes to prove something. They're fighting as if they plan on being immortalized here. We're also making our way toward you. It will be bloody, but we will be there."

"All right, keep heading this way!" Anabelle shouted before flipping her HUD down. "You hear that, Tesla? You better quit while you're ahead. We have the numbers to take you down."

Another bolt of lightning hit Tesla. "Not if I get rid of you three first. Do you think I care about your silly Path? A bygone remnant of the past. I am the future. Even Abby saw the superiority of my tech."

Martin's image projected in front of Abby. "He does have a point. I mean, his tech is pretty out of control."

Anabelle laughed. "Yeah, okay, I'm supposed to believe that a reanimated Tesla is going to pose a challenge to us? This guy lost to Thomas Edison. I hardly know human history, and even I know how badly he got his ass kicked."

Tesla's eyes narrowed. "Do not speak his name in my presence."

The mad scientist teleported and reappeared in front of Anabelle, who tossed up her arms to block the lightning bolt he held. But Tesla didn't pull away. The rods on his back flashed brightly as the air filled with sounds of gears. Tesla's arms lengthened and forced their way through Anabelle's defense.

The ball of lightning hit Annabelle in the chest, shocking her into screams as she flew backward.

Tesla teleported above her, driving his elbow down into her stomach.

Anabelle hit the ground hard as Tesla floated above her, gathering electricity. He divebombed her, his body crackling with energy.

Abby slammed into his side, knocking him off course.

Tesla hit the ground hard, tearing open the earth and sending souls flying, then he jumped to his feet. He dashed forward, moving at the speed of light, and hit Terra with a jab in the jaw.

The force of the impact sent a shockwave past Terra, who tried to turn her face to meet Tesla's. Before she could, he teleported behind her and cracked his knee across her neck.

She stumbled forward, then swung her axe as she whirled toward him again.

Tesla's torso separated at the waist, allowing the axe to carve through the empty space. Then he reconnected, his hands glowing with electricity, and clapped them to Terra's head.

Anabelle rushed the man, and her fist connected with his chest. She let out a wild scream as she launched a flurry of attacks. Tesla blocked them all but only narrowly. Then he slipped up, and Anabelle saw her chance. She harnessed the power of the Path of the Lost while holding true to her knowledge of the ways of the Traveler and burst into a green mist, reforming behind Tesla. She grabbed him by the throat, spun and lifted him, then flung him to the ground. She remained in the air as her body flooded with mana, and then she dove at him and drove her fists into his chest. They disappeared into a crater.

As the resulting shockwave spread, Terra swung her axe in a circle, cleaving through the ghouls who were slowly gathering around them. Abby fired a precise laser, slicing up the remaining ghouls.

Anabelle leapt out of the crater and wiped a few drops of sweat off her brow. "What the hell did I tell you guys? Hardly even broke a sweat. We got this in the bag."

Terra walked over to her as Abby landed by her side. "Yeah, this was a cakewalk compared to Grok or Rasputina."

Abby's armor pulled back and she crossed her arms. "We didn't know you two had gotten so strong. Our upgrades look lame next to yours."

Terra shoved the girl. "Don't be stupid. You got all this practical shit. Nullifying a new microchip is kinda a big deal."

Abby kicked one of the leftover ghoul hands. "Yeah, but it doesn't *look* nearly as cool."

A chuckle came from the crater.

Anabelle and the rest of the DGA leaned in to check what was happening.

Tesla lay in the crater, his head crushed, brain and blood leaking from the hole. His legs were broken, and his left arm was a few feet from his torso. Yet he was laughing.

Anabelle's fist caught fire. "Hm. Thought you were dead."

He spoke in a dead, mechanical voice. "Reconfiguring based on combat data." The brain matter and blood were sucked back into the skull, which regrew its armor as his legs straightened out and his arm was magnetically drawn back to his body. A bolt of lightning hit him, and when the dust settled, he floated into the air. "Thank you for the data. Shall we proceed?"

Anabelle stepped forward. "Let me handle this." She leapt at him, her fists flaming as she swung.

Tesla teleported to the side and grabbed Anabelle's hand. "Elemental damage increased through an oscillating mana reserve. Simple enough." He let go, and she backhanded him.

The attack did no damage. Tesla looked at the elf curiously. "Also bolstered physical force. Calibrating."

Tesla emitted a burst of energy that sent her flying.

Terra tossed her axe on the ground. "Fuck this. I'm just gonna beat his ass."

Tesla landed on the ground and spread his arms, waiting for the attack.

Terra rushed him, slugging him in the face with everything she had. Tesla stood his ground, and the shockwave ripped the ground around him open as if it had been hit with an earth-destroying quake.

He blinked. "Pure blunt force, five megatons' worth. No elemental discharge. Calibrating."

"Calibrate this," Terra screamed as her energy swirled around her, causing her muscles to bulk up. She grabbed Tesla's skull and slammed her knee into his forehead.

The scientist landed on his feet. "Calibrations complete. Matching force." He backhanded Terra, sending her flying into one of the jagged rocks floating above. Then he turned to Abby. "Would you like to try now?"

Before Abby could answer, a voice said, "That will not be necessary."

Tesla turned to find the source of the voice and a blast of magical energy the size of a train hit him, sending him flying into the distance. It was impossible to see where he landed.

In the space where Tesla had stood was Myrddin, his raised wand still smoking. José stood by his side. "Shame to waste that on him," the wizard said. "This is the only time it will work."

Anabelle walked over to the two shades as Terra fell from the rock above and Abby flew over to them. "Fancy seeing you here."

"It shouldn't be. We've been searching for you for hours. The Netherverse is not a small place. It figures you would be on the opposite side from us."

Terra and Abby stared at Myrddin as if they'd seen a ghost. "You're...you're here?" the girl stammered.

Myrddin smiled kindly at her. "Yes, but we will have to save the celebration of our reunion for another time."

Terra shrugged. "Why? We have this thing in the bag. That nerd didn't even hit hard. What's the big deal?"

"'That nerd' is able to adjust to anything he's attacked by. Now, one of my strongest spells won't even affect him, so we must work fast."

Terra scoffed as she cracked her shoulders. "What for? The horde is taking care of those weak-ass ghouls, and Sarah and Kravis have the rest taken care of. And the ether dragons are still coming. We've won."

José chuckled to himself and raised his sword, which cast a shining light that cut through the darkness of the Netherverse.

In the distance was a tall tower covered in eyes and tentacles. The thousands of ghouls milling around it screeched and started to move toward the DGA, Myrddin, and José.

"That's where we need to go, and that's what we have to fight through," the MERC said.

"What the hell? Is that, like, an Elder God version of Mordor?" Anabelle asked.

Abby and Terra glanced at Anabelle, their eyes wide with surprise. "I thought you didn't know nerd stuff?" Abby asked.

The elf shrugged. "It's Tolkien. Everyone knows Tolkien. Come on, you didn't think I'd watch the movies? Legolas is...never mind."

Myrddin sighed. "Never mind, indeed. It's worse than Mordor. We call it the Heart of the Netherverse, and Tesla might very well be in control of it."

Anabelle nodded as she stared at the Hearth. "Cool. Let's go fuck it up."

PART 3

CHAPTER ONE

Terra took in the mass of ghouls. Even though she knew she should have been worried about them, she could not take her eyes off the tower. When she'd first seen it, the edifice had been connected to the ground. Now it had broken off and was floating up into the purple and red sky as asteroids zoomed past it and a heavy black fog Terra could hardly see through spread and obscured the tower.

At the tower's zenith, a bolt of purple lightning cracked. Then a thunderous roar ushered from the tower as the air around the tip started to twist and split as if a new portal were opening. Instead, a giant purple eye emerged.

As the eye glared around, casting purple light everywhere it looked, more eyes began to open all over the tower, creaking as if they were snakes trying to force their way through their soft eggshells.

Anabelle whistled, looking slightly worried. "Okay, I see the Mordor resemblance now. I swear, the Dark One must be a huge fantasy nerd. This is copyright infringement."

Myrddin, who was still gazing solemnly at the tower, shook his head. "It doesn't matter what he is a fan of. It goes much deeper than that. The Dark One is plugged into our universe. Whatever we've written, whatever we've seen, he consumes. It is his way of existing in our plane, and it makes him all the more dangerous."

Abby landed next to Terra and scanned at the tower. "So, what do we do now?"

Myrddin's blue eyes crackled as he turned to face the DGA agents. "That is the Dark One's stronghold. If we remove him from there, we might be able to stop him or possibly even kill him."

"Then what are we waiting for?"

Terra's HUD pinged, along with the rest of the DGA agents'. She looked down. It was a video transmission from Sarah. Her face was panicked, and the destruction could be seen around her. Gnomes were fighting ghouls, magic and plasma darting back and forth behind Sarah as she ran. As they watched, she took cover, gripping her pistol tightly, then popped out and fired.

The confidence in her eyes was gone, replaced by an almost bestial fear. "We're being overrun. I don't know what the hell happened, but the number of the ghouls tripled. We're going to have to fall back. There's no way we can take them."

Anabelle shouted into her HUD, "What about the dragons? Where are they?"

"Still en route. Alex says they'll be here, but I'm not sure if we can stay alive until then. If we retreat, we can at least keep them at bay at the Gate. It'll funnel all the ghouls through a killing hole. If we can defend that, we have a chance at holding out until the dragons ether-nuke this whole place."

The HUDS pinged again. This one was a message from Roy from within his dragon mech. "There are too many of them. What the hell are you guys doing over there?"

A few miles away, ghouls were starting to build up. They had pulled their rancid, rotting bodies from the corpses of the Elder Ones' dreams, the Dark Melody spreading over their flesh as they shook, wailing into the darkness as if their very existence was pain.

Anabelle glanced at them and grimaced. "We're having our own problems here. Did you call just to complain?"

"No," Roy shouted back. "We're retreating. We figure—"

"You can post up at the Gate and use it as a killing tunnel. Yeah, I figured."

Roy smiled. Even over the video, you could tell that he was impressed with what he thought was Anabelle's strategic knowledge. "Yeah, that's exactly what we were planning. Don't know how we got so many ghouls so fast. Just a couple of minutes ago, we were tearing through those sons of bitches. Now there's so fucking many of them."

Abby, who was pacing, snapped her fingers. "It's Tesla. He's using teleportation to jump to different areas and activate more of the ghouls."

An idea sparked in Terra's head. "Can't you track him? Teleport to wherever he is and keep him from resurrecting the ghouls?"

Abby shook her head, looking frustrated. "No, we can't. It eats up a lot of power. If we were to jump more than once, we would be so low on power, we wouldn't be able to defend ourselves, let alone fight Tesla."

Terra raised her hands to the thundering sky and screamed, "Damn you, Nikola Tesla, and your fucking science magic."

There had to be a better plan than this. All that Terra had heard was that everyone was going to need to retreat, putting the entirety of the fight with the Dark One on the DGA, Myrddin, and José. She knew that wasn't going to be nearly enough. "What are we supposed to do?" she asked, turning to Myrddin. "Don't you have a plan for this? What is your long game?"

Myrddin was silent, watching at the horde of ghouls approaching from the tower. "There was only a list of variables, and I perhaps put too much stock in one of them."

"What was that?"

The wizard's eyes darted from Terra to Anabelle. "The Path of the Lost. You and Anabelle are not the only ones who can channel that kind of power. Sarah can as well. I believed that if you three gathered, it would be enough to destroy the Dark One. I was not anticipating this kind of force from him."

"You thought our strength was enough to take him out?"

Myrddin nodded. "The Dark One is not like many of the trials you have faced. He is pure raw strength. His machinations and plans are only for him to deal with what happens in our physical realm. When we are alone with him, we will have only our strength."

Anabelle crouched, staring at the ground beneath her. "That's all we need? Raw power?" She looked at the Elder Gods floating above. "I have a plan."

Myrddin looked uneasy.

Anabelle stood and walked over to him. "You and I have had our issues, and I'll admit, you're the wise old man who knows everything that's going on all the time. But you put me in charge for a reason, and I'm asking you right now: do you trust me?"

There was no hesitation in Myrddin's answer. "Yes. Completely."

Anabelle turned to Terra. "Do you think you can punch through this with me? All the way to the tower?"

Terra looked at the floating tower as the ghouls continued to shamble in their direction. The feeling that came over her was difficult to describe. It was as if the fear melted, showing something else beneath, something she had only seen in glimpses and had once thought was the entirety. "I can make it to the tower as long as you don't slow me down."

Anabelle smiled, a glint of hope in her eyes. "Good. Here's the plan. Sarah, Rasputina, Grok, and Cire will meet us at the tower."

Myrddin's eyes went wide as he opened his mouth to speak.

Anabelle raised her hand, cutting him off. "Myrddin, you head to Roy's Gate and help command the troops. José, you go to the other Gate. Abby, you have the most important job. Bring Persephone to meet us."

Abby's face hardened with fear. "We told you, if we teleport all over the place, we won't have the power to fight Tesla. We'll be a sitting—"

"Cut it out, Abby."

Abby jumped at the sharpness in the elf's voice.

Anabelle's eyes were cool and stony as she stepped to Abby. "You're more than all that tech. You're strong. *You* are, not all the bells and whistles, and if there's anything you should have learned by now, it's that your strength comes from within.."

Abby shook her head. "No, it's not like that. We don't have magic like you, and we're not...we're not like Terra. We can't just will ourselves to be strong."

Anabelle rested her hand on the girl's shoulder and smiled. "That's not true." She tapped the side of Abby's head. "That's all magic. And that's all strength," she said as she pointed at her heart.

Terra stepped over. She knew the truth in Anabelle's words. "You got this, Abby."

The scientist's bottom lip trembled as she opened and closed her hands rapidly. "What if we...what if *I* screw up?"

Terra didn't think, she just acted. She wrapped her arms around her and hugged as tight as she could, lifting Abby into the air. "You're not going to fail. None of us are. You understand?"

She put her back on her feet as Anabelle threw her arm over Abby's shoulder. "And if you don't, you die, and we die, and that's pretty much the end of our problems."

Abby's laugh burst out of her as if she'd been trying to stifle it. "Okay, okay. Terra, you're killing it with the motivation. Anabelle, you could still use a little work. So, are we supposed to say something before our last big fight?"

Terra felt like there was too much to say, so instead, she pressed her fist to her chest. Anabelle and Abby did the same. "All right," the human mumbled. "I love you guys."

Anabelle faced the ghouls heading toward them. "Yeah. Couldn't ask for better friends."

Energy started to flow through Abby's body. "We love y'all too. See you at the eye."

Terra cocked her head sideways as she looked at the tower. "Actually, I think it looks more like an asshole."

"All right, we'll see you at the asshole."

The air crackled, and Abby was gone in a flash of bright blue light.

Terra didn't feel any fear. Only a strong sense of calm. When she looked around, Myrddin and José were gone. She took a deep breath and held it in. Felt her lungs burning. "You ready to do this?"

Mana burst from Anabelle as her eyes turned white. "Watch my back, and I'll watch yours."

Terra flexed, casting her own aura. "Sounds good."

Alex and the rest of Boundless shot out of the Netherverse Gate, following the gnomes, who were retreating.

Sarah, Rasputina, and Grok were behind Boundless, firing plasma weapons and magically attacking the ghouls who were trying to force their way out of the Gate.

Creon was at Sarah's side, armed along with everyone else. He ran to the Gate, attached his HUD to it, and shut it down. "This will buy us a little time."

Sarah's HUD pinged, along with everyone else's. She quickly read her new orders. "Goddamn! That'll leave you without some of your heaviest hitters. We can't leave you like this. There's got to be another way."

Alex closed her HUD and glanced at each member of Boundless before turning to Sarah. She had the look of someone who had accepted a heavy fate. "How much do you trust your commander?"

Sarah didn't answer immediately, but when she did, her voice did not waver. "Almost as much as I trust Kravis."

"Okay, then you need to follow that order. We'll figure something out. We don't really have a choice."

A caravan of tanks filled with gnomes who were armed to the teeth came over the hills in the distance.

Kravis and Persephone were sitting in the gunner's position in the tank leading the reinforcements. They pulled up to the Netherverse Gate as energy pulsed through it, threatening to break free. "What do we have going on?" Kravis asked.

Sarah explained the situation, still expressing doubt about leaving the gnome army to fight without her, Grok, and Rasputina. "I need to help them through the portal, then find Anabelle and Abby. Fuck. I don't like leaving you."

Kravis shrugged off the information as if he'd been told he was going to miss teatime. "You gotta do what you gotta do. Simple as that."

Alex agreed. "We all know we can't make it out of here alive. This is where we make our stand against the Dark One, whatever it takes."

Grok's laughter rang out.

Sarah spun, her eyes narrowing. "What the hell do you find so funny?"

She folded her arms, returning Sarah's hateful stare. "You are all acting like you're defenseless. Persephone is standing right there."

All eyes went to the drow, shrank from the attention.

"No offense, Persephone, but I don't get what the fuck is so funny, Grok. Persephone's tough, but she's not packing nearly as much power as you or the lich."

"None taken," Persephone said, her voice barely above a whisper.

Grok sneered as she spoke. "Rasputina, why don't you go ahead and tell them what Persephone and Abby have been hiding from everyone?"

The lich, who did not seem to find any of this amusing, nodded slowly. "None of you ever stopped to ask yourselves why Persephone was a lieutenant of the Dark One. Grok can wipe out entire armies single-handed, and you know my former strength. Didn't you think it odd that Persephone's power paled compared to ours?"

The thought had crossed Sarah's mind a handful of times, but she had left it at that. "We don't have time to play games. What are you saying?"

Grok walked over to Persephone and looked the drow in the eye. "Now is the time, girl. Show them what you truly are."

Persephone's eyes welled, and she sniffed the tears back as she clenched her jaws. "No, I can't! What if—"

Rasputina interrupted her. "If you do not, all of these people will die. Grok and I have seen what you are capable of. Leave your shame behind. Now is not the time for such childishness. You must play your role."

Persephone looked down at her hand and slowly nodded. "You're right. I'll do what I have to do."

Kravis grunted as he walked over to the Netherverse Gate, checking the readings Creon was looking at. "I like a surprise as much as the next person, but we don't have any time to waste. I'm going to set up our defenses. You all can keep having your hidden-potential moment."

Sarah joined Kravis near Creon. "He's right. Creon, we're going to need help finding the rest of the DGA. Can you stay alive long enough to help us?"

Creon swiped through a couple of screens on his HUD. "I'll do what I can here, but my priority will be guiding you. I have the route planned. Once I open the Gate, you'll have to move fast."

Sarah understood all she needed to. She wished she could have a moment alone with Kravis, but there wasn't time. Each second counted. "Rasputina, Grok, are you ready to go?"

The lich and the orc nodded.

"Boundless, we're putting a lot on you."

Alex and the rest of Boundless saluted Sarah as their dragons roared, preparing to take to the air.

"All right," Sarah shouted. "Creon, let us through."

Creon hit a switch on his HUD, and the Netherverse Gate opened.

A blast of purple energy shot out of the Gate, slamming into Sarah, Grok, and Rasputina.

As the smoke from the energy cleared, a ten-foot-tall giant stepped out of the portal. The ghoul's skin had rotted but was stitched together by the inky texture of the Dark Melody along with Tesla's bizarre technology, giving the giant the look of a spectral set of skeletons glued together. It held an axe made of moving flesh in one hand as it loosed an ungodly roar.

Before anyone could react, Persephone stepped between the army and the giant ghoul. She flexed her hand and her arm splitting down the middle, releasing her tentacles. That was not all that changed.

Four leathery wings sprouted from her back as her neck stretched, five eyes opening on her face in the shape of a pentagram and red cracks appearing in her skin and shining as a fiery black halo formed above her head.

Persephone slammed her hand to the ground, causing thousands of tentacles to burst forth and surround the giant. They grabbed his arms and legs and dragged him to the earth as a siren's scream erupted from the drow, black energy flying from her mouth and tearing through the ghoul's body as if it were paper.

Sarah stared at the eldritch celestial. "Fuck. Uh, well, I guess you guys are all set. Good luck."

She walked past Persephone, who let out another screech as Grok and Rasputina joined her at the Gate. "You guys could have told me she could do that. What the hell is that, by the way?"

Rasputina took a step toward the portal. "It is difficult to explain. Perhaps over a drink, if we survive."

Sarah grinned. "Never thought I'd say this, but sure."

Then the three of them stepped into the Netherverse Portal.

CHAPTER TWO

Roy, Blackwell, Naota, and the Mundanes were with the orc army a few miles east of the Netherverse Gate as Cire stood before them. The orcs had hardly lost anyone in the retreat from the Netherverse. They had fought valiantly, and now they awaited Cire's words.

The mech rider noted that the demeanor of the new shaman had changed a great deal since they first met. Cire had come to HQ as a former slave, a beaten, broken orc uncertain of his place in the grand scheme of his life. Now he stood before the horde, the de facto leader of a race that had been enslaved by the Dark One.

There weren't a lot of soft spots in Roy's heart, but he had one for the Shaman.

Cire pressed his hand to his chest. "My brothers and sisters, we've only started this battle. My strength is needed within the Netherverse, where the final stand will be made. Your strength will keep our home-world safe."

An orc in the crowd shouted, "Why not take us with you? The horde would overrun the Netherverse."

Cire smiled, and even from a distance, Roy could feel its warmth.

"No, the afterlife is too small for your heart. Leave this foul business to me and show these humans what it means to fight like an orc."

The horde roared in anticipation as Cire turned and stepped into the Gate.

Blackwell was sitting on the knee of Roy's mech, smoking a cigarette. "Glad we're not the ones going on a suicide mission to the afterlife. I'd like the chance to actually die rather than closing my eyes and waking up in hell."

Suzuki, who was talking to Naota, chuckled. " I agree with you about that. At least we get to mount our own suicide mission."

Naota had ingratiated himself into the Mundanes' group. He paused his conversation with Beth and Sandy, smiling his usual goofy smile. "Wouldn't be a good last mission if we didn't risk something, right? This is what makes all of the great story arcs, you know. Heroes pushed to their limits. That's how you can tell who deserves to win."

Blackwell put out his cigarette. "Call me a cynic, but I would prefer the odds to be a little more in my favor. I still think I would be in the pretty badass group if there were a couple thousand less ghouls to deal with."

Roy climbed into his mech as he went over the plans left by Cire. They'd talked their strategy over briefly after they'd received the order from Anabelle. What they had wasn't really a plan since it boiled down to a single point: stay alive. "You think he's going to make it to the rest of them by himself?"

"He won't be."

At the base of Roy's mech was Myrddin, smiling at Roy. "How are you doing, old friend?"

Roy jumped out of his mech, slid down its legs, and ran toward Myrddin. He threw his arms around the wizard, his eyes widening as he let out a yelp when he passed straight through Myrddin, whose form wavered like a ghost's. Roy hit the ground and rolled over, cursing under his breath. "Would be doing better if you'd let me know you were incorporeal. Is this a beyond-the-grave kind of thing or out-of-body-experience kind of thing?"

"A bit of both, mostly out of body. I've made a slight adjustment to Anabelle's plan. Giving José and me a body would take too much energy. I've sent José to help on the gnome world, and I will help Cire make it to the Dark One's tower, but I wanted to check on you. Just in case."

Myrddin's eyes wandered to the horde in the distance. "Looks like you've been keeping busy."

Roy crossed his arms as Naota and Blackwell walked over to him. "It's been a joint effort. You set me up with some good agents. Strong-willed. Capable of taking care of themselves and talented leaders. You did good with the DGA."

"I like to think so."

The Netherverse Gate shook violently, sending a slight aftershock toward Roy and the rest of them.

Myrddin walked toward it, growing fainter with each step. "Just wanted to stop by, Roy. Wish you all good luck and say goodbye if this is to be our last meeting."

Roy lit a cigar as he climbed back into his mech and shouted, "You gotta get better at goodbyes, old man."

Myrddin looked over his shoulder, his smile and eyes twinkling like stars. "That is one thing a wizard never learns."

The old man vanished in front of the Gate as it exploded open, purple flames flying everywhere.

The Mundanes drew their weapons. Stew stared hungrily at the portal while Suzuki whirled his battle-axe. Beth impatiently tapped her daggers, and Sandy floated serenely, her wand gripped tight.

Roy slapped the side of his mech. "Okay, assholes, let's make sure that we leave a huge fucking bloody mess, all right? Let's get 'em!"

A serpent's head came through the portal. It was nearly the size of a minivan, its eyes flashing as its tongue flicked out and the rest of its body made its way through the portal. It was the Dark Melody stretching out, the liquid taking a sharp shape. As more of its body became visible, Roy could see that its skin was rotting, and some of its organs were visible through the thin skin.

Ghouls came through behind the snake once the serpent was on the orc world, and had floated up into the sky. The ghouls looked around dumbly as if they were not certain of their purpose since there were no bodies in front of them.

Above them, the snake's mouth split down the middle and another head shot out, screeching a call for war and pain and suffering.

The first line of ghouls raced toward the orcish army.

Roy looked down at Blackwell and Naota as Nib-Nib trotted over to join them. "Make me proud, people. Start shooting. Use that portal as a funnel to get as many of them as you can, not that you'll get them all. There's too many, but at least you'll even the playing field." He turned to the Mundanes. "Do what you guys do best."

Roy slipped back into his mech, fired the thrusters, and headed toward the serpent.

The sky-snake spun and spat thick globs of venom.

Roy barrel-rolled out of the way as he locked onto the sky-snake with his missiles and fired.

The missiles tore through the snake, raining a torrent of intestines covered in the Dark Melody on the battlefield as ghouls and orcs clashed below, plasma weapons and steel meeting the hardened and sharpened Dark Melody weapons the ghouls wielded.

The sky-snake wrapped around Roy's dragon mech, its tail bashing the mech's head.

Roy killed the thrusters and let the weight of the mech pull the sky-snake out of the air. At the last second, Roy hit the thrusters and vented the excess heat from the mech, burning through the reptile's skin.

The sky-snake released the mech and it darted to the side and fired, shredding the construct with dozens of plasma blasts. "Looks like this will be easy enough," he said as he turned back toward the Gate.

He spoke too soon. The Gate was expanding up and outward. As it continued to grow, more sky-snakes came through the portal. "Shit!" Roy muttered.

Down below, Naota and Blackwell were standing back to back, firing at the ghouls surrounding them.

Blackwell emptied his magazine and loaded another, then another. Soon he was out, so he tossed his rifle aside and drew his pistols, then resumed firing. Naota swung his chained electric blades, an upgrade Abby had provided—granted, after she gave him a two-hour lecture about safety.

Naota cleaved through a ghoul that had launched at Blackwell, who ducked, barely seeing Naota's movement, operating mostly out of instinct built between the two over the last few months.

As Naota pulled his blades back, Blackwell tapped him on the shoulder. The former security guard bent over, and Blackwell rolled over his shoulder and kicked an approaching ghoul.

Not far off, Nib-Nib and the tribe leaders led the charge, the old shaman among them, pulling lightning from the sky as the orcs made their push.

Nib-Nib sliced through a ghoul before tearing into the creature with her mandibles.

Stew, who was admiring Nib-Nib's kill, whistled before spinning and cutting a ghoul giant in half down the middle. He kicked the corpse out of the way as Suzuki launched a fireball that tore through a ghoul at Stew's side.

Sandy and Beth were wading through a sea of goblin ghouls, the hunched creatures jittering, their jaws clenching and unclenching as if they were possessed by spirits and their bodies were not their own.

Beth flipped backward to put some distance between her and the ghouls as she fired three arrows, nailing three ghouls in the head. "I'm at three, Suzy!"

Sandy sent a bolt of lightning through the horde of ghouls, skewering a few of them. "Psh, ten souls have already fallen to me."

Scaly claws gripped Sandy's shoulders, and she looked up to see a vrosk infused with the Dark Melody and Tesla's tech. The creature's beak was nearly gone and cracked down the middle, and its eyes were lifeless. It lifted Sandy into the air.

An electric blade struck the vrosk in the chest.

Naota flipped up his sunglasses and winked at Sandy before yanking the vrosk toward him with his chains. Then he jumped and brought the other blade down on the creature's neck.

Roy scanned the battlefield. "Looks like we've got this."

As Roy spoke, the sky-snakes above, which had been floating ominously but not attacking, screeched. The portal grew once more, this time stretching to the height of a skyscraper. "What the fuck is going to come through this time?"

A foot, the largest Roy had ever seen, stepped out. Then came a leg, and soon a waist and torso.

The giant, a creature thirty feet in height with dead, dull eyes and a grizzled bear-face, gripped the sides of the Netherverse Gate and pulled himself onto the orc world.

Everyone who saw the giant froze.

Stew chopped off a ghoul's head and then leaned on his axe. "Whoa. I didn't know giants got that big."

Sandy shook her head as her mask disappeared. "That's not... Oh. Oh, no. That's an ancient giant. They've been extinct for centuries."

Blackwell, who wasn't far off, shouted, "So, it's bigger. What's the big deal?"

Before the grinning Naota could say anything, Blackwell raised his hand to cut him off. "Do *not* comment on the pun."

"Everyone is going to want to get real fucking far away!" Sandy shouted.

The ancient giant opened its mouth and unleashed an icy blast, freezing everything beneath it as it conjured an ice axe. It slammed the axe into the ground, causing a ripple to pulse through it.

Suzuki pointed his axe at the giant. "Beth, you, me, and Stew are taking that thing down."

Sandy shoved Suzuki. "Wait, what about me?"

Suzuki shook his head. "I thought you might want to take care of *that*."

Sandy followed Suzuki's line of sight. A cloaked figure had just exited the portal, its eyes glowing. It tossed back its cloak, revealing a gaunt man covered in tattoos, holding a birch wand. "Oh, mage fight? On it!"

The mage raised his wand, conjuring a murder of flaming crows.

Roy, who was flying above, trying to pick off vrosks while avoiding the sky-snakes, finally saw the ancient giant. "Fuck. Well, at least the Dark One is keeping it interesting."

CHAPTER THREE

Abby hadn't thought about how the teleporting tech was going to work. Once Martin told her he and the consciousness had copied and repurposed the tech, she assumed that either of the two extra minds in her head had figured out how to use it. Turns out, the only thing that had been figured out was how they could turn it on.

When the bright light around Abby faded, she found herself in a plane of existence much different from the nine realms or the Netherverse. At first she couldn't tell what she was looking at, but the more attention she paid to the shimmering lights and the cacophonous noises around her, the more sense it all started to make.

Bright lights moved here, the inverse of shadows. They would stop from time to time, and their voices could be heard echoing throughout the plane. The ground she stood on was not earth, it was solidified light. Millions of suns and moons hung above Abby as she slowly took her first few steps.

On closer observation, she could see multiple versions of herself stretching to infinity. There were not only versions of herself, but there were also versions of the DGA standing next to her, or at least some of them were. Some versions had walked away. Others had disappeared almost instantly, and still more shimmered in and out of existence. "The multiverse," Abby muttered. "That's how Tesla travels. He's not teleporting. he's slipping between dimensions."

Martin appeared in front of Abby, a human-sized paperclip with googly eyes and a cup of coffee. "Correction, *we're* slipping between dimensions."

A rumbling voice from within answered—the nanobot consciousness. Since their first conversation, it had grown difficult to understand. Martin interpreted for the others. It hadn't caused a problem yet.

"So, what now?" Abby asked.

"The consciousness and I are still trying to map the area and see how this all works. Keep looking around. We need as much visual information as possible. We have the same tech as Tesla. All we need to do is learn how to implement it."

Abby barely heard Martin since her mind was focused on something else. If she could travel like Tesla, she might be able to undo his work. An increase in nanobots would allow her to short-circuit at least some of Tesla's army, and it would also afford her more power. As long as she kept moving, dumping the nanobots, she wouldn't burn out.

Having come to a decision, Abby silently concentrated on producing more nanobots. She instantly felt the increase in power.

In the distance, Abby saw a flash of purple light and she instinctively took cover behind a set of lights. Her eyes zoomed in on the source of the flash.

Tesla stood there, smoke coming up from his body. He'd shed a lot of his armor. He looked sleeker and faster than before. Bursts of purple energy crackled off his skin.

He's not drawing lightning to him, Abby thought. *He's creating the power himself.*

Tesla knelt and slipped his hand into the light as the purple energy crackled around him. There was another flash, and he was gone.

"We'll keep an eye out for him," Martin said. "I have a feeling he's going to keep popping in and out."

Abby crossed to what looked like a multidimensional version of the Netherverse Gate. It was farther from the one she'd come from but not too far. Besides the distance, it seemed like everything moved much faster in this plane than the other.

Something caught Abby's eye, and she watched a light version of herself walking backward, away from the Netherverse Gate. "What is going on? Might as well check it out. We still can't figure out how to get out of here."

"We think we have an idea," Abby murmured as she reached for the light version of herself. She slipped her hand into its body and concentrated on venting every source of energy in her body outward.

The light version of Abby exploded and the universe was sucked into the vacuum created, Abby along with everything else.

Another bright flash. When her sight returned, she was standing on solid ground.

The air was heavy with the scent of iron. Abby looked down. She was on the orc world, but something terrible had happened in her absence.

Dead orcs littered the ground, the earth moist with their blood. Among the bodies, Abby could see Roy and Blackwell. Next to their corpses was Naota, kneeling, his hands covered in blood, his face streaked with dirt and tears. He looked up at Abby as she walked toward him. "How are you... You died," Naota said. "I watched you die."

Abby didn't say anything. There was too much to take in. She wasn't overwhelmed, she simply knew she couldn't waste time asking unnecessary questions. "Where is our body?"

Naota pointed, his finger trembling, toward a pile of dead bodies to the right. "What's happening, Abby?"

"We don't know."

Abby walked over to the pile, trying to keep from freaking out. On an intellectual level, she knew this was not her reality. She had stepped into one of the infinite variations of the timeline. That didn't change that she wanted to run over to Naota and hold him and promise that everything would be okay, nor did it keep her from screaming when she saw Terra's and Anabelle's broken bodies.

Abby collapsed at their side, and she picked up the elf's head and held it in her arms. "Belle. Terra."

There was a rustle from the pile of the dead, and Abby jumped. Across from her, a black arm forced itself up.

The alternate dimension version of Abby sat up. She was still in her armor, and the right side of her face had been bashed in. Her eye hung from its socket, connected only by a cord. This version of Abby was much more machine than human.

The two Abbys met each other's eyes. "What are you...how is this?"

"Another timeline. Are you—"

The alternate version of Abby shook her head as she coughed blood. "We're not going to make it. But you know, Rasputina was right." She laughed softly. There was no joy in it.

"What are you talking about?"

"None of us matter. None of our lives do. I didn't get that until now."

Abby shook her head, fighting back her tears. "No, we do. All of us do."

"That's not what I meant. This is, though."

The alternate Abby lightly touched their hand to their chest, which split open to reveal a nano-core, an energy source with roughly the power of a small nuclear bomb. "We tried to fight our way to the Dark One's tower, but we underestimated Tesla. If you're trying what we did, you won't make it. Take out Tesla, and get Suzuki and Alex to the tower to take your place."

She reached in and ripped out the nano-core, tossing it to Abby. "None of our lives matter in the long run like we thought. Do you understand what I'm saying? From Tesla's power, I think he understood that, too."

She closed her eyes, sighing, then opened them no more.

Abby had to push down the urge to vomit. She turned away, concentrating on the nano-core. "We don't have one of these, do we?"

"No," Martin said. "This Abby must have done something different with her nanobots than we did. We can still use the tech, though. It'll make you stronger. A lot stronger."

"How many dead versions of me do you think there are?"

Martin appeared in front of her. "Are you sure you want to do this? It seems...I don't know, wrong."

Abby's nanobots covered the nano-core like ants at a picnic. When the nanobots retreated, the core was gone. The girl went over to the corpse of her alternate self and pressed her palm to her cheek, tears flowing as her nanobots rolled over the other Abby, assimilating everything they could. "We all need to make sacrifices, and ours will not be in vain."

She stood and glanced at Naota, who was staring at her in horror.

Abby's body started to hum with energy. "We're sorry, Naota. We are so sorry."

There was a flash, and the universe was gone. Abby was back in the plane of lights and possibilities. She watched as another version of her sprinted off and stopped in its tracks, then took a deep breath and tore into a new reality.

The gnome world was burning. The Netherverse Gate had opened and unleashed a wellspring of fire elementals infused with the Dark Melody. They had sprinted from the darkness, the Gate opening before anyone had realized it, racing about and setting the land aflame.

Persephone quickly ended them. Both of her arms now dozens of tentacles and her many eyes watched for the next attack. Nothing came for some time, so she reverted to her more subdued drow appearance.

Kravis and Boundless were coordinating their next defensive move, and Persephone joined them at the war table while a group of gnomes and dwarves watched over the Gate.

José, who had come through the Gate with the fire elementals, needed no introduction. Kravis knew the man, and the rest of the team had received an update through their HUDs.

Alex filled the MERC in on the details of what they were up

against. She was surprised they'd only seen base-level ghouls. The elementals had been a pleasant surprise. They meant the Dark One was going to get this fight started.

José listened intently to Alex's words. When she was done, he gave a hearty laugh. "It would seem that even the children here are experienced warriors."

Alex, who was working on her bionic arm, smiled slightly. "Yeah, we all had to grow up pretty fast."

"Hopefully, not grown up enough to want to throw your lives away."

Kravis stared uneasily at José and Alex. "I'm not planning on dying today. I have a wedding to go to after this."

Persephone nodded, her eyes resolute and her jaw tight. "Neither am I. We all walk off this field today, and this planet stays free."

Kravis laughed, slapping his knee and nearly falling out of his chair. "That's easy to say. Not all of us can turn into an eldritch god!"

"Rasputina was exaggerating; I'm not a god. But it is draining since the form consumes my life force. If I stay like that for too long, it will take years off my life."

Alex went sheet-white. "Shit, why didn't you say something earlier? Let's not have you pulling that shit every couple of minutes. We'll be conservative with what we have. Same with the dragons. We don't have the tech to replace our augments, so we'll mostly rely on breath weapons and our anchor weapons. Looks like Persephone and me are our heaviest hitters. What else do we have to work with?"

Kravis jerked his thumb over his shoulder. "Got a pretty sizable army, and I can get into places pretty quickly and silent-like. I don't see how that would be helpful at the moment."

"Good to keep in mind. José?"

José was eyeing a glass of mead on the table. "Might I?" he murmured as he gestured toward the mead. "It has been some time since I've had a body."

Alex shrugged. "Knock yourself out."

José grabbed the glass and downed the mead, then let out a belch nearly as loud as his previous laughter. "As for me, I will be where the most enemies are. I don't know how long I will be able to stay on the physical plane, but I plan on taking a bunch of those sons of bitches with me."

"Good. I guess we just have to wait then. Fortify our defenses. Prepare for the worst."

Kravis, who was pacing, jumped up on the war table to get a better look at the map. "What are you riders going to do if there aren't any airborne nemeses? We can probably—"

His words were cut off as a steel crossbow bolt hit him in the shoulder.

Persephone rushed to Kravis' side and pulled the bolt out. "Any higher and that would have been your throat."

Kravis grabbed a handful of herbs from his pouch and slapped them on the wound, healing it instantly.

The Gate had opened.

The dwarves and gnomes guarding the Gate unsheathed their weapons.

It had happened faster than anyone could have seen other than José and Persephone.

Dozens of sprites, fae creatures larger than pixies and fairies but not nearly as large as gnomes, zoomed out of the Netherverse Gate, their faces rotted and sullen and gray, wings half eaten through. They were firing crossbows infused with the Dark melody, powered by Tesla's dark tech.

The first line of defenses fell as the sprites retreated toward the Gate, holding the line as orcish ghouls lumbered through the portal.

"Gods be damned," Kravis shouted. "What manner of creature won't we have to fight?" He pulled up his HUD. "First fleet to the Gate! The fight is here."

Alex leapt on Chine and spoke into her anchor. "Boundless, we have fast-moving bogies. Damage control now. Everyone in the air."

From all over the camp came the roar of dragons as Boundless took to the air, Jollies the pixie leading the fight. The sprites were zooming across the battlefield, sniping as many gnomes as possible.

José unsheathed his sword and stretched his shoulders. "Come, my drow friend. Let us make memories on this glorious field of death."

Persephone's five eyes opened as her arms transformed into tentacles. "Yeah. Let's."

C H A P T E R   F O U R

Anabelle and Terra approached the army of ghouls that lay before them. The elf was brimming with nervous energy. She still wasn't used to being on the Path of the Lost. Her body felt like it was made out of raw power.

Even with all that power, what lay before them seemed impossible. There was still so much distance between them and the Dark One's tower. She'd hoped Myrddin would have stayed to guide both her and Terra to the tower. She wasn't sure if the two of them could do it on their own.

Strength was what Anabelle needed since fear wasn't going to help her. Terra was at her side, seething with power as well, yet there was something about the multitude of eyes that stared at them from the Dark One's tower that made Anabelle hesitant about blasting through the ghouls to get there.

The Dark One had conquered multiple universes. What could Anabelle and Terra do to stop him once they got to the tower?

The sound of Terra's knuckles cracking brought Anabelle out of her thoughts.

Terra glanced at the elf, a wry smile on her lips. "I bet I'll get there first."

"You're not worried?"

"Fuck, yeah, I'm worried, so let's get to it. I'm tired of standing around all pensive and shit."

The ground beneath her exploded as she sprinted toward the oncoming horde.

Anabelle couldn't help but laugh. There was something irresistible about Terra's lust for a good fight. It was infectious. She raced after Terra, trying her best to catch up.

Terra flung herself at the first wave of ghouls. She hadn't bothered with her axe or sword. Instead, she grabbed one of the ghouls and spun with the creature in her hand, smashing through the others that surrounded her to make room to breathe.

Anabelle hit them as well after charging her arm with mana. The electricity running up and down her body connected with a ghoul, causing lightning to chain to ten other ghouls, frying them on the spot.

They carved their way through the creatures, the two of them fighting in their own style. Anabelle slipped between the different forms of a Traveler, drawing more and more power from the Path of the Lost, losing herself in the fight for the first time. She let her body speak for itself, guiding her fists, her eyes constantly roaming, looking for the next kill.

So this is the Path of the Lost, she thought. It was different from the frantic, psychotic energy she'd felt when she was trying to kill Grok or even what she felt when she and Terra had fought their way through the spirits of the Hands. This was more than peace. Part of her soul came alive as she glided between scores of ghouls, slipping through their shadows and tugging them into the blackness. Then she erupted forward, her body taking on the consistency of lava as she shot flames from her palms, catching up the ashes of the fallen with a whirlwind before bringing her fists down and converting them to water and then ice, impaling the ghouls around her.

Terra didn't use magic. Her power came from the deep wellspring of will within her. Every time a ghoul's Dark Melody claws slashed her and cut her skin open, her will grew stronger, and more power flowed through her muscles. Her vision was the clearest it had been in her life. She saw the world moving before her and she was one step ahead of it, flipping over the bodies of the dead, snatching a ghoul up, cracking its neck, and kicking it into another before taking hold of another, ripping its sharpened arm off, and launching it into a crowd like a spear.

The elf was hardly paying attention to the destruction she wrought, she was so consumed by the pure joy of battle. There was only one thing wrong; in the back of her mind, she felt a whisper, and it was growing louder with each fallen ghoul.

What if someone here was a real challenge?

Anabelle pushed the feeling away. That wasn't why she was here. Defeating the Dark One was the point of the mission. But the thought persisted, calling to her.

She pulled mana from everywhere around her, channeled it into her fists, and slammed it into the ground, sending a rippling energy attack through the mass of ghouls.

Terra glared at Anabelle as she punched in the face of a ghoul. "Hey! I was still enjoying this!"

"We're not here to have a good time. We're supposed to be making our way to the Dark One."

The smile left Terra's face. "Oh, yeah. Guess I kind of forgot."

"There will be more. Come on. Let's go."

The two of them headed toward the tower. All around them, the texture of the world was beginning to change. The bodies of the defeated ghouls melted into the earth, which was becoming more liquid while also seeming less tangible. "We should probably get off this," Anabelle suggested, pointing at the rocks floating above.

Terra went for them first, leaping onto one and then bounding to the other. Anabelle followed closely.

Even in the Netherverse, the wind felt great on Anabelle's face. She wished she could feel like this all the time—confident and consumed. It was like the rest of the world had faded. There was only the battle at hand.

She knew it couldn't last, but she could enjoy it while it did. That was enough. And maybe it shouldn't last. Its rarity was what made it feel so special.

"I've never felt like this my entire life," Terra shouted.

The elf laughed, letting herself fully embrace what she was experiencing. "Me neither. I love it."

The rocks started to fall.

Terra's eyes sparkled with delight. "Oh, what is this?"

The ghouls' corpses swirled into a vortex, combining with each other to form a giant worm. The thousands of mouths on its body were screaming, and more ghouls rose as the Dark One put more bodies between the two women and the tower.

"Looks like the Dark One might be getting scared. He's pullin' out all the stops," Terra joked.

Anabelle could hardly contain herself at the sight of the worm. "I wonder what its guts look like?"

"Only one way to find out."

The two of them leapt at the corpse worm and drove the creature to the ground, where it writhed and screeched as it floundered, its tail slapping and crushing ghouls beneath it.

Terra grabbed the worm's soft skin and tore it open, sending viscera and blood flying everywhere.

The two were ecstatic in their power, watching the worm wiggle in its death throes.

As the worm's soft body exploded, its guts falling out like a black tidal wave, the Dark Melody animating it lashed out and grabbed any nearby souls. It sucked the spirits into its body, causing it to grow larger and stretch out. The Melody contorted and squeezed material out of its orifices and open wounds that solidified and became legs, giving the creature the look of a demonic centipede. Eyes opened all over its body, searching for Terra and Anabelle.

`The creature thrashed, collecting souls in its ever-expanding skin and growing larger still. Another head appeared in its back end, its teeth sharp and vile, black gas leaking from its mouth.

Terra pulled her axe from her back. "That's disgusting."

Anabelle examined the worm. The section she and Terra had

attacked earlier had hardened and had a crust. ""Do you want the worm or the ghouls?"

"We should both take the worm. As long as there is an infinite number of bodies, we're going to have problems with that long, disgusting, freakish sack of crap."

"Sometimes I forget how elegant you are with words."

They headed toward the creature as its heads whipped around, both sides exuding noxious fumes.

Anabelle hit it first. She drove her fist into the closest head and broke its jaw.

The creature recoiled, its broken jaw splitting down the middle, then two more heads formed from the jaw fragments. One of the heads snapped at Anabelle, who fell to the ground, dodging to the side as the other surged forward, its neck elongating, and narrowly missed the elf before driving itself into the ground.

Terra ran up the length of the worm, sidestepping the ghouls crawling up the sides of the beast.

One slashed at Terra's shin.

She tossed her axe at the ghoul almost as an afterthought. The blade sliced through it, and she had to turn back to grab her axe.

The worm rolled onto its side, trying to knock both Terra and Anabelle off its body.

Anabelle gripped tight, letting the flaming aura around her die so that she wouldn't scorch the skin she was holding onto.

Terra, near one head, held on tight as well, screaming. Anabelle was unable to discern if it was fear or joy.

The worm's underbelly was on top now, and hundreds of skeletal hands reached up from its quivering flesh. As Terra crawled up the worm, she ripped out arm after arm as well as beating them back lest they take hold of her.

Anabelle was in a slightly different position. She could see the arms, but they posed no threat to her. "Hold on, Terra!' she shouted as she fired a blast of fiery mana down the worm's side, tearing up the flesh and unleashing hot geysers of black sludge.

Terra covered her face as the black gunk hit her. "Thanks, Belle."

Anabelle ran toward her compatriot, dragging her right arm across the side of the worm. It cut through the creature's flesh until she got to Terra, and she helped the human to her feet.

Terra wiped off the black sludge. "Okay, my turn. You take the ass head. That would make us even."

Anabelle cast a doubtful glance at where she had come from as the worm's body began to convulse. "Fine, but then we *are* even."

Terra took off toward the front head of the worm and unsheathed her sword, screaming as she cut down the dozens of ghouls who stood in her path.

Anabelle doubled back toward the worm's ass, occasionally firing bolts of mana, incapacitating the ghouls who tried to slow her down.

They arrived at the same time. Terra drove her sword deep into the soft flesh of the worm's head as Anabelle burst into flames, consuming the other head of the worm in fire.

The worm writhed, screeching in its death throes as it went limp.

The women fell off the worm in a hailstorm of thick, sticky entrails.

Anabelle let out a flash of mana that burned the crap on her to ash. "Whew. Now that was fun."

Terra pointed at the second wave of ghouls pulling themselves out of the earth. "We're just getting started."

CHAPTER FIVE

The Netherverse spread out before Rasputina, Sarah, and Grok. They'd been traveling for nearly two hours, but the Netherverse that they walked through was much different than the one Terra and Anabelle were experiencing. The Gate had tried to transport them into the path of the ghouls who were invading the gnomish world, but Rasputina was familiar with the Netherverse. She was able to exert a small amount of influence over where it took her.

Now the lich, the assassin, and the disgraced Hand stood on a mountain of souls overlooking the spiraling madness of the Netherverse. The place they were located had a smaller concentration of souls to build upon. More of the elder gods were floating above, which meant the composition of this part of the Netherverse was in a greater state of flux. The realm wavered like water, looking as if it could come apart at any moment or sink into itself like Atlantis.

One could even say the vista the three of them looked out upon was peaceful. Those were the words that Rasputina would have used.

Grok seemed to think so as well since she took a seat and hung her feet over a ledge. "When was the last time you were here?"

Rasputina tried to remember, but her memories were fractured. She still wasn't certain who she was. At first, she'd felt like she was the old Rasputina, her soul having bestowed her humanity back on her, forcing the insane beast into a pit within her. She had thought that all she had to do was keep the creature at bay. Recently, that had changed.

They had become one, the old Rasputina and the lich. There was no separation between the two, and this Rasputina, as different as she was from the old version of herself, was very much a lich. She was only now starting to understand the depth of her illness. The voices in her head were constantly whispering and occasionally screaming, each saying something different. Sometimes it was her voice, sometimes it was the one she had grown accustomed to referring to as the lich. Other times it was the voices of the dead, those she had condemned to an afterlife with no peace.

"I don't know," Rasputina finally said. "I spent a long time here."

"And you didn't know this was where the Dark One was all along?" asked Sarah.

"By the time I arrived, I was broken and had forgotten why I had been searching for magic and knowledge. I was insane, or at least, that's what I've been telling myself. I don't think that was why. There are many insane people, and not all of them do what I did. Very few do, even on a smaller scale. I wasn't insane; I can say that now. I was just evil."

Rasputina sat down beside Grok and pulled back her hood. "This is a terrible feeling. All of these are. It reminds me of why I distorted myself to begin with. Guilt. The constant guilt of failure. Now I've compounded it. I also have the guilt of my actions reverberating in my head until it's all I can think of."

Grok nodded as she stared into the contorting Netherverse, the bleak sky occasionally brightening before slipping back into a darkness that seemed never to end. "It's good to hear you say that. Hiding behind excuses is weakness."

Sarah nodded. "Do either of you ever feel guilt?"

Grok did not answer at first. Instead, she looked down at her hands, which were scarred, callused things. It was apparent that her fingers had been broken many times. "Only if there is a point to it, and there hardly ever is for most mortals. What good is the feeling unless it prompts action? So, yes, sometimes I do feel guilt. Rarely. My decisions were mine, and I do not have to work hard to live with them. I sleep quite well at night."

Rasputina was unsatisfied with Grok's answer. She wasn't sure if it was because it sounded like the orc was trying to avoid telling the complete truth or because she wished she felt like Grok. "I didn't feel guilt before, or anything, really. Sometimes there were moments of clarity. After a time, there was only...I don't even know what to call it. A desire....yes, that would be it. A desire to destroy."

Grok's gaze went to the burning eye. "You aren't that much different from him."

"No, I do not think I am. Why did you do it? What did you have to gain from the Dark One? And don't you dare tell me power. I can see through that nonsense."

Grok sighed as she hung her head. She looked as if all of the strength had been sucked out of her, the years of fighting gone, leaving only tired flesh. "Fear. I was afraid to die. I saw what the Dark One was doing to the orcs, what he was capable of, and I realized that I had a better chance of survival if I was on the winning side. There were small things here or there I could attribute my service to the Dark Lord to, anything that would make me sound noble in my own mind. But it was fear that made me abandon my people, and the Dark One knows how to use fear better than anyone else."

Rasputina could understand that. "Do you think there's any hope for us? Those who have done the things we have?"

Grok shook her head. "No, there isn't. No matter what heroics we perform, it won't change anything. We will always be butchers. Monsters. It is what we are."

"Then why do any of this?" asked Sarah.

Grok looked at her companions, her eyes deep, sad wells. There was a person there, trapped behind walls of hatred and sorrow. "Because I might be wrong. Maybe. Hopefully."

Rasputina stood and pulled up her hood. "Come. We should keep going. We don't want to disappoint our heroes."

"True. That is what they are expecting."

It was the 322nd reality Abby had gone to. The vast majority of them had been filled with death. There were one or two where the orc world didn't exist. Abby had stepped out into space, gasping for air until Martin righted the situation. She visited no realities where anyone survived.

This was to be her last trip. Something had happened with each multiverse version of her whose nanobots she'd consumed. There was something that was left—an imprint, not quite a memory. It was slightly different, like a personality. As Abby absorbed the last moments of her life, she felt as if she were growing into herself, as if one less Abby made her more Abby than anyone else.

There was also a substantial increase in power. The whole time she was absorbing nanobots, she'd been producing more of her own. The increase wasn't stressing her system at all. Her capacity had increased substantially.

The girl appeared on the final orc world. She was greeted with the death she'd grown accustomed to. She scanned the area, looking for her corpse.

Instead, another Abby stood before her. This Abby was older by a few years, and her hair had already started to gray. Most of her body was tech. Much like Tesla's, it was difficult to tell where flesh ended and robotics began. "Fancy seeing you here," the older Abby said.

Abby took a step back, uncertain what she should make of the situation. She was frightened, excited, and oddly attracted to the older version of herself. "What—"

"You don't need to assume the worst. We're here for variations of the same reason. You want to stop the Dark One. I'm finished stopping the Dark One."

"Wait, you destroyed him?"

The older Abby smiled, and it haunted her younger counterpart. It was not the smile she wore, but she could see hints of what it had once been. Now that she was looking closer, Abby could see that the older version of herself looked frail despite all the armor she wore.

"There are some realities where the Dark One is no longer the problem, and that is what brings me here."

The older Abby's HUD started to beep. She sighed, looking even more tired than before. "He's coming. He never stops looking. It's exhausting. I want it to stop. That's why I came here."

Abby didn't need to be told who it was. "Tesla. Why? Why us?"

"You haven't just been wandering through realities, Abby. You've been going through time and space, as has he. Millions of years have passed here. Worlds have come and gone, and he's seen our tech improving. He wants it, so I've come to ask you to do me a favor."

"What is it?"

"I want you to make it stop. I'm the last one other than you, and you're the only person I trust enough for this."

The older Abby opened her palm, all of her nanobots converging into her hand to form a small, black pill. "If you take this, he won't chase me anymore. He'll only look for you. I can't keep on fighting."

Abby let out a sigh of relief. "Holy shit, we thought you were going to ask us to kill you!"

The older Abby laughed, showing her crow's feet in the corners of her eyes. "Hell, no! I don't think any of our alternate reality versions could even get that dramatic."

"Give me the pill. I'll deal with him."

The older Abby looked over her shoulder, her gray hair mixed shimmering slightly from the intermixed tech. "He's coming. Could you send me home? My coordinates are uploaded to your HUD. By now, it should all be instinct."

The older Abby walked over to her younger counterpart and handed her the nanobot pill.

Abby was impressed by how good her older self looked. She hoped she made it to that age.

The older Abby held Abby's hand. "Thank you so much, Abby Prime."

"We thought we didn't have a flair for the dramatic."

Both Abbys smiled at each other.

Lightning crashed behind them, and a purple tint overtook the sky.

"He's here," the older Abby said.

Abby swallowed the pill and pointed her palm at the older Abby. "Get out of here. Enjoy your life."

"Thank you. And I will."

The older Abby vanished into thin air.

Tesla's scream boomed through the air.

Abby turned to see the mad scientist making his way toward her. Whatever Tesla had been doing between realities and through time, it had resulted in a substantial number of upgrades.

Tesla raised his hand, purple electricity pooling in his palm. "Finally. Are you done running, child?"

Abby clenched her fists, allowing herself to feel the complete range of power she'd acquired. Her head and body flooded with nanobots, quickening every facet of her existence. "We think you might be confused, old man. You may have been chasing the other Abbys, but I came here for you."

Tesla bowed in a grotesque parody of a gentleman's gesture. "Well, my dear girl, let us begin." He launched himself at her, palm outstretched, lightning crackling in it as the conductors on his back filled with energy.

Abby reacted instinctively. Martin and the consciousness merged with her mind, activating a part of herself she didn't know existed.

Tesla swung at Abby as she caught the lightning ball.

The girl's eyes flashed as nanobots poured over her face, covering it in a blank black mask. She absorbed the energy from Tesla's attack, drawing it into her body and releasing it in a shockwave, tossing Tesla back. "Yeah, I think it's about that time."

CHAPTER SIX

Abby and Tesla stared each other down as they circled, sizing each other up.

Abby wasn't certain how much power she'd received from her upgrades, but she hadn't been able to recycle energy before, especially not an attack of that magnitude.

Tesla had upgraded himself as well. She'd only seen a small part of Tesla's potential in their last fight, but it had been enough to keep Anabelle, Terra, and her at bay.

He didn't seem to have any idea what Abby was capable of. Abby could tell because he still hadn't attacked. He was fighting like a scientist. Gathering data. Hypothesizing. Adjusting.

"You're a smart girl," Tesla shouted. "It would be a shame to end a life with so much potential. Think of what you and I could do together. Infinite realities and timelines to explore. Things to see and learn that no other human being could ever dream of. Do you really want to throw that away?"

Abby was beyond taking this man seriously. "You're working for the Dark One! Do you think I believe any of that? The only thing he wants to do is enslave. There won't be anything in any timeline worth seeing once he's made it over in his image. If you think anything else is possible, you're the dumbest Tesla out there."

For a moment, the man's eyes seemed human again, the ethereal otherness leaving them. "Do you think I don't know what he's capable of? He's unstoppable, and if the best I can do is preserve what little I can across all realities, then so be it."

"You aren't preserving anything other than your ego."

Tesla's eyes flashed, his hands glowed purple, and his body began to hum. "Fine. Let us settle this."

Abby didn't respond. Instead, she fired her thrusters and went at Tesla, allowing her body to run automatically, accepting the synthesis of her mind with Martin's and the nanobot consciousness.

She stopped a few feet in front of him and skidded to the side, then slammed her elbow into his face. The side of her arm opened and vented energy in a slicing arc, cutting Tesla's face and sending him stumbling backward.

She didn't let up. Abby charged her body with kinetic energy and rushed Tesla, slamming her fist into him before converting her hands to plasma cannons and lining up her shot.

He appeared behind her, much to her surprise. She'd assumed that it would be impossible to teleport like that since they were already in a fluctuating space between time and space. Or were they?

"You still don't get it," Tesla shouted as he backhanded her.

Abby hit the ground and skidded across it, then scrambled to her feet.

Electrical blasts landed only a few feet away as her before she took off and circled back toward Tesla.

"All time and reality are the same to me!" he shouted.

Abby didn't understand what he was saying, but she didn't have time to think about it—and maybe that was the trick. When she'd teleported Persephone, it had been without thinking. She knew who she wanted to see, even if she didn't know how it worked. Granted, she did have Persephone's projected coordinates, but that wasn't the same thing as knowing where the drow was. And it had worked. Maybe

Tesla didn't understand how his own tech worked. Why did she have to?

She blinked out of existence and appeared behind Tesla, who whipped around, swinging an arm charged with electricity.

She blocked the attack as he vanished, the two dodging each other and firing energy blasts as they flickered in and out of the plane.

Each attack was faster than she could have ever seen. She didn't understand how she could move so fast. Obviously, neither could Tesla. Abby caught glimpses of his face, which grew angrier the longer they fought.

Tesla jumped away from the girl, putting a little distance between them. He stretched his hands out and fired a blast of lightning.

Abby tried to teleport, but nothing happened. She raised her hands, projecting an energy shield that only partially deflected the attack. "What's going on?" she mentally shouted to Martin.

"Different power core," the AI replied. "Teleportation has its limits once you exhaust it. Must work the same for him. Don't rely on one trick."

Abby nodded and charged Tesla, stopping at the last minute and punching him in the face. She fired the thrusters on her leg and kicked him in the jaw.

Tesla grabbed Abby's ankles and swung her around.

She sent an electric charge through her body, shocking the scientist, who fired an electric bolt at her that hit her in the face, knocking her through the air.

Before she could stabilize, Tesla appeared in front of her. He cupped his hands as they filled with lightning and brought them down on Abby's head.

She hit the ground hard enough to form a crater.

Tesla floated above her. "Can't you see, I've won? Every move you make, I calculate and adapt to. You don't have anything new. It doesn't matter how strong you are. I've seen it all before. You're finished, and I don't have time to play with you anymore. I have a war to win."

Tesla raised his hands to the sky as it darkened with clouds, purple lightning striking all around. Some of it hit Tesla, charging his conduits.

Abby watched as a ball of lighting grew. It was already the size of an airplane and continued to grow. Within seconds, it could have been the size of the moon.

Tesla was right. Even if Abby was stronger, he knew everything she had—and that was his mistake.

Abby had the thought, and the nanobots' consciousness and Martin instantly took care of it. All of Abby's energy was diverted to teleportation—weapons, armor, life support. Everything, saving only a little bit for her thrusters.

As Tesla charged his electrical attack, Abby charged him.

Tesla laughed maniacally as he continued to charge. "Are you that dense, girl? I've already adjusted for the attack. It won't do anything to me, and I'll burn you to ashes!"

Abby didn't hit Tesla. She stopped right in front of him. "You can't adjust for this." She grabbed Tesla's head and turned herself into a conductor, draining energy from Tesla's body and venting it out of her own.

Her body started to burn. She was releasing billions of watts of energy. It was all she needed.

Tesla panicked as he grew weaker, only now starting to understand what it was Abby was doing. That was all she needed. He might have been able to account for her tech, but he couldn't account for her mind.

Abby held Tesla tight, teleporting again, but this time, taking him to a place she knew had to exist—the grooves between space and time. Negative space.

The two of them appeared in pure infinite whiteness, a place devoid of anything, including energy.

Before Tesla could react, Abby converted all of the energy she had drained from Tesla and transferred it to her nanobots, powering up again. Her arms grew smooth, metallic, and sharp.

She pierced his chest, and with her other arm, she stabbed him through the throat. She didn't stop there. She spun, slashing through the conduits on his back, then ran her blade through his heart.

Tesla fell over, grabbing his neck as he bled out. "Just...flesh wounds. All I need..."

"Is to draw energy to fix yourself, right? We don't think you'll find that here."

"How... This can't be. This place can't exist..."

Abby walked out from behind the man and knelt in front of him. "Infinite universes and timelines. There was bound to be one without any energy, and it seems the layer between time and space is exactly that—a universe without energy, at least not what we understand energy to be."

With that, the girl vanished, stepping into the place of infinite possibilities and then back to the gnomish world. She looked around and saw the Gate in the distance. "We'll get the hang of it eventually."

Abby closed her eyes, preparing to teleport again. Her body hummed, and the hum turned into a slow whine. Instead of teleporting, she fell forward, her body seizing up as she tried to move. "What the hell is happening?"

Martin appeared in Abby's field of vision. "We're having some problems. Looks like you absorbed too much energy and fried your system. We have to make some repairs immediately to keep your organs from failing. You'll be good as long as no one tries to kill you. Then you'll be fucked."

Abby, whose mouth was filled with dirt, groaned as she tried to relax and let the nanobots heal her body.

A handful of miles away, Kravis, Persephone, and the Boundless team were fighting for their lives. The ghouls had not stopped coming through the Gate, and none of the remote attempts to close the Gate off for a time had worked. The forces had been pushed back miles from the Gate, a retreat that could not be fully committed to because Kravis knew they were only killing time.

The gnome was leading the retreat of a squadron of gnome and goblin soldiers while Boundless tried to keep the vrosks and harpies that had come through the portal at bay. He needed to reach the platoon of soldiers heading toward him. They needed more bodies.

Two giants had come through the Gate. They were not as large as the ancient one that had appeared on the orc homeworld but they were still exceptionally large. Persephone was handling both of them.

On paper, it looked good. There seemed to be a glimmer of hope. Kravis knew better than that, though. Whatever was behind that Gate was still coming, and there wasn't anything to stop them.

The other platoon was close enough to see. Kravis waved them down, then kicked his hoverbike into upper gear and sped toward them. "We need to bring up the ground troops now!"

The platoon sergeant looked at Kravis warily. "Are you serious? Already?"

Kravis grabbed the gnome. "I said *now*."

The platoon leader hit his comm and shouted, "Deep gnomes! It's your time to shine."

"Tell them to head toward the Gate. We're going back. If we can push the dark forces back, we can bottleneck them."

The platoon leader's face was grave. "Wasn't that always the plan? It didn't work. What's going to make it work now?"

Kravis didn't have an answer, or not one that he wanted to give. He'd seen how these kinds of missions worked. The truth was best left unsaid, but he knew. This was bigger than the lives of the gnomish resistance. There were families squirreled far from the fight, and they were the ones he was fighting for. Those were the lives he fought to continue, not the lives of his soldiers. They were meant to slow the ghouls, just like him.

The platoon leader saluted Kravis. "You don't have to say anything, sir. I understand."

"You do?"

"Sacrifices. We all know when we have to make 'em. Some people balk, but not the resistance. The deep gnomes are heading toward the coordinates. We might as well get going too."

Kravis turned his hoverbike around, bolstered by the soldiers behind him in gearbox tanks and on hoverbikes. They had superior firepower and higher numbers now. All they had to do was their job.

Alex was drenched in blood as she waded through the battlefield. She'd ditched her dragon, realizing that the two of them could do more damage apart than together. The sky was full of harpies and vrosks, so many they were nearly blocking out the sky. It wasn't any better on the ground. It was hard to see anything other than the dead. Team Boundless and some of the other forces that could fly were dealing with them, but there were so many, and even with Alex's enhanced eyes, she struggled to understand what was going on.

Too many bodies, all fighting for…what? Freedom? Control?

A heavy fog rolled over the battlefield, moving too fast to be natural.

Alex scanned the area until she honed in on where the fog was coming from. A ghoul mage was standing atop a pile of bodies, casting a spell.

That fog wasn't going to make anything easier for the gnomes or the goblins, and it was a terrible idea to leave a mage unattended.

Alex reached out to Chine. *Hey, buddy, I need a lift!*

Chine swooped in, and Alex leapt onto his back. The dragon flew toward the mage.

How much longer until the ether dragons get here? Alex asked.

A half-hour or so! he replied.

They closed on the mage. Alex disengaged her anchor and leapt off Chine to land in front of the mage.

It rolled its head and glared at Alex, raising its staff as it prepared a curse.

"Not today," Alex said as she flexed her telekinesis, freezing the mage in place. She then conjured her scythe and decapitated the ghoul.

As the body dropped, Alex looked out over the grizzly battle. Dead gnomes and goblins were everywhere. It was difficult to tell the difference between their trampled bodies and the ground the ghouls marched relentlessly across.

In the distance, Alex could see Kravis returning with reinforcements and the deep gnomes' mining tanks erupting from the ground, surrounding the Gate and the ghouls. Above, the dragonriders of Boundless were still trying to rid the skies of the harpies who swooped down and carried away gnomish soldiers.

It was a good effort. Alex could see that, but it wasn't enough. She checked her Anchor, watching the estimated arrival of the ether dragons. "Remember…Thirty minutes. That's all we gotta hold out for. Thirty minutes."

Alex slid down the hill, hacking through the ghouls in front of her as she went and praying that the army could hold off for another half-hour.

CHAPTER SEVEN

Terra could nearly make out the pupils of the eyes looking down at them from the Dark One's tower. She didn't need to see them, though. She could feel the eyes creeping over her skin. They were a tangible presence, the feeling akin to having cold grapes rubbed over her.

She and Anabelle had fought through three waves of ghouls, each stronger than the one before. Terra had thought the Dark One was arrogant enough in his power to skimp on the defenses. She'd been very wrong.

The two Dark Gate Angels were catching their breath, having found a small cave away from the horde of ghouls ahead of them.

Even though Terra had felt her strength increase along with her drive for a good fight, she was exhausted. Passion wasn't enough to get her through this; she needed rest. She hadn't thought that she and Anabelle would have to fight through a gauntlet to get to the Dark One.

The elf pulled out a flask and took a swig, wincing as she downed the liquid. "You want some? I brought it along to share. Figured if this was going to be our last hurrah, I might as well make sure to have a good drink before it all goes down."

Terra took the flask and smelled its contents. "And what exactly is your idea of a good last hurrah?"

"Dwarfish whiskey aged three hundred years in barrels above their smithing fires. A shot of that is usually enough to knock a human out. I figured you could probably handle it."

Terra gulped down a slug of the whiskey. She felt like her whole body was on fire. It was hot enough to scream, but the feeling quickly subsided, replaced by warmth radiating from her stomach to the rest of her body. "Goddamn, that's some good shit. How did you get your hands on this? Somehow, I imagine it's not easy to find."

"It might not look like it, but I hung out with a pretty rough and tumble bunch of dwarves back in the day."

"Anabelle, we just fought our way through over two hundred ghouls. Why would I find it hard to believe that you hung out with tough dwarves?"

Anabelle laughed, an odd sound in the Netherverse. "Really, what do you think our odds are?"

Terra hadn't thought much about it. She didn't think in odds to begin with. Years ago, she would not have thought herself capable of something this important. There would never have been a reason for her to question the odds because she wouldn't have had the confidence to try. Now there wasn't even a conversation in her head about succeeding or failing. All she could do was try. That was the only thing she expected of herself.

"Not really thinking about it. We're here to stop the Dark One, and that's what we're going to do."

Anabelle leaned against the cave's wall, wincing when she noticed it was composed of souls. "Ugh. Can you believe this is where we go when we die? Honestly, I would have preferred something a lot less hellish. I'm not saying I bought into the elvish stories about the afterlife, but you know, it would have been nice if it wasn't this shithole."

"It's not like that for everyone, remember? The lich said everyone experiences their own version of the afterlife, at least the people who aren't ripped out of it to serve the Dark One."

Anabelle glanced around the dismal cave and shrugged. "Eh. I'd still prefer for my soul not to be piled on top of other souls."

Outside, there was a low, mournful wailing. It was greeted by another wail, slightly higher in pitch but sad all the same—the song of the Elder Ones. "What do you think they're up there doing?" Terra asked. "You'd think they'd notice or care about all the shit going on beneath them?"

She poked her head out of the cave and watched the tentacles swaying behind the dark clouds. "Maybe that's why they're still around. They stopped caring about all this shit and just let what happens happen. We'd all be in a better situation if the Dark One didn't care so fucking much about conquering all of existence."

Terra took another swig from the flask. "Yeah, it's a pretty shitty thing to care so much about. He could care about gardening. Or fly fishing. If every asshole cared more about gardening than whatever their passion project is, the realms would be nicer places."

She handed the flask back to Anabelle, who drained it and reattached it to her hip. "We're going to make it there, right?" the elf asked.

Terra stood and stretched her legs and arms. "You know, I thought that once I unlocked all this hidden potential, I'd be unstoppable. I remember watching Grok and seeing how she tore through everything. It's funny, but it didn't even cross my mind that she might have been getting tired."

Anabelle joined Terra at the mouth of the cave. "You know, that's not an answer."

"That's because I already answered it. We're stopping the Dark One. You ready to get going?"

"Yeah. Yeah, let's go."

They walked out of the cave, heading toward the Dark One's tower as the masses of screaming, unholy ghouls gathered before them. Terra knew they had to cut through the monsters, but even though she wanted to fight, her body was tired. Whatever pool of strength she was drawing from was not infinite.

Anabelle pointed to an area under the tower. "You see that up ahead? We need to cut through that."

That was where the highest concentration of ghouls was. It was also the quickest route. "Okay. Let's go for it."

They quickened their pace, and Terra could feel the thirst for a fight growing in her again. It pounded along with her heartbeat. If this was going to be her last day among the living, she was glad to be spending it fighting with everything she had.

They let their bodies slip into the Path of the Lost. Terra was about to bring her wrath down on everything that stood between her and the Dark One when a loud voice boomed through the air.

The ghouls ahead froze, their dead mouths ajar as they craned their heads toward the sound.

Terra and Anabelle looked in the same direction, morbidly interested in the new danger that loomed ahead of them, but it was hidden by a fog that had descended without either of them noticing.

Cire stepped out of the dark fog, holding a staff in his hand. He was naked, his body covered in ashen war paint that gave him the look of a spirit, his dark and fiery eyes flashing in the dim light. He raised his staff, and the air rippled out from him. It headed for Anabelle and Terra, passed through them, and hit the ghouls behind them, eviscerating the creatures and leaving nothing in its wake.

Terra's heart raced as she ran toward Cire. "Holy shit, you made it here all the way by yourself?"

Cire kissed her forehead, a gesture Terra would have once avoided and decried. Now, she prized this brief moment of intimacy before the Shaman turned his eyes to the tower. "There were no resources to spare," he explained. "Their fight is difficult enough."

Anabelle walked over to the orc and clasped his forearm, shaking it vigorously. "You have no idea how happy I am to see you."

He smiled wearily. "Only the three of us are going to stand before the Dark One and challenge him? Where is Abby?"

Anabelle and Terra exchanged glances. Neither of them had spoken about Abby's absence since she left to get Persephone. She should have been back, but the fact that she wasn't meant she had run into trouble.

Terra had tried to keep from thinking the worst, but her heart was full of worry. Neither of them had heard from the girl. Anything could have happened.

The elf interrupted Terra's thoughts. "Abby will get here when she gets here. We need to worry about getting to that tower. Now let's go."

She took off toward the ghouls who were beginning to rise from the ground, Tesla's energy still flowing through them.

Cire caressed Terra's cheek as he stared into her eyes. "If there is a better place to die beside my love, I cannot think of one."

Terra blushed before leaning forward and kissing him. "Okay, can the romantic shit until we're done with this, all right? And yeah, there really couldn't be a better place."

The two of them headed after Anabelle. Terra's body flooded with the power of the Path and Cire rose into the air, his strange lich magic stretching from his body, causing roots to spring out of the ground and grip ghouls as Terra and Anabelle cut through them.

The agents made their way through the mass of ghouls, goblins, orcs, giants, and everything in between. Flames and electricity burst from Anabelle's fists and feet, and Terra tore through anything she could get her hands on, ripping the soul-flesh. Cire's arcane magicks conjured trees and roots with eyes and hands and mouths that grabbed ghouls and bit into them, tearing them asunder and tossing their bodies to the side as if they were garbage.

In this fashion, the three carved their way to the Dark One's tower as the multitude of eyes glowered down on them, never taking their eyes off of the goal.

Finally, they were less than two hundred feet from the thing, which floated above as if taunting them.

Anabelle leaned over, her hands on her knees as she breathed heavily. "Okay, now what? Are we supposed to tear that thing down with our hands?"

A flash of light caused all three to jump.

Abby stood next to Anabelle, Terra at her side. "So, this is the big showdown, huh?"

Terra screamed when she saw Abby, a sound of pure joy. She grabbed the girl, hugged her tightly, and lifted her into the air. "Oh, my God, you're alive!"

Abby tried to pry herself away from Terra. "Of course we're alive. Did you think we couldn't handle ourselves?"

Terra let her go, backing away and composing herself. "No. No, it's just that you went after a big bad all on your own, one that gave us all a pretty hard time. You know, the mind wanders is all."

Anabelle smiled lovingly at Abby as she embraced her. "I'm glad you're safe."

"You too," Abby said. "Now hold on. I have a couple more loose ends to tie up."

Abby vanished and reappeared within seconds, José and Myrddin at her side. The men looked extremely confused. She disappeared once more, reappearing with Suzuki, Alex, José, and Persephone a moment later.

"What about Rasputina and Grok? Sarah?" Anabelle asked. Abby shook her head. "Couldn't get a lock on them. Wherever they are in this hell, they must be deep to block me."

Myrddin's eyes widened as he took in the scene. He finally spat, "What's happening here?"

Abby answered, "We made adjustments to the plan. We've seen what happens if we don't give this everything we have. All our heavy hitters—that's the only way we have a chance."

Terra looked at the girl, her heart swelling with pride. The kid had come a long way. "Okay, so we're all here. What now?"

Myrddin stepped forward, averting his eyes from the tower that loomed overhead. "Whatever we do, we must not look into the Dark One's eye. It would be our doom."

Abby walked over to him, shaking her head. "All we have are his eyes, though. Why shouldn't we look?"

The wizard, whose face had gone sheet-white, turned to her. "Because that is where his power lies. Within those eyes."

"Then that's what we need to attack."

Terra laughed as she blinked rapidly. "Great. I always thought you should look your enemy in the eye."

Cire nodded as he stared up at the tower. "I agree. One should meet their opponent's gaze."

Abby's nanobots rolled off her face. "Trust me. We've listened to multiple versions of us explain what went wrong, and none of them stared Death in the eye."

Anabelle's gaze wandered over everyone present. "Then that's what we'll do. We face Death straight on, and we look the son of a bitch in the eye."

The members of the DGA stared up at the shifting eye above them. After a few seconds, Cire, Alex, and José looked up at the Dark One's eye as well. The only holdout was Myrddin, who had not taken his eyes off his hands. "So, this is it?" he murmured. "To finally look him in the eye?"

Anabelle clasped Myrddin's shoulder. "Together. We look Death in the eye together."

Myrddin sighed and turned his eyes to the Dark One's. "Then let us see Death for what he truly is."

CHAPTER EIGHT

The eye of the Dark One widened, seeming to take up more space, expanding deeper and further into the Netherverse.

Everyone watched the eye, unable to look away as a chill wind blew past them, freezing them to the bone. Not one of them was free of the sense of dread that came with that wind, cutting straight to their hearts.

The eye continued to expand, growing watery and dripping on the tower it stood on as well as the earth beneath the feet of the combatants. In very little time, the Netherverse ceased to exist. There was only the all-encompassing gaze of the eye leering down on the mortals who stood beneath it.

The wind kicked up, turning to a howling sonata that was deafening to the ear. Anabelle covered hers, trying to block the incessant noise. The world around her continued to contort and change.

They were in a place that did not seem to exist within the realm of logic. Snippets of other universes, moments in time that none of them had experienced, shifted in and out of sight while the ground beneath them ran red as if it were a river of blood.

Myrddin whipped around, trying to make sense of what it was that he saw. "This…are we…we are…"

The old wizard's face went white. "Prepare yourselves, for we face the Dark One!"

The eye was gone. In its place was a vacant space that seemed to swallow time and space. A cavernous, multitude of voices echoed in that space. "Who dares present themselves before me?"

No one answered. Even Myrddin was frozen.

"Your end," a weak voice said.

It was Abby, standing defiantly against the voice that spoke down to her and her companions.

Anabelle stepped forward. "Show yourself. Or are you too afraid?"

The Dark One boomed out a laugh as the world shook. "Afraid? Of you?"

A small child wearing a deer-head mask walked into the gathering of heroes. He paused for a second, looking at them as if confused, then continued walking as the DGA and the rest watched him. "Uh, okay. That was kind of weird."

Alex's eyes followed the boy as he wandered into a world that shifted and changed around him, resulting in the child not being there. "Huh. I haven't seen that kid in a bit. Wasn't sure if he was real."

Anabelle turned to Alex. "Wait! You've fought the Dark One before. What are we supposed to do?"

"When I fought with him, it was all telepathic. It wasn't anything like this."

The ground rumbled, nearly knocking everyone off of their feet. "Perhaps this is no different. We could have been pulled into his mental space. That is why it seems as if reality is inconsistent."

Terra slowly cracked each of her knuckles. "I didn't come here to talk about beating the Dark One. I came here to do it. How the hell do I get up there to hit him in his stupid eye?"

Alex thought about it before answering. "We have to bring him down here."

Suzuki nodded as he unsheathed his sword. "She's right. He needs to be on our playing ground. You're telekinetic, right? Can you bring him down to us?"

Alex's face was grim and determined. "I've done it before." She reached out, closing her eyes as she levitated, the air swirling around her. When she opened her eyes, they flashed.

What could have been called the sky started to change color, producing shades none of them had ever seen. Out of nowhere, a screech tore through their minds, sending them to their knees—all but Alex, who continued to hold her hand high as reality began to warble.

A hole opened above them, and a shooting star came through it and crashed in front of them. Black smoke wafted from the stone and it bubbled, then cracked open like an egg, lumpy black sludge oozing from the shell.

The sludge swirled as it folded in on itself, building until it was near Cire's height. It solidified into a hooded figure that grew taller still, towering over everyone. "How dare you?" the Dark One shouted.

Anabelle and almost everyone else backed away. "What do we do now?"

"Fuck him up!" Terra shouted as she darted at the Dark One. She swung at him wildly, tackling the Dark One to the ground.

He tossed Terra off, then reached into his cloak and pulled out a scythe.

Alex conjured her scythe. "I would have thought you'd be a little less predictable. Death? Yeah, I get it." She ran toward the Dark One, blade raised.

The Dark One shifted into a black dragon. He swiped his tail at Alex, catching her in the stomach and knocking her away.

When Alex fell, Abby and Persephone joined the fray, Abby firing her shoulder and hand cannons and Persephone's arms splitting open. Wings spreading, she swooped down on the Dark One, who shifted into a giant wielding two axes. He swiped at Abby, who was barely able to throw up a shield in time. Simultaneously, a second torso tore out of the Dark One's back, its hands batting at Persephone, knocking her away.

José went for the Dark One's legs, slashing at them with his massive broadsword. It cut straight through them.

The Dark One toppled to the ground, his body bursting into a black mist that reconfigured itself as a chimera with two heads, a goat's and a lion's, atop the upper body of a huge hawk with the lower torso of a snake. It slithered away and wrapped around Terra, who struggled to break free of its grip.

Anabelle flew at it, arms and legs flaming, and burned through its tail.

After the tail was separated, it split into thousands of snakes, each of them growing to the size of a freight train.

Abby took to the air and fired at the snakes, trying to take down as many as she could. Alex ran to the Dark One's body and slid her scythe into him, slashing him down the middle.

The Dark One's guts exploded outward. His heart, liver, lungs, and stomach grew to the size of a human and sprouted fur, their arms growing and heads hunching over, wolf-like.

The four Lycans darted into the fray as the rest of the Dark One's body reformed as the original hooded figure.

The Dark One spread his cloak, unleashing dozens of pale-skinned harpies, who lunged at the group.

Abby flew past the Dark One and grabbed Alex. "You ready for this?"

Before Alex had a chance to answer, Abby disappeared, only to reappear seconds later, Alex behind her, riding Chine.

The dragon unleashed a torrent of ether fire, burning through the harpies as the Dark One grew to the height of a skyscraper and unleashed a freezing cold breath.

Anabelle leapt into the air, spinning like a top and shooting fire from her body to dispel the cold.

The Dark One's shadow form screeched in anger as he sliced at the mortals with his scythe.

Myrddin stepped forward, holding his wand high, and fired a magical blast that tore through the Dark One's body, cutting him in half.

As he fell, the two halves of him grew eight legs and scurried away from each other.

Persephone's tentacles shot out, wrapping around one of the

halves and crushing it. A wave of black blood gushed out and began to take a new form.

José ran to one of the half-formed parts and drove his sword into it. A blade shot from the Dark One and stabbed José through the stomach.

Terra tackled the enemy, then ripped the blade from José's stomach and jammed it into the hood of the Dark One. "Are you okay?" she asked, helping the MERC to his feet.

José touched his stomach, bloodying his hand. "Tis only a flesh wound," he said as he picked up his sword and charged the remainder of the Dark One, slashing it to ribbons.

Abby flew past, peppering the remainder of the Dark One with plasma blasts as Chine and Alex rained down ether fire.

The pieces of the Dark One rejoined, swirling into the hooded figure of Death once more as he cackled. The scythe appeared in his hand again as he turned and slashed behind him, tearing through the fabric of the reality.

A portal opened and the vacuum sucked everyone toward it.

"Everyone, let the portal suck you in!" Anabelle shouted.

No questions were asked. They gave in to the portal's pull.

Terra tackled the little bit of the Dark One she could get her hands on, forcing him into the portal as well.

The Dark One and everyone else toppled out on the gnome world, plowing through a mass of ghouls fighting the gnomes and goblins.

"Hold on, I have a lock on a friend." Abby smiled and ignited her thrusters, disappearing and reappearing with Sarah, who she dropped into the fray.

Sarah growled as she fell from the sky before unlocking the ninth gate, her aura exploding around her as she fell on the Dark One. His cloak stretched around her, its threads taking the form of hands that grabbed at anything near him.

Anabelle and Terra ran up his length, cutting through his arms. They had entered the Path of the Lost, and Anabelle set fire to the Dark One's hulking body. He screeched as Abby flew across him, firing her plasma cannons. Chine launched ether fire at him.

"Rasputina and Grok?" Terra yelled at Abby. "We could really use them right about now."

The girl nodded. "On their way. They're fighting a bunch of undead beasts, keeping them off our asses."

Terra sucked in air. "Damn. I wish I could see that, but we have a beast of our own to fight."

There were dozens of roars in the distance as the Dark One swelled, growing larger still.

Hundreds of ether dragons were heading toward the Gate, spewing fire at the ghouls below and peppering the Dark One as they passed.

The Dark One writhed in pain as he screeched and spread his cloak once more, pulling out his scythe and opening another tear in reality.

Abby landed and dug her feet into the earth, nanobots constructing a cannon on her back as she leaned over. A plasma blast tore a hole down the middle of the Dark One as he stumbled through the portal.

Anabelle once more led the party through the portal after the Dark One. It opened up above the Gate on the orc world.

Persephone scooped everyone up in her tentacles as she spread her wings, slowing their descent as the Dark One fell on the army of ghouls beneath him and the ether dragons burst through the Gate.

The Dark One's cloak seemed to be independent of the rest of him. It stretched out, attacking everything near him.

Anabelle grabbed Abby and shouted, "Can you take us back?"

Abby looked at the elf warily and then at the Dark One, who was growing larger and writhing, destroying everything near him.

"He'll kill everyone around him!" Anabelle shouted.

The girl's body hummed with energy as she nodded. "We got it."

She waved her hands, spreading an energy field over them all. In a flash of light, they disappeared, reappearing in the Netherverse.

The Dark One reassembled himself from the shreds of his cloak, once more towering over them.

Anabelle loosed a blast of mana at him. "We're ending this. Now."

CHAPTER NINE

The Dark One let out a hiss that slithered down the backs of their necks.

Despite everything that had been thrown at him, he'd hardly taken a scratch.

Anabelle, Terra, and Sarah had attacked using the power of the Path of the Lost, and it seemed to have done nothing.

Abby, with all her upgrades and newfound strength, hadn't managed to leave a mark on him.

José, Suzuki, and Alex had not fared any better.

Even Myrddin, with all of his arcane powers and knowledge, couldn't harm the Dark One.

Everyone was tired, the battles fought previously weighing on them.

Terra leaned on Anabelle, sighing. "What the hell else are we supposed to throw at this guy?"

Anabelle shook her head and gave no answer, looking at Myrddin instead. The wizard looked exasperated.

The Dark One leaned forward and breathed his words with the finality of death. "There is nothing you can do. I am the end of life as you know it. It is my image all living things will be cast into. All you have done, all you have ever done, is slow the inevitable. I *will* destroy you."

Terra groaned as she straightened. "God, can I just say, fuck this guy? How the hell did you deal with him before, Alex?"

Alex, who was staring up at the looming figure, said, "It was only a piece of him. For all I know, this could be as well. What I fought was purely mental. I have no idea what's going on here."

Abby spun to face the rest of the group. "That's it! This whole thing is about energy! See, we've been sitting here chatting, and he hasn't attacked us. We might not have been able to hurt him, but we've tired him out. Everything he's doing must take energy."

Abby's words sparked a memory in Anabelle, something she'd heard repeated during her training as a Traveler. "Energy drains energy," she muttered to herself.

Myrddin's face brightened when he heard Anabelle's words, and he expanded on them. "The law of energy exchange. Every action requires energy."

Abby also seemed to understand Anabelle's cryptic words. "Just like Tesla."

Suzuki and Alex, along with the rest of them, seemed to be at a loss. "Okay, I know we don't have time for a mystic arts lesson, but what the hell does that mean?" Alex shouted.

Abby pointed at the Dark One. "It means that just like we all have our limits, the Dark One does too. Like an electric transformer, he can be overloaded. We just need a way to conduct the energy."

Myrddin stepped forward. His wand shot out a bright white light that caused the Dark One to recoil in anger. "Feed your energy into me. I'll be the conductor."

Abby looked at the wizard, her mask pulling back. She fully understood what had been left unspoken.

The damage to Abby's body from doing the same thing while fighting Tesla had been extensive. She had only survived because of her nanobots. Myrddin might not live through the exchange.

He met Abby's eyes, no doubt realizing the same thing about his physical limitations, but he remained quiet. "Hurry! We need to do this fast!"

Anabelle, Terra, and Sarah stood behind Myrddin. The elf clenched her fist and let her body exude mana, dumping it all out and sending it toward Myrddin. Terra and Sarah did the same. Their energy swirled together, taking on a myriad of bright colors as it fed into the wizard.

The Dark One lunged forward, his cloak spreading, unspeakable terrors screaming from his eyes.

Alex jumped in front of Myrddin, her fingers on her temples. "I'll keep him at bay!" She shut her eyes, and a psychic wall spread in front of Myrddin and the rest.

The Dark One collided with the wall, shrieking as he was repelled.

Alex fell to her knees, swaying as she tried to keep from passing out. She loosed a scream, erupting in flames as she accessed the dragon blood in her anchor to bolster her defense. She wished Chine was with her, but her dragon was off fighting other enemies.

So many enemies…

As if he heard her—and perhaps the dragon did. They were bound, after all—Chine dropped to her side and fed her energy.

So many enemies, Alex thought again. And so many friends.

Cire joined Anabelle, Terra, and Sarah, lending his power to Myrddin, staff raised high. The earth around him grew fertile, flowers and sprouts springing up and encircling him.

The Dark One shrieked with rage, the fabric of reality tearing. The space surrounding the Dark One's body looked to be unraveling, a vast cosmos of stars, suns, and infinity shining through the tear.

"It's not enough!" Alex shouted. "He's breaking through!"

The Dark One reached back and swung his scythe, hitting the shield Alex was projecting. The force of the attack shook the barrier, nearly cracking it, but Alex held it together, blood pouring from her nose and ears. This shield would not crack. "Give it everything you got," she shouted.

A bolt of energy shot into Myrddin from behind, which caused the ball of energy forming around the tip of his wand to explode in size.

Anabelle, Terra, and Sarah looked over the shoulders to see where the energy was coming from.

Grok walked toward the group, the ground shattering beneath her feet with each step as her body pulsed with energy. She stopped walking and stood beside Anabelle, Sarah, and Terra.

Anabelle grimly nodded at the orc, and she returned the gesture.

The Dark One sliced at Alex's shield again.

A deep gash appeared on the rider's face, blood pouring from it.

Abby landed at her side and threw up an energy shield as well, doubling their defense against the Dark One as he slashed at the barrier, screaming in rage.

The Dark One finally slammed the tip of his scythe into the barrier, barely cutting through. "You are nothing to me," he howled. "Nothing!"

Then there was another surge of energy. Bright green flames flew toward Myrddin, tinting the color of the magical energy.

Rasputina appeared from whatever hell she had been in, breathing heavily, and approached the group, her green eyes locked onto the Dark One. "Today I come for Death himself. I wish to look him in the eyes for the first time in thousands of years and extinguish him."

The lich walked up to Myrddin and pulled a bone from her ribcage, fashioning it into a wand. She pointed it at the Dark One as she muttered lost arcane words under her breath.

The enemy recoiled as Myrddin's and Rasputina's wands swirled with magical energy.

Suzuki plunged his sword into the ground at Alex's and Abby's side, screaming as he lent his energy to the barrier.

The cloak of the Dark One blew away as if it were caught in a wind, and they beheld his true form for the first time.

He was an alabaster giant, white as bone, gaunt and fragile-looking, his ribs visible through tightly stretched skin. Dying stars glowed beneath the thin skin, covered by straggly blond hair that reached his stomach. His legs were spindly, splitting at the kneecap into multiple appendages without shape or form, melding together. His mouth hung open without a jaw, stretching wider and wider still, billions of teeth growing far back in his throat, which was as black as space.

Anabelle loosed another burst of mana, pushing her body. "We got this!"

Rasputina looked over her shoulder at Persephone. "Now is the time, child. Can you do what you must?"

The drow slowly nodded.

Rasputina's right hand grew long and crooked, her fingers ending in barbed points. She slashed to her right, tearing a wound in reality. The song of the Elder Ones floated through the tear.

Persephone knelt, singing softly under her breath. Her hand turned to tentacles and snaked into the tear.

Rasputina sliced up, and the tear stretched above the Dark One into the Netherverse.

The drow's arm split into thousands of tentacles as she screamed.

The unworldly shapes of the Elder Ones descended from the tear.

The Dark One looked up as unknowable shapes wrapped around his arms and legs and neck, forcing him to the ground as he screamed and writhed.

Persephone's arm disintegrated as it flowed into the mass of the Elder Ones, and her eyes were wide with fear as she reached out to Abby. "I love you!" she shouted as her skin began to crack. "I love you so much!"

Abby stretched her hand out to the drow. "I love you too! I'll always love you!"

Alex grabbed Abby's arm. "You can't! Hold the barrier!"

The lovers' eyes met as Persephone's body floated into the Netherverse.

Rasputina's voice rose above the cacophony. "Now! Give it everything you have!"

There was a collective scream as everyone unloaded.

Rasputina and Myrddin, the wizard and the lich, one-time enemies, not allies, looked at each other briefly, then they shouted a word none could place. A word from long ago that held meaning.

A thin spark flew from their wands, floating as lightly as a petal caught in a gentle breeze. It landed on the nose of the struggling Dark One.

Green flames spread from the spark and consumed the Dark One as he tried to stand. The bodies of the Elder Ones held him down as the flames spread, burning through the moonlight skin and scorching to the bone as the Dark One screamed, a haunting sound of pain and hatred that continued to echo even after his bones had been consumed.

Everything vanished.

Anabelle looked around, confused.

They were back on the gnome world.

On the battlefield, the ghouls dropped to the ground. Harpies and vrosks fell from the sky like rotten fruit falling from a tree.

The gnomish army, all of whom were covered in the filth of battle, stood dumbfounded, staring at each other.

Kravis raised his fist, screaming triumphantly. A riotous cheer rang out from the troops.

Abby was curled in a ball beside the Gate, wailing and screaming for Persephone.

Terra and Anabelle ran to her side and tried to help her up, but Abby would not allow them to. She pushed them away and crawled toward the Gate, shouting, "She's gone! She's gone!"

"Abby! Abby, listen to me," Anabelle shouted.

Abby's nanobots peeled away, showing her face, which was crumpled in despair and pain. "She's gone!"

She collapsed into her friends' arms, sobbing bitterly as the two held her tightly. Everyone else watched silently since there were no words to be said.

Myrddin walked over to the three of them, his face somber and haggard. "Abby…"

Abby glared at him. "What? What can you say to make this better?"

He said nothing.

As Abby sobbed, the Gate opened once more.

Anabelle and Terra got to their feet as Sarah stepped to the Gate. "Impossible," Anabelle muttered. "He can't still be alive."

Rasputina and Grok stepped through the Gate. The lich was holding a jar, and she knelt in front of Abby. "I know what it means to lose someone you love. I know that pain deeply." She took Abby's chin in her hand. "It is not a pain either of you deserve. There's little I can do to make amends for what I've done, but this I can do." She looked at Grok. "This, we both can."

The orc nodded slowly. "A soul for a soul."

Rasputina met Myrddin's eyes. "Let it be known that monsters do not always remain such." Then she stood and walked back through the Gate, Grok following her.

The portal exploded outward, and a gelatinous sac landed in front of Abby. Then the Gate collapsed, sucking inward into the Netherverse.

A tentacled hand burst from the sac and Persephone tumbled out, gasping for breath.

Abby burst into tears as she threw herself onto Persephone, holding the drow tightly and crying softly as she covered the drow's head with kisses.

Anabelle's and Terra's HUDs pinged. The elf pulled up a message from Roy. He was smiling widely, displaying a boyish charm she'd never seen. "They're down! Every fucking ghoul! They're done!"

Myrddin stared at the spot the Netherverse Gate used to occupy. "He's gone. The Dark One has been defeated. He's *gone*."

Two weeks had passed since the Netherverse Gate battle, and there were no remnants of Gates on the orc or gnome homeworlds. It was as if they had never existed.

There had been no formal declaration of peace throughout the realms. That seemed like too big a step for many, almost as if saying it was all over would prove it wasn't true. Those who were there that day knew what they had seen.

The nine warriors who had stood before the Dark One had walked away with their lives intact. Changed somewhat, but nonetheless alive.

Terra still couldn't wrap her mind around what had happened. Not just the Dark One's death, but how drastically her life had changed. Her current existence was a far cry from getting shitfaced in a bar and blacking out. She had fought a force that had destroyed universes, traveled to different planets and realms, and had forged friendships she could never have imagined. And she was going to be a bridesmaid.

Sarah and Kravis were finally going to tie the knot. The wedding was later in the day. The war was over. It was time for everyone to get back to their lives. Or, as Sarah had put it, for some of them to start living.

There was a knock on Terra's door. "Come on in."

Anabelle and Abby stepped into the room wearing their DGA uniforms, the spaces over their hearts bearing several medals.

Anabelle's hair was combed straight back and arranged in a tight bun. Her makeup was understated, almost plain. It allowed her natural beauty to radiate.

Abby had created a metallic collar out of her nanobots, giving the impression that she was only human from the neck up—a severe and futuristic look she seemed to enjoy for public appearances.

"Terra, you're supposed to be ready!" the girl lectured.

"Don't get your wires in a bunch. All I have to do is a quick shave, and I'm good to go."

Abby crossed her arms as she sat on Terra's bed. "We don't have wires, and you know that."

Anabelle plopped down next to Abby and shoved her. "You two cut it out. Remember what Kravis and Sarah told us? This is a gnomish wedding. No stress, just chill out. I think we could all do with a little chilling out."

Abby relaxed as Terra bustled around, changing out of her pajamas and into her DGA uniform. Terra looked at Abby and pointed to her head. "Hey, can you help me with this?"

"Sure. We got you," Abby said as she came up behind Terra. Raising one finger, she ran a thin laser over Terra's short buzz cut to remove the hair.

Terra ran her hand over her freshly shaved head. "Damn. Great. Real high-quality work. When we get back to Earth, you have a career in hair."

"Yeah, we guess we will have to figure out something to do with our lives. Do you think we'll still need a college degree?"

Anabelle stood and stepped between Terra and Abby, looking at them both sternly. "Nope. Not happening right now. We are not discussing this today. We are going to enjoy Sarah and Kravis' wedding, then we are going to finish our vacation. After that, we can talk about the future."

A voice shouted from outside the room, "Bridesmaids check!"

Terra jumped at the shout, but the door was already opening. Sarah stepped into the room wearing a pair of rust-covered jeans and a t-shirt, and her hair was tangled.

Abby's jaw dropped. "Sarah! You're not ready yet!"

Sarah laughed as she walked over to Terra's mirror, picked up a hairbrush, and started to try to handle the mess on top of her head. "Oh, I'm ready. Gnomish culture dictates you dress comfortably if you're the couple getting hitched, and you have no idea how long I have wanted to wear a pair of jeans. Do you know the last time I wasn't in uniform?"

"We always thought those were your only clothes."

Sarah laughed as she put on lip gloss. "Yeah, that's pretty much what everyone thinks." She turned around, her smile blinding in its brightness. "You guys ready to do this?"

Terra clasped her hands together and leaned forward, smiling sweetly. "Aren't you forgetting something?"

Sarah shook her head. "Nope. I'm not doing a big mushy speech or anything. I love you guys. I'm happy to be getting married. Kicking the Dark One's ass felt great. We're leaving it at that."

Terra jabbed Anabelle in the side. "Hey, did you hear her say she loved us?"

Sarah sighed as she headed toward the door. "All right, all right. Come on. Everyone's waiting for me."

She walked out of the room, leaving the rest of the DGA to follow her.

The ceremony took place at the foot of a waterfall not far from the newly erected town of Grindlehok. Terra wouldn't have thought it possible to build a new city in two weeks, but she didn't know much about gnomes.

The world was rebuilding with stunning speed. As Kravis put it, "Elves talk, dwarves mine, and gnomes build."

Anabelle hadn't been able to disagree.

Their ceremony was short and very difficult for Terra to follow. Much of it was in gnomish, and there didn't seem to be a priest or an officiator. The couple occupied a grand table, surrounded by their wedding party, the DGA on Sarah's side and Cire, Roy, Blackwell, and Naota on Kravis'. As everyone ate appetizers, the guests approached the table, delivered a gift or a kind word, and returned to their table. About halfway through, Terra and Cire were instructed to tie a wreath to Kravis' and Sarah's wrists.

Kravis and Sarah kissed each other and the gnomes in the crowd cheered, leaving the humans a little confused. It wasn't until Sarah turned to her bridesmaids, her face bright with joy, that Terra realized Sarah and Kravis were married.

Myrddin stood and raised his glass. "Sarah asked me to give a speech on this momentous occasion. Initially, I said no. We all know how my speeches go."

Laughter echoed through the crowd.

Myrddin cleared his throat and continued, "But that was precisely why Sarah asked me to speak. Because we cannot recognize the joy without acknowledging the sacrifice. We stand where many of our comrades and friends once stood. Their blood runs deep in the soil. Without their sacrifices, we would not be standing here today, enjoying the union of our friends. Let us celebrate the living and remember the dead."

Myrddin raised his glass, as did everyone else.

Terra leaned over to Anabelle. "I know it's respectful and all, but who is going to get up and dance after that?"

She was right. The band had started to play, and it didn't look like anyone was going to move.

Then Nib-Nib waddled onto the dance floor. She stood there for a moment, extremely still. Then she swayed, bobbing her head to the music, and finally spun in a circle before moonwalking backward.

Terra, Anabelle, and Abby stared at her in disbelief. That was all it took to get the party started. Most of the guests were on the dance floor within moments. Even Kravis and Sarah managed to dance for a little bit, looking much happier than they had for a long time.

The three members of the DGA split up, Terra trying to get Cire to dance with her, Roy and Anabelle playfully bickering over his flamboyant suit choice, and Abby sitting with Persephone near the waterfall, watching the rainbows shifting across the lake.

The party went on long into the afternoon and evening. When the booze turned the party into a mellower event, Terra, Anabelle, and Abby met near the water, where the pixies had come out to dance.

Myrddin was there, looking at the pixies.

Terra clapped Myrddin on the back as she stood next to him. "Didn't think you could suck the fun out of a wedding, but you always impress."

Myrddin didn't take his eyes off the pixies. "So much left to do. So many wrongs left to right, although some have been remedied. José is free of death. Made whole again, riding with the Horsemen in Middang3ard. Boundless has been exonerated, by the way. I, ah, fixed the memories of those who witnessed their betrayal. They are now free."

"You can do that? Fix memories?" Abby asked.

If Myrddin heard her question, he ignored it. "I never thought you three would come so far. It doesn't even seem like it was a gamble at this point."

Anabelle knelt and ran her hand over the grass, watching the pixies as well. "We had a lot of help. But what now? The Dark One is defeated and the Netherverse Gates are closed, which means we won't be hearing from Rasputina or Grok. The orc and gnome worlds are rebuilding. Looks like everything is wrapped up in a nice little package. Where does that leave us?"

Myrddin turned to face the DGA. "If you prefer, you can return to civilian life, but like I said, there is much left to do. The nine realms are open to each other now. That will need…policing. And as for the Dark One, many of his agents have not been brought to justice. Such work would need the patience and power of an angel or three."

The Dark Gate Angels looked at one another, not saying anything. They weren't going anywhere. They were a team. A family.

And families stuck together, no matter what.

Then the old man sighed and shook his head. "Besides, the Dark One is never truly gone."

Terra couldn't believe she'd heard what she thought Myrddin had said. "What is that supposed to mean?"

"All we did was speed up a process. The Dark One travels from universe to universe, destroying and enslaving. He was going to move on eventually. We just managed to make it on our terms."

Abby looked at Terra and Anabelle. "Then why would we disband? If the Dark One is still out there, he still has an ass to kick."

Myrddin smiled, his eyes glinting. "I had a feeling you might think something like that. For now, we should enjoy the evening."

And with that, Myrddin walked back to the afterparty, leaving the DGA agents to talk briefly before following him.

If the Dark One was still out there, they could allow themselves one day to pretend he was not.

EPILOGUE

"I still don't understand why we have to do this right now," Stew whined. "Everything worked out, and we're still alive. We should just cut our losses and get out of here."

The Mundanes were wandering through a dungeon. Specifically, the dungeon the DGA had explored and failed to conquer. Throughout the complexities of defeating the Dark One, the original plan of using the Soul Jar had been forgotten. That is, by everyone but Suzuki, who had brought it up during the wedding.

Most of the Mundanes were indifferent to going back to the dungeon. Suzuki had been the only one excited. Stew had the opposite opinion.

Suzuki was staring at a door with a lock mechanism. Nothing about this dungeon matched the information the DGA had given him. The puzzles were different, as were the enemies. Anabelle, the leader of the DGA, had said there was a rogue named Maurice hidden somewhere in the dungeon, doomed to fight his way through it for eternity. Suzuki hadn't seen him. That being said, the coordinates were right.

Sandy came over to check out the door as well, while Beth and Stew walked around the small room, looking for something to entertain themselves. "You really want to find out what's going on with this place, don't you?" she asked.

Suzuki nodded absentmindedly. "I don't know. I'm kinda curious. We went through all that effort to get the Soul Jar, and then it got dropped like a boring plot point in a convoluted fantasy story. How can I just let that go? And the DGA doesn't care about it, which means if there's any loot in there, it's all ours."

Across the room, Stew perked up. "Wait, what did you say about loot? Why the hell are we just standing around? Let's break this door down!"

Stew charged the door, hunkering down and breaking through it with a shoulder hit. Rock and debris went flying.

The Mundanes walked down a long corridor until they came to a gold door with elvish writing scrawled on it.

Suzuki held up his torch to see better. "Anabelle didn't mention anything about elvish."

Beth, who had walked over carrying her torch as well, shrugged. "It's pretty obvious things changed. Let's just finish this up as fast as we can."

Sandy was studying the inscription. "It's what they described. This is a riddle door. The damn thing doesn't want to wake up for us, but it's still the same door."

Suzuki pulled the Soul Jar out of his inventory and looked down at it. "Okay, who's going to step up for this one?"

The Mundanes looked at each other. Stew cleared his throat. "Well, I don't know, man. This was kind of your idea. I figured you were going to do the big hero thing and sacrifice yourself...since it was your idea."

Suzuki stared at the gold door. "I assumed we were going to be adults about this and draw lots or something, but I can see that you're all terrified of what's on the other side."

Beth drew her dagger and flipped it in one hand. "Stop stalling. How do you want to die, slow and painful or long and drawn out?"

Suzuki rolled the Soul Jar in his hand. "Hm. If I had to choose..." He leaned over and whispered in Beth's ear.

Beth's eyes widened, and she slapped Suzuki. "That's disgusting." Then her face went red and she grinned, turning to Stew and Sandy. "You two need to leave for like ten minutes."

Stew crossed his arms and shook his head. "Nope. If Suzuki's going to die, I want to see it."

Beth tossed a dagger at Stew, the blade passing only a few centimeters beneath his crotch.

Stew threw his hands up and turned around, and Sandy followed him. "Fine, fine. Cut me and Sandy out of all the fucking fun."

As Sandy walked away, she threw an invisible spell at Suzuki and Beth.

As Stew and Sandy waited on the other side of the wall, a litany of sounds came through from the other room. Not many of them were pleasant.

"All right, you two can come in," Beth shouted.

The two Mundanes walked back into the room. Beth was panting heavily, her face sheened with sweat. Suzuki lay at her feet, his chest carved open and blood smeared all over the ground.

Stew winced at the scene. "Ugh. You two are into some weird-ass shit."

Beth pointed her dagger at Stew. "Don't even start with me. I've heard you and Sandy. Come on, let's see what's behind this door." Beth raised the Soul Jar to the gold door.

A face appeared and looked down at the Mundanes. "Hmph. Looks like you figured this one out."

With that, the door opened. A room full of jewels and weapons shimmered before the Mundanes, as well as piles of gold that reached the ceiling.

Beth smiled as Stew and Sandy ran into the room, Stew leaping into the largest pile of loot, screaming as he stood up, a knife in his thigh. "Goddamn it!"

Beth went over to Suzuki's corpse and held the Soul Jar to his mouth.

Suzuki's wounds healed, and his eyes snapped open. "Did it work?"

Beth pointed at the room of glowing loot. "We just might be the richest MERCs ever."

Who would have thought that vanquishing the Dark One would only be the start of their problems? Stay tuned for the epic conclusion of the Dark Gate Angels Saga – coming soon!

Have you tried the Dragon Approved series from Ramy Vance and Michael Anderle? Book one is The First Human Rider and it's available now from Amazon and through Kindle Unlimited.

Dragonriders are all that stand between Middang3ard and total annihilation.

But their numbers are dwindling.

With every passing day, more and more Dragonriders are falling under the scourge of the Dark One.

The forces of humanity and their allies are desperate. They need a new hero to step up and turn the tide.

Myrddin, the resistance's leader, thinks he might have found that someone…on *Earth*, of all places.

Word has just come from the east that the Dark One is launching his largest assault yet, but there is still time to stop him. If, that is, they can find someone good enough to take him on.

Alex Bound just might be the rider they need.

But a human has never been accepted as a Dragonrider.

Let alone a blind human...

Alex isn't someone to step away from a fight.

Not now, not ever, and she has no plans to start—even if she needs to ride a real dragon to make it happen.

Grab your copy of The First Human Rider at Amazon or through Kindle Unlimited

So I thought I would share a little story with you all. Let's call this one **Covid Check-In #2:**

So my son developed a fever a few weeks back. Plus a whole bunch of canker sores in his mouth. Normally we wouldn't be too worried – kids get sick all the time. Right?

Well, my son almost never gets sick. In the last year, he's only needed paracetamol once.

The kid's immune system is something from the gods.

So when he got sick enough that he actually put himself to bed at 3 PM, my wife and I got a little bit worried. We started googling.

Google is evil.

Google gives you cancer.

By the time we were done googling his symptoms, he had at least seven diseases that were terminal.

In normal times, we book an appointment with the doctor and go in. But in the era of 'Love in the Time of Covid' *going in* isn't easy. You need to call a hotline and confirm 'yay' or 'nay' to having the virus.

Now this isn't bashing the UK health system. It is incredible here. Anyone who's ever heard the story of my son's birth will know how badass the health system is in this country.

But still – a Covid test for a five-year-old? Seriously!

We went in for a test and let me just put it this way - The Walking Dead got it right.

The test was conducted in a drive-through – we never got out of the car.

I had to navigate a maze of pylons I haven't seen since taking my driving test at the age of 16. It put all my driving skills to the test, and I'm glad to report I only ran over 2 pylons and one dude's foot in a Hazmat suit. (I might be exaggerating a little bit here – but hey, I'm a fiction writer that's what we do.)

Finally we made it to Medical Bay 2 to conduct the dreaded *Test*.

The Test, for those interested, involves sticking in a 9-inch Q-tip down my son's throat and up his nose (if he develops any weird nose fetishes when he gets older, we will know where that started). Again – not bashing the health system here. They were incredible. Polite, efficient, professional and absolutely confidence inspiring. It was an incredible operation to witness.

But a 9-inch Q-tip? What the hell kind of medieval torture device is that?

My son took it like a champ. No tears, just a morbid fascination with a device that he's only ever seen going into his father's ear.

The results came in later that week – negative. So, 9-inch cotton swaps aside, good news.

All this to say – it really reminded me of what's important. There is no doubt that we are living in incredibly strange and trying times, where the simple act of going to the doctor, something we previously took for granted, has a whole new layer of 'WTF' on it.

It was a stressful few days, but I am grateful. Grateful that we have the technology to make things better. Grateful for my family. Grateful that all in all these are just minor inconveniences - a blimp in unusual times.

(I'm also grateful that I have a whole bunch of fodder for my next book – apocalyptic plague anyone?)

I hope everyone is staying safe. There is no doubt that living through 'Love in the Time of Covid' is one of the strangest episodes of the Twilight Zone ever.

Here's a picture of watermelon to brighten your day.

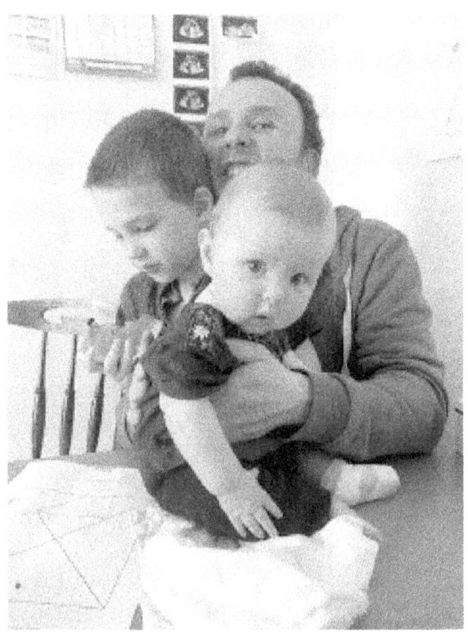

AUTHOR NOTES MICHAEL ANDERLE
AUGUST 15, 2020

Here I am thousands of miles away from Ramy (he lives in Edinburgh, Scotland, and I live in Henderson (right outside of Las Vegas) Nevada.) Yet, both of us have a similar concern about what is going on outside our doors and to people we love and care about.

And many we don't know, but we still care.

I'm fifty-two, but I feel like I'm just past forty. It's peculiar because I don't feel that much older mentally but every morning, I seem to be aging quickly.

(*Editor's note: It gets worse from here. You'll stay in your forties in your head and wonder why the heck you're so tired. I know this.*)

A reason might be I am having to unpack, build furniture, walk on stone floors or ceramic-made-to-look-like-wood floors and *believe it or not that affects one's bones.*

Wall to wall carpet isn't a bad thing. Well, not a bad thing for walking in bare feet or socks, not so great for allergies.

I'm napping after lunch. I'm waking up WAY too early in the morning. I'm sitting at my desk, sometimes, watching the grass grow.

Sure, it could be old(er) age setting in, but I refuse to believe it. I'm not going down without a fight, or at least an effort to call it something else and make it stick.

I don't have COVID, but perhaps my immune system is fighting a dark scourge trying to take over humanity and produce brain-eating zombies. Unfortunately, the sheer amazeballs abilities my body possesses (heretofore unknown) are fighting—and winning—the battle with the scourge.

However, it's causing me to wake early, want a nap after lunch, and occasionally go into a netherverse with my thoughts (also called watching the grass grow), allowing the energy to fight an ongoing internal battle as I take my physical being back inch-by-inch.

Sure …that's it. That's believable, right?

What do you mean, *no?!* You gave Ramy a pass for his driving comment, so I should totally get a zombie apocalypse over a getting older pass.

ONE HUNDRED AND THIRTEEN!

Consider this the epilogue. I just looked at the temperature outside here in Henderson, and it's @#@#%!#%!#~#TY!! Hot.

I'm not sure I wasn't hallucinating from the heat, but I just noticed two red guys in bodysuits saying they are going to stay out of my backyard because, and I quote, "It's hotter than hell here. Let's go back downstairs!"

(*Editor's note: Must be friends of Pandora's.*)

Damn, folks, I don't care who you are, that's *hot*.

Ad Aeternitatem,

Michael Anderle

OTHER BOOKS BY RAMY VANCE

Sacrifices
Love And Aliens
An Alien Affair
Dragons in Space
The Beginning of the End
Death of the Mind
Boundless